a **Kleypas** is the author of a number of historical and
ntemporary romance novels that have been published
  fourteen languages. In 1985, she was named Miss
lassachusetts and competed in the Miss America pageant in
tlantic City. After graduating from Wellesley College with
political science degree, she published her first novel at age
renty-one. Her books have appeared on the *New York Times*
stseller lists. Lisa is married and has two children.

Visit Lisa Kleypas online:

www.lisakleypas.com
www.facebook.com/LisaKleypas
www.twitter.com/LisaKleypas

*Praise for Lisa Kleypas*:

'Kleypas launches the Friday Harbour trilogy with a
elightful portrait of a picturesque town where people know
everything about everyone and look out for each other . . .
e enchantingly weaves together additional connections with
atives and friends, leaving many dangling threads that will
lead the reader straight to book two'
*Publishers Weekly*

'Flawlessly written . . . Kleypas brings together richly
inced characters, an emotionally riveting plot, and a subtle
uch of the paranormal to create an unforgettable romance
that is pure reading magic'
*Booklist*

'Magical'

# Lisa KLEYPAS

## Cold-Hearted Rake

piatkus

PIATKUS

First published in the United States in 2015 by Avon Books,
an imprint of HarperCollins Publishers
First published in Great Britain in 2015 by Piatkus

1 3 5 7 9 10 8 6 4 2

Copyright © 2015 by Lisa Kleypas

The moral right of the author has been asserted.

A CIP catalogue record for this book
is available from the British Library.

ISBN 978-0-349-40760-9

Printed and bound in Great Britain by
Clays Ltd, St Ives plc

Papers used by Piatkus are from well-managed forests
and other responsible sources.

MIX
Paper from
responsible sources
FSC
www.fsc.org   FSC® C104740

Piatkus
An imprint of
Little, Brown Book Group
Carmelite House
50 Victoria Embankment
London EC4Y 0DZ

An Hachette UK Company
www.hachette.co.uk

www.piatkus.co.uk

*To my wonderful and gifted editor, Carrie Feron—*
*thank you for making my dreams come true!*
*Love always,*
*L.K.*

# Cold-Hearted Rake

# *Chapter 1*

"THE DEVIL KNOWS WHY my life should be ruined," Devon Ravenel said grimly, "all because a cousin I never liked fell from a horse."

"Theo didn't fall, precisely," his younger brother, Weston, replied. "He was thrown."

"Obviously the horse found him as insufferable as I did." Devon paced around the receiving room in restless, abbreviated strides. "If Theo hadn't already broken his damned neck, I'd like to go and break it for him."

West sent him a glance of exasperated amusement. "How can you complain when you've just inherited an earldom that confers an estate in Hampshire, lands in Norfolk, a house in London—"

"All entailed. Forgive my lack of enthusiasm for land and properties that I'll never own and can't sell."

"You may be able to break the entailment, depending on how it was settled. If so, you could sell everything and be done with it."

"God willing." Devon glanced at a bloom of mold in the corner with disgust. "No one could reasonably expect me to live here. The place is a shambles."

This was the first time either of them had ever set foot

in Eversby Priory, the ancestral family domain built over the remains of a monastic residence and church. Although Devon had become ennobled shortly after his cousin's death three months ago, he had waited as long as possible before facing the mountain of problems he now confronted.

So far he had seen only this room and the entrance hall, the two areas that were supposed to impress visitors the most. The rugs were worn, the furniture threadbare, the plaster wall moldings dingy and cracked. None of this boded well for the condition of the rest of the house.

"It needs refurbishing," West admitted.

"It needs to be razed to the ground."

"It's not so bad—" West broke off with a yelp as his foot began to sink into a depression in the rug. He hopped away and stared at the bowl-shaped indentation. "What the deuce . . . ?"

Devon bent and lifted the corner of the rug to reveal a rotting hole in the flooring beneath. Shaking his head, he dropped the rug back into place and went to a window fitted with diamond-shaped panes. The lead came that joined the window glass was corroded, the hinges and fittings rusted.

"Why hasn't that been repaired?" West asked.

"For want of money, obviously."

"But how could that be? The estate comes with twenty thousand acres. All those tenants, the annual yields—"

"Estate farming is no longer profitable."

"In Hampshire?"

Devon sent him a dark glance before returning his attention to the view. "Anywhere."

The Hampshire scenery was green and bucolic, neatly divided by bottle-green hedgerows in bloom. However, somewhere beyond the cheerful huddles of thatched-roof cottages and the fertile tracts of chalk down and ancient woodland, thousands of miles of steel track were being laid out for an onslaught of locomotive engines and railcars. All across England, new factories and mill towns had begun to appear faster than hazel catkins in the spring. It had been Devon's bad luck to inherit a title just as a tide of industry was sweeping away aristocratic traditions and entitled modes of living.

"How do you know?" his brother asked.

"*Everyone* knows, West. Grain prices have collapsed. When did you last read an issue of the *Times*? Have you paid no attention to the discussions at the club or the taverns?"

"Not when the subject was farming," came West's dour reply. He sat heavily, rubbing his temples. "I don't like this. I thought we had agreed never to be serious about anything."

"I'm trying. But death and poverty have a way of making everything seem rather less amusing." Leaning his forehead against the windowpane, Devon said morosely, "I've always enjoyed a comfortable life without having to perform a single day of honest labor. Now I have *responsibilities*." He said the word as if it were a profanity.

"I'll help you think of ways to avoid them." Rummaging in his coat, West pulled a silver flask from an inside pocket. He uncapped it and took a long swallow.

Devon's brows lifted. "Isn't it a bit early for that? You'll be stewed by noon."

"Yes, but it won't happen unless I start now." West tilted the flask again.

The habits of self-indulgence, Devon reflected with concern, were catching up with his younger brother. West was a tall and handsome man of four-and-twenty, with a wily intelligence that he preferred to use as seldom as possible. In the past year, an excess of strong drink had lent a ruddy cast to West's cheeks, and softened his neck and waistline. Although Devon had made a point of never interfering in his brother's affairs, he wondered if he should mention something about his swilling. No, West would only resent the unwanted advice.

After replacing the flask in his coat, West steepled his hands and regarded Devon over the tips of his fingers. "You need to acquire capital, and sire an heir. A rich wife would solve both problems."

Devon blanched. "You know I'll never marry." He understood his limitations: He wasn't meant to be a husband or father. The idea of repeating the travesty of his childhood, with himself in the role of the cruel and indifferent parent, made his skin crawl. "When I die," he continued, "you're next in line."

"Do you actually believe I'll outlive you?" West asked. "With all my vices?"

"I have just as many."

"Yes, but I'm far more enthusiastic about mine."

Devon couldn't hold back a wry laugh.

No one could have foreseen that the two of them, from a far-flung branch of the Ravenels, would be the last in a lineage that could be traced back to the Norman Conquest. Unfortunately, Ravenels had always been too hot-blooded and impulsive. They yielded to every temptation, indulged in every sin, and scorned every virtue, with the result that they tended to die faster than they could reproduce.

Now there were only two left.

Although Devon and West were wellborn, they had never been part of the peerage, a world so rarefied that the highest levels were impermeable even for minor gentry. Devon knew little of the complex rules and rituals that distinguished aristocrats from the common masses. What he did know was that the Eversby estate was no windfall, but a trap. It could no longer generate enough income to sustain itself. It would devour the modest annual income from his trust, crush him, and then it would finish off his brother.

"Let the Ravenels come to an end," Devon said. "We're a bad lot and always have been. Who will care if the earldom goes extinct?"

"The servants and tenants might object to losing their incomes and homes," West said dryly.

"They can all go hang. I'll tell you how what's to be done: First I'll send Theo's widow and sisters packing; they're of no use to me."

"Devon—" he heard his brother say uneasily.

"Then I'll find a way to break the entailment, split the estate apart, and sell it piecemeal. If that's not possible, I'll strip the house of everything valuable, tear it down, and sell the stone—"

"*Devon.*" West gestured to the doorway, where a small, slim woman veiled in black stood at the threshold.

Theo's widow.

She was the daughter of Lord Carbery, an Irish peer who owned a stud farm in Glengarrif. She had been married to Theo only three days before he had died. Such tragedy coming on the heels of a customarily joyful event must have been a cruel shock. As one of the last few members of a dwindling family, Devon supposed he should have sent her a letter of sympathy when Theo's accident had occurred. But somehow the thought had never translated into action, only stayed in his mind like a bit of lint caught on a coat lapel.

Perhaps Devon might have forced himself to send condolences if he hadn't despised his cousin so much. Life had favored Theo in many ways, gifting him with wealth,

privilege, and handsomeness. But instead of being grateful for his good fortune, Theo had always been smug and
superior. A bully. Since Devon had never been able to
overlook an insult or provocation, he had ended up brawl-
ing with Theo whenever they were together. It would have
been a lie to say he was sorry that he would never see his
cousin again.

As for Theo's widow, she had no need of sympathy. She
was young and childless, and she had a jointure, which
would make it easy for her to marry again. Although she
was reputed to be a beauty, it was impossible to judge; a
heavy black veil obscured her in a mist of gloom. One
thing was certain: After what she had just overheard, she
must think Devon despicable.

He didn't give a damn.

As Devon and West bowed, the widow responded with
a perfunctory curtsy. "Welcome, my lord. And Mr. Ravenel. I will provide a list of the household inventory as
soon as possible, so that you may loot and pillage in an
organized fashion." Her voice was refined, the cut-glass
syllables frosted with dislike.

Devon watched alertly as she came farther into the
room. Her figure was too slender for his taste, wandlike
in the heft of mourning clothes. But there was something
riveting about her controlled movement, a subtle volatility
contained within stillness.

"My condolences for your loss," he said.

"My congratulations for your gain."

Devon frowned. "I assure you, I never wanted your
husband's title."

"It's true," West said. "He complained about it all the
way from London."

Devon sent his brother a damning glance.

"The butler, Sims, will be available to show you the

house and grounds at your leisure," the widow said. "Since I am, as you remarked, of no use to you, I will retire to my room and begin to pack."

"Lady Trenear," Devon said curtly, "we seem to have started off on bad footing. I apologize if I've given offense."

"No need to apologize, my lord. Such remarks are no less than what I expected of you." She continued before Devon could reply. "May I ask how long you intend to stay at Eversby Priory?"

"Two nights, I expect. At dinner, perhaps you and I could discuss—"

"I'm afraid my sisters-in-law and I will not be able to dine with you. We are overset by grief, and shall take our meals separately."

"Countess—"

Ignoring him, she left the room without another word. Without even a curtsy.

Stunned and outraged, Devon stared at the empty doorway with narrowed eyes. Women *never* treated him with such contempt. He felt his temper threatening to break loose. How the hell could she hold him at fault for the situation when he'd had no choice in any of it?

"What did I do to deserve that?" he demanded.

West's mouth twitched. "Aside from saying you were going to cast her out and destroy her home?"

"I apologized!"

"Never apologize to women. It only confirms that you were wrong, and incenses them further."

Devon would be damned if he'd tolerate the insolence of a woman who should have been offering to help him, instead of heaping blame on his head. Widow or not, she was about to learn a much-needed lesson.

"I'm going to talk to her," he said grimly.

Lifting his feet onto the upholstered settee, West stretched out and arranged a pillow beneath his head. "Wake me when it's over."

Devon left the receiving room and followed the widow with long, ground-eating strides. He caught a glimpse of her at the end of the hallway, her dress and veil rippling as she sped away like a pirate ship at full sail.

"Wait," he called after her. "I didn't mean what I said earlier."

"You *did* mean it." She stopped and whirled to face Devon in an abrupt motion. "You intend to destroy the estate, and your family legacy, all for your own selfish purposes."

He stopped in front of her, his hands gripped into fists. "Look here," he said coldly, "the most I've ever had to manage is a terrace apartment, a cookmaid, a valet, and one horse. And now I'm expected to look after a foundering estate with more than two hundred tenant farms. I would think that merits some consideration. Even sympathy."

"Poor you. How trying it must be, how inconvenient, for you to have to think about someone other than yourself."

With that parting jab, she tried to leave. However, she had stopped near an arched niche in the wall, intended for the display of statuary or art objects on pedestals.

Devon had her now. Deliberately he braced his hands on either side of the recess, blocking her retreat. He heard her breath catch, and—although he wasn't proud of it—he felt a bolt of satisfaction at having unnerved her.

"Let me pass," she said.

He didn't move, keeping her captive. "First tell me your name."

"Why? I would never give you leave to use it."

Exasperated, he studied her shrouded form. "Has it

occurred to you that we have more to gain from mutual cooperation than hostility?"

"I've just lost my husband and my home. What precisely do I have to gain, my lord?"

"Perhaps you should find out before you decide to make an enemy of me."

"You were the enemy before you ever set foot here."

Devon found himself straining to see through the veil. "Must you wear that blasted head covering?" he asked irritably. "It's like conversing with a lampshade."

"It's called a weeping veil, and yes, I must wear it in the presence of a visitor."

"I'm not a visitor, I'm your cousin."

"Only by marriage."

As he contemplated her, Devon felt his temper begin to subside. How small she was, as fragile and quick as a sparrow. He gentled his tone. "Come, don't be stubborn. There's no need to wear the veil around me unless you're literally weeping, in which case I would insist that you put it back down immediately. I can't abide a woman crying."

"Because you're secretly soft-hearted?" she asked sarcastically.

A distant memory stung him, one he hadn't allowed himself to think about in years. He tried to shake it off, but his mind stubbornly retained the image of himself as a boy of five or six, sitting at the closed door of his mother's dressing room, agitated by the sounds of weeping on the other side. He didn't know what had made her cry, but it had undoubtedly been a failed love affair, of which there had been many. His mother had been a renowned beauty who often fell in and out of love in a single night. His father, exhausted by her caprices and driven by his own demons, had rarely been at home. Devon remembered the suffocating helplessness of listening to her sob but not being able to reach her. He had settled for pushing handkerchiefs under the door, begging her to open it, asking repeatedly what was wrong.

"Dev, you're sweet," she had said through her sniffles. "All little boys are. But then you all grow up to be so selfish and cruel. You were born to break women's hearts."

"I won't, Mummy," he had cried in alarm. "I promise I won't."

He had heard a laughing sob, as if he'd said something foolish. "Of course you will, poppet. You'll do it without even trying."

The scene had been repeated on other occasions, but that was the one Devon remembered most clearly.

As it had turned out, his mother had been right. Or at least, he'd often been accused of breaking women's hearts. But he had always made it clear that he had no intention of marrying. Even if he fell in love, he would never make that kind of promise to a woman. There was no reason for it, when any promise could be broken. Having experienced the pain that people who loved each other could inflict, he had no desire to do that to anyone.

His attention returned to the woman in front of him. "No, I'm not soft-hearted," he said in answer to her question. "In my opinion, a woman's tears are manipulative and even worse, unattractive."

"You," she said with certainty, "are the vilest man I have ever met."

Devon was amused by the way she enunciated every word as if it had been shot from a bow. "How many men have you met?"

"Enough to recognize a wicked one when I see him."

"I doubt you can see much of anything through this veil." He reached out to finger the edge of the black gauze. "You can't possibly like to wear it."

"As a matter of fact, I do."

"Because it hides your face when you cry," he said rather than asked.

"I never cry."

Taken aback, Devon wondered if he had heard her correctly. "You mean not since your husband's accident?"

"Not even then."

What kind of woman would say such a thing, even if it were true? Devon gripped the front of the veil and began to hike it upward. "Hold still." He pushed handfuls of the crepe back over the little headpiece that anchored it. "No, don't pull away. The two of us are going to stand face-to-face and attempt a civilized conversation. Good God, you could rig a merchant ship with all this—"

Devon broke off as her face was uncovered. He found himself staring into a pair of amber eyes that tilted at the outer corners in a catlike slant. For a moment he couldn't breathe, couldn't think, while all his senses struggled to take her in.

He had never seen anything like her.

She was younger than he had expected, with a fair complexion and auburn hair that looked too heavy for its pins. A set of wide, pronounced cheekbones and a narrow jaw imparted an exquisite feline triangularity to her features. The curves of her lips were so full that even when she pressed them together tightly, as she was doing now, they still looked soft. Although she was not conventionally beautiful, she was so original that it rendered the question of beauty inconsequential.

Her mourning dress was slim and tightly fitted from the neck to the hips before flaring into a series of complex pleats. A man could only guess at the figure encased in all that boning and ruching and intricate stitching. Even her wrists and hands were obscured by black gloves. Aside from her face, the only visible skin was at her throat, where the front of her high collar parted with a U-shaped notch. He could see the vulnerable movement of her swallow. It looked so very soft, that private place, where a man might press his lips and feel the rhythm of her pulse.

He wanted to start there, kissing her throat, while he undressed her like an intricately wrapped gift until she was gasping and squirming beneath him. If she were any other woman, and they had found themselves in any other circumstances, Devon would have seduced her on the spot. Realizing that it would not do to stand there gaping a landed trout, he searched through his hot, disordered thoughts for some conventional remark, something coherent.

To his surprise, she was the first to break the silence. "My name is Kathleen."

An Irish name. "Why do you have no accent?"

"I was sent to England as a child, to live with family friends in Leominster."

"Why?"

A frown knit between her winged brows. "My parents were very much occupied with their horses. They spent several months of each year in Egypt to purchase Arabian bloodstock for their farm. I was . . . an inconvenience. Their friends Lord and Lady Berwick, who were also horse people, offered to take me in and raise me with their two daughters."

"Do your parents still live in Ireland?"

"My mother has passed away, but my father is still there." Her gaze turned distant, her thoughts chasing elsewhere. "He sent Asad to me as a wedding present."

"Asad," Devon repeated, puzzled.

Refocusing on him, Kathleen looked perturbed, color sweeping from her neck to her hairline.

Then Devon understood. "The horse that threw Theo," he said quietly.

"It wasn't Asad's fault. He was so badly trained that my father bought him back from the man who had originally purchased him."

"Why give a problem horse to you?"

"Lord Berwick often allowed me to help him train the young colts."

Devon ran a deliberate glance over her fine-boned frame. "You're no bigger than a sparrow."

"One doesn't use brute force to train an Arabian. They're a sensitive breed—they require understanding and skill."

Two things that Theo had lacked. How bloody stupid he had been to risk his neck and a valuable animal along with it.

"Did Theo do it on a lark?" Devon couldn't resist asking. "Was he trying to show off?"

A glint of searing emotion appeared in those luminous eyes before it was quickly extinguished. "He was in a temper. He wouldn't be dissuaded."

That was a Ravenel for you.

If anyone had ever dared to contradict Theo, or refuse him anything, it had ignited an explosion. Perhaps Kathleen had thought she could manage him, or that time would mellow him. She couldn't have known that a Ravenel's temper usually outweighed any sense of self-preservation. Devon would have liked to consider himself above that sort of thing, but he had succumbed to it more than once in the past, throwing himself into the volcanic pit of consuming fury. It always felt glorious until one had to face the consequences.

Kathleen folded her arms tightly, each small, black-gloved hand forming a clamp around the opposite elbow.

"Some people said I should have had Asad put down after the accident. But it would be cruel, and wrong, to punish him for something that wasn't his fault."

"Have you considered selling him?"

"I wouldn't want to. But even if I did, I would have to retrain him first."

Devon doubted the wisdom of allowing Kathleen anywhere near a horse that had just killed her husband, albeit inadvertently. And in all likelihood, she wouldn't be able to stay at Eversby Priory long enough to make any progress with the Arabian.

However, now wasn't the time to point that out.

"I'd like to see the grounds," he said. "Will you walk with me?"

Looking perturbed, Kathleen retreated a half step. "I'll arrange for the head gardener to show them to you."

"I would prefer you." Devon paused before asking deliberately, "You're not afraid of me, are you?"

Her brows rushed downward. "Certainly not."

"Then walk with me."

Ignoring his proffered arm, she slid him a wary glance. "Shall we invite your brother?"

Devon shook his head. "He's napping."

"At this hour of the day? Is he ill?"

"No, he keeps the schedule of a cat. Long hours of slumber interrupted by brief periods of self-grooming."

He saw the corners of her lips deepen with reluctant amusement. "Come, then," she murmured, brushing by him to walk briskly along the hallway, and he followed without hesitation.

# Chapter 2

AFTER ONLY A FEW minutes in Devon Ravenel's company, Kathleen had no doubt that every damning rumor she had heard about him was true. He was a selfish ass. A repellent, boorish rake.

He was handsome . . . she would give him that. Although not in the way of Theo, who had been blessed with the refined features and golden hair of a young Apollo. Devon Ravenel's dark good looks were bold and raffish, weathered with a cynicism that made him look every bit his twenty-eight years. She felt a little shock every time she looked up into his eyes, the blue of a rough winter ocean, the vivid irises rimmed with blue-black. His face was smooth shaven, but the lower half was shadowed with a beard grain that even the sharpest razor would not completely remove.

He seemed exactly like the kind of man that Lady Berwick, who had raised Kathleen, had warned her about. "You will encounter men who will have designs on you, my dear. Men without scruple, who will employ charm, lies, and seductive skills to ruin innocent young women for their own impure gratification. When you find yourself in the company of such a scoundrel, flee without hesitation."

"But how will I know if a man is a scoundrel?" Kathleen had asked.

"By the unwholesome glint in his eye and the ease of his charm. His presence may excite rather lurid sensations. Such a man has a certain something in his physical presence . . . a quality of 'animal spirits,' as my mama used to call it. Do you understand, Kathleen?"

"I think so," she had said, although she hadn't at the time.

Now Kathleen knew exactly what Lady Berwick had meant. The man strolling beside her possessed animal spirits in abundance.

"From what I've seen so far," Devon remarked, "it would be far more sensible to set fire to this rotting heap of timber rather than to try and repair it."

Kathleen's eyes widened. "Eversby Priory is historic. It's four hundred years old."

"So is the plumbing, I'll wager."

"The plumbing is adequate," she said defensively.

One of his brows arched. "Sufficiently adequate for me to take a shower bath?"

She hesitated before admitting, "You won't have a shower bath."

"A regular bath, then? Lovely. What kind of modern vessel shall I find myself soaking in tonight? A rusted pail?"

To Kathleen's chagrin, she felt her mouth quiver with the beginnings of a smile. She managed to batten it down before replying with great dignity. "A portable tin bath."

"There are no cast-iron baths in any of the bathrooms?"

"I'm afraid there are no bathrooms. The bath will be brought to your dressing room and removed after you are finished."

"Is there any piped water? Anywhere?"

"The kitchen and the stables."

"But there are water closets in the house, of course."

She sent him a reproving glance at the mention of such an indelicate subject.

"If you're not too delicate to train horses," he pointed out, "who are generally not known for their discretion about bodily functions, surely you can bring yourself to tell me the number of water closets in the mansion."

She colored as she forced herself to reply. "None. Only chamber pots at night, and an outdoor privy by day."

He gave her an incredulous glance, seeming genuinely offended by the idea. "*None?* At one time this was one of the most prosperous estates in England. Why the devil was the house never plumbed?"

"Theo said that according to his father, there was no reason for it when they had so many servants."

"Of course. Such a delightful activity, running up and down the stairs with heavy cans of water. Not to mention chamber pots. How thankful the servants must be that no one has yet deprived them of such enjoyment."

"There's no need for sarcasm," she said. "It wasn't my decision."

They proceeded along a curving path bordered with yews and ornamental pear trees, while Devon continued to scowl.

A pair of miscreants was how Theo had described Devon and his younger brother. "They avoid polite society and prefer to associate with people of low character," Theo had told her. "One may generally find them in East End taverns and sporting houses. Education was wasted on them. In fact, Weston left Oxford early because he didn't want to stay there without Devon." Kathleen had gathered that although Theo had no great fondness for either of his distant cousins, he had reserved a special dislike for Devon.

What a strange turn of fate, that this man would be the one to take his place.

"Why did you marry Theo?" Devon startled her by asking. "Was it a love match?"

She frowned slightly. "I would prefer to limit our conversation to small talk."

"Small talk is a crashing bore."

"Regardless, people will expect a man of your position to be accomplished at it."

"Was Theo?" he asked snidely.

"Yes."

Devon snorted. "I never saw him demonstrate that particular skill. Perhaps I was always too busy dodging his fists to notice."

"I think it's safe to say that you and Theo didn't bring out the best in each other."

"No. We were too much alike in our faults." Mockery edged his tone as he added, "And it seems I have none of his virtues."

Kathleen remained silent, letting her gaze pass over a profusion of white hydrangea, geraniums, and tall stalks of red penstemon. Before her marriage, she had assumed that she knew all about Theo's faults and virtues. During their six-month courtship and betrothal, they had attended dances and parties and had gone on carriage and horseback rides. Theo had been unfailingly charming. Although Kathleen had been warned about the infamous Ravenel temper by friends, she had been too infatuated to listen. Moreover, the constraints of courtship— chaperoned visits and limited outings—had kept her from understanding Theo's true nature. Only too late had Kathleen learned a crucial fact of life: One could never truly know a man until one lived with him.

"Tell me about his sisters," she heard Devon say. "There are three, as I recall. All unmarried?"

"Yes, my lord."

The oldest Ravenel daughter, Helen, was one-and-twenty. The twins, Cassandra and Pandora, were nineteen. Neither Theo nor his father had made arrangements for the girls in their wills. It was no easy task for a blue-blooded young woman with no dowry to attract an appropriate suitor. And the new earl had no legal obligation to provide for them at all.

"Have any of the girls been out in society?" he asked.

Kathleen shook her head. "They've been in more or less constant mourning for four years. Their mother was the first to pass, and then the earl. This was their year to come out, but now . . ." Her voice faded.

Devon paused beside a flower bed, obliging her to stop beside him. "Three unmarried gentlewomen with no income and no dowries," he said, "unfit for employment, and too elevated to marry commoners. And after spending years secluded in the country, they're probably as dull as porridge."

"They are not dull. As a matter of fact—"

She was interrupted by a high-pitched scream.

"*Help!* I'm being attacked by vicious beasts! Have pity, you savage mongrels!" The voice was young and female, pierced with convincing alarm.

Reacting instantly, Devon ran full-bore along the path and around the open gate of a walled garden. A girl in a black dress rolled on a patch of lawn bordered by flowers while a pair of black spaniels jumped on her repeatedly. Devon's steps slowed as her screams broke into wild fits of giggling.

Reaching his side, Kathleen said breathlessly, "The twins—they're only playing."

"Bloody hell," Devon muttered, coming to a halt. Dust swirled around his feet.

"*Back*, scurvy dogs," Cassandra cried in a piratical

brogue, feinting and parrying with a branch as if it were a sword. "Or I'll carve up yer worthless hides and feed ye to the sharks!" She broke the branch in two by snapping it deftly over her knee. "Fetch, ye swabbers," she told the dogs, flinging the pieces to the far side of the lawn.

The spaniels raced after the sticks with joyful barks.

Lifting herself to her elbows, the girl on the ground— Pandora—shaded her eyes with a bare hand as she saw the visitors. "Ahoy, landlubbers," she called out cheerfully. Neither of the girls wore bonnets or gloves. The cuff of one of Pandora's sleeves was missing, and a torn ruffle hung limply from the front of Cassandra's skirt.

"Girls, where are your veils?" Kathleen asked in a chiding tone.

Pandora pushed a swath of hair away from her eyes. "I made mine into a fishing net, and we used Cassandra's to wash berries."

The twins were so dazzling in their long-limbed grace, with the sunlight dancing over their disheveled hair, that it seemed entirely reasonable to have named them for Greek goddesses. There was something lawless and cheerfully feral in their rosy-cheeked disarray.

Cassandra and Pandora had been kept away from the world for far too long. Privately Kathleen thought it a pity that Lord and Lady Trenear's affection had centered almost exclusively on Theo, the only son, whose birth had secured the future for the family and the earldom. In their hopes of having a second heir, they had viewed the arrivals of three unwanted daughters as nothing less than unmitigated disasters. It had been easy for the disappointed parents to overlook Helen, who was quiet and obedient. The ungovernable twins had been left to their own devices.

Kathleen went to Pandora and helped her from the ground. Industriously she whacked at the scattering of leaves and grass on the girl's skirts. "Dear, I did remind you this morning that we would have visitors today." She brushed ineffectually at a scattering of dog hair. "I was rather hoping you might find some quiet occupation. Reading, for example—"

"We've read every single book in the library," Pandora said. "Three times."

Cassandra came to them with the yapping spaniels at her heels. "Are you the earl?" she asked Devon.

He bent to pet the dogs, and straightened to face her with a sober expression. "Yes. I'm sorry. There are no words to express how much I wish your brother were still alive."

"Poor Theo," Pandora said. "He was always doing reckless things, and nothing ever came of it. We all thought him invincible."

Cassandra's tone turned pensive as she added, "Theo thought so too."

"My lord," Kathleen interceded, "I would like to introduce Lady Cassandra and Lady Pandora."

Devon studied the twins, who resembled a pair of unkempt woodland fairies. Cassandra was possibly the more beautiful of the two, with golden hair, large blue eyes, and a Cupid's-bow mouth. Pandora, by contrast, was more slender and spare in form, with dark brown hair and a more angular face.

As the black spaniels danced and circled them, Pandora said to Devon, "I've never seen you before."

"You have, actually," he said. "At a family gathering in Norfolk. You were too young to remember."

"Were you acquainted with Theo?" Cassandra asked.

"A little."

"Did you like him?" she surprised him by asking.

"I'm afraid not," he said. "We brawled on more than one occasion."

"That's what boys do," Pandora said.

"Only bullies and lackwits," Cassandra told her. Realizing she had inadvertently insulted Devon, she sent him an ingenuous glance. "Except for *you*, my lord."

A relaxed grin crossed his mouth. "In my case, I'm afraid the description is not inaccurate."

"The Ravenel temper," Pandora said with a sage nod, and whispered theatrically, "we have it too."

"Our older sister Helen is the only one who doesn't," Cassandra added.

"Nothing provokes her," Pandora said. "We've tried ever so often, but it never works."

"My lord," Kathleen said to Devon, "shall we proceed to the glasshouses?"

"Of course."

"May we go with you?" Cassandra asked.

Kathleen shook her head. "No, dear, I think it best if the two of you went inside to tidy up and change your dresses."

"It will be lovely to have someone new to dine with," Pandora exclaimed. "Especially someone who has just come from town. I want to hear everything about London."

Devon cast a questioning glance at Kathleen.

She answered the twins directly. "I have already explained to Lord Trenear that as we are in strict mourning, we shall dine separately."

The statement was met with a flurry of protests. "But Kathleen, it's been so dull without any visitors—"

"We'll behave perfectly, I promise—"

"They're our cousins!"

"What harm would it do?"

Kathleen felt a twinge of regret, knowing that the girls were eager for any kind of diversion. However, this was the man who intended to cast them out of the only home they had ever known. And his brother, Weston, from all appearances, was already half in his cups. A pair of rakes was unsuitable company for innocent girls, particularly when the girls themselves could not be trusted to conduct themselves with restraint. No good could come of it.

"I'm afraid not," she said firmly. "We will allow the earl and his brother to dine in peace."

"But Kathleen," Cassandra pleaded, "we've had no amusement for so long."

"Of course you haven't," Kathleen said, steeling herself against a stab of guilt. "People aren't supposed to have amusements when they're in mourning."

The twins fell silent, glowering at her.

Devon broke the tension by asking Cassandra lightly, "Permission to go ashore, Captain?"

"Aye," came the sullen reply, "you and the wench can leave by way of the plank."

Kathleen frowned. "Kindly do not refer to me as a wench, Cassandra."

"It's better than 'bilge rat,'" Pandora said in a surly tone, "Which is the term *I* would have used."

After giving her a chiding glance, Kathleen returned to the graveled walk, with Devon by her side. "Well?" she asked after a moment. "Aren't you going to criticize as well?"

"I can't think of anything to add to 'bilge rat.'"

Kathleen couldn't hold back a rueful grin. "I will admit, it doesn't seem fair to require a pair of high-spirited young women to endure another year of seclusion, when they've already gone through four. I'm not certain how to manage them. No one is."

"They've never had a governess?"

"From what I understand, they've had several, none of whom lasted for more than a few months."

"Is it so difficult to find an adequate one?"

"I suspect the governesses were all perfectly capable. The problem is teaching deportment to girls who have no motivation to learn it."

"What about Lady Helen? Is she in need of similar instruction?"

"No, she's had the benefit of tutors and separate lessons. And her nature is far gentler."

They approached a row of four compartmented glasshouses that glittered in the late afternoon light. "If the girls wish to romp outdoors instead of sitting in a cheerless house," Devon said, "I don't see what harm it would do. In fact, what reason is there to hang black cloth over the windows? Why not take it down and let in the sun?"

Kathleen shook her head. "It would be scandalous to remove the mourning cloth so soon."

"Even here?"

"Hampshire is hardly at the extremity of civilization, my lord."

"Still, who would object?"

"I would. I couldn't dishonor Theo's memory that way."

"For God's sake, he won't know. It helps no one, including my late cousin, for an entire household to live in gloom. I can't conceive that he would have wanted it."

"You didn't know him well enough to judge what he would have wanted," Kathleen retorted. "And in any case, the rules can't be set aside."

"What if the rules don't serve? What if they do more harm than good?"

"Just because *you* don't understand or agree with something doesn't mean that it lacks merit."

"Agreed. But you can't deny that some traditions were invented by idiots."

"I don't wish to discuss it," Kathleen said, quickening her step.

"Dueling, for example," Devon continued, easily keeping pace with her. "Human sacrifice. Taking multiple wives—I'm sure you're sorry we've lost that tradition."

"I suppose you'd have ten wives if you could."

"I'd be sufficiently miserable with one. The other nine would be redundant."

She shot him an incredulous glance. "My lord, I am a *widow*. Have you no understanding of appropriate conversation for a woman in my situation?"

Apparently not, judging by his expression.

"What does one discuss with widows?" he asked.

"No subject that could be considered sad, shocking, or inappropriately humorous."

"That leaves me with nothing to say, then."

"Thank God," she said fervently, and he grinned.

Sinking his hands into the pockets of his trousers, he swept an intent gaze over their surroundings. "How many acres do the gardens cover?"

"Approximately twenty."

"And the glasshouses? What do they contain?"

"An orangery, a vinery, rooms for peaches, palms, ferns, and flowers . . . and this one is for orchids." She opened the door of the first glasshouse, and Devon followed her inside.

They were suffused with the perfume of vanilla and citrus. Theo's mother, Jane, had indulged her passion for the exotic blooms by cultivating rare orchids from all over the world. A year-round midsummer temperature was maintained in the orchid house by means of an adjacent boiler room.

As soon as they entered, Kathleen caught sight of Helen's slender figure between the parallel rows. Ever since her mother, the countess, had passed away, Helen had taken it upon herself to care for the two hundred potted bromeliads. It was so difficult to discern what each troublesome plant required that only a select few of the gardening staff were allowed to help.

Seeing the visitors, Helen reached for the veil that draped down her back and began to pull it over her face.

"Don't bother," Kathleen told her dryly. "Lord Trenear has taken a position against mourning veils."

Sensitive to the preferences of others, Helen left off the veil at once. She set aside a small kettle filled with water and came to the visitors. Although she didn't possess the robust sunstruck prettiness of her younger sisters, Helen was compelling in her own way, like the cool glow of moonlight. Her skin was very fair, her hair the lightest shade of blond.

Kathleen found it interesting that although Lord and Lady Trenear had named all four of their children after figures of Greek mythology, Helen was the only one who had been given the name of a mortal.

"Forgive me for interrupting your task," Devon said to Helen after they were introduced.

A hesitant smile emerged. "Not at all, my lord. I'm merely observing the orchids to make certain there is nothing they lack."

"How can you tell what they lack?" Devon asked.

"I see the color of their leaves, or the condition of the petals. I look for signs of aphids or thrips, and I try to remember which varieties prefer moist soil and which ones like to be drier."

"Will you show them to me?" Devon asked.

Helen nodded and led him along the rows, pointing

out particular specimens. "This was all my mother's collection. One of her favorites was *Peristeria elata*." She showed him a plant with marble-white blossom. "The central part of the flower resembles a tiny dove, you see? And this one is *Dendrobium aemulum*. It's called a feather orchid because of the petals." With a flash of shy mischief, Helen glanced back at Kathleen and remarked, "My sister-in-law isn't fond of orchids."

"I despise them," Kathleen said, wrinkling her nose. "Stingy, demanding flowers that take forever to bloom. And some of them smell like old boots or rancid meat."

"Those aren't my favorite," Helen admitted. "But I hope to love them someday. Sometimes one must love something before it becomes lovable."

"I disagree," Kathleen said. "No matter how much you bring yourself to love that bulgy white one in the corner —"

"*Dressleria*," Helen supplied helpfully.

"Yes. Even if you come to love it madly, it's still going to smell like old boots."

Helen smiled and continued to lead Devon along the row, explaining how the glasshouse temperature was maintained by means of an adjacent boiler room and a rainwater tank.

Noticing the speculative way Devon glanced down at Helen caused the hairs on the back of Kathleen's neck to lift unpleasantly. He and his brother, West, seemed exactly like the amoral rakes in one of the old silver-fork novels. Charming on the outside, conniving and cruel on the inside. The sooner Kathleen could manage to remove the Ravenel sisters from the estate, the better.

She had already decided to use the annuity from her jointure to take all three girls away from Eversby Priory. It was not a large sum, but it would be enough to support them if it were supplemented with earnings from gentle occupations such as needlework. She would find a small cottage where they could all live together, or perhaps a set of rooms for lease in a private house.

No matter what difficulties they might face, anything would be better than leaving three helpless girls to Devon Ravenel's mercy.

# Chapter 3

ʟATER IN THE EVENING, Devon and West had dinner in the dilapidated splendor of the dining room. The meal was of far better quality than they had expected, consisting of cold cucumber soup, roast pheasant dressed with oranges, and puddings rolled in sweetened bread crumbs.

"I made the house steward unlock the cellar so I could browse over the wine collection," West remarked. "It's gloriously well provisioned. Among the spoils, there are at least ten varieties of imported champagne, twenty cabernets, at least that many of bordeaux, and a large quantity of French brandy."

"Perhaps if I drink enough of it," Devon said, "I won't notice the house falling down around our ears."

"There are no obvious signs of weakness in the foundation. No walls out of plumb, for example, nor any visible cracks in the exterior stone that I've seen so far."

Devon glanced at him with mild surprise. "For a man who's seldom more than half sober, you've noticed a great deal."

"Have I?" West looked perturbed. "Forgive me—I seem to have become accidentally lucid." He reached for his wineglass. "Eversby Priory is one of the finest sporting estates in England. Perhaps we should shoot grouse tomorrow."

"Splendid," Devon said. "I would enjoy beginning the day with killing something."

"Afterward we'll meet with the estate agent and solicitor, and find out what's to be done with this place." West glanced at him expectantly. "You haven't yet told me what happened this afternoon while you were out walking with Lady Trenear."

Devon shrugged irritably. "Nothing happened."

After introducing him to Helen, Kathleen had been abrupt and cool for the rest of the tour through the glasshouses. When they parted company, she had worn the relieved air of someone who had concluded an unpleasant duty.

"Did she wear the veil the entire time?" West asked.

"No."

"What does she look like?"

Devon shot him a derisive glance. "Why does that matter?"

"I'm curious. Theo had his pick of women—he wouldn't have wed an ugly one."

Devon turned his attention to his wineglass, swirling the vintage until it glittered like black rubies. There seemed no way to accurately describe Kathleen. He could say that her hair was red and that her eyes were golden-brown and tip-tilted like a cat's. He could describe her fair skin and the rosy undertone that rose to the surface like a winter sunrise. The way she moved, her supple athletic grace constrained by laces and stays and layers. But none of that explained the fascination she held for him . . . the sense that somehow she had the power to unlock some altogether new feeling inside him, if only she cared to try.

"If one were to measure strictly by appearance," Devon said, "she's pleasing enough to bed, I suppose. But she has the temperament of a baited badger. I'm going to boot her from the estate as soon as possible."

"What of Theo's sisters? What will become of them?"

"Lady Helen is suited for employment as a governess, perhaps. Except that no married woman in possession of her wits would ever hire a girl that pretty."

"She's pretty?"

Devon gave him a forbidding glance. "Stay away from her, West. *Far* away. Don't seek her out, don't speak to her, don't even look at her. The same goes for the twins."

"Why not?"

"They're innocent girls."

West gave him a caustic glance. "Are they such fragile flowers that they couldn't tolerate a few minutes of my company?"

" 'Fragile' is not the word I would use. The twins have spent years scampering about the estate like a pair of foxes. They're unworldly and more than a little wild. God knows what's to be done with them."

"I pity them, if they're sent out into the world without a man's protection."

"That's not my concern." Devon reached for the carafe of wine and refilled his glass, trying not to think of what would become of them. The world wasn't kind to innocent young women. "They were Theo's responsibility. Not mine."

"I believe this is the part in the play," West mused, "when a noble hero would appear to save the day, rescue the damsels, and set everything to rights."

Devon rubbed the corners of his eyes with the pads of his thumb and forefinger. "The truth is, West, I couldn't salvage this damned estate, or save the damsels, even if I wanted to. I've never been a hero, nor do I have any wish to be."

". . . IN LIGHT OF the late earl's failure to provide legitimate male issue," the family solicitor droned the next morning, "according to the legal rule of perpetuities, which renders the devise of entail void for remoteness, the settlement has expired."

As an expectant silence filled the study, Devon looked up from a pile of leases, deeds, and account books. He was meeting with the estate agent and solicitor, respectively Mr. Totthill and Mr. Fogg, neither of whom appeared to be a day under ninety.

"What does that mean?" Devon asked.

"The estate is yours to do with as you please, my lord," Fogg said, adjusting his pince-nez to regard him owlishly. "At present, you are not bound by entail."

Devon's gaze shot to West, who was lounging in the corner. They exchanged relieved glances. *Thank God.* He could sell the estate in parts or in its entirety, pay off the debt, and go on his way with no further obligation.

"I will be honored to assist you in resettling the entail, my lord," Fogg said.

"That won't be necessary."

Both the estate manager and solicitor looked perturbed at Devon's reply.

"My lord," Totthill said, "I can assure you of Mr. Fogg's competence in such matters. He has twice assisted in resettling the entail for the Ravenels."

"I don't doubt his competence." Relaxing back in his chair, Devon propped his booted feet on the desk. "However, I don't want to be limited by an entail, since I intend to sell the estate."

A shocked silence greeted his pronouncement.

"What portion of it?" Totthill dared to ask.

"All, including the house."

Aghast, the two men burst out with protests . . . Eversby Priory was a historic inheritance, won through the service and sacrifice of his ancestors . . . Devon would have no respectable position without retaining at least a fragment of the estate . . . Surely he could not mean to disgrace his future offspring by leaving them a landless title.

Exasperated, Devon gestured for the pair to be silent. "Trying to preserve Eversby Priory would involve far more effort than it's worth," he said flatly. "No rational man would conclude otherwise. As for my future offspring, there won't be any, since I have no intention of marrying."

The estate manager cast an imploring glance at West. "Mr. Ravenel, you cannot support your brother in this folly."

West extended his hands as if they were a set of weighing scales, and compared invisible counterbalances. "On one hand, he has a lifetime of responsibility, debt, and drudgery. On the other, he has freedom and pleasure. Is there really a choice?"

Before the elderly men could respond, Devon spoke briskly. "The course is set. To begin with, I want a list of investments, deeds, and interests, as well as a complete inventory of every item in the London house and the estate. That includes paintings, tapestries, rugs, furniture, bronzes, marbles, silverware, and the contents of the glasshouses, the stables, and the carriage house."

Totthill asked dully, "Will you want an estimate of all the livestock, my lord?"

"Naturally."

"Not my horse." A new voice entered the conversation. All four men looked to the doorway, where Kathleen stood as straight and rigid as a blade. She stared at Devon with open loathing. "The Arabian belongs to me."

Everyone rose to his feet except for Devon, who remained seated at the desk. "Do you ever enter a room the ordinary way?" he asked curtly, "or is it your usual habit to slink past the threshold and pop up like a jack-in-the-box?"

"I only want to make it clear that while you're tallying the spoils, you will remove my horse from the list."

"Lady Trenear," Mr. Fogg interceded, "I regret to say that on your wedding day, you relinquished all rights to your movable property."

Kathleen's eyes narrowed. "I'm entitled to keep my jointure and all the possessions I brought to the marriage."

"Your jointure," Totthill agreed, "but *not* your possessions. I assure you that no court in England will regard a married woman as a separate legal being. The horse was your husband's, and now it belongs to Lord Trenear."

Kathleen's face went skull-white, and then red. "Lord Trenear is stripping the estate like a jackal with a rotting carcass. Why must he be given a horse that my father gave to me?"

Infuriated that Kathleen would show him so little deference in front of the others, Devon stood from the desk and approached her in a few strides. To her credit, she didn't cower, even though he was twice her size. "Devil take you," he snapped, "none of this is my fault."

"Of course it is. You'll seize on any excuse to sell Eversby Priory because you don't want to take on a challenge."

"It's only a challenge when there's some small hope of success. This is a debacle. The list of creditors is longer than my bloody arm, the coffers are empty, and the annual yields have been cut in half."

"I don't believe you. You're planning to sell the estate to settle personal debts that have nothing to do with Eversby Priory."

Devon's hands knotted with the urge to destroy something. His rising bloodlust would only be satisfied with the sound of shattering objects. He had never faced a situation like this, and there was no one to give him trustworthy advice, no kindly aristocratic relation, no knowledgeable friends in the peerage. And this woman could only accuse and insult him.

"I had no debt," he growled, "until I inherited this mess. God's bollocks, did your idiot husband never explain any of the estate's issues to you? Were you completely ignorant of how dire the situation was when you married him? No matter—someone has to face reality, and Christ help us all, it seems to be me." He turned his back on her and returned to the desk. "Your presence isn't wanted," he said without looking back. "You will leave now."

"Eversby Priory has survived four hundred years of revolutions and foreign wars," he heard Kathleen say contemptuously, "and now it will take but one self-serving rake to bring it all to ruins."

As if he were entirely to blame for the situation. As if he alone would be accountable for the estate's demise. Damn her to hell.

With effort, Devon swallowed back his outrage. Deliberately he stretched out his legs with relaxed indolence and glanced at his brother. "West, are we quite certain that Cousin Theo perished in a fall?" he asked coolly. "It seems far more likely that he froze to death in the marital bed."

West chuckled, not above the enjoyment of a malicious quip.

Totthill and Fogg, for their part, kept their gazes down.

Kathleen crossed the threshold and sent the door shuddering with a violent slam.

"Brother," West said with mock chiding, "that was beneath you."

"Nothing's beneath me," Devon replied, stone-faced. "You know that."

FOR A LONG time after Totthill and Fogg had left, Devon remained at the desk and brooded. Opening an account book, he paged through it without absorbing anything. He was barely aware of the moment when West wandered out of the study, yawning and grumbling. Feeling strangled, Devon unknotted his necktie with a few impatient tugs and opened the front of his collar.

Christ, how he wanted to be back at his London terrace, where everything was well maintained and comfortable and familiar. If Theo were still the earl, and he were still merely the black sheep cousin, he would have gone for a morning ride on the Hyde Park bridle path, and afterward he might have enjoyed a good meal at his club. Later he would have met with friends to watch a boxing match or a horse race, attend the theater, and chase after lightskirts. No responsibility, nothing to worry about.

Nothing to lose.

The sky rumbled as if to underscore his sullen spirits. Devon cast a murderous glance at the window. Rain-tumbled air had pushed inland to settle over the downs, darkening the sky to vestment-black. It would be a ripper of a storm.

"My lord." A timid rap at the doorjamb drew his attention.

Recognizing Helen, Devon rose to his feet. He tried to make his expression pleasant. "Lady Helen."

"Forgive me for disturbing you."

"Come in."

Helen entered the room cautiously. Her gaze swerved to the window before moving back to him. "Thank you, my lord. I came to tell you that with the storm moving in so fast, I would like to send out a footman to search for Kathleen."

Devon frowned. He hadn't been aware that Kathleen had left the house. "Where is she?"

"She has gone to visit the tenant farm on the other side of the hill. She took a basket of broth and elderberry wine to Mrs. Lufton, who is recovering from childbirth fever. I asked Kathleen if I could accompany her, but she insisted on walking alone. She said she needed the solitude." Helen's fingers wove together into a pale knot. "She should have returned by now, but the weather has come in so quickly that I fear she might be caught out in it."

There was nothing in the world that Devon would love more than the sight of Kathleen rain-soaked and bedraggled. He had to restrain himself from rubbing his hands together in villainous glee.

"There's no need to send a footman," he said casually. "I'm certain that Lady Trenear will have the sense to stay at the tenant farm until the rain passes."

"Yes, but the downs will have turned to mud."

Better and better. Kathleen, wading through mud and clay. Devon fought to keep his expression grave, when inside all was joy and exploding Roman candles. He went to the window. No rain yet, but dark clouds seeped through the sky like ink on wet parchment. "We'll wait a bit longer. She could return momentarily."

Lightning bolts pierced the firmament, a trio of brilliant jagged streaks accompanied by a series of cracks that sounded like shattering glass.

Helen drew closer. "My lord, I am aware that you and my sister-in-law exchanged words earlier—"

" 'Exchanged words' would imply that we had a civilized debate," he said. "Had it lasted any longer, we would have torn each other to shreds."

A frown corrugated her smooth brow. "You both find yourself in difficult circumstances. Sometimes that causes people to say things they don't mean. However, if you and Kathleen could manage to set aside your differences—"

"Lady Helen—"

"Do call me cousin."

"Cousin, you will avoid much future distress if you learn to see people as they really are, instead of as you wish them to be."

Helen smiled faintly. "I already do."

"If that were true, you would understand that Lady Trenear and I are correct in our assessments of each other. I am a scoundrel, and she is a heartless bitch who's entirely capable of looking after herself."

Helen's eyes, the silvery-blue of moonstones, widened in concern. "My lord, I have come to know Kathleen very well in our shared grief over my brother's passing—"

"I doubt she feels much grief," Devon interrupted brusquely. "By her own admission, she hasn't shed a single tear over your brother's death."

Helen blinked. "She told you that? But she didn't explain why?"

Devon shook his head.

Looking perturbed, Helen said, "It isn't my story to tell."

Concealing an instant flare of curiosity, Devon shrugged casually. "Don't concern yourself with it, then. My opinion of her won't alter."

As he had intended, the show of indifference pushed Helen into talking. "If it helps you to understand Kathleen a little better," she said uncertainly, "perhaps I should explain something. Will you swear on your honor to keep it in confidence?"

"Of course," Devon said readily. Having no honor, he never hesitated to promise something on it.

Helen went to one of the windows. Fissures of lightning crackled across the sky, illuminating her delicate features with a blue-white flash. "When I didn't see Kathleen cry after Theo's accident, I assumed it was because she preferred to keep her emotions private. People have different ways of grieving. But one evening as she and I sat in the parlor with needlework, I saw her prick her finger, and . . . she didn't react. It was as if she hadn't even felt it. She sat watching a drop of blood form, until I couldn't bear it any longer. I wrapped her finger with a handkerchief, and asked what was the matter. She was ashamed and confused . . . she said she never cried, but she thought that she would have at least been able to shed some tears for Theo."

Helen paused, seeming preoccupied with removing a flake of peeling paint from the wall.

"Go on," Devon murmured.

Meticulously Helen set the flake of paint on the windowsill, and picked at another, as if she were pulling scabs from a half-healed wound. "I asked Kathleen if she could ever remember crying. She said yes, when she was a little girl, on the day she left Ireland. Her parents had told her they were all traveling to England on a three-masted steamer. They went to the docks and made as if to board the ship. But as Kathleen and her nanny stepped onto the gangplank, she realized that her parents weren't following. Her mother told her that she was going to stay with some very nice people in England, and they would send for her someday when they didn't have to travel abroad so often. Kathleen became quite frantic, but her parents turned and walked away, while the nanny dragged her aboard." Helen sent him a sidelong glance. "She was only five years old."

Devon swore quietly. He flattened his palms on the desk, staring at nothing as she continued.

"For hours after Kathleen had been brought to the ship's cabin, she screamed and sobbed until the nanny became very cross and said, 'If you insist on making such a horrid fuss, I shall go away, and you'll be alone in the world with no one to look after you. Your parents sent you away because you're a nuisance.'" Helen paused. "Kathleen quieted at once. She took the nanny's warning to mean that she must never cry again; it was the price of survival."

"Did her parents ever send for her?"

Helen shook her head. "That was the last time Kathleen ever saw her mother. A few years later, Lady Carbery succumbed to malaria during a return voyage from Egypt. When Kathleen was told about her mother's passing, she felt the pain of it acutely, but she couldn't find the relief of tears. It was the same with Theo's death."

The sound of hard-falling rain was like the clatter of coins.

"Kathleen is not heartless, you see," Helen murmured. "She feels very deep sorrow. It's only that she can't show it."

Devon wasn't certain whether to thank or curse Helen for the revelations. He didn't want to feel any compassion for Kathleen. But the rejection by her parents at such a tender age would have been devastating. He understood all about the desire to avoid painful memories and emotions . . . the compelling need to keep certain doors closed.

"Were Lord and Lady Berwick kind to her?" he asked gruffly.

"I believe so. She speaks of them with affection." Helen paused. "The family was very strict. There were many rules, and they were enforced with severity. They value self-restraint perhaps too much." She smiled absently. "The only exception is the subject of horses. They're all quite horse-mad. The night before Kathleen's wedding, at dinner, they had an enthusiastic conversation about pedigrees and equine training, and rhapsodized about the fragrance of the stables as if it were the finest perfume. It went on for nearly an hour. Theo was a bit annoyed, I think. He felt somewhat left out, since he didn't share their passion for the subject."

Biting back an observation about his cousin's lack of interest in any subject except himself, Devon glanced outside.

The storm had settled over the brow of the high grazing fell, water pouring into the chalk streams and flooding the downs. Now the idea of Kathleen being caught out in that tempest alone was no longer enjoyable.

It was intolerable.

Cursing beneath his breath, Devon pushed back from the desk. "If you'll excuse me, Lady Helen . . ."

"You'll send a footman after Kathleen?" Helen asked hopefully.

"No. I'll fetch her myself."

She looked relieved. "Thank you, my lord. How kind you are!"

"It's not kindness." Devon headed to the doorway. "I'm only doing it for the chance of seeing her ankle-deep in mud."

KATHLEEN STRODE BRISKLY along the dirt path that snaked between an overgrown hedgerow and an expanse of ancient oak woodland. The forest rustled from the approaching storm as birds and wildlife took cover, while leaves descended in pale currents. A bolt of thunder unfurled with ground-shaking force.

Pulling a shawl more tightly around herself, she considered going back to the Luftons' farm. There was no doubt that the family would provide shelter. But she had already reached the halfway point between the tenant farm and the estate.

The sky seemed to break open, and rain lashed the ground, blanketing the path until it was puddled and streaming. Finding a gap in the hedgerow, Kathleen left the path to head across a sloped field of old grassland. Beyond the downland fields, the chalk soil was mingled with clay, a rich and sticky composite that would make for an unpleasant slog.

She should have heeded earlier signs that the weather would turn; it would have been wiser to delay her visit to Mrs. Lufton until tomorrow. But the clash with Devon had unsettled her, and her thinking had been muddled. Now after the conversation she'd had with Mrs. Lufton, the red mist of fury had faded enough to allow her to see the situation more clearly.

While sitting at Mrs. Lufton's bedside, Kathleen had asked after her health and that of her newborn daughter, and eventually discussion had turned to the farm. In answer to Kathleen's questions, Mrs. Lufton had admitted that it had been a long time, longer than anyone could remember, since the Ravenels had made improvements on the estate land. Moreover, the terms of their leases had discouraged the tenants from making changes on their own. Mrs. Lufton had heard that some leaseholders on other estates had adopted more advanced farming practices, but on the Eversby Priory land, things remained as they had been for the past hundred years.

Everything the woman had said confirmed what Devon had told her earlier.

Why hadn't Theo explained anything to her about the estate's financial troubles? He had told Kathleen that the house had been neglected because no one had wanted to change his late mother's decorations. He had promised that Kathleen would be in charge of ordering silk damask and French paper for the walls, new velvet curtains, fresh plasterwork and paint, new carpets and furniture. They would make the stables beautiful, he had told her, and install the latest equipment for the horses.

Theo had spun a fairy story, and it had been so appealing that she had chosen to believe it. But none of it had been true. He had known that she would eventually find out that they couldn't begin to afford any of what he'd promised. How had he expected her to react?

She would never know the answer. Theo was gone, and their marriage had ended before it had even begun. The only choice was to forget the past and set her life on a new course.

But first she had to face the uncomfortable truth that she had hadn't been fair to Devon. He was an arrogant cad, to be certain, but he had every right to decide the fate of Eversby Priory. It was his now. She had spoken out of turn and behaved like a shrew, and for that she would have to apologize, even knowing that he would throw every word back in her face.

Glumly Kathleen trudged across the spongy turf. Water seeped through seams and welts of her shoes, soaking into her stockings. Soon her widow's veil, which she had folded back to hang behind her, was sodden and heavy. The smell of aniline, used in the dye for mourning clothes, was especially pungent when wet. She should have changed the indoor headpiece to a bonnet instead of dashing out impulsively. It seemed she was no better than the twins; a fine example she had set, running about like a madwoman.

She jumped as lightning split the angry sky. Her heart began to thump, and she grabbed up handfuls of her skirts to run faster across the field. The ground had softened, causing her heels to sink deep with each step. Rain came down in violent whooshes, bending the stems of blue scabious and knapweed until bright flower heads were lodged into the grass. The clay soil beyond the field would turn to mud by the time she reached it.

Another lightning bolt struck, the sound so explosive that Kathleen flinched and covered her ears. Realizing she had dropped her shawl, she turned to look for it, shielding her eyes with one hand. The limp mass of wool lay on the ground, several yards away. "Bother," she exclaimed, heading back to retrieve it.

She stopped with a low cry as a massive dark blur hurtled toward her, too fast to evade. Instinctively she turned and covered her head with her arms. Deafened by the sound of thunder mingled with the roar of the pulse in her ears, she waited, shivering, for whatever would happen. When it seemed that no immediate disaster had befallen her, she straightened and swiped at her wet face with her sleeve.

A huge shape loomed beside her . . . a man mounted on a sturdy black dray. It was Devon, she realized in bewilderment. She couldn't say a word to save her life. He wasn't dressed for riding—he wasn't even wearing gloves. More perplexing still, he was wearing a stableman's low-crowned felt hat, as if he had borrowed it while departing in haste.

"Lady Helen asked me to fetch you," Devon called out, his face unfathomable. "You can either ride back with me, or we'll stand here and argue in a lightning storm until we're both flambéed. Personally I'd prefer the latter—it would be better than reading the rest of those account ledgers."

Kathleen stared at him with stunned confusion.

In practical terms, it was possible to ride double with

Devon back to the estate. The dray, broad-built and calm-tempered, would be more than equal to the task. But as she tried to imagine it, their bodies touching . . . his arms around her . . .

No. She couldn't bear being that close to any man. Her flesh crawled at the thought.

"I . . . I can't ride with you." Although she tried to sound decisive, her voice was wavering and plaintive. Rain streamed down her face, rivulets trickling into her mouth.

Devon's lips parted as if he were about to deliver a scathing reply. As his gaze traveled over her drenched form, however, his expression softened. "Then you take the horse, and I'll walk back."

Dumbstruck by the offer, Kathleen could only stare at him. "No," she eventually managed to say. "But . . . thank you. Please, you must return to the house."

"We'll both walk," he said impatiently, "or we'll both ride. But I won't leave you."

"I'll be perfectly—"

She broke off and flinched at a bone-rattling peal of thunder.

"Let me take you home." Devon's tone was pragmatic, as if they were standing in a parlor instead of a violent late-summer storm. Had he said it in an overbearing manner, Kathleen might have been able to refuse him. But somehow he'd guessed that softening his approach was the best way to undermine her.

The dray bobbed its head and pawed the ground with one hoof.

She would have to ride back with him, she realized in despair. There was no alternative. Wrapping her arms around herself, she said anxiously, "F-first I have something to say to you."

Devon's brows lifted, his face cold.

"I . . ." She swallowed hard, and the words came out in a rush. "What I said in the study earlier was unkind, and untrue, and I'm s-sorry for it. It was very wrong of me. I shall make that very clear to Mr. Totthill and Mr. Fogg. And your brother."

His expression changed, one corner of his mouth curling upward in the hint of a smile that sent her heartbeat into chaos. "You needn't bother mentioning it to them. All three will be calling me far worse before all is said and done."

"Nevertheless, it wasn't fair of me—"

"It's forgotten. Come, the rain is worsening."

"I must fetch my shawl."

Devon followed her glance to the dark heap in the distance. "Is that it? Good God, leave it there."

"I can't—"

"It's ruined by now. I'll buy you another."

"I couldn't accept something so personal from you. Besides . . . you can't afford extra expenses, now that you have Eversby Priory."

She saw the flash of his grin.

"I'll replace it," he said. "From what I gather, people at my level of debt never concern themselves with economizing." Sliding back against the cantle of the saddle, he extended a hand down. His form was large and lean against the rioting sky, the hard lines of his face cast in shadow.

Kathleen gave him a doubtful glance; it would require considerable strength for him to lift her while he was mounted. "You won't drop me?" she asked uneasily.

Devon sounded insulted. "I'm hardly some limp-wristed fop, madam."

"My skirts are heavy and wet—"

"Give me your hand."

She approached him, and his hand took hers in a strong clasp. A nervous shiver went through her.

She hadn't touched any man since Theo's death three months ago. Lord Berwick had attended the funeral, and afterward had offered Kathleen an awkward embrace, but she had given him her gloved hand instead. "I can't," she had whispered to him, and Lord Berwick had nodded in understanding. Although he was a kind man, he had seldom been disposed to demonstrations of affection. Lady Berwick was the same, a benevolent but self-contained woman who had tried to teach her daughters and Kathleen the value of self-restraint. "Rule your emotions," she had always advised, "or they will most certainly rule you."

An icy runnel of rain ran down Kathleen's sleeve, contrasting sharply with the heat of Devon's grip, and she shivered.

The dray waited patiently in the thrashing wind and rain.

"I want you to spring up," she heard Devon say, "and I'll lift you until you can find the stirrup with your left foot. Don't try to swing a leg over. Just mount as if it were a sidesaddle."

"When should I jump?"

"Now would be convenient," he said dryly.

Gathering her strength, Kathleen leaped from the ground with as much force as her legs could produce. Devon caught the momentum and lifted her with shocking ease. She didn't even have to find the stirrup; she landed neatly on the saddle with her right leg folded. Gasping, she fought for her balance, but Devon had already adjusted, his left arm enclosing her in a secure hold. "I have you. Settle . . . easy."

She stiffened at the feel of being clasped firmly, his muscles working around her, his breath at her ear.

"This will teach you to bring baskets to ailing neighbors," he said. "I hope you realize that all the selfish people are safe and dry at home."

"Why did you come after me?" she managed to ask, trying to calm the little shocks that kept reverberating through her.

"Lady Helen was worried." Once assured of her seat, Devon reached up with his left hand, tugged at her veil and headpiece, and tossed them to the ground. "Sorry," he said before she could protest. "But that dye smells like the floor of an East End tavern. Here, slide your leg to the other side of the saddle."

"I can't, it's caught in my skirts." The horse's weight shifted beneath them. Unable to find purchase on the smooth, flat saddle, Kathleen fumbled and accidentally gripped Devon's thigh, the surface hard as stone. Gasping, she drew her hand back. It seemed that no matter how much air she took in, it wasn't enough.

Temporarily transferring the reins to his left hand, Devon removed his felt hat and pushed it over Kathleen's head. He proceeded to pull at the twisted, bunched layers of her skirts until she was able to unbend her knee enough to slide her leg over the horse's withers.

In childhood she had ridden double with the Berwicks' daughters when they had gone on pony rides. But there was no possible comparison with this, the feeling of a powerfully built man right behind her, his legs bracketing hers. Aside from the horse's mane, there was nothing to hold on to; no reins to grasp, no stirrups for her feet.

Devon urged the horse into a canter, a gait that was impeccably fluid and smooth in an Arabian or Thoroughbred. But it was different for a wide-chested dray, whose legs were spaced farther from its center of gravity, the three-beat rhythm shorter and rounder. Kathleen perceived immediately that Devon was an accomplished rider, moving easily with the horse and communicating with explicit signals. She worked to find the rolling motion of the canter, but it wasn't at all the same as riding alone, and she was mortified to find herself bouncing in the saddle like a novice.

Devon's arm latched more tightly around her. "Easy. I won't let you fall."

"But there's nothing for me to—"

"Just relax into it."

Feeling how capably he maintained the center of their combined weight, she tried to soften her clenched muscles. The slope of her back came to rest exactly against his chest, and then as if by magic, she found the bend and balance of the horse's motion. As she melted into the cadence, there was a curious satisfaction in the sensation of their bodies moving in perfect tandem.

Devon's hand splayed across her midriff with supportive pressure. Even through the mass of her skirts, she could feel the robust muscles of his thighs, flexing rhythmically. An unbearable sweet ache began inside her, intensifying until it seemed as if something might fracture.

As they began up the hill, Devon slowed the dray to a walk and leaned to distribute more weight over the horse's front legs. Obliged to lean forward as well, Kathleen grasped the dray's rough black mane. She heard Devon's voice, muffled by a peal of thunder. Turning her head to hear him better, she felt the electrifying texture of shaven bristle as his jaw brushed her cheek. It sent a ticklish feeling into her throat, as if she'd just bitten into a honeycomb.

"We're almost there," Devon repeated, his breath searing against her wet skin.

They ascended the hill and cantered toward the stable block, a two-story building constructed of plum-colored brick, with arched entrances and molded stone surrounds. A dozen saddle horses were housed on one side of the structure, and ten harness horses and a mule on the other side. The stable also housed a saddle room, harness room, tack room, a forage loft, a coach house, and grooms' chambers.

Compared to the manor house at Eversby Priory, the stables were in far superior condition. Without a doubt that was because of the influence of the stable master, Mr. Bloom, a stout Yorkshire gentleman with white muttonchop whiskers and twinkling blue eyes. What Bloom lacked in height, he made up for in brawn, his hands so meaty and strong that he could crush walnuts with his fingers. No stable had ever been run with more exacting standards: The floors were always scrupulously clean, every piece of tack and leather highly polished. The horses in Bloom's care lived better than most people. Kathleen had met the stable master approximately a fortnight before Theo's accident, and she had liked him immediately. Bloom had known about the Carbery Park Stud Farm, and the exceptional Arabian strain that Kathleen's father had developed, and he had been delighted to include Asad in the Ravenel stables.

In the aftermath of Theo's accident, Mr. Bloom had supported Kathleen's decision to keep Asad from being put down, in spite of the demands made by Theo's friends and peers. Bloom had understood that Theo's recklessness had contributed to the tragedy. "A horseman should never approach his mount with anger," Bloom had told Kathleen privately, weeping in the aftermath of Theo's death. He had known Theo since he'd been a young boy, and had taught him how to ride. "Especially an Arabian.

I told Lord Trenear, 'If tha goes into a pitch battle with Asad, tha'll excite him to wildness.' I could see his lordship was having one of his spates. I told him there was a dozen other mounts that were better for him to ride that day. He wouldn't listen, but I blame mi'sell all the same."

Kathleen hadn't been able to make herself return to the stables since Theo's death. She didn't blame Asad in the least for what had happened, but she was afraid of what she might feel when she saw him. She had failed Asad, just as she had failed Theo, and she didn't know when—or how—she could ever come to terms with any of it.

Realizing that they were riding through the stable's main arch, Kathleen closed her eyes briefly and felt her stomach turn to ice. She clamped her lips together and managed to keep silent. With every breath, she took in the familiar scents of horses and bedding and feed, the comforting smells of her childhood.

Devon stopped the dray and dismounted first, while a pair of stable hands approached.

"Spend extra time caring for his feet, lads," came Mr. Bloom's genial voice. "This kind of weather brings thrush." He looked up Kathleen, his manner changing. "Milady. 'Tis gradely to see thee here again."

Their gazes met. Kathleen expected a hint of accusation in his eyes, after the way she had avoided the stables and abandoned Asad. But there was only friendliness and concern. She smiled tremulously. "It's good to see you too, Mr. Bloom."

As she dismounted, Kathleen was surprised to find Devon assisting her. His hands fit at her waist to ease her descent. She turned to face him, and he removed the hat carefully from her head.

Handing the dripping felt object to the stable master,

Devon said, "Thank you for the loan of your hat, Mr. Bloom."

"I'm glad tha managed to find Lady Trenear in all that rain and wuthering." Noticing that Kathleen's gaze had flickered to the row of stalls, Bloom commented, "Asad is in fine fettle, milady. These past weeks, he's been the best-behaved lad i' the stable. Reckon he'd be pleased wi' a word or two from thee."

Kathleen's heart thumped erratically. The stable floor seemed to move beneath her feet. She nodded jerkily. "I—I suppose I could see him for a moment."

To her astonishment, she felt Devon's fingers slide beneath her jaw, gently urging her to look up at him. His face was wet, his lashes spiked, the dripping locks of his hair as shiny as ribbons. "Perhaps later," he said to Mr. Bloom, his intent gaze remaining on Kathleen. "We don't want Lady Trenear to catch a chill."

"Aye, reckon not," the stable master said hastily.

Kathleen swallowed hard and tore her gaze from Devon's. She was shaking deep inside, dull panic rising. "I want to see him," she whispered.

Wordlessly Devon followed as she went to the row of stalls. She heard Mr. Bloom giving directions to the stable hands about seeing to the dray. "No faffin' about, lads! Gi' the horse a good rubdown an' warm mash."

Asad waited in one of the end stalls, watching alertly as Kathleen approached. His head lifted, his ears perking forward in recognition. He was a compact gelding with powerful hindquarters, an elegant conformation that afforded both speed and endurance. His coloring was a shade of chestnut so light it appeared golden, his mane and tail flaxen. "There's my boy," Kathleen exclaimed gently, reaching out to him with her palm upward. Asad sniffed at her hand and gave her a welcoming nicker. Lowering his finely modeled head, he moved to the front of the stall. She stroked his nose and forehead, and he reacted with pure gladness, blowing softly and nudging closer.

"I shouldn't have waited so long to see you," she said, overcome with remorse. Clumsily she leaned to kiss the space between the horse's eyes. She felt him nibble delicately at the shoulder of her dress, trying to groom her. A crooked grin twisted her lips. Pushing his head away, she scratched his satiny neck in the way she knew he liked. "I shouldn't have left you alone, my poor boy." Her fingers tangled in his white-blond mane.

She felt the weight of his head come to rest on her shoulder. The trusting gesture caused her throat to cinch around a quick breath. "It wasn't your fault," she whispered. "It was mine. I'm sorry, I'm so sorry—"

Her throat had cinched painfully tight. No matter how hard she swallowed, the sharp constriction wouldn't dissolve. It was cutting off her breath. Her arms loosened from Asad's neck, and she turned away. Wheezing, staggering, she crashed into the hard wall of Devon's chest.

He gripped her elbows, steadying her. "What is it?" She could scarcely hear his voice over her frantic heartbeat.

She shook her head, struggling not to feel, not to give in.

"Tell me." Devon gave her a soft, urgent shake.

No words would come. Only a raw breath that fractured into coughing sobs. The pressure in her throat released with startling suddenness, and her eyes filled with liquid fire. She shoved at Devon in blind desperation. *God, no, please . . .* She was losing control in the most humiliating circumstances imaginable, with the last person in the world she would ever want to witness it.

Devon's arm clamped around her shoulders. Ignoring her efforts to twist away, he guided her past the stalls.

"Milor'?" Mr. Bloom asked in mild alarm. "Wha' does the lass need?"

"Privacy," Devon said curtly. "Where can I take her?"

"The saddle room," the stable master said, pointing to the arched opening beyond the stalls.

Devon half pushed, half carried Kathleen into the windowless room lined with match-boarded walls. She grappled with him, flailing like a drowning woman. He said her name repeatedly, patiently, his arms tightening to contain her. The more she struggled, the more firmly he held her, until she was gathered against his chest in a nerveless bundle. Trying to swallow back the shuddering sounds that came from her throat only made them worse.

"You're safe," she heard him say. "Easy . . . you're safe. I won't let go."

Dimly she realized that she was no longer trying to escape but fighting to press closer and hide against him. Her arms clutched around his neck, her face against his throat as she sobbed too hard to think or breathe. Emotion came in a deluge, impossible to separate into its parts. To feel so much all at once seemed a kind of madness.

Her corset was too tight, like a living thing intent on crushing her in its jaws. She went weak, her knees giving way. Her body folded in a slow collapse, and she felt herself being caught up and lifted in strong arms. There was no way to find her bearings, no way to control anything. She could only surrender, dissolving into the devouring shadows.

# Chapter 4

$\mathcal{A}$FTER A MEASURELESS INTERVAL, awareness returned by slow degrees. Kathleen stirred, aware of a brief murmured conversation and retreating footsteps, and the relentless patter of rain on the roof. Irritably she turned her face away from the sounds, wanting to drowse a little longer. Something soft and warm touched the crest of her cheek, lingering gently, and the feel of it teased her senses awake.

Her limbs were heavy and relaxed, her head comfortably supported. She was held firmly against a solid surface that rose and fell in a steady rhythm. With every breath, she drew in a fragrance of horses and leather, and something fresh like vetiver. She had the confused impression that it was morning . . . but that didn't seem quite right . . .

Recalling the storm, she stiffened.

A dark murmur tickled her ear. "You're safe. Rest against me."

Her eyes flew open. "What . . ." she faltered, blinking. "Where . . . *oh.*"

She found herself staring up into a pair of dark blue eyes. A little pang, not entirely unpleasant, pierced somewhere beneath her ribs at the discovery that Devon was holding her. They were on the floor of the saddle room, on a stack of folded horse blankets and rugs. It was the warmest, driest place in the stables, located close to the stalls for easy access. An overhead skylight illuminated the rows of saddle racks affixed to the white pine walls; rain streamed over the glass and sent dappled shadows downward.

Deciding that she wasn't ready to confront the sheer awfulness of how she had just behaved, Kathleen shut her eyes again. Her lids felt itchy and swollen, and she fumbled to rub them.

Devon caught one of her wrists, easing it away. "Don't, you'll make them worse." He pressed a soft cloth into her hand, one of the rags used for polishing tack. "It's clean. The stable master brought it a few minutes ago."

"Did he . . . that is, I hope I wasn't . . . like this?" she asked, her voice thin and scuffed.

He sounded amused. "In my arms, you mean? I'm afraid so."

A moan of distress trembled on her lips. "What he must have thought . . ."

"He thought nothing of it. In fact, he said it would benefit you to do a bit of 'screetin,' as he put it."

The Yorkshire word for bawling like an infant.

Humiliated, Kathleen blotted her eyes and blew her nose.

Devon's hand slid into her tumbled hair, his fingertips finding her scalp and stroking gently as if she were a cat. It was wildly improper for him to touch her in such a way, but it was so shockingly pleasant that Kathleen couldn't quite bring herself to object.

"Tell me what happened," he said softly.

Her insides turned hollow. Her body was as limp as an empty flour sack. Even the effort to shake her head was exhausting.

His soothing hand continued to play in her hair. "Tell me."

She was too exhausted to refuse him. "It was my fault," she heard herself say. A continuous hot rivulet leaked from the outside corner of her eye and disappeared into her hairline. "I'm the reason Theo is dead."

Devon was silent, waiting patiently for her to continue.

The words came out in a shamed rush. "I drove him to it. We had been quarreling. If I had behaved the way I should, if I'd been kind instead of spiteful, Theo would still be alive. I had planned to ride Asad that morning, but Theo wanted me to stay and battle it out with him, and I said no, not when he was in such a state—then Theo said he would go riding with me, but I told him—" She broke off with a wretched sob, and continued resolutely. "I said he wouldn't be able to keep pace with me. He had been drinking the night before, and he still wasn't clearheaded."

Devon's thumb stroked across her temple, through the trail of salt water. "So he decided to prove you wrong," he said after a moment.

Kathleen nodded, her jaw trembling.

"He dashed out to the stables, half drunk and in a fury," Devon continued, "and insisted on riding a horse that he probably wouldn't have been able to control even sober."

The tiny muscles of her face spasmed. "Because I didn't manage him as a good wife would have—"

"Wait," Devon said, as a hiccupping sob escaped her. "No, don't start that again. Hush, now. Take a breath."

His hand slid from her hair, and he propped her higher in his lap until their gazes were almost level. Taking up a fresh cloth, he blotted her cheeks and eyes as if she were a child. "Let's consider this rationally," he said. "First, as to this business of managing Theo—a husband isn't a horse to be trained. My cousin was a full-grown man in command of his own fate. He chose to take a stupid risk, and he paid for it."

"Yes, but he'd been drinking—"

"Also his choice."

Kathleen was struck by his blunt words and matter-of-fact manner. She had expected him to blame her, perhaps even more than she blamed herself, if that were possible. No one could deny her culpability; it was too obvious. "It was my fault," she insisted. "Theo wasn't in command of himself when he was angry. His judgment was impaired. I should have found a way to appease him, and instead I pushed him over the edge."

"It wasn't your responsibility to save Theo from himself. When he decided to act like a hotheaded fool, no one could have stopped him."

"But you see, it wasn't a *decision*. Theo couldn't help it that I set off his temper."

Devon's mouth twisted as if she had said something ridiculous. "Of course he could."

"How do you know that?"

"Because I'm a Ravenel. I have the same damned evil temper. Whenever I yield to it, I'm perfectly aware of what I'm doing."

She shook her head, unwilling to be pacified. "You didn't hear the way I spoke to him. I was very sarcastic and unkind . . . Oh, you should have seen his face . . ."

"Yes, I'm sure you were a perfect little hornet. However, a few sharp words weren't sufficient reason for Theo to dash off in a suicidal tantrum."

As Kathleen considered that, she realized with a start that her fingers had slid into the thick, closely shorn locks of hair at his nape. Her arms were around his neck. When had that happened? Blushing furiously, she jerked her hands from him.

"You have no sympathy for Theo because you didn't like him," she said awkwardly, "but—"

"I haven't yet decided whether I like you either. That doesn't change my opinion of the situation."

Kathleen stared at him with wide eyes. Somehow his cool, unsentimental assessment was more comforting than sympathy.

"They ran to fetch me, after it happened," she found herself telling him. "Theo was lying on the ground. His neck was broken, and no one wanted to move him until the doctor arrived. I leaned over him and said his name, and when he heard my voice, he opened his eyes. I could see that he was dying. I put my hand on his cheek and told him that I loved him, and Theo said, 'You're not my wife.' Those were the last words he ever spoke. He was unconscious by the time the doctor arrived . . ." More tears sprang from her eyes. She didn't realize she was twisting the polishing cloth in her fists until one of his hands settled over both of hers, calming the agitated movement.

"I wouldn't dwell on Theo's last words," Devon said. "One could hardly expect him to be sensible. For God's sake, his neck was broken." His palm passed over her knuckles in a repeated caress. "Listen, my little watering pot, it was in my cousin's nature to do something rash at any given moment. It always would have been. The reckless streak in the Ravenel family has persevered for centuries. Theo could have married a saint, and he would have lost his temper regardless."

"I'm certainly not a saint," she said woefully, ducking her head.

Amusement rustled through his voice. "I knew that within the first minute of meeting you."

Keeping her head down, Kathleen stared at the hand over hers, elegant but brutally strong, with a faint scattering of hair on the back of it. "I wish I had it to do over again," she whispered.

"No one could blame you for what happened."

"I blame myself."

" 'Let her cover the mark as she will,' " he quoted sardonically, " 'the pang of it will always be in her heart.' "

Recognizing the words from *The Scarlet Letter*, Kathleen glanced up at him miserably. "You liken me to Hester Prynne?"

"Only in your aspirations to martyrdom. Although even Hester had a bit of fun before her comeuppance, whereas you've apparently had little."

"Fun?" Despair gave way to bewilderment. "What are you talking about?"

His gaze was intent on her face. "I would think that even a proper lady might find some pleasure in the conjugal embrace."

She gasped in befuddled outrage. "I—you—that you would dare bring up such a subject—" He had been so gentle and comforting, and now he had changed back into the insufferable cad of before. "As if I would ever discuss that with anyone, least of all you!" As she writhed and began to crawl from his lap, he held her in place easily.

"Before you charge away in righteous indignation," he said, "you might want to refasten your bodice."

"My—" Glancing down at her front, Kathleen saw to her horror that the first few buttons of her dress and the top two hooks of her corset had been undone. She went scarlet. "Oh, how could you?"

A flare of amusement lit his eyes. "You weren't breathing well. I thought you needed oxygen more than modesty." After watching her frantic efforts to rehook the corset, he asked politely, "May I help?"

"*No.* Although I'm certain you're quite accomplished at 'helping' ladies with their undergarments."

"They're hardly ever ladies." He laughed quietly as

she worked at the placket of the corset with increasing panic.

The strain of the afternoon had left her so enervated that even the simplest task was difficult. She huffed and wriggled to pull the edges of the corset together.

After watching her for a moment, Devon said brusquely, "Allow me." He brushed her hands away and began to hook the corset efficiently. She gasped as she felt the backs of his knuckles brush the skin of her upper chest. Finishing the hooks, he started on the row of buttons at her bodice. "Relax. I'm not going to ravish you; I'm not quite as depraved as my reputation might indicate. Besides, a bosom of such modest proportions—albeit charming—isn't enough to send me into a frenzy of lust."

Kathleen glowered and held still, secretly relieved that he'd given her a reason to hate him again. Nimbly his long fingers worked at the buttons until each one was neatly secured in its small silk loop. His lashes cast brindled shadows down his cheeks as he glanced along her front.

"There," he murmured.

She clambered out of his lap with the haste of a scalded cat.

"Careful." Devon flinched at the heedless placement of her knee. "I have yet to produce an heir, which makes certain parts of my anatomy more valuable to the estate than the actual family jewels."

"They're not valuable to me," she said, staggering to her feet.

"Still, I'm quite fond of them." He grinned and rose in an easy movement, reaching out to steady her.

Dismayed by the deplorably rumpled and muddy condition of her skirts, Kathleen whacked at the bits of hay and horsehair that clung to the black crepe fabric.

"Shall I accompany you into the house?" Devon asked.

"I prefer to go separately," she said.

"As you wish."

Straightening her spine, she added, "We will never speak of this."

"Very well."

"Also . . . we are still not friends."

His gaze held hers. "Are we enemies, then?"

"That depends." Kathleen took a wavering breath. "What . . . what will you do with Asad?"

Something in his face softened. "He'll remain at the estate until he can be retrained. That's all I can promise for now."

Although it wasn't precisely the answer she'd wanted, it was better than having Asad sold right away. If the horse could be retrained, he might at least end up in the possession of someone who valued him. "Then . . . I suppose . . . we're not enemies."

He stood before her in his shirtsleeves, with no necktie or collar in sight. The hems of his trousers were muddy. His hair needed combing, and there was a bit of hay caught in it, but somehow in his disarray, he was even more handsome than before. She approached him with abashed tentativeness, and he held very still as she reached up to pull the little wisp of hay from his hair. The dark locks were invitingly disheveled, a cowlick on the right side, and she was almost tempted to smooth it.

"How long is the mourning period?" he surprised her by asking abruptly.

Kathleen blinked, disconcerted. "For a widow? There are four mourning periods."

"*Four?*"

"The first one lasts a year, the second for six months, the third for three months, and then half mourning lasts for the rest of one's life."

"And if the widow wishes to marry again?"

"She may do so after a year and a day, although it is frowned upon to marry so quickly unless she has children, or lacks income."

"Frowned upon but not forbidden?"

"Yes. Why do you ask?"

Devon shrugged casually. "I'm merely curious. Men are required to mourn only for six months—probably because we wouldn't tolerate anything longer than that."

She shrugged. "A man's heart is different from a woman's."

His gaze turned quizzical.

"Women love more," she explained. Seeing his expression, she asked, "You think I'm wrong?"

"I think you know little of men," he said gently.

"I've been married: I know all I wish to." She went to the threshold and paused to look back at him. "Thank you," she said, and left before he could reply.

DEVON WANDERED TO the doorway after Kathleen had gone. Closing his eyes, he leaned his forehead against the frame and expelled a controlled sigh.

Dear God . . . he wanted her beyond decency.

He turned and set his back against the match-boarded wall, struggling to understand what was happening to him. A euphoric, disastrous feeling had invaded him. He sensed that he'd undergone a sea change from which there was no return.

He *hated* it when women cried. At the first sign of tears, he had always bolted like a hare at a coursing. But as soon as his arms had gone around Kathleen, in one ordinary instant, the world, the past, everything he'd always been certain of had all been obliterated. She had reached for him, not out of passion or fear, but the simple human need for closeness. It had electrified him. No one had ever sought comfort from him before, and the act of giving it had felt more unspeakably intimate than the most torrid sexual encounter. He'd felt the force of his entire being wrap around her in a moment of sweet, raw connection.

His thoughts were in anarchy. His body still smoldered with the feeling of Kathleen's slight weight in his lap. Before she had fully come back to herself, he had kissed her silky cheek, damp with salt tears and summer rain. He wanted to kiss her again, everywhere, for hours. He wanted her naked and exhausted in his arms. After all his past experience, physical pleasure had lost any trace of novelty, but now he wanted Kathleen Ravenel in ways that shocked him.

What a damnable situation, he thought savagely. A ruined estate, a depleted fortune, and a woman he couldn't have. Kathleen would be in mourning for a year and a day, and even after that, she would be out of his reach. She would never lower herself to be any man's mistress, and after what she had endured with Theo, she would want nothing to do with another Ravenel.

Brooding, Devon went to pick up his discarded coat from the floor. He shrugged into the rumpled garment and wandered from the saddle room back to the stalls. At the far end of the building, a pair of stable boys talked as they cleaned a box stall. Becoming aware of his presence, they quieted instantly, and all he could hear was the rasp of the broom and the scrape of a shovel. Some of the horses in the row watched him curiously while others affected disinterest.

Keeping his movements relaxed, Devon went to the Arabian's stall. Asad turned his head sideways to view him, his teacup muzzle tightening in a sign of unease. "No need for concern," Devon murmured. "Although one can't blame you for wrinkling your nose at a Ravenel's approach."

Asad shuffled and swished his tail nervously. Slowly he came to the front of the stall.

"Look sharp, milor'," came Mr. Bloom's calm voice from somewhere behind Devon. "The lad's a biter—he may take a nip of tha, if he doesn't know tha. He prefers a lass's company to a man's."

"That shows your judgment is sound," Devon told the horse. He extended a hand palm-up, as he had seen Kathleen do earlier.

Carefully Asad sniffed. His eyes half closed. Working his mouth, he lowered his head in submission and pressed his muzzle against Devon's hands. Devon smiled and stroked the horse's head on both sides. "You're a handsome fellow, aren't you?"

"And well he knows it," the stable master said, approaching with a chuckle. " 'He smells her ladyship on thee. Now he'll take to thee like ha'penny sweets. Once they know they're safe with thee, they'll do anything tha asks.''

Devon ran his hand along Asad's graceful neck, from the narrow, refined throatlatch down to the sturdy shoulder. His coat was sleek and warm, like living silk. "What do you make of his temperament?" he asked. "Is there any danger to Lady Trenear if she continues to train him?"

"Nowt a bit, milor'. Asad will be a perfect lady's mount, once he's trained right. He's not obstracklous, only sensitive. He sees, hears, smells everything. The fine ones are canny like that. Best to ride 'em wi' soft tack and gentle hands." Bloom hesitated, idly tugging on his white whiskers. "A week before the wedding, Asad was brought here from Leominster. Lord Trenear came to the stables to see him. 'Twas a mercy that her ladyship wasn't here to witness: Asad nipped at him, and his lordship delivered a hard clout to his muzzle. I warned him, 'If tha use a fist against him, milor', tha may earn his fear but not his trust.' " Bloom shook his head sadly, his eyes moistening. "I knew the master since he was a dear little lad. Everyone at the Priory loved him. But none could deny he was a fire-flaught."

Devon gave him a quizzical glance. "What does that mean?"

"In Yorkshire it's what they call the hot coal that bounces out of the hearth. But it's also the name for a man who can't bide his temper."

Asad raised his head and delicately touched his muzzle to Devon's chin. Resisting the urge to jerk his head back, Devon held still.

"Breathe soft into his nose," Bloom murmured. "He wants to make friends wi' thee."

Devon complied. After blowing back gently, the horse nudged his chest and licked his shirtfront.

"Tha has won him over, milor'," the stable master said, a smile splitting his round face until his cheeks bunched over the cottony bolsters of his whiskers.

"It has nothing to do with me," Devon replied, stroking Asad's sleek head, "and everything to do with Lady Trenear's scent."

"Aye, but tha has a good touch wi' him." Blandly the stable master added, "An' wi' her ladyship, it seems."

Devon sent him a narrow-eyed glance, but the elderly man returned it innocently.

"Lady Trenear was distressed by the memory of her husband's accident," Devon said. "I would offer assistance to any woman in such a state." He paused. "For her sake, I want you and the stablemen to say nothing about her loss of composure."

"I told the lads I'd flay the hide off them if there's so

much as a whisper of't." Bloom frowned in concern. "That morning . . . there was a scruffle between her ladyship and the master, before he came running to the stables. I worrit she might fault hersel' for it."

"She does," Devon said quietly. "But I told her that she is in no way accountable for his actions. Nor is the horse. My cousin brought the tragedy upon himself."

"I agree, milor'."

Devon gave Asad a last pat. "Good-bye, fellow . . . I'll visit you in the morning before I leave." He turned to walk along the stalls to the entrance, while the elderly man accompanied him. "I suppose rumors ran rife around the estate after the earl's death."

"Rumors? Aye, the air was fat wi' them."

"Has anyone said what Lord and Lady Trenear were arguing about that morning?"

Bloom was expressionless. "I couldn't say."

There was no doubt that the man had some idea as to the nature of the conflict between Theo and Kathleen. Servants knew everything. However, it would be unseemly to persist in questioning him about private family matters. Reluctantly Devon set aside the subject . . . for now.

"Thank you for your help with Lady Trenear," he told the stable master. "If she decides to continue training Asad, I'll allow it on condition of your oversight. I trust your ability to keep her safe."

"Thank you, milor'," Bloom exclaimed. "Tha intends for the lady to remain at Eversby Priory, then?"

Devon stared at him, unable to answer.

The question was simple on the surface, but it was overwhelmingly complex. What did he intend for Kathleen? For Theo's sisters? What did he intend for Eversby Priory, the stables and household, and the families that farmed the estate?

Could he really bring himself to throw them all upon the mercy of fate?

But damn it, how could he spend the rest of his life with unimaginable debt and obligations hanging over his head like the sword of Damocles?

He closed his eyes briefly as the realization came to him: It was already there.

The sword had been suspected above him from the moment he'd been informed of Theo's death.

There was no choice to make. Whether or not he wanted the responsibility that came with the title, it was his.

"I do," he finally said to the stable master, feeling vaguely nauseous. "I intend for all of them to stay."

The older man smiled and nodded, seeming to have expected no other answer.

Exiting through the wing of the stables that connected to the house, Devon made his way to the entrance hall. He had a sense of distance from the situation, as if his brain had decided to stand back and view it as a whole before applying itself to the particulars.

The sounds of piano music and feminine voices drifted from one of the upper floors. Perhaps he was mistaken, but Devon thought he could hear a distinctly masculine tone filtering through the conversation.

Noticing a housemaid cleaning the stair rails of the grand staircase with a banister brush, he asked, "Where is that noise coming from?"

"The family is taking their afternoon tea in the up-stairs parlor, milord."

Devon began to ascend the staircase with measured footsteps. By the time he reached the parlor, he had no doubt that the voice belonged to his incorrigible brother.

"Devon," West exclaimed with a grin as he entered the room. "Look at the charming little bevy of cousins

I've discovered." He was sitting in a chair beside a game table, pouring a hefty splash of spirits from his flask into a cup of tea. The twins hovered around him, busily constructing a dissected map puzzle. Sliding a speculative glance over his brother, West remarked, "You look as though you'd been pulled backward through the hedgerow."

"You shouldn't be in here," Devon told him. He turned to the room in general. "Has anyone been corrupted or defiled?"

"Since the age of twelve," West replied.

"I wasn't asking you, I was asking the girls."

"Not yet," Cassandra said cheerfully.

"Drat," Pandora exclaimed, examining a handful of puzzle pieces, "I can't find Luton."

"Don't concern yourself with it," West told her. "We can leave out Luton entirely, and England will be none the worse for it. In fact, it's an improvement."

"They are said to make fine hats in Luton," Cassandra said.

"I've heard that hat making drives people mad," Pandora remarked. "Which I don't understand, because it doesn't seem tedious enough to do that."

"It isn't the job that drives them mad," West said. "It's the mercury solution they use to smooth the felt. After repeated exposure, it addles the brain. Hence the term 'mad as a hatter.'"

"Then why is it used, if it is harmful to the workers?" Pandora asked.

"Because there are always more workers," West said cynically.

"Pandora," Cassandra exclaimed, "I do wish you wouldn't force a puzzle piece into a space where it obviously does not fit."

"It does fit," her twin insisted stubbornly.

"Helen," Cassandra called out to their older sister, "is the Isle of Man located in the North Sea?"

The music ceased briefly. Helen spoke from the corner, where she sat at a small cottage piano. Although the instrument was out of tune, the skill of her playing was obvious. "No, dear, in the Irish Sea."

"Fiddlesticks." Pandora tossed the piece aside. "This is *frustraging.*"

At Devon's puzzled expression, Helen explained, "Pandora likes to invent words."

"I don't *like* to," Pandora said irritably. "It's only that sometimes an ordinary word doesn't fit how I feel."

Rising from the piano bench, Helen approached Devon. "Thank you for finding Kathleen, my lord," she said, her gaze smiling. "She is resting upstairs. The maids are preparing a hot bath for her, and afterward Cook will send up a tray."

"She is well?" he asked, wondering exactly what Kathleen had told Helen.

Helen nodded. "I think so. Although she is a bit weary."

Of course she was. Come to think of it, so was he.

Devon turned his attention to his brother. "West, I want to speak to you. Come with me to the library, will you?"

West drained the rest of his tea, stood, and bowed to the Ravenel sisters. "Thank you for a delightful afternoon, my dears." He paused before departing. "Pandora, sweetheart, you're attempting to cram Portsmouth into Wales, which I assure you will please neither party."

"I told you," Cassandra said to Pandora, and the twins began to squabble while Devon and West left the room.

# Chapter 5

"LIVELY AS KITTENS," WEST said as he and Devon walked to the library. "They're quite wasted out here in the country. I'll confess, I never knew that the company of innocent girls could be so amusing."

"What if they were to take part in the London season?" Devon asked. It was one of approximately a thousand questions buzzing in his mind. "How would you rate their prospects?"

West looked bemused. "At catching husbands? Nonexistent."

"Even Lady Helen?"

"Lady Helen is an angel. Lovely, quiet, accomplished . . . she should have her pick of suitors. But the men who would be appropriate for her will never come up to scratch. Nowadays no one can afford a girl who lacks a dowry."

"There are men who could afford her," Devon said absently.

"Who?"

"Some of the fellows we're acquainted with . . . Severin, or Winterborne . . ."

"If they're friends of ours, I wouldn't pair Lady Helen with one of them. She was bred to marry a cultivated man of leisure, not a barbarian."

"I would hardly call a department store owner a barbarian."

"Rhys Winterborne is vulgar, ruthless, willing to compromise any principle for personal gain . . . qualities I admire, of course . . . but he would never do for Lady Helen. They would make each other exceedingly unhappy."

"Of course they would. It's marriage." Devon sat in a musty chair positioned behind a writing desk in one of the deep-set window niches. So far the library was his favorite room in the house, paneled in oak, with walls of floor-to-ceiling bookshelves that contained at least three thousand volumes. One bookcase had been fitted with narrow stacked drawers for storing maps and documents. Agreeable hints of tobacco, ink, and book dust spiced the air, overlaying the sweetness of vellum and parchment.

Idly Devon reached for a wooden cigar holder on the nearby desk and examined it. The piece was carved in the shape of a beehive, with tiny brass bees scattered on its surface. "What Winterborne needs most is something he can't purchase."

"Whatever Winterborne can't purchase isn't worth having."

"What about an aristocrat's daughter?"

West wandered past the bookshelves, perusing titles. He pulled a volume from a shelf and examined it dispassionately. "Why the devil are we talking about arranging a match for Lady Helen? Her future is none of your concern. After we sell the estate, you'll likely never see her again."

Devon traced the pattern of inset bees as he replied, "I'm not going to sell the estate."

West fumbled with the book, nearly dropping it. "Have you gone mad? *Why?*"

He didn't want to have to explain his reasons, when he was still trying to sort through them. "I have no desire to be a landless earl."

"When has your pride ever mattered?"

"It does now that I'm a peer."

West gave him a sharply assessing glance. "Eversby Priory is nothing you ever expected to inherit, nor desired, nor prepared for in any way whatsoever. It's a millstone tied around your neck. I didn't fully grasp that until the meeting with Totthill and Fogg this morning. You'd be a fool if you do anything other than sell it and keep the title."

"A title is nothing without an estate."

"You can't afford the estate."

"Then I'll have to find a way."

"How? You have no bloody idea how to manage complex finances. As for farming, you've never planted so much as a single turnip seed. Whatever you're qualified for, which isn't much, it's certainly not running a place like this."

Oddly, the more that his brother echoed the doubts that were already in his mind, the more stubborn Devon became. "If Theo was qualified, I'll be damned if I can't learn to do it."

West shook his head incredulously. "Is that where this nonsense is coming from? You're trying to compete with our dead cousin?"

"Don't be an idiot," Devon snapped. "Isn't it obvious there's far more at stake than that? Look around you, for God's sake. This estate supports hundreds of people. Without it, many of them won't survive. Tell me you'd be willing to stand face-to-face with one of the tenants and tell him that he has to move his family to Manchester so they can all work in a filthy factory."

"How can the factory be any worse than living on a muddy scrap of farmland?"

"Considering urban diseases, crime, slum alleys, and

abject poverty," Devon said acidly, "I'd say it's considerably worse. And if my tenants and servants all leave, what of the consequences to the village of Eversby itself? What will become of the merchants and businesses once the estate is gone? I have to make a go of this, West."

His brother stared at him as if he were a stranger. "*Your* tenants and servants."

Devon scowled. "Yes. Who else's are they?"

West's lips curled in a derisive sneer. "Tell me this, oh lordly one . . . what do you expect will happen when you fail?"

"I can't think about failure. If I do, I'll be doomed from the start."

"You're *already* doomed. You'll preen and posture as lord of the manor while the roof caves in and the tenants starve, and I'm damned if I'll have any part of your narcissistic folly."

"I wouldn't ask you to," Devon retorted, heading for the door. "Since you're usually as drunk as a boiled owl, you're of no use to me."

"Who the hell do you think you are?" West called after him.

Pausing at the threshold, Devon gave him a cold glance. "I'm the Earl of Trenear," he said, and left the room.

# Chapter 6

FOR THE FIRST TIME since Theo's accident, Kathleen had slept without nightmares. After emerging from a deep rest, she sat up in bed as her lady's maid, Clara, brought her breakfast tray.

"Good morning, milady." Clara placed the tray on Kathleen's lap while a housemaid opened the curtains to admit a spill of weak gray light from the cloud-hazed sky. "Lord Trenear gave me a note to set by your plate."

Frowning curiously, Kathleen unfolded the small parchment rectangle. Devon's penmanship was angular and decisive, the words written in black ink.

*Madam,*

*As I will soon depart for London, I would like to discuss a matter of some consequence. Please come to the library at your earliest convenience.*

*Trenear*

All her nerves jumped at the notion of facing Devon. She knew why he wanted to speak to her . . . he was going to ask her to leave the estate as soon as possible. He would not want to be burdened by the presence of Theo's widow, or his sisters, and certainly no one would expect it of him.

Today she would send out inquiries to find a house.

With strict economizing, she, Helen, and the twins could live on the income from her jointure. Perhaps it was for the best to make a new beginning somewhere else. Very little good had come to her in the three months she had lived at Eversby Priory. And although Helen and the twins loved the only home they had ever known, they would benefit from a change. They had been secluded from the world for too long . . . They needed new people, new scenery, new experiences. Yes . . . the four of them, together, would manage.

But Kathleen was worried about what would become of the servants and tenants. It was a pity too that with Theo's death, the Ravenel family and its proud legacy had essentially come to an end.

Filled with melancholy, she dressed with Clara's assistance in multiple layers of petticoats, a corset, and a petite padded bustle. Next came a black crepe dress, fitted close to the body with pleated tiers that draped down the back and ended in a slight train. The dress was fastened down the front with jet buttons, the long sleeves fitted closely to her wrists and finished with detachable cuffs made of white linen. She considered and rejected the idea of a veil, deciding wryly that she and Devon were beyond such formalities.

While Clara arranged Kathleen's hair in plaits that had been twisted and pinned tightly to the back of her head, she asked cautiously, "Milady, has his lordship said anything about what he plans to do with the staff? Many are worried about their positions."

"So far he has said nothing to me of his plans," Kathleen said, inwardly chafing at her own helplessness. "But your position with me is safe."

"Thank you, milady." Clara looked marginally relieved, but Kathleen understood her conflicting emotions.

After being an upper servant at a grand estate, it would be a comedown to work at a cottage or a set of rented rooms.

"I'll do what I can to influence Lord Trenear on behalf of the servants," Kathleen told her, "but I'm afraid I have no sway over him."

They exchanged bleak smiles, and Kathleen left the room.

As she approached the library, she felt her heartbeat quicken uncomfortably. Squaring her shoulders, she crossed the threshold.

Devon appeared to be browsing over a row of books, reaching up to straighten a trio of volumes that had fallen sideways.

"My lord," Kathleen said quietly.

Devon turned, his gaze finding hers at once. He was stunningly handsome, dressed in a dark suit of clothes that had been tailored in the new looser-fitting fashion, the coat, waistcoat, and trousers all made of matching fabric. The informal cut of the suit did nothing to soften the hard lines of his body. For a moment Kathleen couldn't help remembering the feel of his arms around her, his solid chest beneath her cheek. Heat swept over her face.

Devon bowed, his face inscrutable. He appeared relaxed at first glance, but a closer look revealed faint shadows beneath his eyes, and finespun tension beneath his calm veneer. "I hope you're well this morning," he said quietly.

Her blush deepened uncomfortably. "Yes, thank you." She curtsied and wove her fingers together in a stiff knot. "You wished to discuss something before you depart?"

"Yes, regarding the estate, I've come to some conclusions—"

"I do hope—" she began, and broke off. "Forgive me, I didn't mean to—"

"Go on."

Kathleen dropped her gaze to her clenched hands as she spoke. "My lord, if you decide to dismiss any of the servants . . . or indeed all of them . . . I hope you take into account that some have served the Ravenels for their entire lives. Perhaps you might consider giving small parting sums to the oldest ones who have little hope of securing other employment."

"I'll bear it in mind."

She could feel him looking at her, his gaze as tangible as the heat of sunlight. The mahogany bracket clock on the mantel measured out the silence with delicate ticks.

His voice was soft. "You're nervous with me."

"After yesterday—" She broke off and swallowed hard, and nodded.

"No one but the two of us will ever know about that."

Even if Kathleen chose to believe him, it didn't set her at ease. The memory was an unwanted bond with him. He had seen her at her weakest, her lowest, and she would have preferred him to be mocking rather than treat her with gentleness.

She forced herself to meet his gaze as she admitted with vexed honesty, "It's easier to think of you as an adversary."

Devon smiled faintly. "That puts us in an awkward situation, then, as I've decided against selling the estate."

Kathleen was too astonished to reply. She couldn't believe it. Had she heard him correctly?

"Eversby Priory's situation is so desperate," Devon continued, "that few men could conceivably make it worse. Of course, I'm probably one of them." He gestured to a pair of chairs positioned near the writing desk. "Will you sit with me?"

She nodded, her thoughts racing as she settled into the

chair. Yesterday he had seemed so resolved—there had been no doubt that he would dispense with the estate and all its problems as expediently as possible.

After she had arranged her skirts and folded her hands in her lap, she sent him a wondering gaze. "May I ask what caused you to change your mind, my lord?"

Devon was slow to reply, his expression troubled. "I've tried to think of every reason why I should wash my hands of this place. But I keep returning to the conclusion that I owe it to every man, woman, and child on this estate to try and save the estate. Eversby Priory has been the work of generations. I can't destroy it."

"I think that's a very admirable decision," she said with a hesitant smile.

His mouth twisted. "My brother calls it vanity. He predicts failure, of course."

"Then I'll be the counterbalance," she said impulsively, "and predict success."

Devon gave her an alert glance, and he dazzled her with a quick grin. "Don't put money on it," he advised. The smile faded except for a lingering quirk at one corner of his mouth. "I kept waking during the night," he said, "arguing with myself. But then it occurred to me to wonder what my father would have done, had he lived long enough to find himself in my position."

"He would have saved the estate?"

"No, he wouldn't have considered it for a second." Devon laughed shortly. "It's safe to say that doing the opposite of what my father would have done is always the right choice."

Kathleen regarded him with sympathy. "Did he drink?" she dared to ask.

"He did everything. And if he liked it, he did it to excess. A Ravenel through and through."

She nodded, thinking of Theo. "It has occurred to me," she ventured, "that the family temperament isn't well suited to stewardship."

Amusement glinted in his eyes. "Speaking as a man who has the family temperament in full measure, I agree. I wish I could claim to have a mother from steady, pragmatic stock, to balance out the Ravenel wildness. Unfortunately she was worse."

"Worse?" Kathleen asked, her eyes widening. "She had a temper?"

"No, but she was unstable. Flighty. It's no exaggeration to say there were days at a time when she forgot she even had children."

"My parents were very attentive and involved," Kathleen volunteered after a moment. "As long as you were a horse."

Devon smiled. He leaned forward and rested his forearms on his legs, dropping his head for a moment. The posture was far too casual to affect in the presence of a lady, but it revealed how very tired he was. And overwhelmed. For the first time, Kathleen felt a stirring of genuine sympathy for him. It wasn't fair that a man should have to contend with so many dire problems all at once, without warning or preparation.

"There's another matter I need to discuss," he said eventually, sitting up again. "I can't, in good conscience, turn Theo's sisters out of the only home they've ever known." One of his brows arched as he saw her expression. "Yes, I have a conscience. It's been abused and neglected for years, but even so, it occasionally manages to be a nuisance."

"If you're considering allowing the girls to remain here—"

"I am. But the scenario presents obvious difficulties.

They'll require a chaperone. Not to mention rigorous instruction, if they're eventually to come out in society."

"Society?" Kathleen echoed in bemusement. "All three?"

"Why not? They're of an age, aren't they?"

"Yes, but . . . the expense . . ."

"That's for me to worry about." He paused. "You would manage the most difficult part of the whole business by taking the twins in hand. Civilizing them to whatever extent you can manage."

"Me?" Her eyes widened. "You . . . you propose that I remain at Eversby Priory with them?"

Devon nodded. "Obviously you're scarcely older than Helen and the twins, but I believe you could manage them quite well. Certainly better than a stranger could." He paused. "They deserve the same opportunities that other young ladies of their rank enjoy. I'd like to make that possible, but I can't do it without you staying here to bring them along." He smiled slightly. "Of course, you would be free to train Asad as well. I suspect he'll learn table manners before Pandora does."

Kathleen's heart was fluttering madly. To stay here with Helen and the twins . . . and Asad . . . it was more than she could have dared to dream. "I suppose you would live here as well?" she asked warily.

"I'll visit infrequently," Devon said. "But most of the work in setting the estate's financial affairs to rights will have to be done in London. In my absence, the entire household will be under your supervision. Would that be inducement enough for you to stay?"

Kathleen began to nod before he'd even finished the sentence. "Yes, my lord," she said, almost breathless with relief. "I'll stay. And I'll help you any way I can."

# Chapter 7

A MONTH AFTER DEVON AND West had left Hampshire, a parcel addressed to Kathleen was delivered to Eversby Priory.

With the Ravenel sisters gathered around her in the upstairs parlor, she opened the parcel and folded back layers of rustling paper. They all exclaimed in admiration as a cashmere shawl was revealed. Such shawls were all the rage in London, hand-loomed in Persia and finished with a border of embroidered flowers and silk fringe. The wefts of wool had been dyed in graduating colors so that it produced the exquisite effect of a sunset, glowing red melting into orange and gold.

"It's called ombré," Cassandra said reverently. "I've seen ribbons dyed that way. How fashionable!"

"It will look beautiful with your hair," Helen commented.

"But who sent it?" Pandora asked. "And why?"

Picking up the note that had been enclosed in the parcel, Kathleen read the boldly scrawled words:

*As promised.*

*Trenear*

Devon had deliberately chosen a shawl with the most vibrant colors imaginable. A garment that a widow could never, ever wear.

"I can't accept this," she said with a scowl. "It's from Lord Trenear, and it is entirely too personal. Perhaps if it were a handkerchief or a tin of sweets—"

"But he's a relation," Helen surprised her by pointing out. "And a shawl isn't all *that* personal, is it? One doesn't wear it next to the skin, after all."

"Think of it as a very large handkerchief," Cassandra suggested.

"Even if I did keep it," Kathleen said, "I would have to dye it black."

The girls looked as aghast as if she had suggested murdering someone. They all spoke at once.

"You mustn't—"

"Oh, but why?"

"To ruin such lovely colors—"

"How could I wear this as it is?" Kathleen demanded. "I'd be as flamboyant as a parrot. Can you imagine the gossip?"

"You can wear it at home," Pandora interrupted. "No one will see."

"Do try it on," Cassandra urged. Despite Kathleen's refusal, the girls insisted on draping it over her shoulders, just to see how it looked.

"How beautiful," Helen said, beaming.

It was the most luxurious fabric she had ever felt, the fleece soft and cushiony. Kathleen ran her hand across the rich hues, and sighed. "I suppose I can't ruin it with aniline dye," she muttered. "But I'm going to tell him that I did."

"You're going to lie?" Cassandra asked, her eyes wide. "That's not setting a very good example for us."

"He must be discouraged from sending unsuitable gifts," Kathleen said.

"It's not his fault if he doesn't know any better," Pandora pointed out.

"He knows the rules," Kathleen said darkly. "And he enjoys breaking them."

*My Lord,*

*It was very kind of you to send the lovely gift, which is very useful now that the weather has turned. I am pleased to relate that the cashmere absorbed an application of black dye quite evenly, so that it is now appropriate for mourning.*

*Thank you for your thoughtfulness.*

*Lady Trenear*

"You *dyed* it?" Devon asked aloud, setting the note on his desk with a mixture of amusement and irritation.

Reaching for a silver penholder, he inserted a fresh nib and pulled a sheet of writing paper from a nearby stack. That morning he had already written a half-dozen missives to lawyers, his banker, and contractors, and had hired an outside agent to analyze the estate's finances. He grimaced at the sight of his ink-stained fingers. The lemon-and-salt paste his valet had given him wouldn't entirely remove the smudges. He was tired of writing, and even more so of numbers, and Kathleen's letter was a welcome distraction.

The challenge could not go unanswered.

Staring down at the letter with a faint smile, Devon pondered the best way to annoy her.

Dipping the pen nib into the inkwell, he wrote,

Madam,

I am delighted to learn that you find the shawl useful in these cooler days of autumn.

On that subject, I am writing to inform you of my recent decision to donate all the black curtains that currently shroud the windows at Eversby Priory to a London charitable organization. Although you will regrettably no longer have use of the cloth, it will be made into winter coats for the poor, which I am sure you will agree is a far nobler purpose. I am confident in your ability to find other ways of making the atmosphere at Eversby Priory appropriately grim and cheerless.

If I do not receive the curtains promptly, I will take it to mean that you are eager for my assistance, in which case I will be delighted to oblige you by coming to Hampshire at once.

Trenear

Kathleen's reply was delivered a week later, along with massive crates containing the black curtains.

My Lord,

In your concern for the downtrodden masses, it appears to have escaped your mind to inform me that you had arranged for a battalion of workmen to invade Eversby Priory. Even as I write,

plumbers and carpenters wander freely
throughout the house, tearing apart
walls and floors and claiming that it is
all by your leave.

The expense of plumbing is
extravagant and unnecessary. The noise
and lack of decorum is unwelcome,
especially in a house of mourning.

I insist that this work discontinue at
once.

Lady Trenear


Madam,

Every man has his limits. Mine happen to be
drawn at outdoor privies.

The plumbing will continue.

Trenear


My Lord,

With so many improvements that
are desperately needed on your lands,
including repairs to laborers' cottages,
farm buildings, drainage systems, and
enclosures, one must ask if your personal
bodily comfort really outweighs all other
considerations.

Lady Trenear

*Madam,*

*In reply to your question,*

*Yes.*

*Trenear*

"Oh, how I despise him," Kathleen cried, slamming the letter onto the library table. Helen and the twins, who were poring over books of deportment and etiquette, all looked up at her quizzically.

"Trenear," she explained with a scowl. "I informed him of the chaos he has caused, with all these workmen tramping up and down the staircases, and hammering and sawing at all hours of the day. But *he* doesn't give a fig for anyone else's comfort save his own."

"I don't mind the noise, actually," Cassandra said. "It feels as if the house has come alive again."

"I'm looking forward to the indoor water closets," Pandora confessed sheepishly.

"Don't tell me your loyalty has been bought for the price of a privy?" Kathleen demanded.

"Not just one privy," Pandora said. "One for every floor, including the servants."

Helen smiled at Kathleen. "It might be easier to tolerate a little inconvenience if we keep reminding ourselves of how pleasant it will be when it's finished."

The optimistic statement was punctuated by a series of thuds from downstairs that caused the floor to rattle.

"A *little* inconvenience?" Kathleen repeated with a snort. "It sounds as if the house is about to collapse."

"They're installing a boiler system," Pandora said, flipping through a book. "It's a set of two large copper cylinders filled with water pipes that are heated by gas burners. One never has to wait for the hot water—it comes at once through expansion pipes attached to the top of the boiler."

"Pandora," Kathleen asked suspiciously, "how do you know all that?"

"The master plumber explained it to me."

"Dear," Helen said gently, "it's not seemly for you to converse with a man when you haven't been introduced. Especially a laborer in our home."

"But Helen, he's *old*. He looks like Father Christmas."

"Age has nothing to do with it," Kathleen said crisply. "Pandora, you promised to abide by the rules."

"I do," Pandora protested, looking chagrined. "I follow all the rules that I can remember."

"How is it that you remember the details of a plumbing system but not basic etiquette?"

"Because plumbing is more interesting." Pandora bent her head over a book on deportment, pretending to focus on a chapter titled "A Lady's Proper Demeanor."

Kathleen contemplated the girl with concern. After a fortnight of tutelage, Pandora had made little headway compared to Cassandra, who had learned far more in the same length of time. Kathleen had also noticed that Cassandra was trying to conceal her own progress to avoid making Pandora look even worse. It had become clear that Pandora was by far the more undisciplined of the pair.

Just then Mrs. Church, the plump and genial housekeeper, came to inform them that tea would soon be brought to the upstairs parlor.

"Hurrah!" Pandora exclaimed, leaping from her chair. "I'm so famished, I could eat a carriage wheel." She was gone in a flash.

Sending Kathleen an apologetic glance, Cassandra scampered after her sister.

Out of habit, Helen began to collect the books and papers, and sort them into stacks. Kathleen pushed the chairs back into place at the library table.

"Has Pandora always been so . . ." Kathleen began, but paused in search of a diplomatic word.

"Yes," Helen said feelingly. "It's why none of the governesses lasted for long."

Kathleen returned to the library table, pushing the chairs back into place. "How am I to prepare her for the season, if I can't manage to keep her seated for more than five minutes?"

"I'm not certain it can be done."

"Cassandra is making excellent progress, but I'm not certain that Pandora will be ready at the same time."

"Cassandra would never go to a ball or soiree if Pandora wasn't with her."

"But it's not fair for her to make such a sacrifice."

Helen's slight shoulders lifted in a graceful shrug. "It's the way they've always been. When they were small, they spoke to each other in their own invented language. When one of them was disciplined, the other would insist on sharing her punishment. They hate to spend time apart."

Kathleen sighed. "They'll have to, if progress is to be made. I'll spend a few afternoons tutoring Pandora in private. Would you be willing to study separately with Cassandra?"

"Yes, of course."

Helen organized the books, tucking in scraps of paper to mark the right place before closing each one. How careful she always was with books: they had been her companions, her entertainment, and her only window to the outside world. Kathleen worried that it would be difficult for her to acclimate to the cynicism and sophistication of London.

"Will you want to take part in society, when the mourning period is over?" she asked.

Helen paused, considering the question. "I would like to be married someday," she admitted.

"What kind of husband do you wish for?" Kathleen asked with a teasing smile. "Handsome and tall? Dashing?"

"He doesn't have to be handsome or tall, as long as he's kind. I would be very happy if he loved books and music . . . and children, of course."

"I promise, we'll find a man like that for you," Kathleen said, regarding her fondly. "You deserve nothing less, dear Helen."

"WHY DIDN'T YOU come to eat at the club?" West asked, striding into the parlor of Devon's terrace apartment. Most of the rooms had been stripped of their furnishings. The stylish modern terrace had just been let to an Italian diplomat for the purpose of keeping his mistress. "They served beefsteak and turnip mash," West continued. "I've never known you to miss—" He stopped abruptly. "Why are you sitting on the desk? What the devil have you done with the chairs?"

Devon, who had been sorting through a stack of mail, looked up with a scowl. "I told you I was moving to Mayfair."

"I didn't realize it would be so soon."

Ravenel House was a twelve-bedroom Jacobean residence of stone and brick, looking as if the manor at Eversby Priory had spawned a smaller version of itself. Thankfully Ravenel House had been kept in better condition than Devon had expected. It was overfurnished but comfortable, the dark wood interior and deeply hued carpets imparting a distinctly masculine ambiance. Although Ravenel House was too large for one person, Devon had no choice but to take up residence there. He had invited West to live with him, but his brother had no desire to give up the comfort and privacy of his stylish terrace.

One couldn't blame him.

"You look rather glumpish," West commented. "I know just the thing to cheer you. Tonight the fellows and I are going to the music hall to see a trio of female contortionists who are advertised as the 'boneless wonders.' They perform in tights and little scraps of gold cloth—"

"Thank you, but I can't."

"Boneless wonders," West repeated, as if Devon must not have heard him correctly.

Not long ago, the offer might have been moderately tempting. Now, however, with the weight of accumulated worry pressing on him, Devon had no interest in flexible showgirls. He and West and their friends had seen similar performances countless times in the past—there was no novelty left in such shenanigans.

"Go and enjoy yourself," he said, "and tell me about them later." His gaze returned to the letter in his hand.

"It does no good to tell you about them," West said, disgruntled. "You have to see them, or there's no point." He paused. "What is so fascinating about that letter? Who is it from?"

"Kathleen."

"Is there news from the estate?"

Devon laughed shortly. "No end of it. All bad." He extended the letter to West, who skimmed it quickly.

*My Lord:*

*Today I received a visit from Mr. Totthill, who appears to be in failing health. It is my private opinion that he is overwhelmed by the demands of his position as your estate agent, and is*

no longer capable of carrying out his
responsibilities to your satisfaction, or
indeed to anyone's.

The issue he brought to my
attention concerns five of your lowland
tenants, who were promised drainage
improvements three years ago. The clay
soil on their farms is as thick and
sticky as birdlime, and nearly impossible
to plow. To my dismay, I have just
learned that the late earl borrowed
money from a private land improvement
company to perform the necessary work,
which was never done. As a result, we
have just been issued an order from the
court of quarter session. Either we must
repay the loan immediately, or install
proper drainage on the tenants' farms.

Please tell me if I may help. I am
acquainted with the tenant families
involved, and I would be willing to
speak to them on your behalf.

Lady Trenear

"What's birdlime?" West asked, handing back the letter.

"A glue made of holly bark. It's smeared on tree branches to catch birds. The moment they alight, they're permanently stuck."

Devon understood exactly how they felt.

After a month of unrelenting work, he had barely scratched the surface of the Eversby Priory's needs. It would take years to acquire an adequate understanding of crop cultivation, land improvement, dairying, animal husbandry, forestry, accounting, investment, property law, and local politics. For now it was essential not to become mired in detail. Devon was trying to think in broad sweeps, seeing ways that problems related to other problems, finding patterns. Although he was beginning to understand what needed to be accomplished, he didn't know precisely *how* it should be done.

He would have to hire men whom he could trust to manage the situation on his terms, but it would take time to find them. Totthill was too old and stubbornly traditional, and so was Carlow, the land agent who worked for him. Replacements were immediately necessary, but throughout England there were only a handful of men equipped for estate administration.

That very morning, Devon had sunk into despair, brooding over his mistake in taking on such a burden. But then Kathleen's letter had arrived, and that had been enough to bolster his resolve.

Anything was worth having her. Anything.

He couldn't explain his obsession with her, even to himself. But it seemed as if it had always been there, woven through the fabric of his being, waiting to be discovered.

"What will you do?" he heard West ask.

"First I'll ask Totthill what he knows about the borrowed funds. Since he probably won't have a satisfactory answer, I'll have to go through the account ledgers to find out what happened. In either event, I'll tell the land steward to estimate what it will take to make the land improvements."

"I don't envy you," West said casually, and paused. His tone changed, sharpening. "Nor do I understand you. Sell the damned estate, Devon. You owe nothing to those people. Eversby Priory isn't your birthright."

Devon sent him a sardonic glance. "Then how did I end up with it?"

"By bloody accident!"

"Regardless, it's mine. Now leave, before I flatten your skull with one of these ledgers."

But West stood unmoving, pinning him with a baleful stare. "Why is this happening? What has changed you?"

Exasperated, Devon rubbed the corners of his eyes. He hadn't slept well for weeks, and his cookmaid had brought him only burned bacon and weak tea for breakfast. "Did you think that we were going to go through life completely unaltered?" he asked. "That we would occupy ourselves with nothing but selfish pleasures and trivial amusements?"

"I was counting on it!"

"Well, the unexpected happened. Don't trouble yourself over it; I've asked nothing of you."

West's aggression weathered down to a core of resentment. He approached the desk, turned, and hoisted himself up with effort to sit next to Devon. "Maybe you should, you stupid bastard."

They sat side by side. In the hard-scoured silence, Devon contemplated his brother's blurred and puffy countenance, the flesh beneath his chin loosening. Alcohol had begun to crosshatch a pattern of threadlike capillaries across his cheeks. It was difficult to reconcile the disenchanted man beside him with the laughing, high-spirited boy West had once been.

It occurred to Devon that in his determination to save the estate, the tenants, servants, and Theo's sisters, he had overlooked the fact that his own brother could do with some saving as well. West had always been so clever that Devon had assumed he could take care of himself. But the cleverest people sometimes caused the worst trouble for themselves.

It had seemed inevitable that Devon and West would turn out to be selfish wastrels. After their father had died in a brawl, their mother had left them at boarding school while she had traveled the continent. She had fluttered from affair to affair, accumulating heartbreak in small fractures that had eventually proved fatal. Devon had never learned whether she had died from illness or suicide, and he didn't want to know.

Devon and West had been shuttled between schools and relations' homes, insisting on remaining together no matter how often people tried to separate them. As Devon reflected on those troubled years, in which each had been the other's only constant, he realized that he had to include West in his new life—even if he didn't want to be included. The strength of their bond would not allow one of them to move in any direction without pulling the other inexorably along.

"I need your help, West," he said quietly.

His brother took his time about replying. "What would you have me do?"

"Go to Eversby Priory."

"You would trust me around the cousins?" West asked sullenly.

"I have no choice. Besides, you didn't seem particularly interested in any of them when we were there."

"There's no sport in seducing innocents. Too easy." West folded his arms across his chest. "What is the point of sending me to Eversby?"

"I need you to manage the tenants' drainage issues. Meet with each one individually. Find out what was promised, and what has to be done—"

"Absolutely not."

"Why?"

"Because that would require me to visit farms and discuss weather and livestock. As you know, I have no interest in animals unless they're served with port wine sauce and a side of potatoes."

"Go to Hampshire," Devon said curtly. "Meet with the farmers, listen to their problems, and if you can manage it, fake some empathy. Afterward I want a report and a list of recommendations on how to improve the estate."

Muttering in disgust, West stood and tugged at his wrinkled waistcoat. "My only recommendation for your estate," he said as he left the room, "is to get rid of it."

# Chapter 8

Madam,

   My sincere thanks for your offer to speak
to the tenants regarding the drainage issues.
However, since you are already burdened with
many demands, I have sent my brother,
Weston, to handle the problem. He will arrive
at Eversby Priory on Wednesday, and stay for
a fortnight. I have lectured him at length
about gentlemanly conduct. If he causes you a
moment's distress, wire me and it will be resolved
immediately.

   My brother will arrive at the Alton rail
station at noon on Saturday. I do hope you'll send
someone to collect him, since I feel certain no one
else will want him.

Trenear

P.S. Did you really dye the shawl black?


My Lord.
   Amid the daily tumult of
construction. which is louder than an

*army corps of drums. your brother's*
*presence will likely go unnoticed.*
*We will fetch him on Wednesday.*
                                    *Lady Trenear*


*P.S. Why did you send me a shawl so*
*obviously unsuitable for mourning?*


In response to Kathleen's letter, a telegram was delivered from the village post office on the morning of West's scheduled arrival.


**Madam,**
  **You won't be in mourning forever.**
                                    **Trenear**


Smiling absently, Kathleen set down the letter. She caught herself wishing, just for a moment, that Devon were coming to Hampshire instead of his brother. She scolded herself for the ridiculous thought. Sternly she reminded herself of how he had distressed and unnerved her. Not to mention the cacophony of plumbing installation that plagued her daily, at his insistence. And she would not overlook the way he had forced her to take down the mourning curtains—although privately she had to admit that everyone in the household, including the servants, took pleasure in the brightened rooms and unencumbered windows.

No, she didn't want to see Devon. Not in the least. She was far too busy to spare a thought for him, or to ponder what the dark, clear blue shade of his eyes reminded her of . . . Bristol glass, perhaps . . . and she had already forgotten the feel of his hard arms around her and the rasp of his whisper in her ear . . . *I have you* . . . and that shiver-inducing scrape of his shaven bristle against her skin.

She had to wonder at Devon's reasons for sending his brother to deal with the tenants. Kathleen had seen little of West during their previous visit, but what she had learned had not been promising. West was a drunkard, and would probably be more of a hindrance than a help. However, it was not her place to object. And since West was the next in line for the earldom, he might as well become familiar with the estate.

The twins and Helen were delighted by the prospect of West's visit and had made a list of planned outings and activities. "I doubt he will have much time, if any, for amusements," Kathleen warned them as they all sat in the family parlor with needlework. "Mr. Ravenel is here on a business matter, and the tenants need his attention far more than we do."

"But Kathleen," Cassandra said in concern, "we mustn't let him work himself into exhaustion."

Kathleen burst out laughing. "Darling, I doubt he's ever worked a day in his life. Let's not distract him on his first attempt."

"Gentlemen aren't supposed to work, are they?" Cassandra asked.

"Not really," Kathleen admitted. "Men of nobility usually concern themselves with the management of their lands, or sometimes they dabble in politics." Kathleen paused. "However, I think even a common workingman could be called a gentleman, if he is honorable and kind."

"I agree," Helen said.

"I wouldn't mind working," Pandora announced. "I could be a telegraph girl, or own a bookshop."

"You could make hats," Cassandra suggested sweetly, arranging her features in a horrid cross-eyed grimace, "and go *mad*."

Pandora grinned. "People will watch me running in circles and flapping my arms, and they'll say, 'Oh, dear, Pandora's a chicken today.' "

"And then I'll remind them that you behaved that way before you ever started making hats," Helen said serenely, her eyes twinkling.

Chuckling, Pandora plied her needle to mend a loose seam. "I shouldn't like to work if it ever prevented me from doing exactly what I wished."

"When you're the lady of a great household," Kathleen said in amusement, "you'll have responsibilities that will occupy most of your time."

"Then I won't be the lady of a great household. I'll live with Cassandra after she marries. Unless her husband forbids it, of course."

"You silly," Cassandra told her twin. "I would never marry a man who would keep us apart."

Finishing the seam of a detachable white cuff, Pandora began to set it aside, and huffed as her skirt was tugged. "Fiddlesticks. Who has the scissors? I've sewed the mending to my dress again."

WEST ARRIVED IN the afternoon, accompanied by an unwieldy assortment of luggage, including a massive steamer trunk that two footmen struggled to carry upstairs. Somewhat to Kathleen's dismay, all three Ravenel sisters greeted him as if he were a returning war hero. Reaching into a leather Gladstone bag, West began to hand out cunning parcels wrapped in delicate layers of paper and tied with matching ribbon as narrow as twine.

Noticing the little tags, each stamped with an ornate letter W, Helen asked, "What does this mean?"

West smiled indulgently. "That shows that it's from Winterborne's department store, where I shopped yesterday afternoon—I couldn't visit my little cousins emptyhanded, could I?"

To Kathleen's dismay, any semblance of ladylike decorum fled. The twins erupted in screams of delight and began to dance around him right there in the entrance hall. Even Helen was pink-cheeked and breathless.

"That will do, girls," Kathleen finally said, struggling to keep her expression neutral. "There's no need to hop about like demented rabbits."

Pandora had already begun to rip one of the parcels open.

"Save the paper!" Helen cried. She brought one of the parcels to Kathleen, lifting one of the layers of paper. "Just see, Kathleen, how thin and fine it is."

"Gloves!" Pandora shouted, having unwrapped a parcel. "Oh, look, they're so stylish, I want to *die*." She held them against her chest. The wrist-length kid gloves had been tinted a soft pink.

"Colored gloves are all the rage this year," West said. "Or so the girl at the department store counter said. There's a pair for each of you." He grinned at Kathleen's obvious disapproval, his gray eyes glinting with mischief. "Cousins," he said, as if that could explain away such unseemly gifts.

Kathleen narrowed her eyes. "My dears," she said calmly, "why don't you open your parcels in the receiving room?"

Chattering and squealing, the sisters hurried into the receiving room and piled the gifts on a satinwood table.

They opened each parcel with scrupulous care, unfolding the gift tissue and smoothing each piece before placing it on an accumulating stack that resembled the froth of freshly poured milk.

There were more gloves, dyed in delicate shades of violet and aqua . . . tins of sweets . . . pleated paper fans with gold and silver embossing . . . novels and a book of poetry, and bottles of flower water to be used for the complexion or the bath, or sprinkled on the bed pillows. Although none of it was appropriate, except perhaps the books, Kathleen couldn't find it in her heart to object. The girls had long been deprived of small luxuries.

She knew that Theo would never have thought of bringing gifts home for his sisters. And despite the family's relative proximity to London, the girls had never been to Winterborne's. Neither had Kathleen, since Lady Berwick had disliked the notion of rubbing elbows in a large store crowded with people from all walks of life. She had insisted instead on frequenting tiny, exclusive shops, where merchandise was kept discreetly out of sight rather than spread willy-nilly over the counters.

Stealing glances at West, Kathleen was disconcerted by the flashes of resemblance he bore to his older brother, the same dark hair and assertive bone structure. But Devon's striking good looks were marred in his brother, whose features were ruddy and soft with dissipation. West was nothing if not well-groomed—in fact, he dressed too lavishly for Kathleen's taste, wearing an embroidered silk waistcoat and jaunty patterned necktie, and gold cuff links set with what were either garnets or rubies. Even now at midday, he smelled strongly of liquor.

"You may not want to glare at me quite so fiercely," West murmured to Kathleen sotto voce, as the sisters gathered up their gifts and carried them from the room. "It would distress the girls if they were to realize how much you dislike me."

"I disapprove of you," she replied gravely, walking out to the grand staircase with him. "That's not the same as dislike."

"Lady Trenear, *I* disapprove of me." He grinned at her. "So we have something in common."

"Mr. Ravenel, if you—"

"Mightn't we call each other cousin?"

"No. Mr. Ravenel, if you are to spend a fortnight here, you will conduct yourself like a gentleman, or I will have you forcibly taken to Alton and tossed onto the first railway car that stops at the station."

West blinked and looked at her, clearly wondering if she was serious.

"Those girls are the most important thing in the world to me," Kathleen said. "I will not allow them to be harmed."

"I have no intention of harming anyone," West said, offended. "I'm here at the earl's behest to talk to a set of clodhoppers about their turnip planting. As soon as that's concluded, I can promise you that I'll return to London with all possible haste."

*Clodhoppers?* Kathleen drew in a sharp breath, thinking of the tenant families and the way they worked and persevered and endured the hardships of farming . . . all to put food on the table of men such as this, who looked down his nose at them.

"The families who live here," she managed to say, "are worthy of your respect. Generations of tenant farmers built this estate—and precious little reward they've received in return. Go into their cottages, and see the conditions in which they live, and contrast it with your own circumstances. And then perhaps you might ask yourself if you're worthy of *their* respect."

"Good God," West muttered, "my brother was right. You do have the temperament of a baited badger."

They exchanged glances of mutual loathing and walked away from each other.

FORTUNATELY THE GIRLS kept the conversation cheerful at dinner. Only Helen seemed to notice the bitter tension between Kathleen and West, sending Kathleen discreet glances of concern. With each course, West asked for new wine, obliging the underbutler to fetch bottle after bottle from the cellar. Fuming at his wastefulness, Kathleen bit her tongue to keep from commenting as he became increasingly soused. At the conclusion of the meal, Kathleen ushered the girls upstairs, leaving West alone at the table with a bottle of port.

In the morning Kathleen rose early, dressed in her riding habit, and went out to the stable as usual. With the assistance of Mr. Bloom, the stable master, she was training Asad to resist shying at objects that frightened him. Bloom accompanied her out to the paddock as she led Asad with a special training halter.

Kathleen had quickly come to value Bloom's advice. He did not believe that physically restraining a horse, especially an Arabian, was the right way to help him overcome his fear. "Tha would only break his spirit, binding him up like a fly in a spider's web. 'Appen he'll take his reassurance from thee, milady. He'll trust tha to keep him safe and know what's best for him."

At Bloom's direction, Kathleen grasped the lead rope under Asad's chin and guided him to take a step forward and then a step back.

"Again," Bloom said approvingly. "Back'ard and for'ard, and again."

Asad was perplexed but willing, moving back and forth easily, almost as if he were learning to dance.

"Well done, lass," Bloom praised, so involved in the training that he forgot to address Kathleen by her title. "Now tha's taking up all his thoughts and leaving no room for fear." He placed a crop in Kathleen's left hand. "This is for tha to tap his side if need be." Standing by Asad's side, he began to unfold a black umbrella. The horse started and nickered, instinctively cringing away from the unfamiliar object. "This umbrolly scares tha a bit, lad, doesn't it?" He closed and opened the umbrella repeatedly, while telling Kathleen, "Make the task tha's given him more important than the thing that scares him."

Kathleen continued to move Asad in the back-and-forth step, distracting him from the threatening movement of the billowing black object. When he tried to swing his hindquarters away, she tapped him back into place with a touch of the crop, not allowing him to put distance between himself and the umbrella. Although Asad was clearly uneasy, his ears swiveling in every direction, he did exactly as she commanded. His hide twitched nervously at the umbrella's proximity . . . but he didn't shy away.

When Bloom finally closed the umbrella, Kathleen grinned and patted Asad's neck with affectionate pride. "Good boy," she exclaimed. "You're a fast learner, aren't you?" She took a carrot stub from the pocket of her skirt and gave it to him. Asad accepted the treat, crunching noisily.

"Next we'll try it as tha rides him—" Bloom began.

He was interrupted by a stable boy, Freddie, who hadn't yet reached his teenage years. "Mr. Bloom," the boy said breathlessly, hurrying up to the paddock railing, "The head groom bade me tell you that Mr. Ravenel has come to the stables for his mount."

"Aye, I told the lads to saddle Royal."

Freddie's small face was pinched with anxiety. "There's a problem, sir. Mr. Ravenel is the worse for drink and isn't fit to ride, but he ordered them to bring the horse to him. The head groom tried to refuse, but the land agent, Mr. Carlow, is there as well, and he said to give Royal to Mr. Ravenel because they're supposed to ride out to a tenant farm."

Once again, Kathleen thought in panicked fury, a drunken Ravenel was going to try to ride a horse from the stables.

Wordlessly she climbed through the paddock rails, in too much of a hurry to bother with the gate. She grabbed handfuls of her riding skirt and ran to the stables, ignoring the sound of Bloom calling after her.

As soon as she entered the building, she saw West gesturing angrily at the head groom, John, whose face was averted. The land agent, Carlow, stood by looking impatient and embarrassed. Carlow, a portly middle-aged man who resided in town, had been employed by Theo's family for more than a decade. It would be his job to escort West to the tenant farms.

One glance was all Kathleen needed to take stock of the situation. West was red-faced and sweating, his eyes bloodshot, and he was swaying on his feet.

"*I'm* the one to judge my capabilities," West was saying belligerently. "I've ridden in far worse condition than this—and I'll be damned if—"

"Good morning, gentlemen," Kathleen interrupted, her heart hammering. Without warning, the image of Theo's stricken face appeared in her mind . . . the way he had looked at her, his eyes like cooling embers as the last seconds of his life had ticked away. She blinked hard, the memory vanishing. The reek of alcohol drifted to her nostrils, provoking a touch of nausea.

"Lady Trenear," the land agent exclaimed with relief. "Perhaps you would be able to talk sense into this half-wit."

"Indeed." Without expression, she took hold of West's arm, digging her fingers in as she felt him resist. "Come outside with me, Mr. Ravenel."

"My lady," the land agent said uncomfortably, "I was referring to the head groom—"

"John is not the half-wit," Kathleen said curtly. "As for you, Carlow . . . you may attend to your other responsibilities. Mr. Ravenel will be indisposed for the rest of the day."

"Yes, my lady."

"What the devil is going on?" West spluttered as Kathleen towed him outside and around to the side of the stables. "I dressed and came to the stables at the crack of dawn—"

"The crack of dawn was four hours ago."

When they had reached a relatively secluded place behind an equipment shed, West shook his arm free of Kathleen's grip and glared at her. "What is the matter?"

"You stink of spirits."

"I always begin the day with brandied coffee."

"How do you expect to ride when you're not steady on your feet?"

"The same way I always ride—badly. Your concern for my welfare is misplaced."

"My concern is not for *your* welfare. It's for the horse you intended to ride, and the tenants you're supposed to visit. They have enough hardship to contend with—they don't need to be subjected to the company of a drunken fool."

West gave her a baleful glance. "I'm leaving."

"Don't you dare take one step away." Discovering that she was still clutching the riding crop, Kathleen brandished it meaningfully. "Or I'll thrash you."

West's incredulous gaze went to the crop. With startling speed, he reached out and wrenched the crop from her, and tossed it to the ground. The effect was ruined, however, as he staggered to regain his balance. "Go on and say your piece," he snapped.

Kathleen folded her arms across her chest. "Why did you bother coming to Hampshire?"

"I'm here to help my brother."

"You aren't helping anyone," she cried with incredulous disgust. "Do you understand *anything* about the burden that Lord Trenear has taken on? About how high the stakes are? If he fails and the estate is divided and sold, what do you think will happen to these people? Two hundred families cut adrift with no means of supporting themselves. And fifty servants, most of whom have spent their entire lives serving the Ravenels."

As she saw that he wasn't even looking at her, she took a quivering breath, trying to contain her fury. "Everyone on this estate is struggling to survive—and we're all depending on your brother, who's trying to solve problems that he had no hand in creating. But instead of doing something to help, you've chosen to drink yourself silly and totter around like a selfish lumping *idiot*—"

Her throat worked around an angry sob, and she swallowed it down before continuing quietly. "Go back to London. You're of no use to anyone here. Blame me if you like. Tell Lord Trenear that I was too much of a bitch to tolerate. He'll have no difficulty accepting that."

Turning, she walked away from him, throwing a few last words over her shoulder. "Perhaps someday you'll find someone who can save you from your excesses. Personally, I don't believe you're worth the effort."

# Chapter 9

To KATHLEEN'S SURPRISE, WEST didn't leave. He returned to the house and went to his room. At least, she thought darkly, he'd made no further attempt to mount a horse while he was drunk, which she supposed put him above her late husband in terms of intelligence.

For the rest of the day, West kept to his room, presumably sleeping, although it was possible he was continuing to pickle himself in strong spirits. He didn't come downstairs for dinner, only requested that a tray be brought up to him.

In response to the girls' concerned inquiries, Kathleen said curtly that their cousin had been taken ill, and would probably return to London in the morning. When Pandora opened her mouth to ask questions, it was Helen who quelled her with a quiet murmur. Kathleen sent her a grateful glance. As unworldly as Helen might be, she was quite familiar with the kind of man who drank to excess and lost his head.

At daybreak, when Kathleen went down to the breakfast room, she was shocked to find West sitting at one of the round tables, staring morosely into the depths of a teacup. He looked ghastly, the skin under his eyes pleated, his complexion pallid and damp.

"Good morning," Kathleen murmured, taken aback. "Are you ill?"

He gave her a bleary glance, his eyes bloodshot and red-rimmed in his gray complexion. "Only if one considers sobriety to be an illness. Which I do."

Kathleen went to the sideboard, took up a pair of silver tongs, and began to heap bacon on a piece of toast. She placed another piece of toast on top, cut the sandwich neatly in two, and brought the plate to West. "Eat this," she said. "Lord Berwick always said that a bacon sandwich was the best cure for the morning after."

He regarded the offering with loathing, but picked up a piece and bit into it while Kathleen made herself breakfast.

Sitting next to him, Kathleen asked quietly, "Shall I have the carriage readied in time for you to catch the late morning train?"

"I'm afraid you won't be that fortunate." West took a swallow of tea. "I can't go back to London. I have to stay in Hampshire until I've met with all the tenants I had planned to visit."

"Mr. Ravenel—"

"I *have* to," he said doggedly. "My brother never asks anything of me. Which is why I'll do this even if it kills me."

Kathleen glanced at him in surprise. "Very well," she said after a moment. "Shall we send for Mr. Carlow to accompany you?"

"I rather hoped that you would go with me." Seeing her expression, West added warily, "Only for today."

"Mr. Carlow is far more familiar with the tenants and their situations—"

"His presence may prove to be inhibiting. I want them to speak to me frankly." He glared at his plate. "Not that I expect more than a half-dozen words from any of them. I know what that sort thinks of me: a city toff. A great useless peacock who knows nothing about the superior virtues of farm life."

"I don't think they'll judge you severely, so long as they believe that you're not judging them. Just try to be sincere, and you should have no difficulty."

"I have no talent for sincerity," West muttered.

"It's not a talent," Kathleen said. "It's a willingness to speak from your heart, rather than trying to be amusing or evasive."

"Please," West said tersely. "I'm already nauseous." Scowling, he took another bite of the bacon sandwich.

KATHLEEN WAS PLEASED to see that despite West's expectation of being treated with insolence, if not outright contempt, by the tenants, the first one he encountered was quite cordial.

George Strickland was a middle-aged man, stocky and muscular, with kind eyes set in a large square face. His land, which he farmed with the help of three sons, was a smallholding of approximately sixty acres. Kathleen and West met him at his cottage, a ramshackle structure propped next to a large barn, where corn was threshed and stored. Livestock were kept in a tumbledown collection of sheds that had been built without plan, placed with apparent randomness around a yard where manure was liquefied by water running from unspouted roofs.

"I'm pleased to meet you, sir," the tenant farmer said, gripping his hat in his hands. "I'm wondering if you and the good lady would mind just walking a piece with me into the field. We could talk while I work. The oats have to be cut and brought in before the rain comes back."

"What if they're not harvested in time?" West asked.

"Too much grain will shed on the ground," Strickland replied. "Once the grain is good and plump, even a gust of high wind could shake it loose from the chaff. We'd lose as much as a third."

As West glanced at Kathleen, she nodded slightly to convey her willingness. They walked out into the field, where the feathery tops of the gold-green oats grew as tall as West's shoulder. Kathleen enjoyed the dusty-sweet smell of the air as a pair of men mowed through the crop with wickedly sharp scythes. A pair of gatherers followed to bind cut stalks into sheaves. After that, bandsters tied the sheaves into stooks, and a young boy cleared loose straw with stubble rakes.

"How much can a man cut in a day?" West asked, while Strickland squatted to deftly bind a sheaf.

"The best scytheman I've seen can cut two acres in a day. But that's oats, which is faster than other grain."

West glanced at the laborers speculatively. "What if you had a reaping machine?"

"The kind with a binder attachment?" Strickland removed his hat and scratched his head. "A dozen acres or more, I'd reckon."

"In one day? And how many laborers would you need to operate it?"

"Two men and a horse."

"Two men producing at least six times the result?" West looked incredulous. "Why don't you buy a mechanical reaper?"

Strickland snorted. "Because it would cost twenty-five pounds or more."

"But it would pay for itself before long."

"I can't afford horses *and* a machine, and I couldn't do without a horse."

Frowning, West watched as Strickland finished tying a sheaf. "I'll help you catch up with the mowers if you'll show me how to do that."

The farmer glanced at West's tailored clothes. "You're not dressed for field work, sir."

"I insist," West said, shrugging out of his jacket and handing it to Kathleen. "With any luck, I'll develop a callus to show people afterward." He squatted beside Strickland, who showed him how to cinch a band around the top of the straw. Just under the grain and not too tight, the farmer cautioned, so that when sheaves were stood on end and bound together, there was enough room between stalks to allow air to circulate and dry the grain faster.

Although Kathleen had expected West to tire quickly of the novelty, he was persistent and diligent, gradually gaining competence. As they worked, West asked questions about drainage and planting, and Strickland answered in detail.

It was unexpected, the way West's politeness seemed to have transformed into genuine interest in the process taking place before him. Kathleen watched him thoughtfully, finding it difficult to reconcile the drunken lout of yesterday with this attentive, engaging stranger. One would almost think he gave a damn about the estate and its tenants.

At the end of the row, West stood, dusted his hands, and pulled a handkerchief from his pocket to mop his face.

Strickland blotted his own brow with his sleeve. "Next I could show you how to mow," he offered cheerfully.

"Thank you, no," West replied with a rueful grin, looking so much like Devon that Kathleen felt a quick pang of recognition. "I'm sure I shouldn't be trusted with a sharp blade." Surveying the field speculatively, he asked, "Have you ever considered dairying, Mr. Strickland?"

"No, sir," the tenant said firmly. "Even with lower yields, there's still more profit in grain than milk or meat. There's a saying about the market: 'Down horn, up corn.'"

"Perhaps that's true for now," West said, thinking out loud. "But with all the people moving to factory towns, the demand for milk and meat will rise, and then—"

"No dairying." Strickland's tentative friendliness faded. "Not for me."

Kathleen went to West, giving him his jacket. She touched his arm lightly to gain his attention. "I believe Mr. Strickland fears you may be trying to avoid paying for the drainage work," she murmured.

West's face cleared instantly as he understood. "No," he said to the farmer, "you'll have the improvements as promised. In fact, Lord Trenear has no choice in the matter: It's his legal obligation."

Strickland looked skeptical. "Beg pardon, sir, but after so many broken promises, it's hard to put faith in another one."

West was silent for a moment, contemplating the man's troubled expression. "You have my word," he said in a way that left no room for doubt. And he extended his hand.

Kathleen stared at him in surprise. A handshake was only exchanged between close friends, or on an occasion of great significance, and then only between gentlemen of similar rank. After a hesitation, however, Strickland reached out and took West's hand, and they exchanged a hearty shake.

"THAT WAS WELL done of you," Kathleen told West as they rode along the unpaved farm road. She was impressed by the way he had handled himself and addressed Strickland's concerns. "It was clever of you to put him at ease by trying your hand at field work."

"I wasn't trying to be clever." West seemed preoccupied. "I wanted to gain information."

"And so you did."

"I expected that this drainage issue would be easily solved," West said. "Dig some trenches, line them with clay pipes, and cover it all up."

"It doesn't sound all that complicated."

"It is. It's complicated in ways I hadn't considered." West shook his head. "Drainage is such a minor part of the problem that it would be a waste of money to fix it without addressing the rest."

"What is the rest?"

"I'm not even sure yet. But if we don't figure it all out, there's no hope of ever making Eversby Priory profitable again. Or even sustaining itself." He gave Kathleen a dark glance as she opened her mouth. "Don't accuse me of scheming to have the estate sold."

"I wasn't," she said indignantly. "I was going to say that as far as I can tell, the Strickland farm is more or less in the same condition as the other tenants."

" 'Down horn, up corn,' " West muttered. "My arse. In a few short years, it's going to be 'Up horn, down corn,' and it's going to stay that way. Strickland has no idea that his world has changed for good. Even I know it, and I could hardly be more ignorant about farming."

"You think he should turn to dairying and livestock," Kathleen said.

"It would be easier and more profitable than trying to farm lowland clay."

"You may be right," she told him ruefully. "But in this part of England, breeding livestock is not considered as respectable as working the land."

"What the devil is the difference? Either way, one ends up shoveling manure." West's attention was diverted as his horse stumbled on a patch of rough road.

"Ease up on the reins," Kathleen said. "Just give the horse more slack and let him pick his way through."

West complied immediately.

"Would a bit more advice be unwelcome?" she dared to ask.

"Fire away."

"You tend to slouch in the saddle. That makes it difficult for you to follow the horse's motion, and it will make your back sore later. If you sit tall and relaxed . . . yes, like that . . . now you're centered."

"Thank you."

Kathleen smiled, pleased by his willingness to take direction from a woman. "You don't ride badly. With regular practice, you would be quite proficient." She paused. "I take it you don't ride often in town?"

"No, I travel by foot or hackney."

"But your brother . . ." Kathleen began, thinking of Devon's assured horsemanship.

"He rides every morning. A big dapple gray that's as mean as the devil if it goes one day without hard exercise." A pause. "They have that in common."

"So that's why Trenear is so fit," Kathleen murmured.

"It doesn't stop at riding. He belongs to a pugilism club where they batter each other senseless, in the savate style."

"What is that?"

"A kind of fighting that developed in the streets of Old Paris. Quite vicious. My brother secretly hopes to be attacked by ruffians someday, but so far, no luck."

Kathleen smiled. "What is the reason for all of his exertion?"

"To keep his temper under control."

Her smile faded. "Do you have a temper as well?"

West laughed shortly. "Without a doubt. It's only that I prefer to drink my demons to sleep rather than battle them."

So did Theo, she thought, but kept it to herself. "I like you better sober," she said.

West slid her an amused glance. "It's only been half a day. Wait a bit longer, and you'll change your mind."

She didn't, however. In the fortnight that followed, West continued to remain relatively sober, limiting his drinking to a glass of wine or two at dinner. His days were divided between visiting tenant farms, poring over rent books, reading books on agriculture, and adding page after page to the report he was writing for Devon.

At dinner one night he told them of his plan to visit many more tenants to form a comprehensive understanding of their problems. With each new piece of information, a picture of the estate's true condition was forming—and it wasn't a pretty sight.

"On the other hand," West concluded, "it's not altogether hopeless, as long as Devon is doing his job."

"What is his job?" Cassandra asked.

"Finding capital," West told her. "A great deal of it."

"It must be difficult for a gentleman to find money without working," Pandora said. "Especially when all the criminals are trying to do the same thing."

West drowned a grin in his goblet of water. "I have every faith," he replied, "that my brother will either outsmart the criminals, or join them." He turned his attention to Kathleen. "I realized this morning that I need to stay here a bit longer than I'd originally planned," he said. "Another fortnight, or better yet, a month. There's still too much I haven't learned."

"Stay then," Kathleen said matter-of-factly.

West glanced at her in surprise. "You wouldn't object?"

"Not if it will help the tenants."

"What if I remained through Christmas?"

"Certainly," she said without hesitation. "You have more claim to stay here than I do. But won't you miss your life in town?"

West's lips quirked as he glanced down at his plate. "I miss . . . certain things. However, there is much to do here, and my brother has a shortage of trustworthy advisors. In fact, few landowners of his rank seem to understand what they're facing."

"But you and Lord Trenear do?"

West grinned suddenly. "No, we don't either. The only difference is, we know it."

# Chapter 10

"Cousin West," Kathleen said a month later, fiercely pursuing him down the grand staircase, "stop running away. I want a word with you."

West didn't slow his pace. "Not while you're chasing me like Attila the Hun."

"Tell me why you did it." She reached the bottom step at the same time he did and swung around to block his escape. "Kindly explain what *deranged* mode of thinking caused you to bring a pig into the house!"

Cornered, he resorted to honesty. "I wasn't thinking. I was at John Potter's farm, and he was about to cull the piglet because it was undersized."

"A common practice, as I understand it," she said curtly.

"The creature looked at me," West protested. "It seemed to be smiling."

"*All* pigs seem to be smiling. Their mouths are curved upwards."

"I couldn't help it; I had to bring him home."

Kathleen shook her head disapprovingly as she looked at him. The twins had already bottle-fed the creature with a formula of cow's milk whisked with raw egg, while Helen had lined a basket with soft cloth for it to sleep in. Now there was no getting rid of it.

"What do you intend for us to do with the pig once it's full-grown?" she demanded.

West considered that. "Eat it?"

She let out an exasperated huff. "The girls have already named it Hamlet. Would you have us eat a family pet, Mr. Ravenel?"

"I would if it turned into bacon." West smiled at her expression. "I'll return the pig to the farmer when it's weaned," he offered.

"You can't—"

He forestalled her by lifting his hand in a staying motion. "You'll have to badger me later; I've no time for it now. I'm leaving for Alton Station, and I can't miss the afternoon train."

"Train? Where are you going?"

West dodged around her, heading to the front door. "I told you yesterday. I knew you weren't listening."

Kathleen glowered and followed him, thinking it would serve him right if bacon were eventually declared off-limits in the Ravenel household.

They paused beside the front receiving room, where workmen pulled up flooring planks and tossed them aside with noisy clatters. Elsewhere, the sound of incessant hammering peppered the air.

"As I explained yesterday," West said, raising his voice to be heard above the infernal racket, "I'm visiting a man in Wiltshire, who's taken over a tenancy to experiment with modern farming methods."

"How long will you be away?"

"Three days," he said cheerfully. "You'll scarcely have time to miss me before I'm back."

"I wouldn't miss you no matter how long you were gone." But Kathleen looked over him with concern as the butler helped him don his hat and coat. When he returned, she thought, they would have to take in his clothes again; he had lost at least another stone. "Don't forget to eat while you're away," she scolded. "You'll soon be mistaken for a scarecrow if you keep missing your dinner."

The constant exercise of riding across the estate lands, walking the fields, helping a farmer repair a gate or retrieve a ewe that had jumped a garden wall, had wrought considerable changes in West. He'd lost so much weight that his garments hung on his frame. The bloat had melted from his face and neck, revealing a firm jawline and hard profile. All the time spent outdoors had imparted healthy color to his complexion, and he appeared years younger, an air of vitality replacing the look of sleepy indolence.

West leaned down to press a light kiss on her forehead. "Good-bye, Attila," he said affectionately. "Try not to browbeat everyone in my absence."

After West's departure, Kathleen headed to the housekeeper's room near the kitchen. It was washing day, the dreaded occasion when the household laundry was sorted, boiled, washed, rinsed, and hung in a drying room attached to the scullery. Together Kathleen and Mrs. Church would take inventory and order fabric.

They had only just begun to discuss the need for new aprons for the housemaids when the butler, Sims, appeared.

"I beg your pardon, milady." Sims's tone was measured, but the wrinkles and crags of his face had scrunched in dissatisfaction. "A tenant and his wife—Mr. and Mrs. Wooten—are asking to meet with Mr. Ravenel. I explained that he was away, but they won't leave. They claim their need is urgent. I thought it best to inform you before I have a footman remove them."

Kathleen frowned. "No, you mustn't do that. The Wootens wouldn't call without good reason. Please show them to the receiving room and I'll meet them there."

"I feared you would say that," Sims said dourly. "I must

protest, milady, that as a widow in mourning, your peace and quiet should not be disturbed."

A crash from the upstairs caused the ceiling to rattle.

"My stars!" the housekeeper exclaimed.

Kathleen fought back a laugh and glanced at the butler.

"I'll show the Wootens in," he said in resignation.

When Kathleen entered the receiving room, she saw that the young couple were distraught. Mrs. Wooten's eyes were swollen and tear-glazed, while her husband's face was pale with anxiety.

"I hope no one is ill or injured?" Kathleen asked.

"No, milady," Mr. Wooten replied, while his wife bobbed a curtsy. He twisted his cap back and forth as he explained that one of his hired workers had encountered a pair of trespassers who had identified themselves as representatives of the railway company.

"They said they was surveying the land," Wooten continued, "and when I asked by whose leave, they said Lord Trenear himself gave them permission." His voice turned unsteady. "They said my farm would be sold to the railway company. I went to Mr. Carlow, but he knows naught about it." His eyes flooded. "My father left this farm to me, milady. They're going to put tracks on it, and plow under my fields, and turn me and my family out of our home without so much as a farthing—" He would have continued, but Mrs. Wooten had begun to sob.

Shocked, Kathleen shook her head. "Mr. Ravenel mentioned nothing of this, and Lord Trenear would not do such a thing without first discussing it with his brother. I am certain this claim is baseless."

"They knew my lease was up," Mr. Wooten said, his eyes haunted. "They knew exactly when, and they said it wouldn't be renewed."

That gave Kathleen pause.

What the devil was Devon up to? Surely he could not be so heartless and cruel as to sell a tenant's farm without notifying him.

"I will find out," she said firmly. "In the meantime, there is no need for distress. Mr. Ravenel is firmly on the side of the tenants, and he has influence with Lord Trenear. Until Mr. Ravenel returns—in only three days—my advice is to carry on as usual. Mrs. Wooten, you really must stop crying—I'm sure such distress isn't good for the baby."

After the Wootens had departed, taking little apparent comfort from her reassurances, Kathleen hurried to the study and sat at the large desk. Fuming, she reached for a pen, uncapped a bottle of ink, and proceeded to write Devon a scathing message, informing him of the situation and demanding to know what was going on.

For good measure, she added a none-too-subtle threat of legal action on behalf of the Wootens. Even though there was nothing a lawyer could do, since Devon had the right to sell any portion of his estate, it would certainly seize his attention.

Folding the message, she tucked it into an envelope and rang for the footman to take it to the telegraph office of the local postmaster. "I'd like this dispatched right away," she told him. "Tell the postmaster that it's a matter of the utmost urgency."

"Yes, milady."

As the footman departed, the housekeeper appeared at the threshold. "Lady Trenear," she said, looking vexed.

"Mrs. Church," Kathleen said, "I promise, I haven't forgotten about the washing book or the aprons."

"Thank you, my lady, but it's not that. It's the workmen. They finished plumbing the master bathroom."

"That's good news, isn't it?"

"So I would think—except that now they've begun to

convert another upstairs room into an additional bathing room, and they must run a pipe beneath the floor of your room."

Kathleen jumped to her feet. "Do you mean to say there are men in my bedroom? No one mentioned anything of the sort to me."

"The master plumber and carpenter both say it's the only way it can be done."

"I won't have it!"

"They have already pulled up some of the flooring without so much as a by-your-leave."

Kathleen shook her head in disbelief. "I suppose it can be tolerated for an afternoon."

"My lady, they say it will take several days, most likely a week, to put it all back to rights."

Her mouth fell open. "Where am I to sleep and dress while my bedroom is torn apart?"

"I've already directed the maids to convey your belongings to the master bedroom," Mrs. Church replied. "Lord Trenear has no need of it, since he is in London."

That did nothing to improve Kathleen's mood. She *hated* the master bedroom, the place she had last seen Theo before his accident. Where they had argued bitterly, and Kathleen had said things she would regret for the rest of her life. Dark memories lurked in the corners of that room like malevolent nocturnal creatures.

"Is there any other room I might use?" she asked.

"Not at the moment, my lady. The workmen have pulled up the floors in three other rooms as well as yours." The housekeeper hesitated, understanding the reason for Kathleen's reluctance. "I'll direct the maids to air out a bedchamber in the east wing and give it a good cleaning— but those rooms have been closed for so long that it will take some work to turn it out properly."

Sighing, Kathleen dropped back to her chair. "Then it seems I'll have to sleep in the master bedroom tonight."

"You'll be the first to try the new copper bathtub," the housekeeper said, in a tone she might have used while offering a bonbon to a sullen child.

Kathleen smiled wanly. "That is some consolation."

As it turned out, her bath in the copper tub was so lovely and luxurious that it almost made up for having to sleep in the master bedroom. Not only was it deeper than any bath she'd ever been in before, it was crowned with a full roll edge upon which she could rest her head comfortably. It was the first bath she'd had ever taken in which she could lean back and submerge herself all the way up to the neck, and it was heavenly.

She stayed in the bath for as long as possible, lazing and half floating until the water began to cool. Clara, her lady's maid, came to wrap her in soft Turkish towels and settle a clean white nightgown over her head.

Covered with gooseflesh, Kathleen went to sit in an upholstered chair by the fire and discovered that her ombré shawl had been draped over the back of the chair. She pulled it over her lap, snuggling beneath the soft cashmere. Her gaze went to the stately bed, with its carved wooden canopy mounted on four elaborately turned posters.

One glance was enough to destroy all the good the bath had done.

She had refused to sleep in that bed with Theo after the debacle of their wedding night. The sound of his slurred, angry voice emerged from her memories.

*Do what you're told, for God's sake. Lie back and stop making this difficult . . . Behave like a wife, damn it . . .*

In the morning, Kathleen was exhausted, her sore eyes undercut with dark shadows. Before she went out to the stables, she went to find the housekeeper at the spice cupboard. "Mrs. Church, forgive me for interrupting you, but I'd like to make certain that you'll have a new bedroom readied for me by this evening. I can't stay in that master bedroom ever again—I'd sooner sleep in the outhouse with a herd of feral cats."

The housekeeper glanced at her in concern. "Yes, my lady. The girls have already begun cleaning a room overlooking the rose garden. They're beating the carpets and scrubbing the floor."

"Thank you."

Kathleen felt her spirits improve as soon as she reached the stables. A morning ride always seemed to restore her soul to rights. Entering the saddle room, she removed the detachable skirt of her riding habit and hung it on a wall bracket.

It was customary for a lady to wear chamois or wool breeches beneath a riding skirt, to prevent chafing. But it was not at all proper to wear *only* the breeches, as Kathleen was doing.

However, she hadn't yet broken Asad to sidesaddle. She had chosen to train him while riding astride, which would be far safer if the horse tried to unseat her. A picturesque riding skirt, with its masses of flowing fabric, was apt to catch on tack or low tree branches, or even become entangled with the horse's legs.

Kathleen had felt more than a little embarrassed the first time she had walked out to the paddock in breeches. The stablemen had stared at her with such astonishment that one might have thought she'd walked out there in the altogether. However, Mr. Bloom, who was more concerned with safety than propriety, had instantly given her his approval. Soon the stablemen had grown accustomed to the sight of Kathleen's unconventional appearance, and now they seemed to think nothing of it. No doubt it helped that her figure was so slight—with her lack of womanly curves, she could hardly be accused of tempting anyone.

Asad was supple and responsive during their practice, moving in half circles and serpentine patterns. His transitions were seamless, his focus perfect. Kathleen decided to take the Arabian outside the paddock for a ride in an enclosed pasture, and he did so well that she extended the morning session.

Glowing and pleasantly tired after the exercise, Kathleen returned into the house and bounded up one of the back staircases. Nearing the top, she realized she had forgotten her detachable skirt at the stables. She would send a footman to fetch it later. As she headed toward the master bedroom, she was obliged to stop and flatten against a wall as a trio of workmen proceeded through the hallway, their arms laden with copper pipes. Noticing Kathleen's breeches, one of the workmen nearly dropped the pipes, and another told him curtly to put his eyes back in his head and carry on.

Blushing, Kathleen hurried into the master bedroom and went directly to the open door of the bathroom, since Clara was nowhere to be seen. Despite her objections to the expense of indoor plumbing, she had to admit that it was lovely to have hot water without having to ring for the maids. After entering the bathroom, she closed the door firmly.

A startled yelp escaped her as she saw that the tub was occupied.

"Dear God!" Her hands flew up to cover her face.

But the image of Devon Ravenel, wet and naked, had already been burned into her brain.

# Chapter 11

*IT COULDN'T BE.* DEVON was supposed to be in London! It was a trick of her imagination . . . a hallucination. Except that the air was hot and humid, spiced with the fragrance that was unmistakably his . . . a spicy, clean incense of skin and soap.

Apprehensively Kathleen parted her fingers just enough to peek through them.

Devon was reclining in the copper tub, looking at her in sardonic inquiry. Hot mist rose around him in a smoke-colored veil. Droplets of water clung to the tautly muscled slopes of his arms and shoulders, and sparkled in the dark fleece of hair on his chest.

Kathleen whirled to face the door, her thoughts scattering like the pins in a game of skittles. "What are you doing here?" she managed to ask.

His tone was caustic. "I received your summons."

"My . . . my . . . you mean the telegram?" It was difficult to pull a coherent thought from the wreckage of her brain. "That wasn't a summons."

"It read like one."

"I didn't expect to see you so soon. Certainly not so much of you!" She went crimson as she heard his low laugh.

Desperate to escape, she seized the door handle, a bit of hardware that had just been installed by the contractor, and tugged. It remained stubbornly closed.

"Madam," she heard Devon behind her, "I suggest that you—"

She ignored him in her panic, yanking violently at the hand grasp. Abruptly the piece pulled free of its rivets, and she staggered back. Bewildered, she looked down at the broken metal part in her hand.

For a moment, there was only silence.

Devon cleared his throat roughly. His voice was thick with suppressed laughter. "It's a Norfolk latch. You have to push down on the thumb piece before pulling the handle."

Kathleen attacked the thumb piece that dangled on the faceplate, jabbing repeatedly until the entire door rattled.

"Sweetheart . . ." Now Devon was laughing almost too hard to speak. "That . . . that's not going to help."

"Don't call me that," she said, keeping her back to him. "How am I going to get out of here?"

"My valet went to fetch some towels. When he returns, he'll open the door from the outside."

With a moan of dismay, Kathleen leaned her forehead against the wood panel. "He mustn't know that I was in here with you. I'll be ruined."

She heard the lazy sluice of water over skin.

"He'll say nothing. He's discreet."

"No, he's not."

The splashing stopped. "Why do you say that?"

"He's provided the servants with no end of gossip fodder about your past exploits. According to my maid, there was a particularly riveting story involving a music hall girl." She paused before adding darkly, "Dressed in feathers."

"Bloody hell," Devon muttered. The splashing resumed.

Kathleen stayed against the door, tense in every limb. Devon's naked body was only a few yards away, in the same bathtub she had used last night. She was helpless to stop herself from imagining the sights that accompanied the sounds, water darkening his hair, soap foam coursing over his skin.

Taking care to keep her gaze averted, she set the latch handle on the floor. "Why are you bathing so early in the day?"

"I came by train, and hired a coach in Alton. A wheel came loose along the way to Eversby. I had to help the driver bolt it back on. Cold, muddy work."

"Couldn't you have asked your valet to do it instead?"

A scoffing sound. "Sutton can't lift a carriage wheel. His arms are no thicker than jackstraws."

Frowning, she drew her finger through a film of moisture that had collected on the door. "You needn't have come to Hampshire in such a hurry."

"The threat of lawyers and Chancery Court impressed me with the need for haste," he said darkly.

Perhaps her telegram had been a bit dramatic. "I wasn't really going to bring lawyers into it. I only wanted to gain your attention."

His reply was soft. "You always have my attention."

Kathleen wasn't certain how to take his meaning. Before she could ask, however, the latch of the bathroom door clicked. The wood panels trembled as someone began to push his way in. Kathleen's eyes flew open. She wedged her hands against the door, her nerves stinging in horror. A violent splash erupted behind her as Devon leaped from the bathtub and flattened a hand on the door to keep it from opening farther. His other hand slid around her to cover her mouth. That was unnecessary—Kathleen couldn't have made a sound to save her life.

She quivered in every limb at the feel of the large, steaming male at her back.

"Sir?" came the valet's puzzled voice.

"Confound it, have you forgotten how to knock?" Devon demanded. "Don't burst into a room unless it's to tell me that the house is on fire."

Distantly Kathleen wondered if she might swoon. She was fairly certain that Lady Berwick would have expected it of her in such circumstances. Unfortunately her mind remained intractably awake. She swayed, her balance uncertain, and his body automatically compensated, hard muscles flexing to support her. He was pressed all along her, hot water seeping through the back of her riding habit. With every breath, she drew in the scents of soap and heat. Her heart faltered between every beat, too weak, too fast.

Dizzily she focused on the large hand braced against the door. His skin was faintly tawny, the kind that would brown easily in the sun. One of his knuckles was scraped and raw—from lifting the carriage wheel, she guessed. The nails were short and scrupulously clean, but ink stains lingered in faint shadows on the sides of two fingers.

"I beg your pardon, my lord," the valet said. With an overdone respect that hinted at sarcasm, he added, "I've never known you to be modest before."

"I'm an aristocrat now," Devon said. "We prefer not to flaunt our assets."

He was wedged against her so tightly that Kathleen could feel his voice resonate through her. The vital, potent maleness of him surrounded her. The sensation was foreign and frightening . . . and bewilderingly pleasant. The motion of his breathing and the heat of him along her back sent little flames dancing through her tummy.

". . . there is some confusion as to the location of your luggage," Sutton was explaining. "One of the footmen carried it inside the house, as I directed, but Mrs. Church told him not to bring it to the master bedroom, as Lady Trenear has taken up temporary residence."

"Has she? Did Mrs. Church enlighten you as to why Lady Trenear has invaded my room?"

"The plumbers are installing pipe beneath the floor in her bedroom. I'm told that Lady Trenear was none too pleased by the situation. One of the footmen said he heard her vow to do you bodily harm."

"How unfortunate." Subtle amusement wove through Devon's voice. She felt his jaw nudge against her hair as he grinned. "I'm sorry to have inconvenienced her."

"It wasn't merely an inconvenience, my lord. Lady Trenear quitted the master bedroom immediately after the late earl's passing, and hasn't spent a night there since. Until now. According to one of the servants—"

Kathleen stiffened.

"I don't need to know why," Devon interrupted. "That is Lady Trenear's concern, and none of ours."

"Yes, sir," the valet said. "More to the point, the footman conveyed your luggage to one of the upstairs rooms, but no one seems to know which one."

"Has anyone thought of asking him?" Devon suggested dryly.

"At present the man is nowhere to be found. Lady Pandora and Lady Cassandra recruited him to assist them in searching for their pig, which has gone missing."

Devon's body tensed. "Did you say 'pig'?"

"Yes, my lord. A new family pet."

Devon's hand slid gently from Kathleen's lips, his fingertips grazing her chin in a whisper of a caress. "Is there a particular reason why we're keeping livestock in the—"

Kathleen had turned to glance up at him just as his head bent. His mouth collided against her temple, the accidental touch causing her senses to reel in confusion. His lips, so firm and smooth, his hot, tickling breath . . . She began to tremble.

"—house?" Devon finished, his voice roughening. He reached out to grasp the door's metal edge plate, preventing it from closing again.

"I needn't point out that such questions do not arise in most well-appointed households," Sutton said primly. "Shall I hand the towels past the door?"

"No, leave them on the other side. I'll retrieve them when I'm ready."

"On the floor?" Sutton sounded appalled. "My lord, allow me to set them on a chair." There were sounds of objects being moved within the room, the thump of a light piece of furniture.

Through heavy-lidded eyes, Kathleen saw that Devon's grip had tightened on the door until the tip of his thumb had turned white. His wrist and arm were corded. How warm he was, and how firmly his chest and shoulders supported her. The only place they didn't quite fit was the place low on her spine, where the pressure of his body was inflexible and stiffly prodding. She squirmed, seeking a more comfortable position. Devon inhaled quickly and reached down to grasp her right hip, forcing her to stay still.

Then she realized what the hard ridge was.

She tensed, her throat closing against a whimper. All the tantalizing heat fled, her flesh turning to ice, the trembling breaking into continuous shivers. She was about to be hurt. Attacked.

Marriage had taught her that men forgot themselves when aroused. They lost control and turned into beasts.

Desperately she calculated how much of a threat Devon might pose, how far he might go. If he hurt her, she would scream. She would fight back, no matter what the consequences to herself or her reputation.

One of his hands came to the side of her waist—she felt the pressure of it even through her corset—and he rubbed in slow circles, the way one would calm a spooked horse.

Through the blood pounding in her ears, Kathleen heard the valet ask if the luggage should be conveyed to the master bedroom. Devon replied that he would decide later, for now just bring some clothes and be quick about it. The valet agreed.

"He's gone," Devon said in a few moments. After taking a deep breath and letting it out slowly, he reached around the edge of the door to tamper with the latch mechanism, bending the thumb-lift bar so it wouldn't close. "Although no one has asked my opinion about the pig," he said, "I'm against any house pet that will eventually outweigh me."

Having braced herself for attack, Kathleen blinked uncertainly. He was behaving so *un*like a lust-crazed beast that it gave her pause.

In response to her frozen silence, Devon lifted a hand to her jaw and nudged her to look at him. Unable to avoid his calm, appraising glance, she realized there was no immediate danger of him forcing himself on her.

"You'd best look away," he advised, "unless you want a big eyeful of Ravenel. I'm going to fetch the towels."

Kathleen nodded, her eyes squeezing shut as he left the bathroom.

She waited, letting the chaos of her thoughts settle. But her nerves still reverberated with the feeling of him against her, the details of his aroused body.

Once, not long ago, she had gone with Lord and Lady Berwick, and their daughters, to visit the National Museum. On their way to view a display of South Seas objects that had been collected by the legendary explorer Captain James Cook, they had passed by a gallery of Italian statuary, where a pair of nude male sculptures had been positioned by the doorway. One of the detachable plaster fig leaves devised by a museum director to conceal the statues' genitals had dropped to the floor and scattered in pieces. Lady Berwick, appalled by what she had considered no less than a visual assault, had whisked Kathleen and her daughters past the offending marble flesh . . . but not before they had seen exactly what the fig leaf had been intended to cover.

Kathleen had been shocked but intrigued by the statue, marveling at how the delicacy of the sculpting had made cold marble look like flesh: veined, vulnerable, smooth everywhere except for the little scruff of hair at the groin. The shy, unobtrusive bud hadn't seemed worth the fuss Lady Berwick had made.

On Kathleen's wedding night, however, she had glimpsed and felt just enough of Theo's body to realize that a living, breathing man was endowed far more substantially than the marble sculpture at a museum.

And just now, the pressure of Devon's body against hers . . .

She wished she'd been able to look at him.

Instantly she chastised herself for the thought. Still . . . she couldn't help being curious. Would it do any harm if she took a quick peek? This was the only chance she would ever have to see a man as God had made him. Before she could talk herself out of it, she inched to the edge of the door and looked around it cautiously.

What a startling sight . . . a healthy, virile male in his prime. Strong and complexly muscled, barbaric and yet beautiful. Fortunately he was facing partially away from her, so that her surveillance went unnoticed. He toweled his hair until the thick locks stood on end and worked down to his arms and chest, scrubbing vigorously. His back was powerful, the line of his spine a pronounced groove. The broad slopes of his shoulders flexed as he draped the towel across and began to dry himself with a sawing motion. A plentitude of hair covered his limbs and the upper portion of his chest, and there was far more at his groin than the decorative tuft she had expected. As for the glimpse she'd had of his male part . . . it was scaled similarly to her husband's, except perhaps even more prodigious. It appeared decidedly inconvenient to have such an appendage. How in the world did men ride horses?

Red-faced, she shrank back behind the door before Devon could catch her spying on him.

Soon she heard him approach, the floor creaking beneath his feet, and a dry Turkish towel was extended through the partially open doorway. She took it gratefully and wrapped it around herself.

"Are you adequately covered?" she brought herself to ask.

"I doubt anyone would call it adequate."

"Would you like to wait in here?" she offered reluctantly. The bathroom was warmer than the drafty bedroom.

"No."

"But it's as cold as ice out there."

"Precisely," came his brusque reply. Judging from his voice, he was standing just on the other side of the door. "What the devil are you wearing, by the way?"

"My riding habit."

"It looks like half a riding habit."

"I leave off the overskirt when I train Asad." At his lack of response, she added, "Mr. Bloom approves of my breeches. He says that he could almost mistake me for one of the stable boys."

"Then he must be blind. No man with eyes in his head

would ever mistake you for a boy." Devon paused. "From now on, you'll ride in skirts or not at all."

"What?" she asked in disbelief. "You're giving me orders?"

"Someone has to, if you're going to behave with so little propriety."

"*You* are lecturing *me* about bloody propriety, you sodding hypocrite?"

"I suppose you learned that filthy language at the stables."

"No, from your brother," she shot back.

"I'm beginning to realize I shouldn't have stayed away from Eversby Priory for so long," she heard him say grimly. "The entire household is running amok."

Unable to restrain herself any longer, Kathleen went to the open gap in the doorway and glared at him. "*You* were the one who hired the plumbers!" she hissed.

"The plumbers are the least of it. Someone needs to take the situation in hand."

"If you're foolish enough to imagine you could take *me* in hand—"

"Oh, I'd begin with you," he assured her feelingly.

Kathleen would have delivered a scathing reply, but her teeth had begun to chatter. Although the Turkish towel had absorbed some of the moisture from her clothes, they were clammy.

Seeing her discomfort, Devon turned and surveyed the room, obviously hunting for something to cover her. Although his back was turned, she knew the precise moment that he spotted the shawl on the fireplace chair.

When he spoke, his tone had changed. "You didn't dye it."

"Give that to me." Kathleen thrust her arm through the doorway.

Devon picked it up. A slow smile crossed his face. "Do you wear it often?"

"Hand me my shawl, please."

Devon brought it to her, deliberately taking his time. He should have been mortified by his indecent state of undress, but he seemed entirely comfortable, the great shameless peacock.

As soon as the shawl was within reach, Kathleen snatched it from him.

Casting aside her damp towel, she pulled the shawl around herself. The garment was comforting and familiar, the soft wool warming her instantly.

"I couldn't bring myself to ruin it," she said grudgingly. She was tempted to tell him that even though the gift had been inappropriate . . . the truth was, she loved it. There were days when she wasn't certain whether the gloomy widow's weeds were reflecting her melancholy mood or causing it, and when she pulled the brilliant shawl over her shoulders, she felt instantly better.

No gift had ever pleased her as much.

She couldn't tell him that, but she wanted to.

"You look beautiful in those colors, Kathleen." His voice was low and soft.

She felt her face prickle. "Don't use my first name."

"By all means," Devon mocked, glancing down at his towel-clad form, "let's be formal."

She made the mistake of following his gaze, and colored deeply at the sight of him . . . the intriguing dark hair on his chest, the way the muscle of his stomach seemed to have been carved like mahogany fretwork.

A knock came at the bedroom door. Kathleen retreated deeper into the bathroom like a turtle withdrawing in its shell.

"Come in, Sutton," she heard Devon say.

"Your clothes, sir."

"Thank you. Lay them out on the bed."

"Won't you require assistance?"

"Not today."

"You will dress yourself?" the valet asked, bewildered.

"I've heard that some men do," Devon replied sardonically. "You may leave now."

The valet heaved a long-suffering sigh. "Yes, sir."

After the door had opened and closed again, Devon said, "Give me a minute. I'll be dressed soon."

Kathleen didn't reply, thinking to her dismay that she would never be able to look at him without being aware of what was beneath those elegant layers of clothing.

Over the rustle of cloth, Devon said, "You're welcome to occupy the master bedroom, if you like. It was your room before it was mine."

"No, I don't want it."

"As you prefer."

She was desperate to change the subject. "We need to discuss the tenants," she said. "As I mentioned in the telegram—"

"Later. There's no point in talking about it without my brother's participation. The housekeeper said that he has gone to Wiltshire. When will he return?"

"Tomorrow."

"Why did he go?"

"To consult with an expert about modern farming methods."

"Knowing my brother," Devon said, "it's more likely he's gone a-whoring."

"Apparently you *don't* know him, then." Not only was she pleased to be able to contradict him, she was affronted on West's behalf. "Mr. Ravenel has worked very hard ever since he arrived here. I daresay he has learned more about the tenants and estate farms than anyone, including the land agent. Spend a few minutes reading the reports and ledgers he keeps in the study, and you'll change your tune."

"We'll see." Devon pushed open the bathroom door. He was fully clothed in a gray wool suit, although he wore no necktie, and his cuffs and collar had been left unfastened. His face was expressionless. "Will you help with this?" he asked, extending his arm.

Hesitantly Kathleen reached out to fasten one of his loose cuffs. The backs of her knuckles brushed the skin on the inside of his wrist, where the skin was blood-heated and smooth. Acutely aware of the measured sound of his breathing, she fastened the other cuff. Reaching up to the sides of his open shirt collar, she drew them together and proceeded to fasten them with a small gold stud that had been left dangling in the buttonhole. As she slid her fingers beneath the front of the collar, she could feel the ripple of his swallow.

"Thank you," Devon said. There was a slight rasp in his voice, as if his throat had gone dry.

As he turned to leave, Kathleen said, "Please take care not to be seen when you leave the room."

Devon paused at the door and glanced back at her. The familiar taunting gleam appeared in his eyes. "Have no fear. I'm accomplished at making a discreet exit from a lady's bedroom." He grinned at her scowl, looked out into the hallway, and slipped from the room.

# Chapter 12

DEVON'S SMILE VANISHED AS soon as he left the master bedroom. With no destination in mind, he wandered along the hallway until he reached a connecting space with an inset window niche. It led to a cramped circular stair that spiraled upward to servants' rooms and garrets. The ceiling was so low that he was obliged to duck his head to pass through. A house as old as Eversby Priory had undergone multiple expansions over the decades, the additions creating odd and unexpected nooks. He found the effect less charming than other people might have; eccentricity was not something he valued in architecture.

Lowering to sit on a narrow step, Devon braced his forearms on his knees and bent his head. He let out a shaking breath. It had been the most exquisite torment he had ever suffered, standing there with Kathleen pressed against him. She had trembled like a newborn foal straining to stand. He'd never wanted anything in his life as much as he'd wanted to turn her to face him, and take her mouth with long, searching kisses until she melted against him.

Groaning faintly, he rubbed the inside of one of his wrists, where a glow of heat lingered as if he'd been branded by her touch.

What had his valet started to say about Kathleen? Why

had she refused to sleep in the master bedroom after Theo's death? The memory of her last argument with her husband must have something to do with it . . . but could it be something more? Perhaps the wedding night had been unpleasant for her. Privileged young women were often kept in ignorance about such matters until they were married.

Devon certainly didn't care to speculate on his cousin's prowess in the bedroom . . . but even Theo would have known to treat a virgin with care and patience . . . wouldn't he? Even Theo would have known enough to soothe and seduce a nervous bride, and ease her fears before taking his own pleasure.

The thought of the two of them together . . . Theo's hands on Kathleen . . . It sent an unfamiliar poisonous feeling through him. Holy hell, was it . . . jealousy?

He'd never been jealous over a woman.

Cursing beneath his breath, Devon stood and raked his hands through his damp hair. Brooding over the past wouldn't change the fact that Kathleen had belonged to Theo first.

But she would belong to Devon last.

Gathering his wits, he walked through Eversby Priory, investigating the changes that had taken place since his last visit. Activity was rampant in the house, with many rooms in various stages of disrepair and construction. So far, repairs on the estate had required a small fortune, and it would take ten times that before all was said and done.

He ended up in the study, where ledgers and bundled papers had been piled high on the desk. Recognizing his brother's precise, compact handwriting, he picked up a report of what West had learned about the estate so far.

It took two hours to read the report, which was more thorough than Devon would have ever expected—and it didn't appear to be finished by half. Apparently West was visiting every tenant farm on the estate, making detailed notes about each family's problems and concerns, the conditions of their property, their knowledge and views of farming techniques.

Sensing a movement, Devon turned in his chair and saw Kathleen in the doorway.

She was dressed in widow's weeds again, her hair pinned in a braided coil, her wrists encircled with demure white cuffs. Her cheeks were very pink.

Devon could have devoured her in one bite. Instead, he gave her a neutral glance as he rose to his feet. "Skirts," he said in a tone of mild surprise, as if it were a novelty to see her in a dress. "Where are you going?"

"To the library for a lesson with the girls. But I noticed that you were in here, and I wondered if you'd read Mr. Ravenel's report."

"I have. I'm impressed by his dedication. Also rather astonished, since West advised me to sell the estate, lock, stock, and barrel, just before he left London."

Kathleen smiled and studied him with those tip-tilted eyes. He could see tiny rays in the light brown irises, like gold threads. "I'm very glad you didn't," she said softly. "I think perhaps he might be too."

All the heat from their earlier encounter came rushing back so fast that it hurt, his flesh rising with a swift ache beneath the layers of his clothes. Devon was profoundly grateful for the concealment of his suit coat.

Kathleen reached for a wood-cased pencil on the desk. The graphite lead had worn down to a dull stub. "Sometimes I wonder . . ." Picking up a pair of scissors, she began to sharpen the pencil with one blade, scraping off thin layers of wood.

"What is it?" Devon asked huskily.

She concentrated on her task, sounding troubled as she replied. "I wonder what Theo would have done with the estate, if he hadn't passed away."

"I suspect he would have turned a blind eye until there were no decisions left to make."

"But why? He wasn't a stupid man."

A latent impulse of fairness moved Devon to say, "It had nothing to do with intelligence."

Kathleen paused and gave him a puzzled glance.

"Eversby Priory was Theo's childhood home," Devon continued. "I'm sure it was painful for him to confront its decline."

Her face softened. "You're confronting it, though, aren't you? You've changed your entire life for it."

Devon shrugged casually. "It's not as though I had something better to do."

"It's not easy for you, however." A faintly apologetic smile whisked across her lips. "I don't always remember that." Lowering her head, she resumed her work on the pencil.

Devon watched, helplessly charmed by the sight of her scraping away like an industrious schoolgirl.

"At this rate," he said after a moment, "you'll spend all day doing that. Why don't you use a knife?"

"Lord Berwick would never allow it—he said scissors were safer."

"Just the opposite. I'm surprised you never lost a finger. Here, set those down." Devon reached across the desk to retrieve a silver penknife resting in the inkwell tray. He unfolded the blade and gave it to Kathleen handle first. "Hold the knife like this." He rearranged her fingers, disregarding her protests. "Always direct the pencil away from your body as you sharpen it."

"Really, there's no need . . . I'm better with scissors . . ."

"Try. It's more efficient. You can't go through life doing this the wrong way. The wasted minutes could add up to days. Weeks."

An unexpected giggle escaped her, as if she were a young girl being teased. "I don't use a pencil *that* often."

Devon reached around her, his hands engulfing hers. And she let him. She stood still, her body wary but compliant. A fragile trust had been established during their earlier encounter—no matter what else she might fear from him, she seemed to understand that he wouldn't hurt her.

The pleasure of holding her washed through him in repeated waves. She was petite and fine-boned, the delicious fragrance of roses rising to his nostrils. He'd noticed it when he'd held her earlier . . . not a cloying perfume, but a light floral essence swept with the sharp freshness of winter air.

"All it takes is six cuts," he said near her ear. She nodded, relaxing against him as he guided her hands with precision. One deep stroke of the blade neatly removed an angled section of wood. They rotated the pencil and made another cut, and then a third, creating a precise triangular prism. "Now trim the sharp edges." They concentrated on the task with his hands still bracketed over hers, using the blade to chamfer each corner of wood until they had created a clean, satisfying point.

Done.

After one last luxurious inhalation of her scent, Devon released her slowly, knowing that for the rest of his life, a single breath of a rose would bring him back to this moment.

Kathleen set aside the knife and pencil, and turned to face Devon.

They were very close, not quite touching, not quite separate.

She looked uncertain, her lips parting as if she wanted to say something but couldn't think of what it should be.

Devon's control began to fray, thread by thread, in that electric silence. He found himself leaning forward by degrees until his hands were anchored on the desk on either side of her. Kathleen was forced to lean back, gripping his forearms to maintain her balance. He waited for her to protest, push him, tell him to move back.

But she stared at him as if mesmerized, her breath coming in fits and starts. Her grip began to tighten and ease on his arms like a cat kneading her paws. Lowering his head, he touched his lips to her temple, where a faint whisk of blue veins was visible. He could sense her bewilderment, the force of her unwilling attraction to him.

Dimly aware that he was burning through the last few shreds of self-control, he forced himself to straighten and take his hands from the desk. He began to move away, but Kathleen stayed with him, still clinging to his arms, her gaze unfocused. *God . . .* this was how it would be, her body following his without effort, while he lifted and filled her . . .

Every heartbeat drove him closer to her.

His hand lifted to the side of her face, tilting it upward, while his other arm drew around her.

Her lashes lowered, settling in dark crescents against her pink skin. Confusion had etched a delicate apostrophe of tension between her brows, and he kissed the fine notches before bringing his mouth to hers.

He expected her to protest, to push him away, but instead she went pliant, making a little pleasured sound that sent burning chills down his spine. Both his hands came to her face, gently adjusting the angle of her jaw as he coaxed her lips to part. He began to search her, wringing sensation and sweetness from her innocently responsive mouth . . . but her tongue retreated instantly at the first touch of his.

Burning with lust and tender amusement, Devon slid his mouth to her ear. "No," he whispered, "let me taste you . . . let me feel how soft you are inside . . ."

He kissed her again, slow and ruthlessly gentle, until her mouth clung to his and he felt the answering touch of her tongue. Her hands inched up his chest, her head tilting backward as she surrendered helplessly. The pleasure was unimaginable, as unfamiliar to him as it must have been to her. Suffused with an agony of need, he moved his hands over her, caressing and trying to grip her closer. He could feel the movements of her body within the rustling dress, firm sweet flesh trussed in all those stiff layers of starch and laces and boning. He wanted to tear it all from her. He wanted her vulnerable and exposed to him, her private skin naked beneath his mouth.

But as he took her face in his hands so his thumbs could stroke her cheeks, he felt a smudge of moisture.

A tear.

Devon went still. Lifting his head, he stared down at Kathleen while their panting breaths mingled. Her eyes were wet and bewildered. She raised her fingers to her lips, touching them tentatively as if they'd been burned.

Silently he berated himself, knowing that he'd pushed her too far, too soon.

Somehow he managed to let go and back away, putting a crucial distance between them.

"Kathleen—" he began gruffly. "I shouldn't have—"

She fled before he could say another word.

THE NEXT MORNING, Devon took the family coach to meet West's train. The market town of Alton was bisected by a long main street lined with prosperous shops, neighborhoods of handsome houses, a bombazine cloth factory, and a paper mill. Unfortunately the sulfurous stench of the paper mill announced itself well before the building came into view.

The footman huddled closer to the station building, taking refuge from the biting November wind. Feeling too restless to stay still, Devon paced along the platform, his hands shoved in the pockets of his black wool great-coat. Tomorrow he would have to return to London. The thought of that silent house, so crowded with furniture and yet so empty, filled him with revulsion. But he had to stay away from Hampshire. He needed distance from Kathleen, or he wouldn't be able to stop himself from se-ducing her long before she was ready for it.

He was playing a long game, and he couldn't let him-self forget that.

Bloody mourning period.

He was obliged to curtail his pacing as the platform became crowded with people holding tickets, and others waiting to greet the arriving passengers. Soon their con-versation and laughter were drowned out by the approach of the locomotive, a thundering, hissing beast that sped forward with impatient clattering and chugging.

After the train had stopped with a metallic screech, porters carried trunks and valises off the train, while ar-riving and departing passengers milled in a roiling crowd. People collided as they headed in a multitude of direc-tions. Objects were dropped and hastily retrieved; travel-ers became separated and searched for each other; names were called out in the cacophony. Devon pushed past the confluence of bodies, looking for his brother. Not finding him, he glanced back at the footman, wondering if he had caught sight of West. The servant gestured and shouted something, but his voice was lost in the clamor.

As Devon made his way to the footman, he saw him talking to a stranger wearing baggy clothes, the kind of good quality but ill-fitting castoffs that a clerk or tradesman might wear. The man was young and slim, with heavy dark hair that wanted cutting. He bore a striking resemblance to West in his days at Oxford, especially the way he smiled with his chin tilted downward, as if reflecting on some private joke. In fact . . .

Holy hell. It was his brother. It was West.

"Devon," West exclaimed with a surprised laugh, reaching out to shake his hand heartily. "Why aren't you in London?"

Devon was slow to gather his wits. West looked years younger . . . healthy, clear-eyed, as he'd never thought to see him again.

"Kathleen sent for me," he finally said.

"Did she? Why?"

"I'll explain later. What has happened to you? I hardly recognize you."

"Nothing's happened. What do you—oh, yes, I've lost a bit of weight. Never mind that, I've just arranged to purchase a threshing machine." West's face glowed with pleasure. At first Devon thought he was being sarcastic.

*My brother,* he thought, *is excited over farming equipment.*

As they proceeded to the coach, West described his visit to Wiltshire and talked animatedly about what he had learned from an agriculturist who was practicing modern techniques on his model farm. With a combination of deep drainage and steam power, the man had doubled the yield on his land using less than half the labor. Furthermore, the agriculturist wanted to acquire the latest machinery and was willing to sell his equipment at a bargain. "It will require some investment," West admitted, "but the returns will be exponential. I have some estimates to show you—"

"I've seen some of them. You've done impressive work."

West shrugged nonchalantly.

They climbed into the coach and settled into the fine leather seats. "You seem to be thriving at Eversby Priory," Devon remarked as their vehicle began to move.

"The devil knows why. There's never a moment's peace or privacy. A man can't sit and think without being jumped on by some overexcited dog, or harassed by gabby females. There's always an emergency: something breaking, exploding, or collapsing—"

"Exploding?"

"One explosion. The laundry drying room stove wasn't properly ventilated—no, don't be alarmed—a brick wall absorbed most of the force. No one was injured. The point is that the house is perpetually topsy-turvy."

"Why don't you come back to London, then?"

"I can't."

"If it's because of your plan to visit every tenant family on the estate, I don't see the need—"

"No, it's not that. The fact is . . . Eversby Priory suits me. Damned if I know why."

"Have you developed an attachment for . . . someone?" Devon asked, his soul icing over with the suspicion that West wanted Kathleen.

"All of them," West admitted readily.

"But not one in particular?"

West blinked. "A romantic interest in one of the girls, you mean? Good God, *no*. I know too much about them. They're like sisters to me."

"Even Kathleen?"

"Especially her." An absent smile crossed West's face.

"I've come to like her," he said frankly. "Theo chose well for himself. She would have improved him."

"He didn't deserve her," Devon muttered.

West shrugged. "I can't think of a man who would."

Devon clenched his hand until the scab over his knuckle pulled stingingly tight. "Does she ever mention Theo?"

"Not often. I can't imagine a more dedicated effort to mourn someone, but it's obvious that her heart isn't in it." Noticing Devon's sharp glance, West said, "She knew Theo for a mere matter of months and was married to him for three days. Three days! How long should a woman grieve for a man she scarcely knew? It's absurd for society to insist upon a fixed mourning period without regard to circumstance. Can't such things be allowed to happen naturally?"

"The purpose of society is to prevent natural behavior," Devon said dryly.

West grinned. "Granted. But Kathleen isn't suited to the role of drab little widow. She has too much spirit. It's why she was attracted to a Ravenel in the first place."

THE AMIABLE RELATIONSHIP between West and Kathleen was immediately obvious upon their return to Eversby Priory. Kathleen came to the entrance hall while the butler was still collecting their hats and coats, and propped her hands on her hips as she viewed West with mock suspicion. "Have you brought back any farm animals?" she asked.

"Not this time." West smiled and went to kiss her forehead.

To Devon's surprise, Kathleen accepted the affectionate gesture without protest. "Did you learn as much as you'd hoped?" she asked.

"Ten times more," West said promptly. "On the subject of fertilizer alone, I could regale you for hours."

Kathleen laughed, but her expression became remote as she turned to Devon. "My lord."

Annoyed by the stilted acknowledgment, Devon nodded in return.

It appeared that she had decided to hold him at arm's length and pretend the kiss had never happened.

"The earl claims that you sent for him, my lady," West said. "Should I assume that you pined for his charming company, or was there another reason?"

"After you left, there was a crisis with the Wootens," Kathleen told him. "I informed Trenear of the situation and asked what he knew about it. So far he's insisted on being mysterious."

"What happened to the Wootens?" West asked, looking from one of them to the other.

"We'll discuss it in the library," Devon said. "Lady Trenear, it's unnecessary for you to be present, however—"

"I *will* be present." Kathleen's brows lowered. "I gave the Wootens my personal assurance that everything would be sorted out."

"They shouldn't have come to you," Devon said bluntly. "They should have waited to speak to my brother or Mr. Carlow."

"They went to Mr. Carlow first," she retorted, "and he knew nothing about the situation. And Mr. Ravenel wasn't here. I was the only person available."

"From now on, I would prefer you not to make yourself available when it comes to discussing leaseholds. You should limit yourself to whatever it is the lady of the manor is supposed to do. Bring them baskets when people are ill, and so forth."

"What smug, condescending—" Kathleen began.

"Are we to stand here squabbling in the entrance hall?" West interceded hastily. "Let's pretend to be civilized and proceed to the library." He pulled Kathleen's arm over his and accompanied her from the entrance hall. "I wouldn't mind sending for some tea and sandwiches," he said. "I'm starved after riding on the train. You're always telling me to eat, remember?"

Devon strode after them, only half listening to the conversation. Scowling, he focused on the sight of Kathleen's arm tucked into West's. Why was he touching her? Why was she allowing it? The unfamiliar poisonous jealousy returned, coiling thickly in his chest.

". . . and Mrs. Wooten couldn't speak for weeping," Kathleen said indignantly. "They have four children, and Mrs. Wooten's elderly aunt to look after, and if they were to lose the farm—"

"Don't worry," West interrupted with a soothing murmur. "We'll sort it all out. I promise."

"Yes, but if Trenear made such an important decision without saying *anything*—"

"Nothing's been decided yet," Devon said stonily, following the pair.

Kathleen glanced over her shoulder, her eyes narrowed. "Then why were there railroad surveyors on the estate land?"

"I prefer not to discuss my business affairs in the hallway."

"You gave them permission to be there, didn't you?" Kathleen tried to stop and face him, but West tugged her inexorably toward the library.

"I wonder if I should have Darjeeling tea?" West mused aloud. "No, perhaps something stronger . . . Ceylon or pekoe . . . and some of the little buns with the cream and jam . . . What were those, Kathleen?"

"Cornish splits."

"Ah. No wonder I like them. It sounds like something I once saw performed at a dance hall."

They entered the library. Kathleen tugged at the bellpull beside the door and waited until a housemaid appeared. After requesting a tea tray and a plate of sandwiches and pastries, Kathleen went to the long table, where Devon had unrolled a map of the estate lands.

"Well, did you?" she asked.

Devon gave her an ominous glance. "Did I what?"

"Did you give the railway men permission to survey your land?"

"Yes," he said flatly. "But they didn't have permission to talk to anyone about it. They should have kept their mouths shut."

Her eyes flashed with outrage. "Then it's true? You've sold the Wootens' farm?"

"No, and I don't intend to."

"Then what—"

"Kathleen," West broke in gently, "we'll be here all night if you don't let him finish."

She scowled and fell silent, watching as Devon weighted the corners of the map with various objects.

Taking up a pencil, Devon drew a line across the east side of the estate. "Recently I met with the director of the London Ironstone railway," he said. For Kathleen's benefit, he explained, "It's a private company, owned by a friend. Tom Severin."

"We're in the same London club," West added.

Devon viewed the map critically before drawing a parallel line. "Severin wants to reduce distance on London Ironstone's existing Portsmouth route. He's also planning to relay the entire sixty-mile line, start to finish, with heavier rails to accommodate faster trains."

"Can he afford such a project?" West asked.

"He's already secured one million pounds."

West uttered a wordless exclamation.

"Precisely," Devon said, and continued in a matter-of-fact tone. "Of all the prospective plans for the shortened route, the natural gradient is best across this area." He shaded lightly between the parallel lines. "If we were to allow London Ironstone to cross the eastern perimeter of the estate, we would receive a large annual sum that would go far toward easing our financial problems."

Kathleen leaned over the table, staring intently at the pencil markings. "But this is impossible," she said. "According to what you've drawn, the tracks would run not only across the Wootens' farm, but at least three other leaseholds as well."

"Four tenant farms would be affected," Devon admitted.

A frown grooved West's forehead as he studied the map. "The tracks appear to cross two private drives. We would have no access to the east side."

"The railroad would build occupation bridges at their own expense, to keep all parts of the estate connected."

Before West could comment, Kathleen stood and faced Devon across the table. She looked stricken. "You can't agree to this. You can't take the farms away from those families."

"The solicitor confirmed that it's legal."

"I don't mean legally, I mean morally. You can't deprive them of their homes and their livings. What would happen to those families? All those children? Even you couldn't live with that on your conscience."

Devon gave her a sardonic glance, annoyed that she would automatically assume the worst about him. "I'm not going to abandon the tenants. I fully intend to help them find new situations."

Kathleen had begun to shake her head before he had even finished. "Farming is what these people have done for generations. It's in their blood. Taking away their land would break them."

Devon had known this was exactly how she would react. People first, business second. But that wasn't always possible. "We're discussing four families out of two hundred," he said. "If I don't strike a deal with London Ironstone, *all* the Eversby Priory tenants may lose their farms."

"There has to be another way," Kathleen insisted.

"If there were, I'd have found it." She knew nothing of all the sleepless nights and exhausting days he'd spent searching for alternatives. There was no good solution, only a choice between several bad solutions, and this was the least harmful.

Kathleen stared at him as if she'd just caught him snatching a crust of bread from an orphan. "But—"

"Don't press me on this," Devon snapped, losing his patience. "It's difficult enough without a display of adolescent drama."

Kathleen's face went white. Without another word, she turned and strode from the library.

West sighed and glanced at Devon. "Well done. Why bother reasoning with her when you can simply crush her into submission?"

Before Devon could reply, his brother had left to follow Kathleen.

# Chapter 13

KATHLEEN WAS HALFWAY DOWN the hallway before West could catch up to her.

Having become acquainted with Kathleen, and knowing Devon as well as anyone could, West could say with authority that they brought out the worst in each other. When they were in the same room, he reflected with exasperation, tempers flared and words became bullets. The devil knew why they found it so difficult to be civil to each other.

"Kathleen," West said quietly as he reached her.

She stopped and turned to face him. Her face was drawn, her mouth tight.

Having endured the lash of Devon's temper more than a few times in the past, West understood how deeply it could cut. "The estate's financial disaster is not of Devon's making," he said. "He's only trying to minimize the casualties. You can't blame him for that."

"Tell me what I can blame him for, then."

"In this situation?" A note of apology entered his voice. "Being realistic."

Kathleen gave him a reproachful glance. "Why should four families pay the price for all the rest of us to survive? He has to find some other way."

West rubbed the back of his neck, which was stiff after two nights of sleeping on a lumpy bed in a cold farmhouse. "Life is hardly ever fair, little friend. As you well know."

"Can't you talk him out of it?" she brought herself to ask.

"Not when I would make the same decision. The fact is, once we lease the land to London Ironstone, that tiny eastern portion of the estate will become our only source of reliable profit."

Her head lowered. "I thought you would be on the tenants' side."

"I am. You know I am." West reached out to take her narrow shoulders in a warm, sustaining grip. "I swear to you, we'll do everything possible to help them. Their farms will be reduced in size, but if they're willing to learn modern methods, they could produce double their annual yields." To make certain she was listening, he gave her the gentlest possible shake. "I'll persuade Devon to give them every advantage: We'll reduce their rents and provide drainage and building improvements. We'll even supply machinery to help them plow and harvest." Staring down into her mutinous face, he said ruefully, "Don't look like that. Good God, one would think we were conspiring to murder someone."

"I have just the person in mind," she muttered.

"You had better pray that nothing ever happens to him, because then I would become the earl. And I would wash my hands of the estate."

"Would you really?" She seemed genuinely shocked.

"Before you could blink."

"But you've worked so hard for the tenants . . ."

"As you yourself once said, Devon is carrying a heavy burden. There's nothing in this world I want badly enough to be willing to do what my brother is doing. Which means I have no choice but to support him."

Kathleen nodded glumly.

"Now you're being practical." West smiled slightly. "Will you accompany me back to the lion's den?"

"No, I'm tired of quarreling." Briefly she rested her forehead against his chest, a close and trusting gesture that touched him nearly as much as it surprised him.

After parting company with Kathleen, West returned to the library.

Devon was outwardly calm as he stood at the table and stared down at the map. However, the pencil had been broken into multiple pieces that were scattered across the carpet.

Contemplating Devon's hard profile, West asked blandly, "Could you try to be a bit more artful in dealing with her? Perhaps use a smidgen of diplomacy? Because even though I happen to agree with your position, you're being a donkey's arse about it."

Devon sent him a wrathful glance. "I'll be damned if I have to win her approval before making decisions about my estate."

"Unlike either of us, she has a conscience. It won't hurt you at all to hear her opinion. Especially since she happens to be right."

"You just said you agreed with my position!"

"From a practical standpoint. Morally, Kathleen is right." West watched as his brother prowled away from the table and back again, pacing like a caged tiger. "You have to understand something about her," he said. "She's spirited on the surface, but sensitive at the core. If you show her just a little consideration—"

"I don't need you to explain her to me."

"I know her better than you," West said sharply. "I've been living with her, for God's sake."

That earned him a chilling glance. "Do you want her?" Devon asked brusquely.

West was baffled by the question, which seemed to have come from nowhere. "*Want* her? In the biblical sense? Of course not, she's a widow. Theo's widow. How could anyone . . ." His voice faded as he saw that Devon had resumed pacing, his expression murderous.

Thunderstruck, West realized what the most likely reason was for all the free-floating hostility and high-riding tension between Devon and Kathleen. He closed his eyes briefly. This was bad. Bad for everyone, bad for the future, just bloody awful compounding badness in all directions. He decided to test his theory in the hope that he was mistaken.

"Although," West continued, "she is a little beauty, isn't she? One could find all kinds of entertaining uses for that sweet mouth. I wouldn't mind catching her in a dark corner and having some fun. She might resist at first, but soon I'd have her writhing like a cat—"

Devon lunged at him in a blur of motion, seizing West by the lapels. "Touch her and I'll kill you," he snarled.

West stared at him in appalled disbelief. "I knew it. Sweet Mother of God! *You* want her."

Devon's visceral fury appeared to fade a few degrees as he realized he had just been outmaneuvered. He released West abruptly.

"You took Theo's title and his home," West continued in appalled disbelief, "and now you want his wife."

"His widow," Devon muttered.

"Have you seduced her?"

"Not yet."

West clapped his hand to his forehead. "*Christ.* Don't you think she's suffered enough? Oh, go on and glare. Snap me in pieces like that blasted pencil. It will only confirm that you're no better than Theo." Reading the outrage in his brother's expression, he said, "Your relationships typically last no longer than the contents of the meat larder. You have a devil of a temper, and if the way you just handled her is an example of how you'll deal with disagreements—"

"That's enough," Devon said with dangerous softness.

Rubbing his forehead, West sighed and continued wearily. "Devon, you and I have always overlooked each other's faults, but that doesn't mean we're oblivious to them. This is nothing but blind, stupid lust. Have the decency to leave her alone. Kathleen is a sensitive and compassionate woman who deserves to be loved . . . and if you have any capacity for that, I've never witnessed it. I've seen what happens to women who care about you. Nothing cools your lust faster than affection."

Devon gave him a cold stare. "Are you going to say anything to her?"

"No, I'll hold my tongue and hope that you'll come to your senses."

"There's no need to worry," Devon said darkly. "At this point I've made her so ill-disposed toward me that it would be a miracle if I ever manage to lure her to my bed."

AFTER CONSIDERING THE idea of missing dinner for the second night in a row, Kathleen decided in a spirit of defiance to join the family in the dining room. It was Devon's last evening at Eversby Priory, and she could force herself to endure an hour and a half of sitting at the same table with him. Devon insisted on seating her, his face inscrutable, and she thanked him with a few clipped words. But even with that civilized distance between them, she was in an agony of nerves and anger . . . most of it directed at herself.

Those kisses . . . the impossible, terrible pleasure of them . . . how could he have done that to her? How could she have responded so wantonly? The fault was more hers than Devon's. He was a London rake; of course he would make advances to her, or to any woman in his proximity. She should have resisted, slapped him, but instead she had stood there and let him . . . let him . . .

She couldn't find the right words for what he had done. He had shown her a side of herself that she had never known existed. She had been raised to believe that lust was a sin, and she had self-righteously considered herself to be above carnal desire . . . until Devon had proven otherwise. Oh, the shocking heat of his tongue against hers, and the shivery weakness that had made her want to sink to the floor and have him cover her . . . She could have wept for shame.

Instead, she could only sit there suffocating while the conversation flowed around her. It was a pity she couldn't enjoy the meal, a succulent partridge pie served with fried oyster patties and a crisp salted salad of celery, radishes, and cucumber. As she forced herself to take a few bites, every mouthful seemed to stick in her throat.

As talk turned to the subject of the approaching holiday, Cassandra asked Devon if he planned to come to Eversby Priory for Christmas.

"Would that please you?" Devon asked.

"Oh, yes!"

"Will you bring presents?" Pandora asked.

"Pandora," Kathleen chided.

Devon grinned. "What would you like?" he asked the twins.

"*Anything* from Winterborne's," Pandora exclaimed.

"I want people for Christmas," Cassandra said wistfully. "Pandora, do you remember the Christmas balls that Mama gave when we were little? All the ladies in their finery, and the gentlemen in formal attire . . . the music and dancing . . ."

"And the feasting . . ." Pandora added. "Puddings, cakes, mince pies . . ."

"Next year we'll make merry again," Helen said gently, smiling at the pair of them. She turned to West. "How do you usually celebrate Christmas, cousin?"

He hesitated before replying, seeming to ponder whether to answer truthfully. Honesty won out. "On Christmas Day I visit friends in a parasitical fashion, going from house to house and drinking until I finally fall unconscious in someone's parlor. Then someone pours me into a carriage and sends me home, and my servants put me to bed."

"That doesn't sound very merry," Cassandra said.

"Beginning this year," Devon said, "I intend for us all to do the holiday justice. In fact, I've invited a friend to share Christmas with us at Eversby Priory."

The table fell silent, everyone staring at him in collective surprise.

"Who?" Kathleen asked suspiciously. For his sake, she hoped it wasn't one of those railway men plotting to destroy tenant farms.

"Mr. Winterborne himself."

Amid the girls' gasping and squealing, Kathleen scowled at Devon. Damn him, he *knew* it wasn't right to invite a stranger to a house of mourning. "The owner of a department store?" she asked. "No doubt accompanied by a crowd of fashionable friends and hangers-on? My lord, surely you haven't forgotten that we're all in mourning!"

"How could I?" he parried with a pointed glance that incensed her. "Winterborne will come alone, as a matter of fact. I doubt it will burden my household unduly to set one extra place at the table on Christmas Eve."

"A gentleman of Mr. Winterborne's influence must already have a thousand invitations for the holiday. Why must he come here?"

Devon's eyes glinted with enjoyment at her barely contained fury. "Winterborne is a private man. I suppose the idea of a quiet holiday in the country appeals to him. For his sake, I would like to have a proper Christmas feast. And perhaps a few carols could be sung."

The girls chimed in at once.

"Oh, do say yes, Kathleen!"

"That would be splendicious!"

Even Helen murmured something to the effect that she couldn't see how it would do any harm.

"Why stop there?" Kathleen asked sarcastically, giving Devon a look of open animosity. "Why not have musicians and dancing, and a great tall tree lit with candles?"

"What excellent suggestions," came Devon's silky reply. "Yes, let's have all of that."

Infuriated to the point of speechlessness, Kathleen glared at him while Helen discreetly pried the butter knife from her clenched fingers.

# Chapter 14

DECEMBER SWEPT OVER HAMPSHIRE, bringing chilling breezes and whitening the trees and hedgerows with frost. In the household's general enthusiasm for the approaching holiday, Kathleen soon gave up any hope of curtailing the celebrations. She found herself surrendering by degrees. First she consented to let the servants plan their own party on Christmas Eve, and then she agreed to allow a large fir tree in the entrance hall.

And then West asked if the festivities could be expanded even more.

He found Kathleen in the study, laboring over correspondence. "May I interrupt you for a few moments?"

"Of course." She gestured to a chair near her writing desk, and set the pen in its holder. Noticing the deliberately bland expression on his face, she asked, "What scheme are you hatching?"

He blinked in surprise. "How do you know there's a scheme?"

"Whenever you try to look innocent, it's obvious you're up to something."

West grinned. "The girls wouldn't dare approach you about it, but I told them I would, since it's been established that I can outrun you when necessary." He paused. "It seems that Lord and Lady Trenear used to invite all the tenant families and some local tradesmen to a party on Christmas Eve—"

"Absolutely not."

"Yes, that was my first reaction. However . . ." He gave her a patient, cajoling glance. "Encouraging a spirit of community would benefit everyone on the estate." He paused. "It's not that different from the charitable visits you pay to those families individually."

Kathleen buried her face in her hands with a groan. A grand party. Music. Presents, sweets, holiday cheer. She knew exactly what Lady Berwick would have said: It was indecent to host such revelry in a house of mourning. It was wrong to steal a day or two of joy out of a year that had been set aside for sorrow. Worst of all, she secretly wanted to do it.

She spoke through her fingers. "It's not proper," she said weakly. "We haven't done anything the way we should: The black was taken from the windows far too early, and no one's wearing veils anymore, and—"

"No one gives a damn," West said. "Do you think any of the tenants would blame you for setting aside your mourning just for one night? To the contrary, they would appreciate it as a gesture of kindness and goodwill. I know next to nothing about Christmas, of course, but even so . . . it strikes me as being in keeping with the spirit of the holiday." At her long hesitation, he went in for the kill. "I'll pay for it out of my own income. After all . . ." A touch of self-pity shaded his voice. ". . . how else am I to learn about Christmas?"

Lowering her hands, Kathleen gave him a dark glance. "You're a shameless manipulator, Weston Ravenel."

He grinned. "I knew you'd say yes."

"IT'S A VERY tall tree," Helen commented a week later, as they stood in the entrance hall.

"We've never had one this large before," Mrs. Church admitted with a perturbed frown.

Together they watched as West, a pair of footmen, and the butler struggled to heft the trunk of an enormous fir into a metal tub filled with stones. The air was filled with masculine grunts and profanity. Shiny green needles sprinkled across the floor, pencil-thin cones scattering as the tree was hoisted upward. Their underbutler stood halfway up the curving grand staircases, holding the end of a cord that had been tied to an upper section of the trunk. On the other side of the hall, Pandora and Cassandra stood at the second-floor balcony, gripping another attached cord. Once the trunk was positioned perfectly, the cords would be tied to the balustrade spindles to keep the tree from tilting to one side or the other.

The underbutler pulled the cord steadily, while West and the footmen pushed from below. Gradually the fir eased upright, its boughs spreading majestically to fan a pungent evergreen scent through the air.

"It smells heavenly," Helen exclaimed, inhaling deeply. "Did Lord and Lady Berwick have a Christmas tree, Kathleen?"

"Every year." Kathleen smiled. "But only a small one, because Lady Berwick said it was a pagan custom."

"Cassandra, we'll need many more ornaments," she heard Pandora exclaim from the second-floor balcony. "We've never had a tree this tall before."

"We'll make another batch of candles," her twin replied.

"No more candles," Kathleen called up to them. "This tree is already a fire hazard."

"But Kathleen," Pandora said, looking down at her,

"the tree will look dreadful if we don't have enough decorations. It will look positively *undressed*."

"Perhaps we could tie some sweets in scraps of netting and ribbon," Helen suggested. "It would be pretty to hang them from the branches."

West brushed leaves from his hands and used his thumb to rub off a spot of sap on his palm. "You all might want to look in the crate that was delivered from Winterborne's this morning," he said. "I'm sure it contains some Christmas finery."

All movement and sound in the hall was instantly extinguished as everyone looked at him.

"What crate?" Kathleen demanded. "Why did you keep it a secret until now?"

West gave her a speaking glance and pointed to the corner, where a massive wooden crate had been set. "It's hardly been a secret—it's been there for hours. I've been too busy with this blasted tree to make conversation."

"Did you order it?"

"No. Devon mentioned in his last letter that Winterborne was sending some holiday trimmings from his store, as a gesture of appreciation for inviting him to stay."

"I did not invite Mr. Winterborne," Kathleen retorted, "and we certainly can't accept gifts from a stranger."

"They're not for you, they're for the household. Hang it all, it's just a few baubles and wisps of tinsel."

She stared at him uncertainly. "I don't think we should. I'm not certain of the etiquette, but it doesn't seem proper. He's an unmarried gentleman, and this is a household of young women who have only me as a chaperone. If I were ten years older and had an established reputation, it might be different, but as things are . . ."

"I'm a member of the household," West protested. "Doesn't that make the situation more respectable?"

Kathleen looked at him. "You're joking, aren't you?"

West rolled his eyes. "My point is, if anyone were to try and attach some improper meaning to Winterborne's gift, the fact that I'm here would—"

He stopped as he heard a choking sound from Helen, who had turned very red.

"Helen?" Kathleen asked in concern, but the girl had turned away, her shoulders shaking. Kathleen sent West an alarmed glance.

"Helen," he said quietly, striding forward and taking her upper arms in an urgent grasp. "Sweetheart, are you ill? What—" He paused as she shook her head violently and gasped out something, one of her hands flailing in the direction behind them. West looked up alertly. His face changed, and he began to laugh.

"What is the matter with you two?" Kathleen demanded. Glancing around the entrance hall, she realized the crate was no longer in the corner. The twins must have raced downstairs the moment it had been mentioned. Clutching it on either side, they lugged it furtively toward the receiving room.

"Girls," Kathleen said sharply, "bring that back here at once!"

But it was too late. The receiving room's double doors closed, accompanied by the click of a key turning in the lock. Kathleen stopped short, her jaw slackening.

West and Helen staggered together, overcome with hilarity.

"I'll have you know," Mrs. Church said in amazement, "it took our two stoutest footmen to bring that crate into the house. How did two young ladies manage to carry it away so quickly?"

"Sh-sheer determination," Helen wheezed.

"All I want in this life," West told Kathleen, "is to see you try to pry that crate away from those two."

"I wouldn't dare," she replied, giving up. "They would do me bodily harm."

Helen wiped at a stray tear of mirth. "Come, Kathleen, let's go see what Mr. Winterborne sent. You too, Mrs. Church."

"They won't let us into the room," Kathleen muttered.

Helen grinned at her. "They will if I ask."

The twins, busy as squirrels, had already unpacked a multitude of wrapped parcels when they finally allowed everyone into the receiving room.

The butler, underbutler, and footmen ventured to the doorway to have a peek at the contents of the crate. It resembled a pirate's treasure chest, overflowing with blown glass spheres painted to look like fruit, papier-mâché birds decorated with real feathers, clever tin figures of dancers and soldiers and animals.

There was even a large box of miniature colored glass cups, or fairy lights, meant to be filled with oil and floating candle wicks and hung on the tree.

"A fire will be inevitable," Kathleen said in worry, looking at the multitude of candle cups.

"We'll station a pair of boys with pails of water next to the tree when it's lit," Mrs. Church reassured her. "If any of the branches catches fire, they'll douse it right away."

Everyone gasped as Pandora unearthed a large Christmas angel from the crate. Her porcelain face was framed by golden hair, while a pair of gilded wings protruded from the back of a little satin gown embellished with pearls and gold thread.

While the family and servants gathered reverently to view the magnificent creation, Kathleen took West's arm and tugged him out of the room. "Something is going on here," she said. "I want to know the real reason why the earl has invited Mr. Winterborne."

They stopped in the space beneath the grand staircase, behind the tree.

"Can't he show hospitality to a friend without an ulterior motive?" West parried.

She shook her head. "Everything your brother does has an ulterior motive. Why has he invited Mr. Winterborne?"

"Winterborne has his finger in many pies. I believe Devon hopes to benefit from his advice, and at some future date enter into a business deal with him."

That sounded reasonable enough. But her intuition still warned that there was something fishy about the situation. "How did they become acquainted?"

"About three years ago, Winterborne was nominated for membership at two different London clubs, but was rejected by both of them. Winterborne is a commoner; his father was a Welsh grocer. So after hearing the sniggering about how Winterborne had been refused, Devon arranged to have our club, Brabbler's, offer a membership to him. And Winterborne never forgets a favor."

"Brabbler's?" Kathleen repeated. "What an odd name."

"It's the word for a fellow who tends to argue over trifles." West looked down and rubbed at a sticky spot of sap on the heel of his hand. "Brabbler's is a second-tier club for those who aren't allowed into White's or Brooks's, but it includes some of the most successful and clever men in London."

"Such as Mr. Winterborne."

"Just so."

"What is he like? What is his character?"

West shrugged. "He's a quiet sort, but he can be as charming as the devil if it suits him."

"Is he young or old?"

"Thirty years, or thereabouts."

"And his appearance? Is he well-favored?"

"The ladies certainly seem to think so. Although with his fortune, Winterborne could look like a toad and they would still flock to him."

"Is he a good man?"

"One doesn't acquire a fortune by being a choirboy."

Holding his gaze, Kathleen realized that was the most she was going to pry from him. "The earl and Mr. Winterborne are scheduled to arrive tomorrow afternoon, are they not?"

"Yes, I'll go to meet them at the Alton Station. Would you like to accompany me?"

"Thank you, but my time will be better spent with Mrs. Church and Cook, making certain everything is prepared." She sighed and cast a rueful glance at the looming tree, feeling guilty and uneasy. "I hope none of the local gentry hears about all our festivities. But I'm sure they will. I shouldn't allow any of this. You know that."

"But since you have," West said, patting her shoulder, "you may as well try to enjoy it."

# Chapter 15

"You're going to be nominated for membership at White's," Rhys Winterborne said as the train rattled and swayed along the route from London to Hampshire. Although their private compartment in the first-class carriage could have easily accommodated four more passengers, Winterborne had paid to keep the seats empty so they could have the space to themselves. Devon's valet, Sutton, was traveling in one of the lower-class carriages farther back in the train.

Devon shot him a look of surprise. "How do you know that?"

Winterborne's only reply was an oblique glance. He often knew about people's private business before they themselves had learned of it. Since almost everyone in London had applied to his store for credit, the man knew intimate details about their finances, their purchases, and their personal habits. In addition, much of what the store employees overheard on the floors was funneled upward to Winterborne's office.

"They needn't bother," Devon said, stretching his legs into the space between the seats. "I wouldn't accept."

"White's is a more prestigious club than Brabbler's."

"Most clubs are," Devon rejoined wryly. "But the air is a bit too thin in such elevated circles. And if White's didn't want me before I was an earl, there's no reason for them to want me now. I'm unchanged in every regard except for the fact that I'm now as deeply in debt as the rest of the peerage."

"That's not the only change. You've gained social and political power."

"Power without capital. I'd rather have money."

Winterborne shook his head. "Always choose power. Money can be stolen or devalued, and then you're left with nothing. With power, one can always acquire more money."

"I hope you're right about that."

"I'm always right," Winterborne said flatly.

Few men could make such a statement convincingly, but Rhys Winterborne certainly did.

He was one of those rare individuals who had been born in the perfect time and place to suit his abilities. In a staggeringly short time, he had built his father's ramshackle shop into a mercantile empire. Winterborne had an instinct for quality and a shrewd understanding of the public appetite . . . somehow he could always identify what people wanted to buy before they themselves knew. As a well-known public figure, he had a vast array of friends, acquaintances, and enemies, but no one could truthfully claim to know the man.

Reaching for a decanter, which had been set on a railed shelf affixed to the teak paneling beneath the window, Winterborne poured two malt whiskeys and handed one to Devon. After a silent toast, they settled back into the plush seats and watched the ever-changing view through the window.

The luxurious compartment was one of three in the carriage, each with its own set of doors that opened to the outside. The doors had been locked by a porter, a standard railway practice to prevent unticketed passengers from sneaking aboard. For the same reasons, the windows had been barred with brass rods. To distract himself from the vague feeling of being trapped, Devon focused on the scenery.

How much smaller England had become, now that it was possible to cover a distance in a matter of hours rather than days. There was scarcely time to absorb the scenery before it had rushed by, which inspired some people to call the railway a "magician's road." The train crossed bridges, pastures, public thoroughfares, and ancient villages, now passing through deep chalk cuttings, now chugging by open heath. The Hampshire hills appeared, slopes of dark wintry green hunkering beneath the white afternoon sky.

The prospect of arriving home filled Devon with anticipation. He had brought presents for everyone in the family, but he had deliberated the longest about what to give to Kathleen. At one of the jeweler's counters in Winterborne's, he had found an unusual cameo brooch, an exquisitely carved scene of a Greek goddess riding a horse. The cream-colored cameo was set against an onyx background and framed with tiny white seed pearls.

Since the cameo was set in onyx, the saleswoman at the counter had told Devon, it was suitable for a lady in mourning. Even the pearls were acceptable, since they were said to represent tears. Devon had purchased it on the spot. It had been delivered to him that morning, and he had slipped it into his pocket before leaving for the railway station.

He was impatient to see Kathleen again, hungry for the sight of her and the sound of her voice. He had missed her smiles, her frowns, her endearing frustrations with impropriety and pigs and plumbers.

Filled with anticipation, he contemplated the scenery

as the train struggled to the summit of a hill and began the downward slope. Soon they would cross the River Wey, and then it would be only a mile to the station at Alton. The railway cars were only half full; a far greater number of passengers would travel the next day, on Christmas Eve.

The train's momentum gathered as they approached the bridge, but the forward-hurtling force of the engine was upset by a sudden jerk and lurch. Instantly Devon's ears were filled with the metallic shrieks of brakes. The carriage erupted with violent shudders. Reflexively Devon grabbed one of the brass window bars to keep from being bounced out of his seat.

In the next second, a tremendous impact jolted his hand loose of the brass bar—no, the bar itself had come loose—and the window shattered as the carriage wrenched free of the rails. Devon was thrown into a chaos of glass, splintering wood, twisting metal, and unholy noise. A wild heave was accompanied by the snap of the couplings, and then there was the sensation of plunging, tumbling, as the two men were thrown across the compartment. Blinding white light filled Devon's head as he tried to find a fixed point in all the madness. He kept falling, helpless to stop the descent, until his body slammed down and a spearlike pain burst in his chest, and his mind reeled and sank into darkness.

# Chapter 16

THE VIOLENT COLD BROUGHT him back to awareness, pulling gasps from the bottom of his lungs. Devon rubbed his wet face and tried to hoist himself upward. Foul-smelling river water was gushing steadily into the train compartment, or what remained of it. Climbing over splintered glass and wreckage, Devon maneuvered to the gap of the shattered window and stared through the brass bars.

It appeared that the locomotive had plummeted over the wing wall of the bridge, and taken three railway carriages with it, leaving two remaining vehicles poised on the embankment above. Nearby, the broken bulk of a railway carriage had settled into the water like a felled animal. Desperate cries for help swarmed through the air.

Turning, Devon searched frantically for Winterborne, shoving aside planks of teak until he found his friend's unconscious form beneath a chair that had broken free of the floor. The water had just begun to close over his face.

Devon hauled him upward, every movement sending an excruciating stab of pain through his chest and side.

"Winterborne," he said roughly, shaking him a little. "Wake up. Come to. *Now.*"

Winterborne coughed and let out a ragged groan. "What happened?" he asked hoarsely.

"The train derailed," Devon replied, panting. "Carriage is in the river."

Winterborne rubbed at his bloody face and grunted in pain. "I can't see."

Devon tried to pull him higher as the water inched steadily upward. "You'll have to move, or we'll drown."

Indecipherable Welsh phrases tore through the air before Winterborne said in English, "My leg is broken."

Cursing, Devon shoved more debris aside and found a brass window bar that had broken from its rivets. He crawled over another seat and reached upward for the locked side door on the downstream side of the current. Gasping with effort, he used the brass rod as a makeshift crowbar to pry open the door. The diagonal tilt of the carriage made it difficult work. And all the while, water rushed in, swirling up to their knees now.

Once the lock was broken, Devon pushed the door open until it swung free and thudded against the outer side of the vehicle.

Poking his head out, he calculated their distance from the riverbank. The water appeared to be no more than hip deep.

The problem was the extreme cold, which would finish them off quickly. They couldn't afford to wait for help.

Coughing from the smoke-glazed air, Devon ducked back into the carriage. He found Winterborne pulling shards of glass from his hair, his eyes still closed, his face scored with a mesh of bloody scratches. "I'm going to pull you outside and guide you to the river's edge," Devon said.

"What's your condition?" Winterborne asked, sounding remarkably lucid for a man who'd just been blinded and had his leg broken.

"Better than yours."

"How far are we from solid ground?"

"About twenty feet."

"And the current? How strong is it?"

"It doesn't bloody matter: We can't stay here."

"Your odds are better without me," came the calm observation.

"I'm not going to leave you in here, you arse-witted bastard." Devon gripped Winterborne's wrist and pulled it across his shoulders. "If you're afraid you'll owe me a favor after saving your life . . ." With effort, he towed him toward the open doorway. ". . . you're right. A *huge* favor." He set a foot wrong and they both stumbled. Reaching out with his free hand, Devon grabbed hold of the doorway to secure their balance.

A lacerating jolt pierced through his chest, momentarily stealing his breath. "Christ, you're heavy," he managed to say.

There was no reply. He realized that Winterborne was fighting not to lose consciousness.

With every excoriating breath, Devon felt the stabs in his chest lengthen into an unbroken shrill of agony. His muscles locked and spasmed.

Too many complications were piling up . . . the river, the cold, Winterborne's injuries, and now whatever was causing him such pain. But there was no choice except to keep moving.

Gritting his teeth, he managed to tug Winterborne upward and out of the carriage. Together they splashed into the water, which caused Winterborne to cry out in agony.

Clutching him, Devon struggled to find purchase, anchoring his feet into the gluey river bottom. The water was higher than he'd estimated, reaching well over his waist.

For a moment the shock of cold paralyzed him. He concentrated on forcing his locked muscles to move.

"Winterborne," he said through gritted teeth, "it's not far. We'll make it."

His friend replied with a succinct curse, making him grin briefly. Laboring against the current, Devon waded toward the reed bed at the riverbank, where other survivors of the accident were crawling out.

It was hard, exhausting work, the mud sucking at his feet, the frigid water sapping his coordination and shutting down all feeling.

"My lord! My lord, I'm here!" His valet, Sutton, was standing at the river's edge, waving to him anxiously. It appeared he had climbed down the escarpment from the derailed carriages still poised on the bridge.

The valet plunged into the shallows, gasping at the bone-chilling temperature.

"Take him," Devon said brusquely, dragging the half-conscious Winterborne through the reed bed.

Sutton locked his arms around the other man's chest and pulled Winterborne to safety.

Devon felt his knees give out, and he staggered among the reeds, fighting not to collapse. His exhausted brain worked to summon his last reserves of strength, and he lurched toward the bank.

He stopped as he became aware of frantic, high-pitched cries. Looking back over his shoulder, he saw that passengers still occupied one of the compartments of a flooded carriage that had landed in the river at a diagonal tilt.

They hadn't been able to break open the locked door. No one had gone to help them; the survivors who had made it out of the water had collapsed from the cold. Rescuers were only now just beginning to arrive, and by the time they made it down the embankment, it would be too late.

Without giving himself time to consider it, Devon turned and sloshed back out into the water.

"*Sir*," he heard Sutton call out.

"Look after Winterborne," Devon said brusquely.

By the time he reached the carriage, he was numb from the waist down and struggling through a haze of confusion. Through pure force of will, he fought his way into a compartment of the carriage, through the space in a wall that had been torn by the force of the accident.

He went to a window and gripped a brass rod. It took immense concentration to make his hand close around it properly. Somehow he managed to wrench it free of the wall, and waded through the carriage to plunge back into the river.

As he used the bar to pry at the door of the locked compartment, he heard screams of relief from inside. The door opened with a protesting groan of metal, and passengers crowded the opening. Devon's bleary gaze took in a middle-aged woman holding a squalling baby, two weeping girls, and a boy in his early teens.

"Are there any more in there?" Devon asked the boy. His voice was slurred, as if he were drunk.

"None alive, sir," the boy said, shivering.

"D'you see those people at the side of the river?"

"I th-think so, sir."

"Go there. Take the girls arm-in-arm. Keep your sides to the current . . . less for it to push against. *Go.*"

The boy nodded and plunged into the river, gasping at the intense cold that reached up to his chest. The frightened girls followed with shrieks, clutching at his arms. Together the trio moved toward the riverbank, steadying one another against the current.

Turning to the terrified woman, Devon said tersely, "Give me the child."

She shook her head wildly. "Please, sir, why—"

"*Now.*" He wouldn't be able to stay on his feet much longer.

The woman obeyed, weeping, and the child continued to wail as he curled his little arms around Devon's neck. His mother gripped Devon's free arm and stepped from the carriage, letting out a shrill cry as she plunged into the water. Step by step, Devon hauled her through the river, the weight of her skirts making progress difficult. He soon lost all sense of time.

He wasn't quite certain where he was, or what was happening. He couldn't be sure that his legs were still working; he couldn't feel them. The baby had stopped crying, his hand groping curiously over Devon's face like a migrating starfish. He was vaguely aware that the woman was shouting something, but the words were lost amid the sluggish pulse in his ears.

There were people in the distance . . . hand lamps . . . lights dancing and bobbing in the smoke-blistered air. He kept pushing on, impelled by the dim understanding that to hesitate even for a moment was to snap the last thread of consciousness.

His mind registered a tug at the child in his arms. Another stronger pull, as he resisted briefly. The child was being gathered up by strangers, while others had come forward to help the woman through the sludge of reeds and mud.

Losing his balance, Devon staggered back, his muscles no longer obeying his commands. The water snatched him instantly, closing over his head and dragging him away.

As he felt himself carried by the current, his brain hovered over the scene, observing the slowly spinning form—his own—in the inky water. He couldn't save himself, he realized with dazed surprise. No one was going to save him. He had met the same untimely fate as all the Ravenel men, leaving far too much unfinished, and he couldn't even bring himself to care. Somewhere in the rubble of his thoughts, he knew that West would manage without him. West would survive.

*But Kathleen . . .*

She would never know what she had meant to him.

That pierced his failing awareness. Dear God, why had he waited, assuming he had time at his disposal? If he could have had five minutes to tell her . . . bloody hell, *one* minute . . . but it was too late.

Kathleen would go on without him. Some other man would marry her . . . grow old with her . . . and Devon would be nothing but a faded memory.

If she remembered him at all.

He struggled and flailed, a silent howl trapped inside. Kathleen was his fate, *his*. He would defy all the hells that ever were to stay with her. But it was no use; the river bore him steadily away into the darkness.

Something caught at him. Tough, sinewed bands twined around his arm and chest like some monster from the deep. An inexorable force wrenched him painfully backward. He felt himself gripped and held fast against the current.

"Oh, no, you don't," a man growled close to his ear, gasping with effort. The secure grip tightened around his midriff, and he began to cough, spikes of agony driving through him as the voice continued. "You're not leaving me to manage that bloody estate on my own."

# Chapter 17

"THE TRAIN MUST HAVE been late," Pandora said crossly, playing with the dogs on the receiving room floor. "I hate waiting."

"You could occupy yourself with a useful task," Cassandra said, poking away at her needlework. "That makes waiting go faster."

"People always say that, and it's not true. Waiting takes just as long whether one is being useful or not."

"Perhaps the gentlemen have stopped for refreshments on the way from Alton," Helen suggested, leaning over her embroidery hoop as she executed a complicated stitch.

Kathleen looked up from an agricultural book that West had recommended to her. "If that's the case, they had better be famished when they arrive," she said with mock indignation. "After the feast Cook has prepared, nothing less than gluttony will suffice." She grimaced as she saw Napoleon settling into the billowing folds of Pandora's dress. "Darling, you'll be covered with dog hair by the time the gentlemen arrive."

"They won't notice," Pandora assured her. "My dress is black, and so is the dog."

"Perhaps, but still—" Kathleen broke off as Hamlet trotted into the receiving room with his perpetual grin. In all the bustle of holiday preparations for that evening, she had forgotten about the pig. She had become so accustomed to the sight of him following Napoleon and Josephine everywhere that she had begun to think of him as a third dog. "Oh, dear," she said, "something must be done with Hamlet. We can't have him wandering about while Mr. Winterborne is here."

"Hamlet is very clean," Cassandra said, reaching down to pet the pig as he came up to her and grunted affectionately. "Cleaner than the dogs, actually."

It was true. Hamlet was so well-behaved that it seemed unjust to banish him from the house. "There's no choice," Kathleen said regretfully. "I'm afraid that Mr. Winterborne can't be expected to share our enlightened view of pigs. Hamlet will have to sleep in the barn. You can make him a nice bed of straw and blankets."

The twins were aghast, both of them protesting at once.

"But that will hurt his feelings—"

"He'll think he's being punished!"

"He'll be perfectly comfortable—" Kathleen began, but broke off as she noticed that both dogs, alerted by a noise, had hurried from the room with their tails wagging. Hamlet rushed after them with a determined squeak.

"Someone is at the front door," Helen said, setting aside her embroidery. She went to the window for a glimpse of the front drive and portico.

It had to be Devon and his guest. Jumping to her feet, Kathleen told the twins urgently, "Take the pig to the cellars! Hurry!"

She suppressed a grin as they ran to obey.

Smoothing her skirts and tugging her sleeves into place, Kathleen went to stand beside Helen at the window. To her surprise, there was no carriage or team of horses on the drive, only a sturdy pony, its sides sweat-streaked and heaving.

She recognized the pony: It belonged to the postmastcr's young son, Nate, who was often sent to deliver telegraph dispatches. But Nate didn't usually ride pell-mell on his deliveries.

Uneasiness slithered down her spine.

The elderly butler came to the doorway. "Milady."

A breath caught in Kathleen's throat as she saw that he held a telegram in his hand. In the time she had known him, Sims had never given her a letter or telegram directly from his own hand, but had always brought it on a small silver tray.

"The boy says it's a matter of great urgency," Sims said, his face tense with repressed emotion as he gave the telegram to her. "A news dispatch was sent to the postmaster. It seems there was a train accident at Alton."

Kathleen felt the color drain from her face. A sharp hum crackled in her ears. Clumsy with haste, she snatched the telegram from him and opened it.

DERAILMENT NEAR ALTON STATION. TRENEAR AND WINTERBORNE BOTH INJURED. HAVE DOCTOR READY FOR THEIR ARRIVAL. I WILL RETURN BY HIRED COACH.

SUTTON

Devon . . . injured.

Kathleen found herself clenching her fists as if the terrifying thought were something she could physically bat away. Her heart had begun to hammer.

"Sims, send a footman to fetch the doctor." She had to force words through a smothering layer of panic. "He must come without delay—both Lord Trenear and Mr. Winterborne will require his attention."

"Yes, my lady." The butler left the receiving room, moving with remarkable alacrity for a man his age.

"May I read it?" Helen asked.

Kathleen extended the telegram to her, the paper's edges fluttering like a captured butterfly.

Nate's breathless voice came from the doorway. He was a small, wiry boy with a mop of rust-colored hair and a round face constellated with freckles. "My dad told me the news from the wire." Seeing that he had gained both women's attention, he continued excitedly, "It happened at the bridge, just before the station. A train of ballast wagons was crossing the line and didn't clear in time. The passenger train crashed into it, and some of the carriages went over the bridge into the River Wey." The boy's eyes were huge and round with awe. "More than a dozen people were killed, and another score are missing. My dad says there's probably some who'll die in the coming days: They might have their arms and legs torn off, and their bones crushed—"

"Nate," Helen interrupted, as Kathleen whirled away, "why don't you run to the kitchen and ask the cook for a biscuit or a heel of gingerbread?"

"Thank you, Lady Helen."

Kathleen pressed her balled fists against her eyes, digging her knuckles hard against the sockets. Anguished fear caused her to shake from head to toe.

She couldn't bear knowing that Devon was hurt. At that very moment, that beautiful, arrogant, superbly healthy man was in pain . . . perhaps frightened . . . perhaps dying. She let out a coughing breath, and another, and a few hot tears slid between her knuckles. No, she couldn't let herself cry, there was too much to do. They had to be ready when he arrived. Everything necessary to help him must be instantly available.

"What can I do?" she heard Helen ask behind her.

She dragged her cuffs over her wet cheeks. It was difficult to think; her brain was in a fog. "Tell the twins what's happened, and make certain they're not present when the men are brought inside. We don't know what their condition is, or how severe the injuries are, and . . . I wouldn't want the girls to see . . ."

"Of course."

Kathleen turned to face her. Blood throbbed in her temples. "I'll find Mrs. Church," she said hoarsely. "We'll need to gather the household medical supplies, and clean sheets and rags—" Her throat closed.

"West is with them," Helen said, settling a gentle hand on her shoulder. She was very calm, although her face was white and tense. "He'll take good care of his brother. Don't forget, the earl is large and very strong. He would survive hazards that other men might not."

Kathleen nodded automatically. But the words gave her no comfort. Yes, Devon was a big, strapping man, but a railway accident was different from any other kind of disaster. Injuries from collisions and derailments were rarely trifling. It didn't matter how strong or brave or clever someone was, when he was hurtling along at sixty miles per hour. It all came down to luck . . . which had always been in short supply for the Ravenel family.

To Kathleen's relief, the footman who had been dispatched to find Dr. Weeks returned with him promptly. Weeks was a competent, skillful physician who had trained in London. He had come to the estate on the morning of Theo's accident, and he had been the one to break the news to the Ravenel girls about their brother's death. Whenever a member of the household was ill, Weeks always arrived promptly, treating the servants with the same consideration and respect that he showed to the Ravenel family. Kathleen had quickly come to like and trust him.

"I haven't yet had the pleasure of meeting Lord Trenear," Weeks said as he opened his medical cases in one of the bedrooms that had been readied for the soon-to-arrive patients. "I regret that the first time will be on such an occasion."

"So do I," Kathleen said, staring fixedly at the contents of the large black cases: plaster bandages, needles and thread, shining metal implements, glass tubes filled with powders, and small bottles of chemicals. A sense of unreality kept sweeping over her as she wondered when Devon would arrive, and what kind of injuries he had sustained.

Dear Lord, this was hideously similar to the morning that Theo had died.

She folded her arms and gripped her elbows, trying to quell the tremors that ran through her frame. The last time Devon had left Eversby Priory, she thought, she had been too cross with him to say good-bye.

"Lady Trenear," the doctor said gently, "I'm sure this unfortunate situation, and my presence here, must remind you of your husband's accident. Would it help if I mixed a mild sedative?"

"No, thank you. I want to keep my wits about me. It's only . . . I can't believe . . . another Ravenel . . ." She couldn't bring herself to finish the sentence.

Weeks frowned and stroked his close-trimmed beard as he commented, "The men of this family don't seem to be gifted with longevity. However, let's not assume the worst just yet. We'll learn about Lord Trenear's condition soon enough."

As the doctor arranged various items on a table, Kathleen could hear Sims in some distant room, telling a footman to run to the stables and fetch a bundle of training poles for makeshift stretchers. There were sounds of rapid feet on the stairs, and the clanks of hot water cans and pails of coal. Mrs. Church was in the middle of scolding a housemaid who had brought her a dull pair of scissors, but she broke off in mid-sentence.

Kathleen tensed at the abrupt silence. After a moment, the housekeeper's urgent voice came from the hallway.

"My lady, the family coach is coming along the drive!"

Leaping forward as if scalded, Kathleen bolted from the room. She passed Mrs. Church on the way to the grand staircase.

"Lady Trenear," the housekeeper exclaimed, following her, "you'll have a tumble!"

Kathleen ignored the warning, racing headlong down the stairs and out to the portico, where Sims and a group of housemaids and footmen were gathering. Every gaze was on the approaching vehicle.

Even before the wheels had stopped moving, the footman riding on the back had leaped to the ground, and the carriage door had flung open from the inside.

Exclamations rippled through the air as West emerged. He was in appalling condition, his clothing filthy and wet. Everyone tried to gather around him at once.

West raised a hand to hold them off, bracing himself against the side of the carriage. Continuous tremors ran through him, his teeth chattering audibly. "No . . . s-see to the earl first. Wh-where's the damned doctor?"

Dr. Weeks was already beside him. "Here, Mr. Ravenel. Are you injured?"

West shook his head. "Only c-cold. H-had to pull my brother fr-fr-from the river."

Having pushed her way through the group, Kathleen took West's arm to steady him. He was shuddering and swaying, his complexion gray. A fetid river smell clung to him, his clothes reeking of mud and polluted water.

"How is Devon?" she asked urgently.

West leaned hard against her. "Barely c-conscious. Not m-making much sense. In the w-water too long."

"Mrs. Church," Weeks said to the housekeeper, "Mr. Ravenel must be carried straight to bed. Stoke the hearth and cover him with blankets. No one is to administer spirits of any kind. That is very important, do you understand? You may give him warm sweet tea, *not* hot."

"I don't need to be c-carried," West protested. "Look, I'm st-standing right here before you!" But even as he spoke, he had begun to sink to the ground. Kathleen braced her legs against his weight, trying to keep him from falling. Hastily a pair of footmen grabbed him and lowered him onto a stretcher.

As West struggled, the doctor spoke sternly. "*Be still*, Mr. Ravenel. Until you've been warmed through and through, any exertion could be the death of you. If the chilled blood in your extremities reaches your heart too fast—" He broke off impatiently and said to the footmen, "Take him inside."

Kathleen had begun to climb the folding step of the carriage. The dark interior was ominously silent. "My lord? Devon, can you—"

"Allow me to see them first," the doctor said from behind her, pulling her firmly away from the vehicle.

"Tell me how Lord Trenear is," she demanded.

"As soon as I can." Weeks climbed into the carriage.

Kathleen clenched every muscle in the effort to be patient. She bit her lower lip until it throbbed.

A half minute later, the doctor's voice emerged with a new note of urgency. "We will remove Mr. Winterborne first. I need a strong fellow to help, immediately."

"Peter," Sims directed, and the footman hastened to comply.

*What about Devon?* Kathleen was maddened with worry. She tried to look into the carriage, but she couldn't see anything with the doctor and footman blocking the way. "Dr. Weeks—"

"In a moment, my lady."

"Yes, but—" She fell back a step as a large, dark, shape clambered from the carriage.

It was Devon, ragged and nearly unrecognizable. He had heard her voice.

"Lord Trenear," came the doctor's terse command, "*do not* exert yourself. I will see to you as soon as I assist your friend."

Devon ignored him, staggering as his feet reached the ground. He clutched the edge of the door opening to keep from falling. He was filthy and battered from head to toe, his shirt wet and bloodstained. But as Kathleen looked over him frantically, she saw with relief there were no missing limbs, no gaping wounds. He was in one piece.

His disoriented gaze found hers in a blaze of unholy blue, and his lips shaped her name.

Kathleen reached him in two strides, and he seized her roughly. One hand clutched the mass of coiled braids at the back of her head in a grip that hurt. A quiet groan vibrated in his throat, and he ground his mouth over hers in a punishing kiss, heedless of anyone who saw them. His body shuddered, his balance ramshackle, and she stiffened her legs to support him.

"You shouldn't be standing," she said unsteadily. "Let me help you—we'll sit on the ground—Devon, please—"

But he wasn't listening at all. With a primitive, impassioned grunt, he turned and pushed her against the side of the carriage and kissed her again. Even hurt and exhausted, he was unbelievably strong. His mouth took hers with bruising force, stopping only when he had to gasp for air. Over his shoulder, Kathleen saw Mrs. Church and a pair of footmen coming to them with a stretcher.

"Devon," she begged, "you must lie down—there's a stretcher right here. They have to bring you into the house. I'll stay with you, I promise."

He was motionless except for the violent shivers that ran through his frame.

"Darling," Kathleen whispered near his ear with anguished worry, "please let go of me."

He responded with an indecipherable sound, his arms cinching harder around her . . . and he began to fall as he lost consciousness.

Thankfully, the footmen were right there to grab Devon before he crushed Kathleen under his solid weight. As they pulled him away from her and lowered him to the stretcher, her dazed brain comprehended the word he'd said.

*Never.*

# Chapter 18

DURING THE PROCESS OF settling Devon onto the stretcher, the hem of his wet shirt rode up. Kathleen and Mrs. Church gasped simultaneously as they saw a hideous purple-black bruise the size of a dinner plate, spreading across the left side of his rib cage and chest.

Kathleen blanched as she thought of the blunt force it had taken to cause such an injury. Surely he must have broken ribs. Desperately she wondered if one of his lungs might have collapsed. Carefully she bent to arrange one of his sprawled arms against his side. How shocking it was to see a man of his vitality lying there so limp and still.

Mrs. Church settled a blanket over him and told the footmen, "Take him up to the master bedroom. Softly . . . no jostling. Treat him as if he were a newborn babe."

After counting in unison, the footmen lifted the stretcher. "A babe that weighs fourteen stone," one of them grunted.

Mrs. Church tried to look stern, but the corners of her eyes crinkled briefly. "Mind your tongue, David."

Kathleen followed behind the footmen, swiping impatiently at the film of tears over her eyes.

Walking beside her, the housekeeper murmured consolingly, "There, there. Don't distress yourself, my lady. We'll soon have him patched up and as good as new."

Although Kathleen longed to believe her, she whispered tightly, "He's so bruised and feeble—he might have internal injuries."

"He didn't seem so feeble as all that, a moment ago," the housekeeper observed dryly.

Kathleen turned scarlet. "He was overwrought. He didn't know what he was doing."

"If you say so, my lady." Mrs. Church's slight smile faded as she continued. "I think we should save our worry for Mr. Winterborne. Just before Mr. Ravenel was carried inside, he said that Mr. Winterborne's leg is broken and he's also been blinded."

"Oh, no. We must find out if he wants us to send for someone."

"I would be surprised if he did," the housekeeper said pragmatically as they entered the house.

"Why do you say that?" Kathleen asked.

"If he had anyone, he wouldn't have come here alone for Christmas in the first place."

WHILE DR. WEEKS attended to Devon's injuries, Kathleen went to visit West.

Even before she reached the open door of his room, she heard noise and laughter drifting into the hallway. She stood at the threshold, watching with a touch of fond resignation as she saw West sitting up in bed, regaling a group that included a half-dozen servants, Pandora, Cassandra, both dogs, and Hamlet. Helen stood beside a lamp, reading the temperature of a glass thermometer.

Thankfully West no longer appeared to be shivering, and his color had improved.

". . . then I glimpsed a man wading back out into the river," he was saying, "toward a half-submerged railway carriage with people trapped inside. And I said to myself,

'That man is a hero. Also an idiot. Because he's already been in the water for too long, and he won't be able to save them, and he's about to sacrifice his life for nothing.' I proceeded to climb down the embankment and found Sutton. 'Where is the earl?' I asked." West paused for dramatic effect, relishing the rapt attention of his audience. "And where do you think Sutton pointed? Out to the river, where that reckless fool had just saved a trio of children, and was wading after them with a baby in one arm and a woman on the other."

"The man was *Lord Trenear*?" one of the housemaids gasped.

"None other."

The entire group exclaimed with pleasure and possessive pride.

"Nothing to it, for a bloke as big as his lordship," one of the footmen said with a grin.

"I should think he'll be put in the papers for this," another exclaimed.

"I hope so," West said, "if only because I know how he would loathe it." He paused as he saw Kathleen in the doorway.

"All of you," she said sotto voce to the servants, "had better clear out before Sims or Mrs. Church catches you in here."

"I was just reaching the best part," West protested. "I'm about to describe my thrilling yet poignant rescue of the earl."

"You can describe it later," Kathleen said, standing in the doorway as the servants hastily filed out. "For now, you should be resting." She glanced at Helen. "How is his temperature?"

"He needs to go up one more degree."

"The devil I do," West said. "With that fire stoked

so high, the room is an oven. Soon I'll be as brown as a Christmas goose. Speaking of that . . . I'm famished."

"The doctor said we can't feed you until you've reached the right temperature," Pandora said.

"Will you take another cup of tea?" Cassandra asked.

"I'll have a brandy," West retorted, "along with a wedge of currant pie, a plate of cheese, a bowl of potato and turnip mash, and a beefsteak."

Cassandra smiled. "I'll ask the doctor if you may have some broth."

"Broth?" he repeated indignantly.

"Come along, Hamlet," Pandora said, "before West decides he wants bacon as well."

"Wait," Kathleen said, frowning. "Isn't Hamlet supposed to be in the cellars?"

"Cook wouldn't allow it," Cassandra said. "She said he would find a way to knock over the bins and eat all the root vegetables." She cast a proud glance at the cheerful-looking creature. "Because he is a *very* creative and enterprising pig."

"Cook didn't say that last part," Pandora said.

"No," Cassandra admitted, "but it was implied."

The twins cleared the dogs and pig from the room and left.

Helen extended the thermometer to West. "Under your tongue, please," she said gravely.

He complied with a long-suffering expression.

"Dear," Kathleen asked Helen, "will you speak to Mrs. Church about dinner? With three invalids in the house, I think it's best if we dine informally tonight."

"*Two* invalids," West mumbled indignantly around the thermometer. "I'm perfectly well."

"Yes, of course," Helen replied to Kathleen. "And I'll make up a tray for Dr. Weeks. He may be occupied for a while with Lord Trenear and Mr. Winterborne, and he's certainly earned his supper."

"Good idea," Kathleen said. "Don't forget to include a dish of lemon syllabub. As I recall, Dr. Weeks has a sweet tooth."

"By all means," West said around the thermometer, "let's talk about food in front of a starving man."

Before leaving, Helen paused to nudge his chin upward, closing his mouth. "No talking."

After Helen had gone, Kathleen brought some tea to West and took the thermometer from his mouth. She examined the line of mercury intently. "A half degree more, and you may eat."

West relaxed against the pillows, his animated expression easing into strained lines. "How is my brother?"

"Dr. Weeks is treating him. Mrs. Church and I saw an appalling bruise on his chest and side—we think he may have broken ribs. But he was conscious when he left the carriage, and he opened his eyes when he was brought to his room."

"Thank God." West sighed heavily. "It's a miracle if it's nothing more than broken ribs. That accident . . . my God, railway cars were strewn about like children's toys. And the people who didn't survive—" He broke off and swallowed hard. "I wish I could forget what I saw."

Sitting on the bedside chair, Kathleen reached out and squeezed his hand gently. "You're exhausted," she murmured.

West let out a brief, mirthless laugh. "I'm so dog-tired that exhaustion would be an improvement."

"I should leave you to rest."

His hand turned and curled around hers. "Not yet," he muttered. "I don't want to be alone."

She nodded, remaining in the chair.

Letting go of her hand, West reached for his tea.

"Is it true?" Kathleen asked. "The story you were telling about Devon?"

After draining the tea in two gulps, West gave her a haunted glance. "All true. The son of a bitch almost succeeded in killing himself."

Kathleen took the cup from his lax fingers.

"I don't know how he did it," West continued. "I was in the water for no more than two minutes, and my legs went numb to the bone. It was agony. By all accounts, Devon was in that river for at least twenty minutes, the reckless lackwit."

"Saving children," Kathleen said, feigning scorn. "How dare he?"

"Yes," West said with no trace of humor. He stared at the leaping fire, brooding. "Now I understand what you once said to me about all the people who depend on him—and I've become one of them. Damn him to hell. My brother can't take arse-headed chances with his life again, or I swear I'll kill him."

"I understand," she said, aware of the fear lurking beneath his caustic words.

"No, you don't. You weren't there. My God, I almost didn't reach him in time. Had I arrived just a few seconds later—" West took a shuddering breath and averted his face. "He wouldn't have done this before, you know. He used to have more sense than to risk his neck for someone else. Especially strangers. The numbskull."

Kathleen smiled. Swallowing back the tightness in her throat, she reached out and smoothed his hair back. "My dear friend," she whispered, "I'm sorry to have to say this . . . but you would have done the same thing."

SOMETIME AFTER MIDNIGHT, Kathleen slipped out of bed to check on the patients. She buttoned a robe over her nightgown, picked up a bedside candlestick, and set off down the hall.

First she ducked her head into Winterborne's room. "May I come in?" she asked Dr. Weeks, who was sitting in a chair by the bed.

"Of course, my lady."

"Do stay seated, please," Kathleen said before he could rise to his feet. "I only wanted to ask after the patient."

She knew it had been a difficult night's work for the doctor, who had needed the assistance of the butler and two footmen to help realign Winterborné's broken leg. As Sims had described it to Kathleen and Mrs. Church afterward, the large muscles of the injured leg had contracted, and it had required great effort to stretch them sufficiently to restore the bone to its original position. Once the leg had been stabilized, Sims had helped the doctor to wrap the limb with strips of damp linen soaked with gypsum plaster, which had hardened into a cast.

"Mr. Winterborne is doing as well as can be expected," Dr. Weeks murmured. "He was fortunate in that the fibula break was clean. Furthermore, after his exposure to the extreme cold, his blood pressure was so low that it reduced blood loss. I expect, barring complications, that the leg will heal well."

"What about his vision?" Kathleen went to Winterborne's bedside, looking down at him in concern. He was in a sedated sleep, the upper half of his face obscured by the bandages around his eyes.

"He has corneal scratches," the doctor replied, "from flying glass. I removed a few splinters and applied salve. None of the abrasions appear to be particularly deep, which gives me good reason to hope he will recover his sight. To give him the best chance of recovery, he must be kept still and sedated for the next few days."

"Poor man," Kathleen said quietly. "We'll take good care of him." Her gaze returned to the doctor. "Will Lord Trenear have to be sedated as well?"

"Only if he has difficulty sleeping at night. I believe his ribs are cracked but not broken. One can usually feel a broken rib move when palpated. Painful, to be certain, but in a few weeks he'll be as good as new."

The candle wavered a little in her hand, a drop of hot wax splashing onto her wrist. "You have no idea how happy I am to hear that."

"I think perhaps I do," Dr. Weeks said dryly. "Your affection for Lord Trenear is impossible to miss."

Kathleen's smile faltered. "Oh, it's not affection, it's only . . . well, my concern for the family, and the estate, and . . . I couldn't become . . . fond . . . of a man when I'm still in mourning. That would be very wrong indeed."

"My lady . . ." Dr. Weeks contemplated her for a long moment, his eyes weary and kind. "I know many scientific facts about the human heart—not the least of which is that it's far easier to make a heart stop beating entirely than to keep it from loving the wrong person."

KATHLEEN WENT TO Devon's room afterward. When there was no response to her soft tap, she let herself in. He was sleeping on his side, his long form motionless beneath the covers. The sound of his breathing was reassuringly deep and steady.

Coming to stand beside the bed, she looked down at him with tender protectiveness. His mouth was relaxed into gentle lines amid the bristle of his jaw. His lashes were long and as black as ink. Two small white plasters had been affixed over cuts on his cheek and forehead. The cowlick on the right side of his forehead had sprung up in a way he would never have allowed during the day.

She tried as hard as she could to keep from smoothing it. Losing the battle, she stroked the tempting lock gently.

Devon's breathing altered. As he came to the surface, his eyes flickered open, drowsy with exhaustion and opiate tonic.

"Kathleen." His voice was low and raw.

"I just wanted to check on you. Is there anything you need? A glass of water?"

"You." He caught at her free hand and pulled it closer. She felt his lips press against her fingers. "Need to talk to you."

Her breath stopped. A pulse began to throb in every vulnerable place of her body. "You . . . you've been dosed with enough laudanum to sedate an elephant," she said, trying to sound light. "It would be wiser not to tell me anything at the moment. Go to sleep, and in the morning—"

"Lie with me."

Her stomach tightened in yearning. "You know I can't," she whispered.

Undeterred, he gripped her wrist and began to tug her toward him with pained determination

"Wait—you'll hurt yourself—" Kathleen fumbled to set the candle on the nearby table, while he continued to exert pressure on her arm. "Don't—your ribs—oh, *why* must you be so stubborn?" Alarmed and anxious, she climbed onto the bed rather than risk injuring him by struggling. "Only for a minute," she warned. "*One* minute."

Devon subsided, his fingers remaining around her wrist in a loose manacle.

Lowering to her side to face him, Kathleen immediately regretted her decision. It was disastrously intimate, lying with her body so close to his. As she stared into his drowsy blue eyes, a bolt of painful longing went through her.

"I was afraid for you," she said faintly.

Devon touched her face with a single fingertip, tracing the edge of her cheek.

"What was it like?" she whispered.

His fingertip followed the slope of her nose down to the sensitive verge of her upper lip. "One moment everything was ordinary," he said slowly, "and the next . . . the world exploded. Noise . . . glass flying . . . things tumbling over and over . . . pain . . ." He paused as Kathleen took his hand and pressed it against her cheek. "The worst part," he continued, "was the cold. Couldn't feel anything. Too tired to go on. Started to seem . . . not so terrible . . . to let go." His voice began to fade as exhaustion overtook him. "My life . . . didn't pass before my eyes. All I saw was you." His lashes fell and his hand slipped from her face. He managed one more whisper before he fell asleep. "The last moment, I thought . . . I would die wanting you."

# Chapter 19

IT WAS THE LAUDANUM.

That was the thought Kathleen repeated to herself last night until she'd fallen asleep, and it was her first thought upon waking. In the fragile gray light of dawn, she climbed out of bed and hunted for her slippers, which were nowhere to be found.

Blearily she padded barefoot to the marble-topped washstand in the corner, scrubbed her face, and brushed her teeth. Staring into the oval pedestal looking glass, she saw that her eyes were bloodshot and dark-ringed.

*I thought I would die wanting you.*

Devon probably wouldn't remember, she thought. People seldom recalled what they had said under the influence of opium. He might not even remember kissing her beside the carriage, although the servants would gossip about it interminably. She would pretend that nothing had happened, and with any luck, he would either have forgotten it, or have the grace not to mention it.

Reaching for the bellpull to summon Clara, she thought better of it and drew her hand back. It was still early. Before she began the complicated process of dressing and arranging her hair, she would look in on the patients. She pulled her cashmere shawl over her nightgown and went to see Devon first.

Although she hadn't expected him to be awake, the

door to his room was ajar and the curtains had been drawn open.

Devon was sitting up in bed, propped on pillows. The thick locks of his hair looked damp and clean, his skin gleaming from a recent shave. Even there in a sickbed, he looked robust and a bit restless, as if he were chafing at his confinement.

Kathleen paused at the threshold. As tense silence filled the distance between them, a wave of excruciating shyness caused her to blush. It didn't help that he was staring at her in a way he never had before . . . bold and vaguely proprietary. Something had changed, she thought.

A faint smile touched Devon's lips as he glanced over her, his gaze lingering at the colorful shawl.

Kathleen closed the door but hesitated, feeling nervous about approaching him. "Why are you awake so early?"

"I woke up hungry, and I needed a wash and shave, so I rang for Sutton."

"Are you in pain?" she asked in concern.

"Yes," he said emphatically. "Come here and make me feel better."

She obeyed cautiously, her nerves stretched as tightly as piano wires. As she drew closer to the bedside, she detected a sharp scent that was out of place on him and yet oddly familiar . . . an effusion of pennyroyal and camphor.

"I smell liniment," she said, perplexed. "The kind we use on the horses."

"Mr. Bloom sent up a pot of it from the stables and demanded that we apply a poultice to my ribs. I didn't dare refuse."

"Oh." Her brow cleared. "It works very well," she assured him. "It heals the horses' pulled muscles in half the usual time."

"I'm sure it does." A rueful grin crossed his lips. "If only the camphor weren't burning a hole through my hide."

"Did Sutton apply it full strength?" she asked with a frown. "That concentration was intended for horses—he should have cut it with oil or white wax."

"No one told him."

"It should be removed right away. Let me help." She began to reach for him but paused uncertainly. The poultice was bound to him beneath his white nightshirt. Either she would have to pull up the shirt and reach beneath the hem, or she would have to unbutton the placket down the front.

Seeing her uneasiness, Devon smiled and shook his head. "I'll wait until Sutton returns."

"No, I'm perfectly able to do it," Kathleen insisted, pink-cheeked. "I was a married woman, after all."

"So worldly," Devon mocked gently, his gaze caressing.

Her lips pressed together in a determined line. Trying to appear composed, she began on the placket of buttons. The garment was made of exceptionally smooth white linen, the fabric heavy with a slight sheen. "This is a very fine nightshirt," she remarked inanely.

"I wasn't even aware that I owned one, until Sutton brought it out."

Kathleen paused, perplexed. "What do you wear to sleep, if not a nightshirt?"

Devon gave her a speaking glance, one corner of his mouth quirking.

Her jaw went slack as his meaning sank in.

"Does that shock you?" he asked, a glint of laughter in his eyes.

"Certainly not. I was already aware that you're a barbarian." But she turned the color of a ripe pomegranate as she concentrated resolutely on the buttons. The nightshirt gaped open, revealing a brawny, lightly furred chest. She cleared her throat before asking, "Are you able to lift up?"

For answer, Devon pushed away from the pillows with a grunt of effort.

Kathleen let her shawl drop and reached beneath him, searching for the end of the cloth binding. It was tucked in at the center. "Just a moment—" She reached around him with her other arm to pull at the end of the cloth. It was longer than she'd expected, requiring several tugs to free it.

No longer able to maintain the position, Devon dropped back to the pillows with a pained sound, his weight pinning her hands. "Sorry," he managed.

Kathleen tugged at her imprisoned arms. "Not at all . . . but if you wouldn't mind . . ."

Recovering his breath, Devon was slow to respond as he took stock of the situation.

She was torn between amusement and outrage as she saw the glint of mischief in his eyes. "Let me up, you *rogue.*"

His warm hands came up to the backs of her shoulders, caressing in slow circles. "Climb into bed with me."

"Are you mad?"

As she strained to free herself, he reached for the loose braid that hung over her shoulder and played with it idly. "You did last night," he pointed out.

Kathleen went still, her eyes widening.

So he did remember.

"You can hardly expect me to make a habit of it," she said breathlessly. "Besides, my maid will come looking for me soon."

Devon moved to his side and tugged her fully onto the bed. "She won't come in here."

She scowled. "You're impossible! I should let the camphor burn a few layers of skin off you."

His brows lifted. "I would think you'd treat me at least as well as one of the horses."

"Any one of the horses is better behaved than you," she informed him, reaching into his nightshirt and around his back with one arm. "Even the mule behaves better." She tugged at the end of the bandage until it came free. The mass of the poultice and bindings loosened, and she managed to pull it off and toss it to the floor.

Devon lay still beneath her ministrations, obviously pleased with himself.

Looking down at the handsome scoundrel, Kathleen was tempted to smile back at him. Instead, she gave him a reproving glance. "Dr. Weeks said you're supposed to refrain from movements that put pressure on your ribs. No pulling or lifting *anything*. You have to rest."

"I'll rest as long as you stay with me."

The feel of him was so clean and warm and inviting that she felt herself weakening. Carefully she eased into the crook of his arm. "Is this hurting you?"

"I'm feeling better by the minute." He pulled the covers over them both, enclosing her in a cocoon of white sheets and soft wool blankets.

She lay against him front to front, shivering with pleasure as she felt how perfectly the hard, warm contours of his body fit against hers. "Someone will see."

"The door's closed." Devon reached up to toy with the delicate curve of her ear. "You're not afraid of me, are you?"

She shook her head, even though her pulse was racing.

Devon nuzzled against her hair. "I worried that I might have hurt or frightened you yesterday, in my . . ." He paused, searching for a word. ". . . enthusiasm," he finished dryly.

"You . . . you didn't know what you were doing."

Self-mockery thickened his voice. "I knew exactly what I was doing. I just wasn't able to do it well." His thumb grazed the edge of her lower lip, teasing the full shape. She caught her breath as his fingers slid across her jaw, nudging the angle upward, stroking the soft skin beneath her chin. "I meant to kiss you more like . . . this."

His mouth covered hers with tantalizing pressure. So hot and slow, his lips coaxing a helpless response before she could think of withholding it. So gentle, his mouth firm and teasing, sending ticklish pangs down to parts of her body that she didn't even have names for. The kisses went on and on, a new one starting before the last had quite ended. Beneath the covers, one of his hair-roughened legs brushed against hers. Reaching around his neck, she let her fingers sink into his silky dark hair, shaping to his skull.

His hand drifted along her spine until he had molded her hips against his. Even through the layers of flannel and linen that separated them, she felt their bodies conform intimately, softness yielding to hardness. He kissed her more aggressively, his tongue probing, searching deeper, and she moaned at the pleasure of it.

Nothing existed outside of this bed. There was only the sensuous friction of tangled limbs and gently wandering hands. She whimpered as he cupped her bottom and brought her against the hard ridge of his aroused flesh. He guided her hips in a slow rhythm, rubbing her sensuously against him until she began to moan with each stroke. The soft place he teased began to swell and twitch with sensation, and she flushed with shame. She shouldn't feel this way, she shouldn't want . . . what she wanted. No matter how close she pressed to him, she needed more. She could almost have attacked him, the desire was so acute.

As she squirmed against him, Devon flinched and gasped, and she realized she had inadvertently pressed against his ribs.

"Oh . . . I'm sorry . . ." Kathleen began to roll away from him, panting.

"No harm done." He kept her in place. "Don't go." He was breathing hard—it must have been hurting him—but he didn't seem to care.

"We have to stop," she protested. "It's wrong, and it's dangerous for you—and I feel—" She paused. No word in her vocabulary could account for the seething desperation that filled her, the agonizing tension coiling inside.

Devon nudged her intimately, the subtle movement drawing a deep shiver from her.

"*Don't*," she moaned. "I feel hot and ill, and I can't think. I can't even breathe."

She couldn't fathom why Devon was amused, but as he brushed his lips against her cheek, she felt the shape of his smile.

"Let me help you, love."

"You can't," she said in a muffled voice.

"I can. Trust me."

He pressed her onto her back, his parted lips dragging over her throat and chest. She didn't realize that he'd been working at the fastenings of her clothes until he spread her gown open.

She started as cool air wafted over her bare skin. "Devon—"

"Hush." The word blew against the tip of her breast.

She moaned as his mouth covered her, drawing in the tender flesh with a firm, warm tug.

It seemed that his notion of how to help was to heap even more torment on her. He cupped her breasts in his hands and suckled with the lightest possible pulls, until her hips stirred helplessly to relieve the merciless tension. His palm slid beneath her nightgown to clasp her bare hip.

"You're so beautiful," he whispered, "your skin, your shape, every part of you." His hand insinuated between her thighs, easing them apart. "Open for me . . . a little more . . . yes . . . God, how soft you are, here . . . and here . . ."

He sifted through crisp curls and stroked into the tender furrow, separating the wetly yielding layers with his fingertips until an aching peak of flesh was revealed. Skillfully he teased around it and traced the melting-soft folds down to the entrance of her body. A jolt of surprise shook her as the tip of his finger slipped inside the tightness. Her eyes flew open, and she reached down reflexively, gripping his thickly muscled wrist.

Devon went still, seeming confounded as he stared down at her scarlet face. His expression changed to a mixture of wonder and pleasure and lust. "Does it hurt, love?" he asked huskily.

Her body had clamped around the intrusion, throbbing and smarting. "A . . . a little." Awkwardly she tugged at his wrist, but he resisted the wordless plea.

Gently his thumb swirled over the tight, sensitive bud. His finger slid deeper inside her, caressing, eliciting such abundant wetness that she cringed and tried to look past the tangled bunch of the nightgown around her waist.

Breathing hard, he pressed his lips to the anxious lines of her forehead. "No, don't worry. You become wet . . . in here . . . when your body is ready for me . . . it's lovely, it makes me want you even more . . . Ah, sweet . . . I can feel you holding me."

She could feel it too, her flesh working in lubricious pulls to welcome him. The invasion withdrew briefly, and then two fingers slipped inside, stretching her uncomfortably tight. His entire hand cupped her, the heel of it pressing against the soft crest of her sex, his fingers thrusting deep, deep, and she couldn't help arching in hot confusion. Too much sensation was rolling up to her, making her heart thump so wildly that it frightened her.

"Stop," she whispered through dry lips. "Please . . . I'm going to faint . . ."

His taunting whisper tickled her ear. "Then faint."

The tension heightened unbearably. She spread her legs, helplessly rocking against his hand. It all began to uncoil with astonishing force, tumbling her headlong through a release so consuming that it felt like dying. The sensation kept opening, flowering, breaking into squeezing shudders. As she moaned and gasped, Devon kissed her, sucking at her lips as if he could taste the sounds of her pleasure. Another surge went through her, the heat spreading in her head, breasts, stomach, groin, while his mouth never stopped ravishing hers.

After the last liquid shivers had faded, she wilted against him, her head swimming. She was vaguely aware of having moved to her side, her face pressed to the softly springy hair on Devon's chest. He had pulled her gown back down over her hip, one hand rubbing her bottom in comforting circles, while his breath eased back to its normal rhythm. She had never wanted to sleep as much as she did right then, steeped in the warmth of his body, snuggled close in his arms. But she could hear the distant sounds of housemaids beginning their morning chores, cleaning the grates, sweeping the carpets. If she stayed much longer, she would be discovered.

"Your body has gone as taut as a bowstring," Devon said drowsily over her head. "And after all the work I just did to relax you." A chuckle escaped him at her mortified silence. His hand came to her back, caressing the length of her spine. "Has that never happened to you before?"

She shook her head. "I didn't know it was possible for women." Her voice sounded strange to her own ears, low and languid.

"No one told you before your wedding night?"

"Lady Berwick did, but I'm sure she didn't know anything about it. Or perhaps . . ." She paused as a discomfiting thought occurred to her. "Perhaps it's not something that happens to respectable women."

His hand continued its slow, reassuring glide up and down her back. "I don't see why it shouldn't." His head lowered, and he whispered near her ear, "But I won't tell."

Timidly she let her fingers trace the edge of the great spreading bruise on his side. "Do other men know how to do . . . that?"

"Pleasure a woman, you mean? Yes, all it takes is patience." He played with a few locks of hair that had come loose from her braid. "But it's well worth the effort. A woman's enjoyment makes the act more satisfying."

"Does it? Why?"

"It flatters a man's pride to know that he can make a woman desire him. Also . . ." His hand drifted to the soft cove between her thighs, and stroked through the layer of her nightgown. ". . . the way you tightened around my fingers . . . that's pleasurable for a man when he's inside you."

Kathleen hid her face against his shoulder. "Lady Berwick made it all sound very simple. But I'm beginning to think that she left out some important details."

He let out a quiet laugh. "Anyone who says the sexual act is simple has never done it properly."

They lay together, listening to the sounds beyond the bedroom. Outside, groundskeepers began to push wheeled mowers and edgers across the lawn, the bladed cylinders whirring smoothly. The sky was the color of steel, a strong wind chafing at the last few bleached brown leaves of an oak tree near the window.

Devon pressed a kiss into her hair. "Kathleen . . . you told me that the last time Theo spoke to you, he said, 'You're not my wife.'"

She froze, alarm stinging the insides of her veins as she realized what he was going to ask.

His voice was gentle. "Was it true?"

She tried to move away, but he kept her firmly against him.

"It doesn't matter how you answer," he said. "I just want to understand what happened."

She would risk everything by telling him. She had far too much to lose. But part of her longed to admit the truth. "Yes," she forced herself to say, her voice thin. "It was true. The marriage was never consummated."

# Chapter 20

"So THAT WAS WHAT you argued about," Devon murmured, his hand moving over her back in slow strokes.

"Yes. Because I wouldn't let Theo . . ." She paused with a shaking sigh. "I have no right to be called Lady Trenear. I shouldn't have stayed at Eversby Priory afterward, except . . . I didn't know if I would be allowed to keep my dowry, and I didn't want to go back to live with Lord and Lady Berwick, and besides all that, it was shameful. So I lied about being Theo's wife."

"Did someone actually ask if you'd slept with him?" he asked, sounding incredulous.

"No, but I lied by omission. Which is just as bad as the other kind of lying. The deplorable truth is that I'm a virgin. A fraud." She was stunned to feel a rustle of suppressed laughter in his chest. "I don't see how you can find cause for humor in that!"

"I'm sorry." But a smile lingered in his voice. "I was just thinking, with the tenants' drainage concerns, the plumbers, the estate's debt, and the hundred other issues I'm facing . . . finally there's a problem around here I can do something about."

She gave him a reproachful glance, and he grinned. He kissed her before moving to find a more comfortable position, levering himself higher. Reaching for the pillows, Kathleen propped them behind his shoulders. She sat to face him with her legs half curled beneath her, and refastened her nightgown.

One of Devon's hands came to rest on her thigh. "Tell me what happened, sweetheart."

It was impossible to hold anything back now. She looked away from him, her fingers gripped around the placket of her bodice. "You must understand . . . I had never been alone with Theo until our wedding night. Lady Berwick chaperoned us every minute, until after the wedding. We were married at the estate chapel. It was a very grand wedding, a week-long affair, and . . ." She paused as a new thought occurred to her. "You and West should have been invited. I'm so sorry that you weren't."

"I'm not," Devon said. "I don't know what I would have done, had I met you before the wedding."

At first she thought he was joking, but his gaze was deadly serious.

"Go on," he said.

"After the ceremony, Theo went to a tavern with his friends, and he stayed away all afternoon and evening. I was obliged to remain in my room because . . . it's very awkward for the bride, you see. It's unseemly to linger and talk to people before the wedding night. So I bathed, and Clara curled my hair with hot tongs, and I dressed in a white lace nightgown, and then I sat alone to wait . . . and wait . . . and wait . . . I was too nervous to eat anything, and there was nothing to do. I went to bed at midnight. I couldn't sleep, I just lay there stewing."

Devon's hand tightened on her thigh.

She glanced at him quickly, and found him staring at her with a concern that turned her insides to molten honey.

"Finally Theo came into the room," she continued, "very much the worse for drink. His clothes were dirty, and he smelled sour, and he didn't even wash, just re-

moved his clothes and climbed into bed, and started—"
Kathleen stopped, reaching for her long braid and fidgeting with the end of it. There was no way to explain the ghastly surprise of being groped and overwhelmed, with no chance to become accustomed to the feel of a man's naked body. Theo hadn't kissed her . . . not that she had wanted him to . . . he hadn't even seemed to be aware of her as a person.

"I tried to hold still at first," she said. "That was what Lady Berwick said I was supposed to do. But he was so heavy and rough, and he was cross because I didn't know what to do. I started to protest, and he tried to quiet me. He put his hand over my mouth—that was when I lost control. I couldn't help it. I fought and kicked him, and suddenly he pulled away, doubling over. I told him that he smelled like a dung mixen, and I didn't want him to touch me."

Pausing, she glanced at him apprehensively, expecting disapproval or mockery. But his expression was inscrutable.

"I ran from the room," she continued, "and spent the rest of the night on the divan in Helen's room. She was very kind and didn't ask questions, and the next morning she helped me to mend the torn lace on my nightgown before the maids could see it. Theo was furious with me the next day, but then he admitted that he shouldn't have had so much to drink. He asked me to begin again. And I . . ." She swallowed hard, flooded with shame as she confessed, "I refused his apology. I said I would never share a bed with him, that night or any other night."

"Good," Devon said, in a different tone than she had ever heard him use before. He had glanced away from her, as if he didn't want her to see what was in his eyes, but his profile was hard.

"No, it was terrible of me. When I went to Lady Berwick and asked what I should do, she said that a wife must tolerate her husband's advances even when he's in his cups, and it's never pleasant, but that's the nature of the marriage bargain. A wife exchanges her autonomy in return for her husband's protection."

"Shouldn't the husband protect her from himself, if necessary?"

Kathleen frowned at the soft question. "I don't know."

Devon was silent, waiting for her to continue.

"During the next two days," she said, "all the wedding guests departed. I couldn't make myself go to Theo's bed. He was hurt and angry, and he demanded his rights. But he was still drinking a great deal, and I said I would have nothing to do with him until he was sober. We argued terribly. He said that he would never have married me, had he known that I was frigid. On the third morning, he went out to ride Asad, and . . . you know the rest."

Devon's hand slipped beneath the hem of her nightgown, lightly stroking her bare thigh. He studied her, his gaze warm and interested. "Do you want to know what I would have done," he asked eventually, "had I made the same mistake as Theo?" At her cautious nod, he continued, "I would have begged you for forgiveness, on my knees, and sworn never to let it happen again. I would have understood that you were angry and frightened, with good reason. I would have waited for as long as you needed, until I had earned back your trust . . . and then I would have taken you to bed and made love to you for days. As for you being frigid . . . I think we've disproved that conclusively."

Kathleen blushed. "Before I leave . . . I know that a man has needs. Is there something I should do for you?"

A rueful smile tugged at his lips. "I appreciate your

offer. But at the moment, it hurts to take a deep breath. Being pleasured by you would finish me off for good." He squeezed her thigh. "The next time."

"But there can't be a next time," she said bleakly. "Everything must go back to the way it was."

His brows lifted fractionally. "Do you think that's possible?"

"Yes, why not?"

"Certain appetites, once awakened, are difficult to ignore."

"It doesn't matter; I'm a widow. I can't do this again."

Devon caught one of her ankles and tugged her toward him despite the pain it must have caused him. "Stop it," she whispered sharply, trying to pull down the hem of her nightgown as it rode higher on her hips. "You'll hurt yourself—"

"Look at me."

He had taken her shoulders in his hands. Reluctantly Kathleen brought herself to look into his eyes.

"I know that you regret Theo's death," Devon said quietly. "I know that you married him with the best of intentions, and you've tried to mourn him sincerely. But Kathleen, love . . . You're no more his widow than you ever were his wife."

The words were like a slap in the face. Shocked and offended, she scrambled from the bed and snatched up her shawl. "I should never have confided in you," she exclaimed.

"I'm only pointing out that—at least in private—you're not bound by the same obligations as a true widow."

"I am a true widow!"

Devon looked sardonic. "You barely knew Theo."

"I loved him," she insisted.

"Oh? What did you love most about him?"

Angrily Kathleen parted her lips to reply . . . but not a single word emerged. She pressed the flat of her hand to her stomach as a sickening realization occurred to her. Now that her guilt over Theo's death had been at least partially assuaged, she couldn't identify any particular feeling for him except the distant pity she would have had for a complete stranger who had met such a fate.

Despite that, she had taken her place as Theo's widow, living in his house, befriending his sisters, enjoying all the benefits of being Lady Trenear. Theo had known that she was a sham. He had known that she didn't love him, even when she herself hadn't known it. That was why his last words had been an accusation.

Furious and ashamed, Kathleen turned and went to the door. She flung it open without pausing to consider the need for discretion, and ran across the threshold. The breath was nearly knocked from her as she collided with a sturdy form.

"What the—" she heard West say, while he reached out to steady her. "What is it? Can I help?"

"Yes," she snapped, "you can throw your brother back into that river." She strode away before he could respond.

WEST WANDERED INTO the master bedroom. "Back to your usual charming self, I see."

Devon grinned and let out a ragged breath, willing the raging heat of the past several minutes to retreat. Having Kathleen there, in his bed, had been the most exquisite torture imaginable. His body was a mass of aches, stabs, and cravings.

He'd never felt better in his life.

"Why was she angry?" West asked. "Never mind, I don't

want to know." Picking up the bedside chair with one hand, he turned it around. "You owe me a pair of shoes." He sat astride the chair and braced his arms on the back of it.

"I owe you more than that." A few months ago, Devon reflected, it was doubtful that West would have had the physical strength, let alone the presence of mind, to haul him out of the river. "Thank you," he said simply, holding his brother's gaze.

"It was wholly self-serving, I assure you. I have no desire to be the Earl of Trenear."

Devon gave a short laugh. "Nor do I."

"Oh? Lately the role seems a better fit for you than I would have expected." West glanced over him speculatively. "How are your ribs?"

"Cracked but not broken."

"You've fared much better than Winterborne."

"He was seated next to the window." Remembering the moment when the trains had collided, Devon grimaced. "How is he?"

"Sleeping. Weeks wants to keep him sedated to help with the pain and improve his chances of healing properly. He also advised sending for an oculist from London."

"Will Winterborne regain his sight?"

"The doctor thinks so, but there's no way of knowing for certain until he's tested."

"And the leg?"

"The break was clean—it will heal well. However, Winterborne will be staying with us for quite a bit longer than we'd planned. At least a month."

"Good. That will give him more time to become acquainted with Helen."

West's face went blank. "You're back to that idea again? Arranging a match between them? What if Winterborne turns out to be lame and blind?"

"He'll still be rich."

Looking sardonic, West said, "Evidently a brush with death hasn't changed your priorities."

"Why should it? The marriage would benefit everyone."

"How exactly would *you* stand to benefit?"

"I'll stipulate that Winterborne settle a large dower on Helen, and name me as the trustee of her finances."

"And then you'll use the money as you see fit?" West asked incredulously. "Sweet Mother of God, how can you risk your life to save drowning children one day, and plot something so ruthless the next day?"

Annoyed, Devon gave him a narrow-eyed glance. "There's no need to carry on as if Helen's going to be dragged to the altar in chains. She'll have a choice in the matter."

"The right words can bind someone more effectively than chains. You'll manipulate her into doing what you want regardless of how she feels."

"Enjoy the view from your moral pedestal," Devon said. "Unfortunately I have to keep my feet on the ground."

West stood and went to the window, scowling at the view. "There's a flaw in your plan. Winterborne may decide that Helen isn't to his taste."

"Oh, he'll take her," Devon assured him. "Marrying a daughter of the peerage is the only way for him to climb in society. Consider it, West: Winterborne is one of the richest men in London and half the nobility is in debt to him—and yet the same aristocrats who beg him to extend their credit refuse to welcome him into their drawing rooms. If he marries an earl's daughter, however, doors that have always been closed to him would instantly open." Devon paused reflectively. "Helen would do well for him."

"She may not want him."

"Would she rather become a penniless spinster?"

"Perhaps," West replied testily. "How should I know?"

"My question was rhetorical. Of course Helen will agree to the match. Aristocratic marriages are always arranged for the benefit of the family."

"Yes, but the brides are usually paired with their social equals. What you're proposing is to lower Helen by selling her to any common lout with deep pockets for your own benefit."

"Not *any* common lout," Devon said. "One of our friends."

West let out a reluctant laugh and turned back to face him. "Being a friend of ours doesn't exactly recommend him. I'd rather let him have Pandora or Cassandra—at least they have enough spirit to stand up to him."

HELEN WAS GLAD and relieved that the Christmas Eve party and servants' ball would be held as planned. It had been discussed among the family, with all of them sensitive to the plight of poor Mr. Winterborne in his invalid condition. However, both Devon and West had said flatly that Winterborne would be the last person to want a holiday to be canceled for his sake, when it would mean so much to the servants and tenants who had worked so hard all year. Going on with the celebration as planned would be good for the morale of the entire household, and in Helen's opinion, it was important to honor the spirit of the holiday. No harm was ever done by encouraging love and goodwill.

The household bustled with renewed excitement as everyone wrapped gifts and made preparations, while rich smells of pastries and joint roasts drifted from the kitchen. Hampers of oranges and apples were set out in the entrance hall, along with baskets containing spinning tops, carved wooden animals, skipping ropes, and cup-and-ball toys.

"I feel sorry for Mr. Winterborne," Pandora remarked. She and Cassandra were busy wrapping sugared almonds in little twists of paper, while Helen arranged flowers in a large vase. "He'll be alone in a dark room," she continued, "while the rest of us are enjoying decorations that he sent to us, and can't even see!"

"I feel sorry for him too," Cassandra said. "But his room is far enough from the noise that it shouldn't bother him. And since the medicine from Dr. Weeks makes him sleep most of the time, he probably won't even know what's happening."

"He's not sleeping now," Pandora said. "According to Mrs. Church, he refused to take his afternoon dose. He knocked a cup out of her hand and said something beastly and didn't even apologize!"

Helen paused in the middle of arranging a large vase of red roses, evergreen branches, white lilies, and chrysanthemums. "He's in a great deal of pain," she said, "and probably frightened, as any man in his situation would be. Don't judge him unfairly, dear."

"I suppose you're right," Pandora said. "It would be awfully dull to lie there with no diversions. Not even being able to read! Kathleen said she was going to visit him, and try to coax him to take some broth or tea. I hope she had more luck than Mrs. Church."

Frowning, Helen trimmed another rose stem and slid it into the arrangement. "I'll go upstairs," she said, "and ask if there's something I can do to help. Cassandra, would you finish these flowers for me?"

"If Mr. Winterborne would like," Pandora offered, "Cassie and I could read *The Pickwick Papers* to him. We'll do all the characters' voices and make it very amusing."

"I could bring Josephine to visit him after I finish the flowers," Cassandra suggested. "She's much calmer than Napoleon, and it always makes me feel better to have a dog with me when I'm ill."

"Perhaps he'd like to meet Hamlet," Pandora exclaimed.

Helen smiled into her younger sisters' earnest faces. "You are both very kind. No doubt Mr. Winterborne will be grateful for the entertainment after he's had a bit more rest."

She left the dining room and crossed through the entrance hall, enjoying the sight of the glittering tree. Beneath the ornamented branches, a housemaid hummed a carol as she swept up fallen needles. She went upstairs and found Kathleen and Mrs. Church standing outside Winterborne's room. Both of them looked concerned and exasperated as they conferred in hushed tones.

"I came to see how our guest was," Helen said, joining them.

Kathleen answered with a frown. "He has a fever and can't keep anything down. Not even a sip of water. It's very worrying."

Helen glanced through the partially open doorway, into the shadowed room. She heard a quiet sound, somewhere between a groan and a growl, and the hairs on the back of her neck lifted.

"Shall I send for Dr. Weeks?" Mrs. Church asked.

"I suppose so," Kathleen said, "although he stayed up most of the night watching over Mr. Winterborne, and he desperately needs a few hours of rest. Furthermore, if we can't persuade our patient to take any medicine or water, I don't know how Weeks could manage it."

"May I try?" Helen offered.

"No," the other women said in unison.

Turning to Helen, Kathleen explained, "So far we've heard nothing but profanities from Mr. Winterborne. Fortunately at least half of it is in Welsh, but it's still too vulgar for your ears. Besides, you're still unmarried, and he isn't decently clothed, so it's out of the question."

A curse emerged from the depths of the room, followed by a wretched groan.

Helen felt a rush of pity. "The sickroom holds no surprises for me," she said. "After Mama was gone, I nursed Father through more than one illness."

"Yes, but Winterborne isn't a relation."

"He's certainly in no condition to compromise anyone . . . and you and Mrs. Church are already burdened with much to do." She gave Kathleen a pleading glance. "Let me see to him."

"Very well," Kathleen said reluctantly. "But leave the door open."

Helen nodded and slipped into the room.

The atmosphere was warm and stuffy, the air pungent with sweat, medicine, and plaster. Winterborne's large, dark form writhed on the bed amid tangled sheets. Although he was dressed in a nightshirt, with one leg encased in a cast from the knee down, Helen had a glimpse of swarthy skin and hairy limbs. The locks on his head were obsidian black and slightly curly. His white teeth clenched with pained effort as he tried to pull the bandages from his eyes. Helen hesitated. Ill though he was, Winterborne seemed like a feral beast. But as she saw the way his hands fumbled and shook, she was filled with compassion.

"No, no . . ." she said, hurrying to him. She laid a gentle hand on his forehead, which was as dry and hot as a stove plate. "Be at ease. Be still."

Winterborne had begun to shove her away, but at the

feel of her cool fingers, he made a low sound and went motionless. He seemed half delirious with fever. His lips were chapped and cracked at the corners. Bringing his head to her shoulder to steady it, Helen restored the bandage around his eyes, tucking in the loose ends. "Don't pull at this," she murmured. "Your eyes must stay covered while they heal." He stayed against her, breathing in short, sharp bursts. "Will you try some water?" she asked.

"Can't," he managed wretchedly.

Helen turned her gaze to the housekeeper, who had remained at the threshold. "Mrs. Church, please open the window."

"Dr. Weeks said to keep the room warm."

"He's feverish," Helen persisted. "I think it would help to make him more comfortable."

Mrs. Church went to the window. As she unlatched the casement and pushed it open, a rush of icy air entered the room, whisking away the sickroom odor.

Helen felt the movement of Winterborne's chest as he drew in a deep breath. The heavy muscles of his back and arms twitched with relief, the ferocious tension draining. His head settled on her shoulder as if he were an exhausted child. Aware of his state of undress, Helen didn't dare look down.

As she held him, she reached for the cup of water on the nightstand. "Try a few drops of water," she coaxed. As he felt her press the cup to his lips, he made a faint protesting sound, but he allowed her to wet his lips.

Realizing it was the most he could do, Helen set the cup aside and whispered, "There, that's better." She continued to hold him while the housekeeper came forward without a word and began to straighten the bedclothes.

It was scandalous, Helen knew, for her to behave this

way with any man, let alone a stranger. There was no question that Kathleen would have been appalled. But Helen had been secluded from society for her entire life, and although she was disposed to follow the rules whenever possible, she was also willing to discard them when necessary. Besides, even though Winterborne was a powerful and influential man in his everyday existence, right now he was suffering and very ill, and she could almost think of him as a child in need of help.

She tried to lower him to the pillows, but he resisted with a grunt. One of his hands clamped around her wrist. Although his grip wasn't painful, she felt the strength of it. If he wished to, he could have easily snapped her bones. "I'll go fetch something to make you feel better," she said gently. "I'll come back soon."

Winterborne let her ease him down to the pillows, but he didn't let go. Perturbed, Helen contemplated his large hand before her gaze traveled to his face. His eyes and forehead were obscured by bandages, but the bone structure beneath his bruised and scratched complexion was austerely angled, the cheekbones paring-knife sharp, the jaw sturdy and emphatic. There were no smile lines around the mouth, no touch of softness anywhere.

"I'll return within a half hour," Helen said. "I promise."

Winterborne didn't relinquish his grip.

"I promise," she repeated. With her free hand, she stroked his fingers lightly, coaxing them to loosen.

He tried to dampen his lips with his tongue before speaking. "Who are you?" he asked hoarsely.

"Lady Helen."

"What time is it?"

Helen sent a questioning glance to Mrs. Church, who went to the mantel clock. "It's four o'clock," the housekeeper reported.

He was going to time her, Helen realized. And heaven help her if she was late.

"I'll return by half past four," she said. After a moment, she added softly, "Trust me."

Gradually Winterborne's hand opened, freeing her.

*Chapter 21*

THE FIRST THING RHYS had become aware of after the railway accident was someone—a doctor, perhaps—asking if there was someone he wanted to send for. He had shaken his head immediately. His father was dead, and his elderly mother, a flinty and humorless woman who lived in London, was the last person he wanted to see. Even if he'd asked her for comfort, she wouldn't have known how to give it.

Rhys had never been seriously injured or ill in his life. Even as a boy he had been big-boned and physically fearless. His Welsh parents had thrashed him with a barrel stave for any misdeed or moment of laziness, and he had taken the worst punishments without flinching. His father had been a grocer, and they had lived on a street of shopkeepers where Rhys had not learned the skills of buying and selling so much as he had absorbed them, as naturally as he breathed air.

After he had built his own business, he never let any personal relationship detract from it. There were women, of course, but only the ones who were willing to have an affair on his terms: purely sexual and devoid of sentiment. Now, as he lay suffocating in an unfamiliar bedroom with pain rioting through him, it occurred to Rhys that perhaps he had been rather too independent. There *should* be someone he could send for, someone who would care for him in this inexplicable situation of being injured.

In spite of the cool breeze that came from the window, every inch of him felt scorched. The weight of the cast on his leg maddened him almost as much as the unrelenting hurt of the broken bone. The room seemed to revolve and swivel, making him violently nauseous. All he could do was wait, minute by helpless minute, for the woman to return.

Lady Helen . . . one of the rarefied creatures he had always regarded with private contempt. One of his betters.

After what seemed an eternity, he was aware of someone entering the room. He heard a quiet rattle, like glass or porcelain against metal. Brusquely he asked, "What time is it?"

"Four twenty-seven." It was Lady Helen's voice, luminous with a hint of amusement. "I have three minutes left."

He listened intently to the rustle of skirts . . . the sound of something being poured and stirred . . . the crackle of water and ice. If she intended for him to drink something, she was mistaken: The idea of swallowing sent a shudder of revulsion through him.

She was close now; he sensed her leaning over him. A length of cool, damp flannel began to stroke over his forehead, cheeks and throat, and it felt so good that a wrenching sigh left him. When the cloth was removed momentarily, he reached for it, gasping, "Don't stop." He was inwardly furious that he'd been reduced to begging for small mercies.

"Shhh . . ." She had freshened the flannel, made it colder and wetter. As the unhurried stroking continued, his fingers encountered the folds of her skirts and closed on them so tightly that nothing could have pried the fabric free. Her gentle hand slid beneath his head and lifted it enough for the cloth to slide underneath to the back of his neck. The pleasure of it drew a mortifying groan of relief from him.

When he had relaxed and was breathing deeply, the cloth was set aside. He felt her maneuver around him, easing his head and shoulders upward, tucking pillows behind him. Perceiving that she intended to give him more water or perhaps some of the foul laudanum tonic from earlier, he protested through gritted teeth.

"No—damn you—"

"Just try." She was gentle but merciless. Her slight weight depressed the side of the mattress, and a slender arm slid behind him. As he was caught in that half-cradling hold, he considered shoving her off the bed. But her hand touched his cheek with a tenderness that somehow undermined his will to hurt her.

A glass was brought to his mouth, and a sweet, very cold liquid touched his lips. As he took a cautious sip, the woolly surface of his tongue absorbed the faintly astringent drink instantly. It was delicious.

"Slower," she cautioned.

He was so parched, as dry as a powder house, and he needed more. Reaching upward, he fumbled for her hand with the cup, gripped it steady, and took a greedy swallow before she could stop him.

"Wait." The cup was pulled from his grasp. "Let's see if you can keep it down."

He was tempted to curse her for withholding the drink, although a distant part of his brain understood the sense of it.

Eventually the glass came to his lips again.

He forced himself to drain the contents slowly rather than gulp. After he had finished, Lady Helen waited patiently, still supporting him. The motion of her breathing was gentle and even, her breast a soft cushion beneath his head. She smelled like vanilla and some faint, flowery essence. He had never been at such a disadvantage in his adult life . . . He was always well dressed and in control, but all this woman saw was a helpless, grossly unkempt invalid. It was infuriating.

"Better?" she asked.

"*Ydw*," Rhys replied in Welsh without thinking. Yes. It seemed impossible, but the room had stopped turning over. Even though shocks of pain still ran up his leg as if bullets were being fired through it at intervals, he could tolerate anything as long as the nausea was gone.

She began to ease him from her lap, but he laid a solid arm across her. He needed everything to stay exactly as it was, at least for a few minutes. To his satisfaction, she settled back beneath him.

"What did you give me?" he asked.

"A tea I made with orchids."

"Orchids," he repeated, puzzled.

He'd never heard of any use for the odd flowers, other than as exotic ornaments.

"Two varieties of *Dendrobium*, and a *Spiranthes*. Many orchids have medicinal properties. My mother collected them, and filled a score of notebooks with information she'd gathered."

Oh, he liked her voice, a low and lulling melody. He felt her move again—another attempt to set him aside—and he slumped more heavily into her lap, his head pinning her arm in a determined effort to make her stay.

"Mr. Winterborne, I should leave you to rest now—"

"Talk to me."

She hesitated. "If you wish. What shall we talk about?"

He wanted to ask her if he'd been permanently blinded. If anyone had said anything to him about it, he'd been too drugged to remember. But he couldn't bring himself to give voice to the question. He was too afraid of the answer. And there was no way to stop thinking about it while he was alone in this quiet room. He needed distraction and comfort.

He needed her.

"Shall I tell you about orchids?" she asked in the silence. She continued without waiting for an answer, adjusting her position more comfortably. "The word comes from Greek mythology. Orchis was the son of a satyr and a nymph. During a feast to celebrate Bacchus, Orchis drank too much wine and tried to force his attentions on a priestess. Bacchus was very displeased, and reacted by having Orchis torn to pieces. The pieces were scattered far and wide, and wherever one landed, an orchid grew." Pausing, she leaned away for a few seconds, reaching for something. Something soft and delicate touched his cracked lips . . . She was applying salve with a fingertip. "Most people don't know that vanilla is the fruit of an orchid vine. We keep one in a glasshouse on the estate— it's so long that it grows sideways on the wall. When one of the flowers is full grown, it opens in the morning, and if it isn't pollinated, it closes in the evening, never to open again. The white blossoms, and the vanilla pods within them, have the sweetest scent in the world . . ."

As her gentle voice continued, Rhys had the sensation of floating, the red tide of fever easing. How strange and lovely it was to lie here half dozing in her arms, possibly even better than fucking . . . but that thought led to the indecent question of what it might be like with her . . . how she might lie quietly beneath him while he devoured all that petal softness and vanilla sweetness . . . and slowly he fell asleep in Lady Helen's arms.

# Chapter 22

LATE IN THE AFTERNOON, Devon left his bed with the intention of joining the rest of the family in the dining room for Christmas Eve tea. He managed to dress with the help of his valet, but it took far longer than he'd anticipated. The process first entailed binding his midsection firmly enough to support the cracked ribs and restrict sudden movements. Even with Sutton's assistance, it was excruciating to slide his arms into the sleeves of his shirt. The slightest twist of his torso sent agony zinging through him. Before Devon was able to don his coat, he was obliged to take a half dose of laudanum to dull the pain.

Eventually Sutton tied his neck cloth in a precise knot and stood back to view him. "How do you feel, my lord?"

"Well enough to go downstairs for a while," Devon said. "But I'm not what anyone would call spry. And if I sneeze, I'm fairly certain I'll start bawling like an infant."

The valet smiled slightly. "You'll have no shortage of people eager to help you. The footmen literally drew straws to decide who would have the privilege of accompanying you downstairs."

"I don't need anyone to accompany me," Devon said, disliking the idea of being treated like some gouty old codger. "I'll hold the railing to keep myself steady."

"I'm afraid Sims is adamant. He lectured the entire

staff about the necessity of protecting you from additional injury. Furthermore, you can't disappoint the servants by refusing their help. You've become quite a hero to them after saving those people."

"I'm not a hero," Devon scoffed. "Anyone would have done it."

"I don't think you understand, my lord. According to the account in the papers, the woman you rescued is a miller's wife—she had gone to London to fetch her little nephew, after his mother had just died. And the boy and his sisters are the children of factory workers. They were sent to live in the country with their grandparents." Sutton paused before saying with extra emphasis, "Second-class passengers, all of them."

Devon gave him a look askance.

"For you to risk your life for *anyone* was heroic," the valet said. "But the fact that a man of your rank would be willing to sacrifice everything for those of such humble means . . . Well, as far as everyone at Eversby Priory is concerned, it's the same as if you had done it for any one of them." Sutton began to smile as he saw Devon's discomfited expression. "Which is why you will be plagued with your servants' homage and adoration for decades to come."

"Bloody hell," Devon muttered, his face heating. "Where's the laudanum?"

The valet grinned and went to ring the servants' bell.

As soon as Devon left his room, he was overwhelmed by a surplus of unwanted attention. Not one but two footmen accompanied him down the stairs, eagerly pointing out dangers such as the edge of a particular step that wasn't quite smooth, or a section of the curved balustrade that might be slippery from a recent polishing. After negotiating the apparent perils of the staircase, Devon continued through the main hall and was obliged to stop along the way as a row of housemaids curtsied and uttered a chorus of "Happy Christmas" and "God bless you, milord," and offered abundant wishes for his good health.

Abashed by the role he seemed to have been cast in, Devon smiled and thanked them. He made his painstaking way to the dining room, which was filled with lavish arrangements of Christmas flowers, and hung with evergreen garlands twined with gold ribbon. Kathleen, West, and the twins were all seated, laughing and chatting with relaxed good humor.

"We knew you were approaching," Pandora said to Devon, "from all the happy voices we could hear in the entrance hall."

"He's not accustomed to people exclaiming happily when he arrives," West said gravely. "Usually they do it when he leaves."

Devon sent his brother a mock-threatening glance and went to the empty place beside Kathleen. Immediately the underbutler, who had been waiting at the side of the room, pulled back the chair and helped to seat him with exaggerated caution.

Kathleen seemed to have difficulty meeting Devon's gaze. "You mustn't overdo," she said with soft concern.

"I won't," Devon replied. "I'm going to have tea, and help the family greet the tenants as they arrive. After that, I expect I'll be done in." He glanced around the table. "Where's Helen?"

"She's keeping company with Mr. Winterborne," Cassandra said brightly.

How had that come about? Devon sent a questioning glance to West, who hitched his shoulders in a slight shrug.

"Mr. Winterborne had a rather difficult day," Kathleen

explained. "He's feverish, and the laudanum makes him ill. It's against all decorum, obviously, but Helen asked if she might try to help him."

"That's very kind of her," Devon said. "And it's kind of you to allow it."

"Mrs. Church told me that Mr. Winterborne isn't snapping and snarling anymore," Pandora volunteered. "He's resting on pillows and drinking orchid tea. And Helen has been chattering like a magpie for hours."

Cassandra looked dumbfounded. "Helen, chattering for hours? That doesn't seem possible."

"I wouldn't have thought she had that much to say," Pandora agreed.

"Perhaps it's just that she's never able to slide a word in edgewise," West remarked blandly.

A few seconds later, he was pelted with a shower of sugar lumps.

"*Girls*," Kathleen exclaimed indignantly. "Stop that at once! West, don't you dare encourage them by laughing!" She sent a threatening glance at Devon, who was desperately trying to suppress his amusement. "Or you," she said severely.

"I won't," he promised, wincing and reflecting ruefully that whoever said laughter was the best medicine had never broken a rib.

KATHLEEN THOUGHT IT was a wonder that the family had managed to adopt a reasonably dignified façade by the time the tenants and townspeople began to arrive.

As they welcomed the procession of guests, Devon was self-assured and gracious, without the slightest hint of arrogance. He exerted himself to be charming, receiving praise and admiring comments with self-deprecating wit. Well-scrubbed children were shepherded forward, the little boys bowing, the girls curtsying, and Devon bowed in response, showing no sign of the pain he had to be feeling.

However, after an hour and a half, Kathleen noticed subtle grooves of strain appearing on his face. It was time for him to stop, she thought. West and the girls could manage the last few arrivals without him.

Before she could draw Devon away, however, a couple approached with a rosy-cheeked infant, a girl with blond curls tied up in a ribbon.

"Will you hold her, milord?" the young mother asked hopefully. "For luck?" Obviously she knew nothing about the injuries that Devon had sustained during the train accident.

"Oh, please let me hold her," Kathleen exclaimed before he could reply. She reached out for the cherub, feeling a bit awkward since she knew little about young children. But the baby relaxed contentedly in her arms and stared up at her with eyes as round as buttons. Kathleen smiled down at the infant, marveling at the delicacy of her skin and the perfect rosebud shape of her mouth.

Turning to Devon, she lifted the baby and suggested, "A kiss for luck?"

He complied without hesitation, bending to press his lips to the infant's head.

As he stood, however, his gaze traveled from the baby to Kathleen's face, and for one brief moment his eyes were the flat, frozen blue of glacier ice. The expression was deftly concealed, but not before she had seen it. Instinctively she understood that the sight of her with the baby had opened a door on emotions he didn't want to confront.

Forcing a smile to her lips, Kathleen gave the baby back to her proud mother, exclaiming, "What a beautiful little girl. An angel!"

Fortunately there was a lull in the line of arriving guests, and Kathleen took swift advantage. Slipping her arm through Devon's, she said quietly, "Let's go."

He escorted her away without a word, letting out a sigh of relief as they walked through the entrance hall.

Kathleen had intended to find a quiet place for them to sit undisturbed, but Devon surprised her by pulling her behind the Christmas tree. He drew her into the space beneath the stairs where heavy-laden evergreen branches obscured them from view.

"What are you doing?" she asked in bemusement.

Lights from hundreds of tiny candles danced in his eyes. "I have a gift for you."

Disconcerted, she said, "Oh, but . . . the family will exchange presents tomorrow morning."

"Unfortunately the presents I brought from London were lost in the accident." Reaching into his coat pocket, he said, "This is the one thing I managed to keep. I'd rather give it to you privately, since I have nothing for the others."

Hesitantly she took the object from his open palm.

It was a small, exquisite black cameo rimmed with pearls. A woman on a horse.

"The woman is Athena," Devon said. "According to myth, she invented the bridle and was the first ever to tame a horse."

Kathleen looked down at the gift in wonder. First the shawl . . . now this. Personal, beautiful, thoughtful things. No one had ever understood her taste so acutely.

Damn him.

"It's lovely," she said unsteadily. "Thank you."

Through a glaze of incipient tears, she saw him grin.

Unclasping the little pin, she tried to fasten it to the center of her collar. "Is it straight?"

"Not quite." The backs of his fingers brushed her throat as he adjusted the cameo and pinned it. "I have yet to actually see you ride," he said. "West claims that you're more accomplished than anyone he's ever seen."

"An exaggeration."

"I doubt that." His fingers left her collar. "Happy Christmas," he murmured, and leaned down to kiss her forehead.

As the pressure of his lips lifted, Kathleen stepped back, trying to create a necessary distance between them. Her heel brushed against some solid, living thing, and a sharply indignant squeal startled her.

"*Oh!*" Kathleen leaped forward instinctively, colliding with Devon's front. His arms closed around her automatically, even as a pained grunt escaped him. "Oh—I'm sorry . . . What in heaven's name—" She twisted to see behind her and broke off at the sight of Hamlet, who had come to root beneath the Christmas tree for stray sweets that had fallen from paper cones as they'd been removed from the branches. The pig snuffled among the folds of the tree skirt and the scattered presents wrapped in colored paper. Finding a tidbit to consume, he oinked in satisfaction.

Kathleen shook her head and clung to Devon as laughter trembled through both of them. "Did I hurt you?" she asked, her hand resting lightly at the side of his waistcoat.

His smiling lips grazed her temple. "Of course not, you little makeweight."

They stayed together in that delicious moment of scattered light and fragrant spruce and irresistible attraction. The entrance hall was quiet now; the guests had proceeded en masse to the drawing room.

Devon's head lowered, and he kissed the side of her

throat. "I want you in my bed again," he whispered. Working his way along her neck, he found a sensitive place that made her shiver and arch, the tip of his tongue stroking a soft pulse. It seemed as if her body had become attuned to his, excitement leaping instantly at his nearness, delight pooling hotly in her stomach. How easy it would be to let him have whatever he wanted of her. To yield to the pleasure he could give her, and think only of the present moment.

And then someday . . . it would all fall apart, and she would be devastated.

Forcing herself to pull away from him, she stared at him with equal parts misery and resolve. "I can't have an affair with you."

Devon's expression was instantly remote.

"You want more than that?"

"No," she said feelingly. "I can't conceive of any kind of relationship with you that would end in anything other than misery."

That seemed to pierce through his detachment like a steel-tipped arrow.

"Would you like references?" he asked, his tone edged with coolness. "Attesting to my satisfactory performance in the bedroom?"

"Of course not," she said shortly. "Don't be snide."

His gaze shot to hers, a smolder awakening in the depths of blue. "Then why refuse me? And why deny yourself something you want? You've been married—no one would expect virginity of you. It would harm no one if you and I took pleasure in each other's company."

"It would harm me, eventually."

He stared at her with baffled anger. "Why do you say that?"

"Because I know myself," she said. "And I know you

well enough to be certain that you would never intentionally hurt any woman. But you're dangerous to me. And the more you try to convince me otherwise, the more obvious it becomes."

HELEN SPENT THREE days in Rhys Winterborne's room, babbling incessantly while he lay there feverish and mostly silent. She became heartily tired of the sound of her own voice, and said something to that effect near the end of the second day.

"I'm not," he said shortly. "Keep talking."

The combination of Winterborne's broken leg, the fever, and the enforced bed rest had made him surly and ill tempered. It seemed that whenever Helen wasn't there to entertain him, he vented his frustration on everyone within reach, even snapping at the poor housemaid who came in the morning to clean and light the grate.

After having run through childhood anecdotes, detailed histories of the Ravenel family, and descriptions of all her tutors, favorite pets, and the most picturesque walks around Eversby, Helen had gone in search of reading material. Although she had attempted to interest Winterborne in a Dickens novel, he had rejected it categorically, having no interest in fiction or poetry. Next Helen had tried newspapers, which had been deemed acceptable. In fact, he wanted her to read every word, including the advertisements.

"I'm amazed that you're willing to read to him at all," Kathleen said when Helen told her about it later. "If it were me, I wouldn't bother."

Helen glanced at her with mild surprise. They were in the orchid house, where Kathleen was helping her with the painstaking task of hand pollinating vanilla blossoms. "You sound as if you don't like Mr. Winterborne."

"He's terrified the housemaids, cursed Mrs. Church, insulted Sims, and was rather short-tempered with me," Kathleen said. "I'm beginning to think the only member of the household he hasn't offended is the pig, and that's only because Hamlet hasn't gone into his room yet."

"He's had a fever," Helen protested.

"You must at least concede that he's grumpy and demanding."

Helen's lips tightened against a smile as she admitted, "Perhaps a little demanding."

Kathleen laughed. "I've never been more impressed with your ability to manage difficult people."

Helen pried a pale yellow flower open to find the pollen-tipped rod within. "If living in a house of Ravenels hasn't been adequate preparation, I can't fathom what would be." Using a toothpick, she collected grains of pollen and applied them to the nectar, which was hidden beneath a tiny flap in the stigma. Her hands were adept from years of practice.

After finishing a flower, Kathleen gave her sister-in-law a puzzled glance. "I've always wondered why you're the only one who doesn't have a temper. I've never seen you in a rage."

"I'm quite capable of anger," Helen assured her wryly.

"Anger, yes. But not the kind of fury in which you shout and throw things, and make nasty remarks you'll later regret."

Helen worked diligently on the vanilla vine as she replied. "Perhaps I'm a late bloomer. I could develop a temper later."

"Heavens, I hope not. If you do, we'll have no kind, calm person to soothe savage beasts such as Mr. Winterborne."

Helen sent her a quick sidelong smile. "He's not savage. He's accustomed to being the center of much activity. It's difficult for a man with a forceful nature to be idle and ill."

"He is better today, however?"

"Decidedly. And the ophthalmologist arrives today to examine his vision." Helen paused, opening another flower. "I expect that Mr. Winterborne's disposition will improve a hundredfold when he's able to see again."

"What if he can't?"

"I pray that he will." Considering the question, Helen looked troubled. "I think . . . he wouldn't be able to bear anything that he thought of as a weakness in himself."

Kathleen regarded her with wry sadness. "There are times in life when all of us have to bear the unbearable."

AFTER THE LAST of the vanilla blossoms had been pollinated, Helen and Kathleen returned to the house and discovered that the ophthalmologist, Dr. Janzer, had already arrived. He was in the process of examining Winterborne's eyes, while Dr. Weeks and Devon stayed in the room with them. Despite a few shameless attempts at eavesdropping, no one had been able to hear anything through the closed door.

"The number of ocular specialists in England, at Janzer's level of expertise," West said as he and the rest of the family waited in the private upstairs parlor, "can be counted on the fingers of one hand. He's been trained to use an ophthalmoscope, which is a device that reflects light to allow him to look directly into the living eye."

"Into the pupil?" Cassandra asked, looking amazed. "What can be seen in there?"

"Nerves and blood vessels, I imagine."

Pandora, who had left the parlor a few minutes earlier,

rushed to the threshold and announced dramatically, "Mr. Winterborne can see!"

Helen drew in a quick breath, her heart clattering. "How do you know, dear?" she asked calmly.

"I overheard him reading letters from an eye chart."

Kathleen gave Pandora a chiding glance. "I asked you not to listen at the door, Pandora."

"I didn't." Pandora held up an empty glass. "I went into the adjoining room and put this against the wall. When you bring your ear close enough, you can make out what they're saying."

"I want to try!" Cassandra exclaimed.

"You will do no such thing," Kathleen told her, motioning for Pandora to come into the parlor and sit. "Mr. Winterborne is entitled to his privacy. We'll learn soon enough if his vision is intact."

"It is," Pandora said smugly.

"Are you certain?" Helen couldn't restrain herself from asking.

Pandora gave her an emphatic nod.

Helen retained her ladylike posture, but inside she wilted with relief, and prayed silently in gratitude.

"Thank God," she heard West, who was lounging beside her on the settee, say quietly.

While the others in the room continued their conversation, Helen asked West, "Were you not optimistic about Mr. Winterborne's vision?"

"I expected it would turn out well enough, but there was still a chance that something might have gone wrong. I would hate for that to happen to Winterborne. He's not one to suffer hard knocks with forbearance and grace."

Helen gathered that not all of Winterborne's impatience was a result of being confined to a sickroom. "I had imagined that a man who owned a department store would be very charming and put people at ease."

West grinned at that. "He can be. But the moments when he's charming and putting people at ease are when he's most dangerous. Never trust him when he's nice."

Her eyes rounded with surprise. "I thought he was your friend."

"Oh, he is. But have no illusions about Winterborne. He's not like any man you've ever known, nor is he someone your parents would have allowed you to meet in society."

"My parents," Helen said, "had no intention of allowing me to meet anyone in society."

Staring at her keenly, West asked, "Why is that, I wonder?"

She was silent, regretting her comment.

"I've always thought it odd," West remarked, "that you've been obliged to live like a nun in a cloister. Why didn't your brother take you to London for the season when he was courting Kathleen?"

She met his gaze directly. "Town held no interest for me; I was happier staying here."

West's hand slid over hers and squeezed briefly. "Little friend . . . let me give you some advice that may prove helpful in the future, when you're in society. When you lie, don't fidget with your hands. Keep them still and relaxed in your lap."

"I wasn't—" Helen broke off abruptly. After a slow breath, she spoke calmly. "I wanted to go, but Theo didn't think I was ready."

"Better." He grinned at her. "Still a lie . . . but better."

Helen was spared the necessity of replying as Devon came to the doorway. Smiling, he spoke to the room in general. "According to Dr. Janzer, Winterborne's eyes have healed well, and his vision is exceptional." He paused as glad exclamations rippled through the group. "Winterborne is tired after the examination. Later we can visit him at intervals, rather than go all at once and gape as if he were a gibbon at the Bristol Zoo."

*Chapter 23*

WITH HIS VISION RESTORED, and the fever gone, Rhys felt almost like his usual self. A surge of impatient energy coursed through him as his mind was overrun with thoughts of his store. He needed to communicate with his managers, his press officer, his private secretary, his suppliers and manufacturers. Although he trusted his staff to carry on competently for the short term, their work would soon become slipshod if he was not there to supervise. The store had just opened a book department—how had the first two weeks of sales gone? An expanded and remodeled refreshment room would be unveiled in a month—had the carpenters and technicians kept to their schedule?

Stroking his jaw, he discovered that he was as bristly as a hedgehog. Disgruntled, he rang the bell at his bed-side. After a half hour had passed and no one had arrived, Rhys was about to reach for the bell again, when a white-haired, elderly man arrived. He was a short, burly fellow, dressed in a simple black swallowtail coat and dark gray trousers. His plain, unremarkable face had the appearance of an unevenly risen bread loaf, the nose somewhat bulbous . . . but the dark currant eyes set beneath the snowy frills of his brows were wise and kindly. Introducing himself as Quincy, the valet asked how he might be of service.

"I need a wash and shave," Rhys said. In a rare self-deprecating moment, he added, "Obviously you have your work cut out for you."

The valet didn't crack a smile, only replied pleasantly, "Not at all, sir."

Quincy left to make preparations, and soon returned with a tray of shaving supplies, scissors and shining steel implements, and glass bottles filled with various liquids. At the valet's direction, a footman brought in a tall stack of toweling, two large cans of hot water, and a washtub.

Clearly the valet intended to groom him beyond a simple wash and shave. Rhys glanced at the accumulation of supplies with a touch of suspicion. He had no personal valet, something he had always considered as an upper-class affectation, not to mention an invasion of his privacy. Usually he shaved his own face, cut his own fingernails, washed with plain soap, kept his teeth clean, and twice a month went to a Mayfair barber for a hair trimming. That was the limit of his primping.

The valet set to work on his hair first, draping toweling around his neck and shoulders, and dampening the unruly locks. "Do you have preferences as to length and style, sir?"

"Do what you think best," Rhys said.

After donning a pair of spectacles, Quincy began to cut Rhys's hair, scissoring through the heavy layers with calm confidence. Answering questions readily, he revealed that he had served as valet to the late Earl of Trenear, and the earl before him, having worked for the Ravenel family for a total of thirty-five years. Now that the current earl had brought his own valet with him, Quincy had been relegated to providing assistance to visiting guests, and otherwise assisted the underbutler with tasks such as polishing the silver and helping the housekeeper with the mending.

"You know how to sew?" Rhys asked.

"Of course, sir. It's a valet's responsibility to keep his master's clothing in perfect repair, with no frayed seams or missing buttons. If alterations are needed, a valet should be able to perform them on the spot."

Over the next two hours, the elderly man washed Rhys's hair and smoothed it with a touch of pomade, steamed his face with hot towels, shaved him, and tended his hands and feet with a variety of implements. Finally Quincy held up a looking glass, and Rhys viewed his reflection with a touch of surprise. His hair was shorter and well shaped, his jaw shaved as smooth as an eggshell. His hands had never looked so clean, the surfaces of his fingernails buffed to a quiet gleam.

"Is it satisfactory, sir?" Quincy asked.

"It is."

The valet proceeded to put away the supplies, while Rhys watched him with a contemplative frown. It seemed that he had been wrong about valets. No wonder Devon Ravenel and his like always appeared so impeccable and smart.

The valet proceeded to help him don a fresh nightshirt, borrowed from West, and a dressing robe made of diamond quilted black velvet, with a silk shawl collar and sash and silk cord trim. Both were finer than any garments that Rhys had ever owned.

"Do you think a commoner should dare to dress like a blue blood?" Rhys asked as Quincy pulled the hem of the robe over his legs.

"I believe every man ought to dress as well as he is able."

Rhys's eyes narrowed. "Do you think it's right for people to judge a man for what he wears?"

"It is not for me to decide whether it is right, sir. The fact is, they do."

No answer could have pleased Rhys more; it was the kind of pragmatism that he had always understood and trusted.

He was going to hire Quincy, no matter what it took. No one else would do: Rhys needed someone old and experienced, who was familiar with the aristocracy's intricate rules of etiquette and fashion. Quincy, formerly a valet to two earls, would provide him with necessary insurance against looking like a fool.

"What is your annual salary?" Rhys asked.

The valet looked taken aback. "Sir?"

"Thirty pounds, I would guess." Reading the other man's expression, Rhys deduced that the figure was a bit high. "I'll give you forty," he said coolly, "if you'll valet for me in London. I have need of your guidance and expertise. I'm an exacting employer, but I'm fair, I pay well, and I'll give you opportunities for advancement."

Buying time, the valet removed his spectacles, cleaned the lenses, and placed them into his coat pocket. He cleared his throat. "At my age," he said, "a man doesn't usually consider changing his life and moving to an unfamiliar place."

"Do you have a wife here? Family?"

After a brief but telling hesitation, the valet replied, "No, sir. However, I have friends in Hampshire."

"You can make new ones in London," Rhys said.

"May I ask, sir, if you reside in a private house?"

"Yes, it's next to my store, in a separate but connected building. I own all the property on Cork Street, and the mews behind it, and I've recently bought the block of Clifford that runs up against Savile Row. My servants work six days a week with the usual holidays off. Like the store employees, you'll have the benefit of a private doctor and a dentist. You can eat at the staff canteen without charge, and you'll be given a discount for anything you wish to buy at Winterborne's." Rhys paused, able to smell indecision as keenly as a foxhound on the hunt. "Come, man," he said softly, "you're wasted here. Why spend the rest of your years dwindling in the country, when you could be of use to me? You have plenty of work left in you, and you're not too old for the delights of London." Reading Quincy's uncertainty, he went for the kill. "Forty-five a year. That's my last offer."

The valet swallowed hard as he considered the proposition. "When shall I begin?" he asked.

Rhys smiled. "Today."

NEWS TRAVELED FAST around the Ravenel household: By the time Devon came to visit Rhys later that evening, he was already aware of Quincy's new position.

"It appears you've begun to hire my servants away from me," Devon said dryly.

"Do you object?" Rhys lifted a glass of wine to his lips. He had just finished his dinner tray, and was in an unsettled, edgy mood. Hiring a valet had given him a sense of satisfaction that had lasted only a few minutes. Now he was hungry to make decisions, accomplish things, take the reins in hand once more. It seemed as if he would be stuck in this small bedroom forever.

"You must be joking," Devon said. "I have too damned many servants. Hire ten more, and I'll dance a jig for joy."

"At least one of us can dance," Rhys muttered.

"You couldn't dance even before you broke your leg."

Rhys grinned reluctantly; Devon was one of a handful of men in the world who had no fear of mocking him.

"You won't go wrong with Quincy," Devon continued. "He's a solid old fellow." Settling in the chair by the bed, he stretched out his legs and crossed them.

"How are you?" Rhys asked, noticing that he was moving with uncharacteristic carefulness.

"Grateful to be alive." Devon looked more relaxed and content than Rhys had ever seen him. "Upon reflection, I realized that I can't expire for at least forty years: There's too much to do at Eversby Priory."

Rhys sighed, his thoughts returning to his department store. "I'll go mad here, Trenear. I have to return to London as soon as possible."

"Dr. Weeks said you could begin to walk on the cast, with the aid of crutches, in three weeks."

"I have to do it in two."

"I understand," Devon said.

"If you have no objections, I want to send for some of my staff, and have them visit for a day. I need to find out what's been happening in my absence."

"Of course. Tell me how I can help."

Rhys was grateful to Devon, to an extent he had never felt before. It wasn't a comfortable feeling: He didn't like being beholden to any man. "You've helped more than enough by saving my neck. Now I want to repay the favor."

"We'll call it even if you'll continue to advise me on the matter of leasing land to Severin's railway."

"I'll do more, if you'll let me look over the estate's finances and rental income calculations. English agriculture is a bad investment. You need revenue from sources other than farming."

"West is making changes that will increase the annual yields by at least half again."

"That's a good start. With skill and luck, you might eventually make the estate pay for itself. But you'll never make a profit. That will only come with ventures in something other than land, such as manufacturing or urban properties."

"Capital is a problem."

"It doesn't have to be."

Devon's gaze turned sharp with interest. Before he could explain further, however, Rhys happened to catch sight of a slim, dark shape walking past the doorway. It was only a fleeting glimpse . . . but it was enough to send a jolt of awareness through him.

"*You*," he said in a voice that carried out into the hallway. "Whoever just passed by the door. Come here."

In the riveting silence, a young woman appeared at the threshold. Her features were delicately angular, her silverblue eyes round and wide-set. As she stood at the edge of the lamplight, her fair skin and pale blond hair seemed to hold their own radiance, an effect he'd seen in paintings of Old Testament angels.

"There's a grain about it," Rhys's father had always said when he'd wanted to describe something fine and polished and perfect, something of the highest quality. Oh, there was a grain about this woman. She was only medium height, but her extreme slenderness gave her the illusion of being taller. Her breasts were high and gently rounded beneath the high-necked dress, and for a pleasurable, disorienting moment Rhys remembered resting his head there as she had given him sips of orchid tea.

"Say something," he commanded gruffly.

The shy glow of her smile gilded the air. "I'm glad to see you in better health, Mr. Winterborne."

Helen's voice.

She was more beautiful than starlight, and just as unattainable. As he stared at her, Rhys was bitterly reminded of the upper-class ladies who had looked at him with contempt when he was a shop boy, holding their skirts back if he passed near them on the street, the way they would seek to avoid a filthy stray dog.

"Is there something I can do for you?" she asked.

Rhys shook his head, still unable to take his gaze from her. "I only wanted a face to go with the voice."

"Perhaps later in the week," Devon suggested to Helen, "you might play the piano for Winterborne, when he's able to sit in the parlor."

She smiled. "Yes, if Mr. Winterborne wouldn't mind mediocre entertainment."

Devon glanced at Rhys. "Don't be deceived by the show of false modesty," he said. "Lady Helen is a fearsomely talented pianist."

"It's not false," Helen protested with a laugh. "In truth, I have little talent. It's only that I've spent so many hours practicing."

Rhys glanced at her pale hands, remembering the way she had smoothed salve over his lips with a light fingertip. It had been one of the most erotic moments of his life. For a man who had indulged his carnal appetites without restraint, that was saying something.

"Hard work often produces better results than talent," he said in response to her comment.

Helen blushed a little and lowered her gaze. "Good evening, then. I will leave you to your conversation."

Rhys didn't reply, only lifted his wineglass and drank deeply. But his gaze followed her every second until she left the room.

Devon leaned back and interlaced his fingers, resting them on his midriff. "Lady Helen is an accomplished young woman. She's been educated in history, literature, and art, and she's fluent in French. She also knows how to manage servants and run an upper-class household.

After the mourning period is over, I intend to take her to London, along with the twins, for her first season."

"No doubt she'll have many splendid offers," Rhys said bitterly.

Devon shook his head. "At best, she'll have a few adequate ones. None will be splendid, nor even appropriate for a girl of her quality." In response to Rhys's perplexed glance, he explained, "The late earl didn't provide for a dowry."

"A pity." If Devon were going to try to borrow money from him to improve Lady Helen's chances of marrying a peer, Rhys would tell him to sod off. "What has any of that to do with me?"

"Nothing, if she doesn't please you." Seeing Rhys's baffled expression, Devon shook his head with an exasperated laugh. "Confound it, Winterborne, don't be obtuse. I'm trying to point out an opportunity, if you have any interest in Lady Helen."

Rhys was silent. Stunned.

Devon chose his words with obvious care. "On the surface, it's not the most obvious match."

Match? *Marriage* match? The bastard clearly didn't understand what he was suggesting. Even so . . . Rhys felt his soul clutch at the idea.

"However," Devon continued, "there are advantages to both sides. Helen would gain a life of security and comfort. She would have her own household. For your part, you would have a well-bred wife whose pedigree would gain you entrance to many of the doors that are closed to you now." After a brief pause, he added casually, "As the daughter of an earl, she would keep her title, even after she became your wife. Lady Helen Winterborne."

Devon was wily enough to understand how the sound of that would affect him. Lady Helen Winterborne . . .

yes, Rhys bloody-fucking-well *loved* that. He had never dreamed of marrying a respectable woman, much less a daughter of the peerage.

But he wasn't fit for her. He was a Welshman with a rough accent and a foul mouth, and vulgar origins. A merchant. No matter how he dressed or improved his manners, his nature would always be coarse and competitive. People would whisper, seeing the two of them together . . . They would agree that marrying him had debased her. Helen would be the object of pity and perhaps contempt.

She would secretly hate him for it.

Rhys didn't give a damn.

He had no illusions of course, that Devon was offering him Lady Helen's hand without conditions. There would be a hefty price: The Ravenels' need for money was dire. But Helen was worth whatever he would have to pay. His fortune was even vaster than people suspected; he could have purchased a small country if he so desired.

"Have you discussed it with Lady Helen yet?" Rhys asked. "Is that why she played Florence Nightingale while I had fever? To soften me in preparation for bargaining?"

"Hardly," Devon said with a snort. "Helen is above that sort of manipulation. She helped you because she's naturally compassionate. No, she has no inkling that I've considered arranging a match for her."

Rhys decided to be blunt. "What makes you think she would be willing to marry the likes of me?"

Devon answered frankly. "She has few options at present. There is no occupation fit for a gentlewoman that would afford her a decent living, and she would never lower herself to harlotry. Furthermore, Helen's conscience won't allow her to be a burden on someone else, which means that she'll have to take a husband. Without a dowry, either she'll be forced to wed some feeble old dotard who

can't work up a cock-stand or someone's inbred fourth
son. Or . . . she'll have to marry out of her class." Devon
shrugged and smiled pleasantly. It was the smile of a man
who held a good hand of cards. "You're under no obligation, of course: I could always introduce her to Severin."

Rhys was too experienced a negotiator to show any reaction, even though a burst of outrage filled him at the
suggestion. Staying outwardly relaxed, he murmured,
"Perhaps you should. Severin would take her at once.
Whereas I would probably be better off marrying the kind
of woman I deserve." He paused, contemplating his wineglass, turning it so one last tiny red drop rolled across the
inside. "However," he said, "I always want better than I
deserve."

All his ambition and determination had converged into
a single desire . . . to marry Lady Helen Ravenel. She
would bear his children, handsome blue-blooded children. He would see that they were educated and raised in
luxury, and he would lay the world at their feet.

Someday, by God, people would *beg* to marry Winter-
bornes.

# Chapter 24

$\mathcal{A}$ WEEK AFTER THE RAILWAY ACCIDENT, Devon had still not healed sufficiently to go on his customary morning ride. He was accustomed to beginning each day with some form of physical exertion, and a simple walk wasn't enough. His temper grew short with the enforced inactivity, and to make things worse, he was as randy as a stoat, with no way to relieve either problem. He was still puzzled over Kathleen's refusal to even consider an affair with him. *You're dangerous to me . . .* The statement had baffled and infuriated him. He would never harm a hair on her head. How could she even think otherwise?

Her proper upbringing by Lady Berwick had given her an overactive conscience, he decided. Obviously she needed time to adjust to the idea that she was no longer bound by the same rules she had always followed so strictly.

For his part, Devon knew that he would have to earn her trust.

Or seduce her.

Whatever happened first.

He struck out for the countryside along a footpath that led through the wood and past the remains of a medieval barn. The day was damp, the air bitten with hoarfrost, but the brisk walk kept him pleasantly warm. Noticing a hen harrier flying low to the ground, he paused to watch it hunt. The bird seemed to drift as it searched for prey, its gray and white plumage ghostlike in the morning light. In the distance, a flock of bramblings in flight quivered against the sky.

Continuing on the footpath, Devon reflected that he'd become attached to the estate. The lifelong responsibility of preserving it, and restoring the house, no longer seemed like a punishment. It called to a deep ancestral instinct.

If only the past few generations of Ravenels hadn't been such shortsighted fools. At least two dozen rooms at Eversby Priory had become uninhabitable. Seeping water had assailed the walls with damp and rot, ruining plasterwork and interior furnishings. Restoration work had to be done soon, before the damage worsened beyond repair.

He needed money, a large sum, without delay. He would have loved to sell Ravenel House in London and immediately pour the profit into Eversby Priory, but that would be seen as a weakness by potential lenders or partners. Perhaps he could risk selling his land in Norfolk? That would attract far less notice. But the proceeds would be unimpressive . . . and he could already hear the howls of complaint from Kathleen and West if he decided to evict his Norfolk tenants.

A self-mocking smile curved his lips as he recalled that not too long ago, his problems had consisted of issues such as his cookmaid bringing weak tea, or his horse needing to be reshod.

Brooding, he headed back to Eversby Priory, its intricate roofline silhouetted against the December sky. As he gazed at the proliferation of openwork parapets, arcade arches, and slender chimneys topped with ornamental finials, he wondered grimly which parts of it were likely to fall to the ground first. He passed by outbuildings and neared the row of chalk paddocks behind the stables. A stable boy stood at the post and rail fencing of the largest enclosure, watching a small, slim rider put a horse through its paces.

Kathleen and Asad.

Devon's pulse quickened with interest. He went to join the boy at the fence, bracing his forearms on the top rail.

"Milord," the boy said, hastily grabbing the cap from his head to give him a respectful nod.

Devon nodded in return, watching intently as Kathleen rode the golden Arabian around the far side of the paddock.

She was dressed in a severely tailored riding jacket and a small hat with a narrow crown—and on her lower half, she wore trousers and ankle boots. Like the breeches he had seen her in before, the trousers had been designed to wear under a riding skirt, never by themselves. However, Devon had to admit that the somewhat outlandish ensemble gave Kathleen a freedom and athletic ease that heavy draped skirts would never have allowed.

She guided Asad into a series of half circles, her weight transferring fluidly with each turn, the inside hip pushing forward with a deep knee. Her form was so perfect and easy that the hairs on Devon's neck lifted as he watched. He'd never seen anyone, man or woman, who could ride with such economy of motion. The Arabian was acutely sensitive to the subtle pressures of her knees and thighs, following her guidance as if he could read her mind. They were a perfect pairing, both of them fine-boned, elegant, quick.

Noticing Devon's presence, Kathleen sent him a brilliant grin. Not above showing off, she urged the horse into a supple trot, the knees elevated, the hind legs flexed. After completing a serpentine pattern, Asad trotted in place before executing a perfect turn on his haunches, spinning in a circle to his right, and then a full spin to his left, his golden tail swishing dramatically.

The damned horse was dancing.

Devon shook his head slightly, watching them in wonder. After taking the horse around the paddock in a rolling, gliding canter, Kathleen slowed him to a trot and then walked him up to the fence. Asad gave a welcoming nicker as he recognized Devon, and nudged his muzzle between the rails.

"Well done," Devon said, stroking the horse's golden hide. He glanced up at Kathleen. "You ride beautifully. Like a goddess."

"Asad would make anyone look accomplished."

He held her gaze. "No one but you could ride him as if he had wings."

Turning pink, Kathleen glanced at the stable boy. "Freddie, will you walk Asad on the lead and then take him to the turn out paddock?"

"Yes, milady!" The boy slipped between the rails, while Kathleen dismounted in an easy motion.

"I would have helped you down," Devon said.

Kathleen climbed through the fence. "I don't need help," she told him with a touch of smugness that he found adorable.

"Are you going into the house now?" he asked.

"Yes, but first I'll collect my overskirt in the saddle room."

Devon walked with her, stealing a surreptitious glance at her backside and hips. The clear outline of firm, feminine curves caused his pulse to quicken. "I seem to recall a rule regarding breeches," he said.

"They're not breeches, they're trousers."

He arched one brow. "So you think you're justified in

breaking the spirit of the law as long as you keep to the letter?"

"Yes. Besides, you have no right to make rules about my attire in the first place."

Devon fought back a grin. If her impudence was intended to discourage him, it had the opposite effect. He was a man, after all, and a Ravenel to boot.

"Nevertheless," he said, "there will be consequences."

Kathleen shot him an uncertain glance.

He kept his expression impassive as they headed through the stables to the saddle room.

"There's no need for you to accompany me," Kathleen said, her pace quickening. "I'm sure you have much to do."

"Nothing as important as this."

"As what?" she asked warily.

"Finding out the answer to one question."

Kathleen stopped near the wall of saddle racks, squared her shoulders, and turned to face him resolutely. "Which is?" She tugged meticulously at the fingers of her riding gloves and pulled them from her hands.

Devon loved her willingness to stand up to him, even though she was half his size. Slowly he reached out and removed her hat, tossing it to the corner. Some of the defiant tension left her slight frame as she realized that he was playing with her. She looked very young with her cheeks flushed and her hair a bit mussed from the ride.

He moved forward, crowding her back against the wall between two rows of empty racks, effectively pinning her into the small space. Gripping the narrow lapels of her riding jacket, he lowered his mouth to her ear and asked softly, "What do ladies wear beneath their riding trousers?"

A breathless laugh escaped her. The gloves dropped to the floor. "I would think an infamous rake would already know."

"I was never infamous. In fact, I'm fairly standard as far as rakes go."

"The ones who deny it are the worst." She strained as he began to kiss along the side of her neck. Her skin was hot from exertion, a little salty, and her scent was divinely arousing: horses, fresh winter air, roses. "I'm sure you caused no end of mayhem in London, with all your drinking, gambling, carousing, chasing lightskirts . . ."

"Moderate drinking," he said in a muffled voice. "Very little gambling. I'll admit to the carousing."

"And the lightskirts?"

"None." At her skeptical snort, Devon lifted his head. "None since I met you."

Kathleen drew back, her perplexed gaze lifting to his. "There haven't been women since . . ."

"No. How could I take someone else to bed? In the morning I would wake up still wanting you." He moved closer, his large feet bracketing her small ones. "You haven't answered my question."

She shrank from him until her head pressed against the wood-planked wall. "You know I can't."

"Then I'll have to find out for myself." His arms slid around her, one hand traveling beneath the hem of her riding jacket to the small of her back. His fingertips drew across the ribbed surface of her riding corset, shorter and lighter than the usual ones. Exploring beneath the waist of her trousers, he encountered thin, silky fabric where he would have expected linen or cotton. Fascinated, he used one hand to unfasten the row of buttons at the front of her trousers, while the other eased into the back. "Are these drawers? What are they made of?"

She began to push at him, but remembering his injury, she stopped. Her hands were suspended in midair as

Devon pulled her hips against his. Feeling how hard he was, Kathleen drew in a quick breath.

"*Someone will see*," she hissed.

He was far too occupied with her drawers to care. "Silk," he said, his hand wandering deeper inside the trousers.

"Yes, so they don't bunch up beneath the . . . Oh, do stop . . ."

The legs of the undergarment were hemmed so that they only just covered the tops of her thighs. As Devon continued to explore, he discovered that there was no split-seam opening in her drawers. "They're sewn shut."

A nervous giggle broke through Kathleen's indignation as she saw his genuinely perplexed expression. "One wouldn't want an opening there while riding." She shivered as one of his hands slid down her front to caress her over the silk.

He traced the delicate swells of feminine flesh, the heat of her radiating through the fabric. His fingertips played over her, tickling and soothing, and he felt a change in her body, the way she began to soften against him. Returning his mouth to her neck, he kissed the smooth curve down to the collar of her jacket. Very gently he used his knuckle to stroke into the furrow between her thighs, the knobbiness drawing a moan from her.

She began to say something on a desperate breath, but he took the words into his mouth, kissing her with avid hunger. Her hands fluttered to his shoulders, and she clung to him with an agitated sound. Her reluctance was collapsing, melting deliciously, and he didn't allow her one second of respite, only kissed and stroked until a little seep of dampness came through the silk.

Kathleen struggled until he let go of her and stepped back. Holding the front of her trousers closed, she went to snatch her overskirt from the hook on the wall. She grappled with the heavy mass of fabric, unable to find the fastenings.

"Would you like me to—" Devon began.

"*No*." Huffing with frustration, she gave up and bundled the skirts in her arms.

Instinctively Devon reached out for her. She hopped back with an anxious froth of laughter.

The sound aroused him unbearably, heat bolting from nerve to nerve.

"Kathleen." He made no attempt to hide the lust in his gaze. "If you hold still, I'll help you with your skirt. But if you run from me, you're going to be caught." He took an unsteady breath before adding softly, "And I'll make you come for me again."

Her eyes turned huge.

He took a deliberate step forward. She bolted across the nearest threshold and fled to the carriage room. Devon was at her heels instantly, following her past the workshop with its long carpenter's benches and tool cupboards. The carriage room smelled pleasantly of sawdust, axle grease, lacquer varnish, and leather polish. It was quiet and shadowy, illuminated only by a row of skylights over massive hinge-strapped doors that could be opened onto the estate's carriage drive.

Kathleen darted through rows of vehicles used for different purposes; carts, wagons, a light brougham, a landau with a folding top, a phaeton, a hooded barouche for summer. Devon circled around and intercepted her beside the family coach, a huge, stately carriage that could only be pulled by six horses. It had been designed as a symbol of power and prestige, with the Ravenel family crest—a trio of black ravens on a white and gold shield—painted on the sides.

Halting abruptly, Kathleen stared at him through the semidarkness.

Taking the overskirt from her, Devon dropped it to the floor, and pinned her against the side of the carriage.

"My riding skirt," she exclaimed in dismay. "You'll ruin it."

Devon laughed. "You were never going to wear it anyway." He began to unbutton her riding jacket, while she sputtered helplessly.

Quieting her with his mouth, he worked on the row of buttons. After the sides of the jacket had listed open, he took the back of her head in his hand and kissed her more deeply, ravishing her mouth, and she responded as if she couldn't help herself. A shock of pleasure went through him as he felt her suck on his tongue with a shy little tug, and he reached out to fumble for the ring-shaped handle of the carriage door.

Realizing what he intended, Kathleen said dazedly, "You can't."

Devon was more aroused and entertained than he'd ever been in his life. After tugging the door open, he pulled down the folding step. "Here's your choice: Out here, in full view of anyone who passes by . . . or in the carriage, where no one will see."

She blinked and stared at him, seeming aghast. But there was no concealing the deep flush of excitement on her face.

"Out here, then," he said ruthlessly, and reached for the waist of her trousers.

Galvanized into action, Kathleen turned with a whimper and climbed into the carriage.

Devon followed instantly.

The interior of the carriage was luxuriously upholstered in leather and velvet, with lacquered wood inlays, compartments for crystal glasses and wine, and silk-fringed damask curtains framing the windows. At first it was too dark to see, but as Devon's vision adjusted, he could make out the pale gleam of Kathleen's skin.

She moved uncertainly, sliding her arms from the riding jacket as he tugged it from her. He reached around her to unfasten the buttons at the back of her blouse, and felt her trembling. Catching the rim of her ear with his teeth, he nipped softly and soothed the little spot with the tip of his tongue.

"I'll stop if you tell me to," he whispered. "Until then, we'll play by my rules." He moved to strip off his coat with a grimace of effort. He pressed a smile against her head as he felt her hands go to the knot of his necktie.

With each item of clothing that was removed . . . waist-coat . . . braces . . . shirt . . . he began to seriously question how much self-control he would be able to maintain. As he eased Kathleen against his naked chest, she slid her arms around him, her palms coming to rest on the backs of his shoulders. Groaning, he kissed his way down to the upper curves of her breasts, where the corset had plumped them high. He longed to unhook her corset, but there was no way he would be able to refasten it in the darkness.

Searching beneath the loosened waist of her trousers, he found the drawstring of the silk drawers, and untied it with a deft tug. Kathleen stiffened, but she didn't pro-test as he eased the garments down past her hips, and lower still, with hands that weren't quite steady. His heart pounded in a rough staccato, every muscle knotted with craving. Kneeling on the carpeted floor, he ran his palms over the smooth curves of her bare hips and along the length of her thighs. The riding trousers had caught on her short boots, bunching at her ankles. Thanks to the gussets on the sides, and the leather tabs at the backs, the boots were easily removed. After divesting her of the trousers, Devon drew a single fingertip along the line of her clenched thighs.

"Open for me," he whispered.

She didn't.

Sympathetic and tenderly amused, Devon caressed her legs with patient hands. "Don't be shy. There's no part of you that isn't beautiful." His hand moved to the top of her thighs, his thumb sliding into the delicate fleece of curls. "Let me kiss you here," he coaxed. "Just once."

"Oh, God . . . no." She reached down and weakly pushed his hand away. "It's a sin."

"How do you know?"

"Because it feels like one," she managed to say.

He laughed quietly and pulled her hips farther toward him with a decisiveness that drew a little yelp from her. "In that case . . . I never sin by half measures."

*Chapter 25*

"WE'RE BOTH GOING TO HELL," Kathleen said as he kissed along the seam of her clenched thighs.

"I've always assumed I would." Devon didn't sound at all troubled by the prospect.

She squirmed in violated modesty, wondering wildly how she had come to find herself half naked in a carriage with him. The air was cold, the velvet upholstery chilled beneath her bare bottom, and his warm hands and mouth raised gooseflesh all over her body.

His hands gripped her legs, not forcing them apart, only squeezing the locked muscles, and it felt so deliriously good that she moaned in despair. His thumbs worked into the top of the soft triangle, kneading gently. A quivery pleasure awakened at the pit of her stomach, and she let him tease her legs apart. She was lost, unable to think, all her senses focused on the kisses that pressed along her inner thigh, straying where the skin was thin and sensitive. Her knees jerked as he reached the tender seam of closed lips and licked upward, parting them with his tongue. He stopped just before he reached the soft bud at the top. Panting, she reached for his head and slid her fingers into his hair, uncertain whether she wanted to push him away or pull him closer. He nibbled the edge of an outer fold, his breath hot and tickling. He searched slowly, never quite reaching the place that ached the most.

A devil whisper sifted through the darkness. "Do you want me to kiss you?"

"No." A half second after that, she took a sobbing breath and said, "Yes."

A quiet laugh vibrated against her wet flesh, and she nearly swooned at the feel of it. "Which is it?" he asked. "Yes or no?"

"Yes. Yes."

It was not pleasant to discover that one's moral resolve had all the strength of wet cardboard.

"Show me where," he murmured.

Breathing hard with excited misery, she made herself do it, reaching down to expose the tiny peak. His mouth covered her slowly, tenderly, the flat of his tongue resting against the intimate throb. Her hands fell away and groped for the velvet cushions beneath her, fingertips digging tightly. His tongue slid over her. Once. Trembling and half fainting, she let out a plangent moan.

Another languid stroke, finishing with a flick. "Tell me you need me." His breath tickled her softness as he waited.

"I need you," she gasped.

He used his tongue in a wickedly teasing circle. "Now say that you're mine."

She would have said almost anything, the desire was so consuming. But she'd heard a subtle change in his tone, a note of possessiveness that warned he was no longer playing.

When she didn't reply, he insinuated a finger into the entrance of her body . . . no, two . . . nudging past sensitive tucks and pleats of flesh. The sense of fullness was uncomfortable but exquisite. She could feel her inner muscles pulsing, striving to pull his fingers even deeper. As he searched, he touched something inside her, some acutely tender place that made her knees draw up and her toes curl.

His voice lowered . . . darkened. "Say it."

"I'm yours," she said brokenly.

He made a sound of satisfaction, almost a purr.

Her hips arched, begging him to touch that soft inner spot again, and she jerked as he found it. All her limbs went weak. "*Oh.* Yes, there, there . . ." Her voice dissolved as she felt his lips open over her, sucking, teasing. He rewarded her with a steady rhythm, his free hand sliding beneath her writhing bottom, guiding her, rocking her more firmly up against his mouth. With every ascent of her hips, he licked upward, the tip of his tongue catching wetly just beneath the little pearl of her sex, again and again. She heard herself breathing in sobs and moaning out words, and there was no controlling anything now, no thought or will, only a terrible need that raced higher and higher, until the wrenching spasms began. With a low cry, she jerked against him, her thighs clamping uncontrollably on his shoulders.

After the last long, helpless shudders had faded, Kathleen fell back on the velvet cushions like a rag doll that someone had tossed aside. Devon kept his mouth on her, easing the pleasure into relaxation. She summoned just enough strength to reach out and caress his hair.

*That might have been worth going to hell for,* she thought, and didn't realize she had mumbled it aloud until she felt him smile.

A FEW GUTTURAL words caused Helen's steps to slow as she neared the upstairs parlor. The sounds of Welsh curses had become quite familiar during the past week, as Mr. Winterborne grappled with the limitations of his injuries and the heavy leg cast. Although he never shouted, something about his voice carried farther than the average man's: It had a deep timbre like bronze bell metal. His accent fell pleasantly on her ears, with singsong vowels and tapped R's that carried the hint of a burr, and consonants as soft as velvet.

Winterborne's presence seemed to fill the household, no matter that he was still confined to the upstairs rooms. He was a vigorous man, easily bored, chafing at any restrictions. He craved activity and noise, having even gone so far as to insist that the carpenters and plumbers resume their daily cacophony of work, despite the fact that Devon had told them to stop while Winterborne recovered. Apparently the last thing Winterborne wanted was peace and quiet.

So far he had kept her father's old valet running on constant errands, which would have been a cause for concern, except that Quincy seemed to be thriving in his new position as Winterborne's manservant. A few days ago, Quincy had told the news to Helen as he had been on his way to the village with some telegraph dispatches from Winterborne.

"I'm so very pleased for you," Helen had exclaimed, after the initial surprise had worn off. "Although I confess, I can't imagine Eversby Priory without you here."

"Yes, my lady." The elderly man had regarded her warmly, his gaze conveying an affection that he would never express in words. He was a disciplined and buttoned-up man, but he had always treated Helen and the twins with unfailing kindness, interrupting his work to help search for a lost doll, or to wrap his own handkerchief around a scraped elbow. Deep down, Helen had always known that of the three sisters, she was Quincy's favorite, perhaps because their natures were somewhat similar. They both liked everything to be peaceful and quiet and in its place.

Helen's unspoken bond with Quincy had been cemented by the shared experience of taking care of her father in his last days, after he had fallen ill from a long day of hunting in the cold and wet. Although Sims and Mrs. Church had done what they could to ease the earl's suffering, it had been Helen and Quincy who had taken turns sitting at his bedside. There had been no one else: The twins hadn't been allowed into his room for fear that the earl's illness was catching, and Theo hadn't come from London in time to say good-bye.

Upon learning that Quincy was leaving Eversby Priory, Helen had tried to be happy for him, rather than selfishly wish for him to stay. "Will you like living in London, Quincy?"

"I expect so, my lady. I will view it as an adventure. Perhaps it will be just the thing to blow the cobwebs out."

She had given him a tremulous smile. "I will miss you, Quincy."

The valet had remained composed, but his eyes had turned suspiciously bright. "When you visit London, my lady, I trust you will remember that I'm always at your service. You have only to send for me."

"I'm glad that you're going to take care of Mr. Winterborne. He needs you."

"Yes," Quincy had said feelingly. "He does."

It would take some time, Helen thought, for Quincy to become familiar with his new employer's habits, preferences, and quirks. Fortunately Quincy had spent decades in the practice of managing volatile temperaments. Winterborne certainly couldn't be any worse than the Ravenels.

During the past two days, a group of Winterborne's employees, including store managers, an accountant, and a pressman, had visited from London. They had spent hours with Winterborne in the family parlor, delivering reports and receiving instructions. Although Dr. Weeks had warned that too much exertion might hinder the healing process, Winterborne seemed to have drawn energy from the interaction with his employees.

"That store is more than a mere business to him," West had told Helen, while Winterborne had been upstairs talking with his managers. "It's who he is. It consumes all his time and interest."

"But what does he do it for?" Helen had asked, perplexed. "Usually a man desires an income so that he can pursue more important things . . . time with family and friends . . . developing his talents, his inner life . . ."

"Winterborne has no inner life," West had replied dryly. "He would probably resent any suggestion that he did."

The employees had left this morning, and Winterborne had spent most of the day either in the parlor or in his bedroom, stubbornly maneuvering on his crutches without assistance, despite the doctor's instructions not to set weight on his injured leg.

Looking around the doorjamb, Helen saw Winterborne sitting alone in the parlor, in a chair beside a walnut marble-topped table. He had accidentally knocked a stack of papers from the table, and they had settled on the floor around him. Leaning over awkwardly, he tried to retrieve the fallen pages without toppling from the chair.

Concern overcame Helen's shyness, and she went into the room without a second thought. "Good afternoon, Mr. Winterborne." She sank to her knees and gathered up the papers.

"Don't trouble yourself with that," she heard Winterborne say gruffly.

"No trouble at all." Still kneeling, she looked up at him uncertainly. Her heart skipped a beat, and another, as she stared into the darkest eyes she had ever seen, a brown so deep it looked black, shadowed by thick lashes and set deep in a complexion of rich umber. His brutal handsomeness unnerved her. He could have been Lucifer himself, sitting there. He was much larger than she'd realized; even the cast on his leg didn't help to make him seem less formidable.

She handed the papers to him, and their fingers touched briefly. Startled by a shock of awareness, she pulled back quickly. His mouth turned grim, his thick brows drawing together.

Helen rose to her feet. "Is there something I can do to make you more comfortable? Shall I send for tea or refreshments?"

He shook his head. "Quincy will bring a tray soon."

She wasn't certain how to reply. It had been easier to talk to him when he had been ill and helpless.

"Mr. Quincy told me that he will be working for you in London. I am glad, for both your sakes, that you've given him such an opportunity. He will be an excellent valet."

"For what I'm paying him," Winterborne said, "he'd better be the best in England."

Helen was briefly nonplussed. "I have no doubt he will be," she ventured.

Meticulously Winterborne neatened the stack of paper. "He wants to start by disposing of my shirts."

"Your shirts," Helen repeated, perplexed.

"One of my managers brought some of my clothes from London. Quincy could tell that the shirts were ready-made." He glanced at her warily, assessing her reaction. "To be accurate," he continued, "they're sold half finished, so they can be tailored to the customer's preference. The quality of the fabric is as high as any bespoke shirt, but Quincy still turns up his nose."

Helen considered her reply carefully. "A man of Quincy's profession has an exacting eye when it comes to details." She probably should have left it at that. The discussion of a man's clothing was entirely improper, but she felt that she should help him to understand Quincy's concerns. "It's more than just the fabric. The stitching is different in a bespoke shirt: The seams are perfectly straight and flat-felled, and the buttonholes are often hand-worked with a keyhole shape at one side to reduce the stress of the button's shank." She paused with a smile. "I would elaborate about plackets and cuffs, but I fear you would fall asleep in the chair."

"I know the value of details. But where shirts are concerned . . ." He hesitated. "I've made a point of wearing the kind that I sell, so that customers know they have the same quality as the store's owner."

"That sounds like a clever sales strategy."

"It is. I sell more shirts than any other store in London. But it didn't occur to me that the upper class pays close attention to buttonholes."

It had chafed his pride, she thought, to realize that he had put himself at a disadvantage when mingling with social superiors.

"I'm sure they shouldn't," Helen said apologetically. "There are far more important things for them to worry about."

His gaze turned quizzical. "You speak as if you're not one of them."

She smiled slightly. "I've lived away from the world for so much of my life, Mr. Winterborne, that I sometimes wonder who I am, or if I belong anywhere."

Winterborne studied her. "Trenear plans to take you and your sisters to London when you've finished mourning."

Helen nodded. "I haven't been to town since I was a child. I remember it as a very large and exciting place."

She paused, vaguely surprised that she was confiding in him. "Now I think I might find it . . . intimidating."

A smile tugged at the corners of his mouth. "What happens when you're intimidated? Run to the nearest corner and hide, do you?"

"I should say not," she said primly, wondering if she were being teased. "I do what has to be done, no matter what the situation."

Winterborne's smile widened until she saw the flash of white teeth against that deep bronze complexion. "I suppose I know that better than most," he said softly.

Understanding that he was referring to how she had helped him through the fever . . . and remembering how she had held that black head in the crook of her arm, and bathed his face and neck . . . Helen felt a blush start. Not the ordinary kind of blush that faded soon after it started. This one kept heating and heating, spreading all through her until she was so uncomfortable that she could scarcely breathe. She made the mistake of glancing into his simmering coffee-black eyes, and she felt positively immolated.

Her desperate gaze settled upon the battered pianoforte in the corner. "Shall I play something for you?" She stood without waiting for a reply. It was the only alternative to bolting from the room. Out of the periphery of her vision, she saw Winterborne automatically grip the arms of his chair in preparation to rise, before he remembered that he was in a leg cast.

"Yes," she heard him say. "I'd like that." He maneuvered the chair a few inches so that he could see her profile as she played.

The pianoforte seemed to offer a small measure of protection as she sat at the keyboard and pushed up the hinged fallboard that covered the keys. Taking a slow, calming breath, Helen arranged her skirts, adjusted her posture, and placed her fingertips on the keys. She launched into a piece she knew by memory: the allegro from Handel's Piano Suite in F Major. It was full of life and complexity, and challenging enough to force her to think about something besides blushing. Her fingers danced in a blur over the keys, the exuberant pace unfaltering for two and a half minutes. When she finished, she looked at Winterborne, hoping he had liked it.

"You play with great skill," he said.

"Thank you."

"Is that your favorite piece?"

"It's my most difficult," Helen said, "but not my favorite."

"What do you play when there's no one to hear?"

The gentle question, spoken in that accent with vowels as broad as his shoulders, caused Helen's stomach to tighten pleasurably. Perturbed by the sensation, she was slow to reply. "I don't remember the name of it. A piano tutor taught it to me long ago. For years I've tried to find out what it is, but no one has ever recognized the melody."

"Play it for me."

Calling it up from memory, she played the sweetly haunting chords, her hands gentle on the keys. The mournful chords never failed to stir her, making her heart ache for things she couldn't name. At the conclusion, Helen looked up from the keys and found Winterborne staring at her as if transfixed. He masked his expression, but not before she saw a mixture of puzzlement, fascination, and a hint of something hot and unsettling.

"It's Welsh," he said.

Helen shook her head with a laugh of wondering disbelief. "You know it?"

" 'A Ei Di'r Deryn Du.' Every Welshman is born knowing it."

"What is it about?"

"A lover who asks a blackbird to carry a message to his sweetheart."

"Why can't he go to her himself?" Helen realized they were both speaking in hushed tones, as if they were exchanging secrets.

"He can't find her. He's too deep in love—it keeps him from seeing clearly."

"Does the blackbird find her?"

"The song doesn't say," he said with a shrug.

"But I must know the ending to the story," Helen protested.

Winterborne laughed. It was an irresistible sound, rough-soft and sly. When he replied, his accent had thickened. "That's what comes o' reading novels, it is. The story needs no ending. That's not what matters."

"What matters, then?" she dared to ask.

His dark gaze held hers. "That he loves. That he's searching. Like the rest of us poor devils, he has no way of knowing if he'll ever have his heart's desire."

*And you?* Helen longed to ask. *What are you searching for?* The question was too personal to ask even of someone she had known for a long time, much less a stranger. Even so, the words hovered on her tongue, begging to be spoken. She looked away and fought to hold them back. When she returned her gaze to Winterborne, his expression had become remote again. Which was a relief, because for a moment she'd had the alarming feeling that she was only a breath away from confiding every private thought and wish that she'd never told anyone.

To Helen's great relief, Quincy arrived with the dinner tray. The valet's white brows lifted fractionally as he saw her alone in the room with Winterborne, but he said nothing. As Quincy proceeded to arrange the flatware, glasses, and plate on the table, Helen regained her composure. She stood from the upholstered bench and gave Winterborne a neutral smile. "I will leave you to enjoy your dinner."

His gaze swept over her, lingering at her face. "You'll play for me again one evening?"

"Yes, if you like." She left the parlor gratefully, steeling herself not to break into a run.

RHYS STARED AFTER HELEN, while his brain sorted through every detail of the past few minutes. It was fairly clear that she had a disgust of him: She had recoiled from his touch, and she had trouble meeting his gaze. She had abruptly changed the conversation when it had strayed toward the personal.

Perhaps his looks weren't to her taste. No doubt his accent was off-putting. And like the other sheltered young women of her class, she probably thought of the Welsh as third-rate barbarians. Helen knew that she was too fine for the likes of him—God knew Rhys wouldn't argue.

But he was going to have her anyway.

"What is your opinion of Lady Helen?" he asked as Quincy arranged the meal on the table in front of him.

"She is the jewel of the Ravenels," Quincy said. "A more kind-hearted girl you'll never meet. Sadly, she's always been overlooked. Her older brother received the lion's share of her parents' interest, and what little was left went to the twins."

Rhys had met the twins a few days earlier, both of them bright-eyed and amusing, asking a score of questions about his department store. He had liked the girls well enough, but neither of them had captured his interest. They were nothing close to Helen, whose reserve was mysterious and alluring. She was like a mother-of-pearl shell that appeared to be one color, but from different angles revealed delicate shimmers of lavender, pink, blue, green. A beautiful exterior that revealed little of its true nature.

"Is she aloof with all strangers?" he asked, arranging a napkin on his lap. "Or is it only with me?"

"Aloof?" The valet sounded genuinely surprised. Before he could continue, a pair of small black spaniels entered the parlor, panting happily as they bounded up to Rhys. "Good heavens," he muttered with a frown.

Rhys, who happened to like dogs, didn't mind the interruption. What he found disconcerting, however, was the third animal that trotted into the room after them and sat assertively by his chair.

"Quincy," Rhys asked blankly, "why is there a pig in the parlor?"

The valet, who was busy shooing the dogs from the room, said distractedly, "A family pet, sir. They try to keep him in the barn, but he will insist on coming into the house."

"But why—" Rhys broke off, realizing that regardless of the explanation, it would make no sense to him. "Why is it," he asked instead, "that if I kept livestock in my home, people would say I was ignorant or daft, but if a pig wanders freely in the mansion of an earl, it's called eccentric?"

"There are three things that everyone expects of an aristocrat," the valet replied, tugging firmly at the pig's collar. "A country house, and a weak chin, and eccentricity." He pushed and pulled at the pig with increasing determination, but the creature only sat more heavily. "I vow," the valet wheezed, budging him only an inch at a time, "I'll have you turned into sausage and collops by tomorrow's breakfast!"

Ignoring the determined valet, the pig stared up at Rhys with patient, hopeful eyes.

"Quincy," Rhys said, "look sharp." He picked up a bread roll from his plate and tossed it casually in the air.

The valet caught it deftly in a white-gloved hand. "Thank you, sir." As he walked to the door with the bread in hand, the pig trotted after him.

Rhys watched with a faint smile. "Desire," he said, "is always better motivation than fear. Remember that, Quincy."

# Chapter 26

*THEO! THEO, DON'T!*

The nightmare was as vivid and intolerable as ever, the ground shifting so that every step landed askew as she ran toward the stables. She could hear Asad's maddened whinnying in the distance. A pair of stablemen held on to the horse's bridle, forcing him to stay still while her husband's dominating figure swung up onto his back. The morning light fell with bright menace onto Asad's golden form as his hooves churned and stomped.

Her heart thudded as she saw that her husband was holding a whip. Asad would die rather than submit to it. *Stop!* she cried, but the stablemen had released the bridle, and the horse had leaped forward. Wall-eyed and panicked, Asad reared, plunged, swelling his body to break his girth. Theo's whip arm lifted and descended, again and again.

The Arabian twisted and bucked, and Theo was flung from the saddle. His body snapped like a length of toweling before hitting the ground with sickening force.

Kathleen staggered the last few yards before she reached his still form, already knowing it was too late. Falling to her knees, she stared into the face of her dying husband.

But it wasn't Theo.

A scream scalded her throat.

Kathleen awakened from the dream and fought to sit up amid the tangle of sheets. Her breath came in hard, corroded bursts. Unsteadily she wiped her wet face with a clutch of the counterpane, and rested her head on her bent knees.

"It wasn't real," she whispered to herself, waiting for the terror to die down. She eased back to the mattress, but the knotted muscles in her back and legs wouldn't allow her to lie flat.

Sniffling, she rolled to her side and sat up again. She let one leg slip over the edge of the mattress, and then the other. *Stay in bed*, she told herself, but her feet were already lowering. The moment they touched the floor, there was no turning back.

Swiftly she left her room and rushed through the darkness, with ghosts and memories at her heels.

She didn't stop until she had reached the master bedroom.

Even as her knuckles rapped against the door, she regretted the impulse that had driven her there, and yet she couldn't seem to make herself stop knocking until the door opened abruptly.

She couldn't see Devon's face, only his huge, dark shape, but she could hear the familiar baritone of his voice.

"What's wrong?" He pulled her inside the room and closed the door. "What happened?"

His arms closed around her trembling body. As she pressed against him, she realized that he was naked except for the binding around his midriff. But he was so hard and warm and comforting that she couldn't make herself pull away.

"I had a nightmare," she whispered, resting her cheek against the silky-coarse hair on his chest.

She heard a soothing, indistinguishable murmur over her head.

"I shouldn't have bothered you," she faltered. "I'm sorry. But it was so real."

"What did you dream about?" he asked gently, smoothing her hair.

"The morning Theo died. I've had the same nightmare so many times. But tonight was different. I ran to him—he was on the ground—and when I looked down at his face, it wasn't him, it was—it was—" She stopped with a sound of grief, closing her eyes more tightly.

"Me?" Devon asked calmly, his hand shaping around the back of her head.

Kathleen nodded with a hiccupping breath. "H-how did you know?"

"Dreams have a way of tangling memories and worries together." His lips brushed her forehead. "After all that's happened recently, it's not surprising that your mind would make connections to your late husband's accident. But it wasn't real." Tilting her head back, he kissed her wet lashes. "I'm here. And nothing's going to happen to me."

She let out a wobbly sigh.

Devon continued to hold her until he felt her shaking ease. "Do you want me to take you back to your room?" he eventually asked.

A long moment passed before Kathleen could respond. The right answer was yes, but the truthful one was no. Damning herself, she settled for a tiny shake of her head.

Devon went still. He took a deep breath and released it slowly. Keeping one arm around her, he guided her to his bed.

Riddled with guilt and pleasure, Kathleen climbed onto the mattress and slid beneath the warm weight of the covers.

Devon lingered at the bedside. A match flared, the brief blue sizzle followed by the glow of candle flame.

She tensed as Devon joined her beneath the covers. There was no doubt where this would lead: One did not share a bed with a naked adult in his robust masculine prime and expect to leave it a virgin. But she also knew where it would *not* lead. She had seen Devon's face on Christmas Eve as she had held the tenant's infant daughter. His expression had frozen for a brief, brutal instant of dread.

If she chose to let this go any farther, she would have to accept that whatever his plans were for the estate, they did not include marrying and siring children.

"This isn't an affair," she said, more to herself than to him. "It's only one night."

Devon lay on his side, a lock of hair falling over his forehead as he looked down at her. "What if you want more than that?" he asked huskily.

"It still won't be an affair."

His hand caressed her over the covers, charting the shape of her hips and stomach. "Why does the word matter?"

"Because affairs always end. So calling it that would make it more difficult when one of us wants to leave."

Devon's hand stilled. He looked down at her, his blue eyes as dark as pitch. Candlelight flickered over the hard, high planes of his cheeks. "I'm not going anywhere." He took her jaw in his hand, his mouth covering hers in a strong, urgent kiss—a kiss of ownership. She opened to him, letting him do as he wished, while he searched her with aggressive ardor.

Pulling the covers away from her body, he bent over her chest. His breath was like steam as it penetrated the thin cambric of her nightgown, causing her nipple to rise. He touched the aching point with his fingers, shaping the tightening flesh before he covered it with his mouth and licked through the fabric. The cambric turned wet beneath his tongue, cooling against the tight bud as he drew back and blew gently.

Moaning, she reached for the placket of tiny buttons that held her bodice together, trying to open them with frantic tugs.

Devon took her wrists and pinned them at her side, easily holding her captive as he continued to suck and nibble over the gown. His body settled between her spread thighs, the weight of him hard and stimulating. As she wriggled and strained against his hold, she felt his shaft swelling tighter against her, the luscious friction making them both breathless.

Releasing her wrists, Devon turned his attention to the line of buttons at her bodice and began to unfasten them with meticulous care. The hem of her nightgown had ridden up to her hips. She could feel the taut, intimate heat of his shaft brushing her inner thigh.

By the time the last button was freed, Kathleen was weak and gasping.

Finally Devon pulled the garment over her head and tossed it aside. Kneeling with his folded legs spread beneath her thighs, he stared intently at her flame-gilded body. Modesty burned through her as she realized it was the first time he'd seen her completely naked. Her hands moved reflexively to cover herself. He caught them and held them wide.

God, the way he stared at her, harsh and tender, his gaze devouring.

"You're the most beautiful thing I've ever seen." His voice was slightly hoarse. Letting go of her hands, he reached down to touch her with spread fingertips that slid over her stomach in burning trails, down to the feathery triangle between her legs. A silent moan stuck in her throat as he played with her, combing through wispy curls, delving to the private skin beneath.

Her hands fisted and fell to her sides. The rhythm of his breathing had roughened with lust, but his hands stayed gentle, teasing softly furled edges of pink and white, kneading with his thumbs, stroking her open. The sensations slid all through her, until she couldn't keep from writhing and twisting helplessly upward.

Flattening a palm on her stomach, he murmured, "Settle." His fingertips slid between her thighs, stroking just above the peak of her sex, awakening delicate throbs of heat. She shivered, her legs closing on either side of his hips.

His thumb swirled at the entrance of her body, gathering wetness before returning to the swelling peak.

It was utterly wicked, the things he knew.

Closing her eyes, she turned her blazing face away while he toyed and teased, eliciting more wetness and fullness until her sex was achingly sensitive. She felt his thumb slide down again, circling and stroking . . . pressing inside her. It stung as he nudged deeper into the tight-rimmed tenderness. But he was exquisitely gentle, his fingers splaying over the mound and massaging in a deliberate rhythm. She gasped at the sensation, pleasure turning her insides molten, her buttocks tensing and relaxing in shameless craving, her insides molten with pleasure.

His hand pulled away, and she whimpered in protest. The dark shape of his head and broad shoulders loomed over her as he gripped her knees and pushed them apart. Her hips rolled upward until her sex was brazenly displayed. She heard herself groan as he bent over her, his tongue dragging moistly along the soft slit. Reaching the peak of her sex, he suckled and stroked without mercy, sending bliss racing through every nerve, driving her relentlessly until release broke and flooded her.

As the climax eased into quicksilver splashes, she felt Devon lowering her hips to the mattress. He kissed her mouth, his tongue salted with a subtle erotic savor. She let her hands wander down to the tough-banded muscle of his stomach, hesitantly touching the stiff length of his erection. It was harder than she had thought human flesh could be, the skin silkier than silk. To her surprise, a distinct pulse beat strongly against her fingers.

With a low sound, Devon settled more heavily between her legs, pushing them wider.

Awkwardly she guided him into place. He pressed until her body began to yield, persisting even as she shrank away from the sharpening ache. He pushed inside the soft, clenching tightness until she gave a faint openmouthed cry, going rigid at the burn of it.

Devon held still, muttering endearments and reassurances. Trying to soothe her, he caressed her hips and thighs, while her body closed over his in knifelike throbs. He gathered her closer, his belly against hers, the heat of him deep inside. Gradually her inner muscles weakened as if recognizing the uselessness of resisting.

"There," he whispered as he felt her relaxing. He kissed her jaw and throat, and stared down at her as he began to move in slow, careful lunges. Pleasure misted his hard features and emblazoned fresh color across the crests of his cheeks. As he reached the flashpoint, he fastened his mouth over hers, while his body worked in vehement shudders.

Withdrawing, he crushed his hard wet length against her stomach. A wash of heat spread between them, while he buried his face in her hair with a groan.

Kathleen held him tightly, savoring the tremors of satisfaction that ran through him. When he recovered his breath, he kissed her lazily, a sated male enjoying his plunder.

Eventually Devon left the bed and returned with a cup of water and a damp cloth. While she drank thirstily, he wiped away the evidence of their lovemaking. "I didn't want to hurt you," he murmured, as the cloth stroked over the sore place between her thighs.

Kathleen handed him the empty cup. "I was worried about you," she confessed. "I was afraid you might injure yourself."

He grinned, setting the cup and cloth aside. "How?" he scoffed. "By falling out of bed?"

"No, with all that vigorous activity."

"That wasn't vigorous. That was restrained." Joining her on the bed, he pulled her against him, his hands wandering boldly over her. "Tomorrow night," he said, kissing her shoulder, "I'll show you some vigor."

Circling her arms around his head, she pressed her lips against his vibrant dark hair. "Devon," she said warily, "I probably won't want to share a bed tomorrow night."

His head lifted as he glanced at her with concern. "If you're too sore, I'll just hold you."

"It's not that." She stroked back a lock that had fallen over his forehead. "As I told you, I can't have an affair."

Devon's gaze turned baffled. "I think we'd better start defining terms," he said slowly. "Now that we've slept together, what difference does it make if we do it again tomorrow night?"

Wondering how to make him understand, she chewed her bottom lip. "Devon," she asked eventually, "what is the pattern of your usual relationships with women?"

He clearly disliked the question. "There's no pattern."

She gave him a skeptical glance. "I'm sure they all began the same," she said in a neutral tone. "You took an interest in someone, and after some flirtation and pursuit, you eventually seduced her."

His brows lowered. "They were always willing."

Gazing at the magnificently formed man beside her, Kathleen smiled slightly. "I'm sure they were," she said. "It's certainly no hardship to go to bed with you."

"Then why—"

"Wait," she murmured. "How long did it usually last after you took up with someone? A few years? A few days?"

"On average," he said curtly, "a matter of months."

"And during that time, you visited the lady's bed whenever it was convenient. Until you eventually grew tired of her." She paused. "I assume you were usually the one to end it?"

He gave her an outright scowl. "I'm beginning to feel as if I'm at Chancery Court."

"I assume that means yes."

Devon's arms withdrew, and he sat up. "Yes. I was always the one to end it. I would bring her a parting gift, tell her I would always treasure the memories, and then I left with all possible haste. What has any of that to do with us?"

Drawing the sheets higher over her breasts, Kathleen said frankly, "*That's* what I mean when I say I don't want an affair. I don't want you to assume I'll be available whenever you wish to satisfy your needs. I don't want either of us to have any claim on the other. I don't want complications or the possibility of scandal, and I don't want a parting gift."

"What the devil *do* you want?"

Diffidently she began to fold the edge of the sheet into

tiny fanlike pleats. "I suppose . . . I would like to spend a night with you every now and then, when we both desire it. With no obligations or expectations."

"Define 'every now and then.' Once a week?"

She shrugged and let out a nonplussed laugh. "I wouldn't want to schedule it. Couldn't we just allow it to happen simply and naturally?"

"No," Devon said stonily. "Men like schedules. We don't like unanswered questions. We'd rather know what's going to happen and when."

"Even in matters of intimacy?"

"Especially in matters of intimacy. Damn it, why can't you be like other women?"

Kathleen's lips quirked with a wry, regretful smile. "And give you all the control? Hop into bed whenever you snap your fingers, as often as you wish, until you lose interest in me? And then I suppose I should stand at the door waiting for my good-bye present?"

A muscle twitched in his jaw, while his eyes flashed. "I wouldn't treat you like that."

Of course he would. That was how he had always treated women.

"I'm sorry, Devon, but I can't do it your way. We'll have to do it my way, or not at all."

"I'm damned if I even understand what your way is," he grated.

"I've made you angry," she said regretfully, beginning to sit up. "Shall I leave?"

Devon pushed her back down and leaned over her. "Not on your life." He stripped away the sheet in an abrupt motion. "Since I have no idea when I'll be allowed to bed you next, I have to make the most of my opportunities."

"But I'm sore," she protested, reflexively covering her breasts and groin with her hands.

His head lowered. "I won't hurt you," he growled against her belly. He nibbled at the edge of her navel, and then his tongue slipped inside the little hollow, making her gasp. He repeated it deliberately, and again, until he felt her quiver.

As his mouth worked downward, her heart began to pound and her vision blurred. Her hands slid away and her thighs loosened, parting easily as he spread them. With diabolical gentleness, he aroused her with lips, teeth, tongue, bringing her to the edge of fulfillment but never letting her go over. He held her between his elbows, the maddening teasing continuing until she heard herself begging. His tongue thrust in silky-wet penetrations, deep and steady, stroking her into a series of wrenching spasms. Reaching down, she clamped her trembling hands around his skull, holding him to her. He licked at the taste of her as if he couldn't have enough, and she purred and arched, her nerves dancing in response. As her pulse quieted, she stretched beneath him with a sigh of exhaustion.

He began again.

"No," she said with a shaky laugh. "Devon, please . . ."

But he was tugging at her sensitive flesh, so relentless and determined that she could only surrender with a groan. The candle burned down and shadows reclaimed the room, until there was nothing left but darkness and pleasure.

# Chapter 27

As the days of January trudged by, Kathleen remained steadfast in her refusal to allow Devon a place in her bed. In one fell swoop, she had assumed control of their relationship. As a result, Devon was perpetually filled with a mixture of outrage, lust, and genuine bewilderment, in varying proportions.

It would have been easier had she either given in to him completely or denied him absolutely, but instead she had made the situation stupefyingly unclear.

How like a woman.

"When we both desire it," she had said—as if she didn't know that he *always* desired it.

If it was a strategy on her part, to make him insane with wanting her and never knowing when he could have her, it was working brilliantly. But he knew her well enough to be certain that it wasn't a deliberate manipulation. Somehow it made the situation even worse to know that she was trying to protect herself from him. He understood her reasons—he thought he might even agree with them in principle—but nevertheless, it was driving him mad.

He couldn't change his nature, and by God, he didn't want to. He would never be able to surrender his heart, or his freedom. However, he hadn't realized until now that it was almost impossible to have an affair with a woman who was equally determined to keep her heart, and her freedom.

For her part, Kathleen was the same as she had always been, talkative, earnest, amusing, ready to argue when she disagreed with him.

He was the one who was different. He had become obsessed with Kathleen, so fascinated by everything she thought and did that he couldn't tear his gaze from her. Half the time he wanted to do everything possible to fill her with happiness, while the rest of the time he was tempted to throttle her. He had never known such agonizing frustration, wanting her, wanting far more than she was willing to give.

He was reduced to pursuing her, trying to catch her in corners like some lecherous lord playing a game of slap-and-tickle with a housemaid. Fondling and kissing her in the library, sliding his hand beneath her skirts on the back stairs. One morning, after having gone out on an early ride with her, he pulled her into a dark corner of the harness room, coaxing and caressing until he'd finally had his way with her against the wall. And even then, in the disorienting seconds after a magnificent release, he wanted more of her. Every second of the day.

The rest of the household had to have noticed how preoccupied he'd become with Kathleen, but so far no one had dared utter a word. However, West eventually asked why Devon had changed his mind about returning to London in the middle of the month.

"You're supposed to leave with Winterborne tomorrow," West said. "Why aren't you going with him? You should be in London, preparing for the land lease negotiations. The last I heard, they were set to begin on the first of February."

"The lawyers and accountants can prepare without

me," Devon replied. "I can stay here where I'm needed for at least another week."

"Needed for what?" West asked with a snort.

Devon's eyes narrowed. "Between the house renovations, the drainage ditches, hedge planting, and corn threshing, I believe I can find something to do."

They were walking back to the house from an outbuilding near the stables, where a newly arrived mechanical steam thresher had just been stored. Although the equipment had been purchased secondhand, it appeared to be in excellent condition. West had devised a plan by which the machine would be used and shared in rotation by several families.

"I can manage the estate," West argued. "You would be of more use in London, working on our financial problems. We need money, particularly now that we've agreed to give rent remissions and reductions to the tenants."

Devon sighed tautly. "I told you we should have waited before doing that."

"Those families can't wait. And unlike you, I can't pluck crusts of bread from the mouths of hungry children."

"You sound like Kathleen," Devon muttered. "I'll come to an agreement with Severin as quickly as possible. It would be easier if he left negotiations to his director, but for some reason he's decided to handle it himself."

"As we both know, Severin loves nothing more than to argue with his friends."

"Which explains why he doesn't have more of them." Pausing before the entrance of the house, Devon slid his hands in his pockets and looked up at the second-floor parlor window. Helen was playing the pianoforte, an exquisite melody rippling from the house with such delicacy that one could almost overlook the fact that the instrument was out of tune.

Holy hell, he was tired of things that needed to be repaired.

West followed his gaze. "Did you speak to Winterborne about Helen?"

"Yes. He wants to court her."

"Good."

Devon's brows lifted. "Now you approve of a match between them?"

"In part."

"What do you mean, in part?"

"The part of me that loves money and wants to stay out of prison thinks it's a splendid idea."

"We wouldn't face prison. Only bankruptcy."

"A fate worse than debt," West quipped, and shrugged. "I've come to the conclusion that it wouldn't be a bad match for Helen. If she doesn't marry him, she'll have to choose from among the dregs of the aristocracy."

Speculatively Devon glanced back at the window. "I've been thinking about bringing the family to London with me."

"The entire family? Good God, why?"

"It will bring Helen into proximity with Winterborne."

"And," West said pointedly, "it will keep Kathleen in proximity with you." Meeting Devon's alert gaze, he continued in an ironic tone. "When I told you not to seduce her, it was out of concern for her well-being. Now it seems I should have been equally as concerned for yours." A deliberate pause. "You're not yourself these days, Devon."

"Let it be," he said tersely.

"Very well. But one more bit of advice—I wouldn't mention anything to Kathleen about your plans for Helen. She's determined to help all three of those girls find happiness." West smiled grimly. "It seems she hasn't yet realized that in this life, happiness is optional."

As KATHLEEN ENTERED the morning room, she discovered that Helen and the twins were not at breakfast. West and Devon sat at the table reading mail and newspapers, while a footman removed used dishes and flatware.

"Good morning," Kathleen said. Both men stood automatically as she entered the room. "Have the girls finished already?"

West nodded. "Helen is accompanying the twins to the Luftons' farm."

"For what purpose?" she asked as Devon helped her into her chair.

"It was my suggestion," West told her. "The Luftons have offered to take Hamlet, provided we undertake the expense of building a pen and covered enclosure. The twins are willing to give the pig away if they have Mr. Lufton's personal guarantee of his welfare."

Kathleen smiled. "How did that come about?" The footman brought a tea tray from the sideboard, and held it while she measured a few spoonfuls of loose leaves into a small pot.

West spread a liberal helping of preserves on a slice of toast. "I told the twins, as tactfully as possible, that Hamlet was never barrowed in infancy, as he should have been. I had no idea the procedure was necessary, or I would have made certain it was done."

"Barrowed?" Kathleen asked, perplexed.

West made a scissoring gesture with two fingers.

"Oh."

"Remaining, er . . . intact," West continued, "has made Hamlet unfit for future consumption, so there's no reason to fear he'll end up on the dinner table. But he'll become increasingly aggressive as he goes through pubescence. It seems he'll become malodorous as well. He's now suited for only one purpose."

"Do you mean—" Kathleen began.

"Might this wait until after breakfast?" Devon asked from behind a newspaper.

West sent Kathleen an apologetic grin. "I'll explain later."

"If you're going to tell me about the inconvenience of having an uncastrated male in the house," Kathleen said, "I'm already aware of it."

West choked a little on his toast. There was no sound from Devon's direction.

The footman returned with the tea, and Kathleen poured a cup for herself. After she added sugar and took a sip of the steaming beverage, the butler approached.

"Milady," he said, proffering a silver tray that contained a letter and an ivory-handled letter knife.

Picking up the letter, she saw to her pleasure that it was from Lord Berwick. She slit the envelope open, set the knife back on the tray, and started to read silently. The letter began innocuously enough, assuring her that all was well with the Berwick family. He proceeded to describe a fine Thoroughbred colt he had just bought. Midway through the letter, however, Lord Berwick had written, *I recently learned some troubling news from your father's farm manager in Glengarrif. Although he did not seem to think it necessary for you to be informed, neither did he oppose my wish to tell you about an injury that your father sustained . . .*

As Kathleen tried to set her teacup on its saucer, the porcelain rattled. Ordinary though the sound was, it attracted Devon's attention. After one glance at her bleach-white face, he folded the paper and set it aside. "What is it?" he asked, his intent gaze on her.

"Nothing serious," she said. Her cheeks felt stiff. Her heart had begun to beat unpleasantly fast and sharp, while her corset seemed to squeeze every breath short. Glancing back down at the letter, she read the paragraph again, trying to make sense of it. "The letter is from Lord Berwick. He relates that my father suffered an injury but has recovered now." She wasn't aware that Devon had moved until she found him sitting in the chair next to hers, his warm hand enclosing hers.

"Tell me what happened." His tone was very gentle.

Kathleen stared down at the letter in one hand, trying to breathe around the suffocating tightness in her chest. "I . . . I don't know long ago it was. It seems my father was riding into an indoor arena, and the horse flung up its head. The momentum knocked my father's skull against a wooden support beam." She paused and shook her head helplessly. "According to the farm manager, he was in pain and disoriented, but the doctor bandaged his head and prescribed rest. He was in bed for three days, and now it appears he's feeling more himself."

"Why weren't you told immediately?" Devon asked with a frown.

Kathleen shrugged, unable to reply.

"Perhaps your father didn't want to worry you," came West's neutral comment.

"I suppose so," she managed to say.

But the truth was that it didn't matter to her father whether she worried over him or not. He had never felt any affection for her. He'd never remembered her birthdays, nor had he ever traveled to spend a holiday with her. After her mother had died, he hadn't sent for Kathleen to come home to live with him. And when she had turned to him for comfort after Theo's passing, he had warned her not to expect that there would be a place for her under his roof, should she want to live in Ireland. She should return to the Berwicks, he had suggested, or strike out on her own.

After so many rejections, Kathleen would have expected it to stop hurting by now. But the pain sank as deep as ever. She had always secretly harbored the fantasy that her father might need her someday, that he would send for her if he were ever injured or ill. She would go to him at once, and care for him tenderly, and they would finally have the relationship she had always longed for. But reality, as usual, bore no resemblance to fantasy. Her father had been injured, and not only had he declined to send for her, he hadn't even wanted her to know about it.

Staring down at the blur of Lord Berwick's letter, Kathleen was unaware of the glance Devon gave his brother. All she knew was that by the time she took her hand from Devon's and reached for her tea, West's place was empty. She cast a bewildered glance around the room. West had left surreptitiously, along with the butler and footman, and they had closed the door behind them.

"You didn't have to make them leave," Kathleen exclaimed, her color rising. "I'm not going to make a scene." She tried to drink her tea, but the hot liquid sloshed over the rim, and she set down the cup with chagrin.

"You're upset," Devon said quietly.

"I'm not upset, I'm merely . . ." She paused and ran a trembling hand across her forehead. "I am upset," she admitted.

Devon reached out to lift her from her chair with astonishing ease. "Sit with me," he murmured, settling her onto his lap.

"I was sitting with you. I don't need to sit *on* you." She found herself perched sideways with her feet dangling. "Devon—"

"Hush." Keeping a supportive arm around her, he reached with his free hand for her teacup and brought it to her lips. She took a sip of the hot, sweet tea. His lips brushed her temple. "Have some more," he murmured, and held the cup as she drank again. She felt rather silly, allowing him to comfort her like a child . . . and yet a sense of relief began to steal over her as she leaned against his broad chest.

"My father and I have never been close," she eventually said. "I've never understood why. Something . . . something about me, I suppose. He only ever loved one person in his life, and that was my mother. She felt the same about him. Which is romantic, but . . . it was difficult for a child to understand."

"Where did you acquire such a perverse view of romance?" Devon asked, now sounding sardonic.

She glanced at him in surprise.

"Loving only one person in the world isn't romantic," he said, "nor is it love. No matter how your parents felt about each other, they had no excuse for relinquishing all responsibility for their only child. Although God knows you were better off living with the Berwicks." His hand tightened on hers. "If it pleases you, I'll telegram the farm manager to find out more about your father's condition."

"I would like that," Kathleen admitted, "but it would probably annoy my father."

"So much the better." Devon reached up to the ebony cameo at her throat and adjusted it.

She looked at him solemnly. "I used to wish I'd been born a boy. I thought he might have taken an interest in me then. Or perhaps if I were prettier or cleverer."

Devon cupped the side of her face, compelling her to look at him. "You're already too pretty and clever by half, darling. And it wouldn't have mattered if you were a boy. That was never the problem. Your parents were a pair of selfish lackwits." His thumb caressed her cheek. "And whatever flaws you might have, being unlovable is not one of them."

During that last extraordinary sentence, the quiet volume of his voice fell to a near whisper.

She stared at him, transfixed.

He hadn't meant to say it, she thought. He undoubtedly regretted it.

But their shared gaze remained unbroken. Looking into his dark blue eyes was like drowning, sinking into unfathomable depths from which she might never resurface. She trembled and managed to look away, severing the connection.

"Come to London with me," she heard Devon say.

"What?" she asked, bewildered.

"Come to London with me," he repeated. "I have to leave within a fortnight. Bring the girls and your maid. It will be good for everyone, including you. At this time of year there's nothing to do in Hampshire, and London offers no end of amusements."

Kathleen looked at him with a frown. "You know that's impossible."

"You mean because of mourning."

"Of course that's what I mean."

She didn't like the sparks of mischief that had appeared in his eyes.

"I've already considered that," he told her. "Not being as familiar with the rules of propriety as yourself, I undertook to consult a paragon of society about what activities might be permissible for young women in your situation."

"What paragon? What are you talking about?"

Shifting her weight more comfortably in his lap, Devon reached across the table to retrieve a letter by his plate. "You're not the only one who received correspondence today." He extracted the letter from its envelope with a flourish. "According to a renowned expert on mourning etiquette, even though attending a play or a dance is out of the question, it's permissible to go to a concert, museum exhibition, or private art gallery." Devon proceeded to read aloud from the letter. "This learned lady writes, *One fears that the prolonged seclusion of young persons may encourage a lasting melancholy in such malleable natures. While the girls must pay appropriate respect to the memory of the late earl, it would be both wise and kind to allow them a few innocent recreations. I would recommend the same for Lady Trenear, whose lively disposition, in my opinion, will not long tolerate a steady diet of monotony and solitude. Therefore you have my encouragement to—*"

"Who wrote that?" Kathleen demanded, snatching the letter from his hand. "Who could possibly presume to—" She gasped, her eyes widening as she saw the signature at the conclusion of the letter. "Dear God. You consulted *Lady Berwick*?"

DEVON GRINNED. "I knew you would accept no one's judgment but hers." He bounced Kathleen a little on his knee. The slim, supple weight of her was anchored amid the rustling layers of skirts and underskirts, the pretty curves of her body corseted into a narrow column. With every movement she made, little whiffs of soap and roses floated around them. She reminded him of one of those miniature sweet-smelling bundles that women tucked into dressers and wardrobes.

"Come," he said, "London isn't such an appalling idea, is it? You've never stayed at Ravenel House—and it's in far better condition than this heap of ruins. You'll have new sights and surroundings." He couldn't resist adding in a mocking tone, "Most importantly, I'll be available to service you whenever you like."

Her brows flew down. "Don't call it that."

"Forgive me, that was uncouth. But I'm an uncastrated male, after all." He smiled as he saw that the stricken look had gone from her eyes. "Consider it for the girls' sake," he coaxed. "They've endured mourning far longer than you have. Don't they deserve a respite? Besides, it would benefit them to become more familiar with London before next year's season."

Her brows drew together. "How long do you propose for us to stay? A fortnight?"

"Perhaps a month."

She played with the ends of his silk necktie as she considered it. "I'll discuss it with Helen."

Sensing that she was leaning toward agreeing, he decided to push her a bit. "You're coming to London," he said flatly. "You've become a habit. If you're not with me, I'm afraid of what I may start doing to replace you. Tobacco. Knuckle cracking."

Kathleen twisted in his lap to face him more fully, her hands coming to the shoulders of his morning coat. Her smiling gaze locked with his. "You could take up an instrument," she suggested.

Slowly Devon brought her forward and whispered against the sweet, full curves of her mouth, "But you're the only thing I want to play."

Her arms reached around his neck.

The position between them was awkward, with her body angled sideways and the stiff corset latched around her torso. They were smothered in layers of clothing that hadn't been designed for freedom of movement. The rigid collar of his shirt pressed into his neck and his shirt had begun to bunch beneath his waistcoat, while the elastic of his braces pulled uncomfortably. But her tongue played against his with a kittenish flick, and that was all it took to send him to full-bore arousal.

Still kissing him, Kathleen struggled within the heap of her dress. She reached down to tug at the great mass of her skirts, and to his amusement, she nearly toppled herself from his lap. He pulled her body higher against his, while her legs churned amid the heavy skirts until she managed to straddle him even with huge swathes of fabric still trapped between them. It was ridiculous, the two of them writhing on this blasted chair, but it felt insanely good to hold her.

One of her hands slipped over his front, and she gripped the hard length of him over the fabric of his trousers. He jolted against her. Before he quite realized what he was doing, his hands were rummaging beneath her skirts. Finding the slit of her drawers, he pulled at the fabric until the seam tore with a satisfying rip, and the soft, moist flesh he craved was exposed.

Kathleen moaned as he sank two of his fingers into her, her hips tilting forward eagerly, her wetness and heat pulsing around him. All reason fled. Nothing mattered except being inside her. Withdrawing his fingers, he fumbled roughly for the fastenings of his trousers. She tried to help him, grappling with the obstinate buttons. Her efforts ended up hindering him in a way that would have made him laugh, if he hadn't been so wild for her. Somehow they ended up on the floor, with Kathleen still straddling him, her skirts billowing and ballooning over them both like some gigantic unearthly flower.

Underneath the tumult of fabric, his naked flesh found hers. He positioned himself, and before he could even guide her, Kathleen had sunk down, her small, wet sex taking him deeper than ever before. They both shivered and gasped at the feel of it, the crushed-velvet texture of her closing on him in rich pulses.

She held on to his shoulders and began to roll to the side, trying to reverse their positions and pull him over her. Resisting, he caught her hips, keeping her on top. While Kathleen stared down at him with bewildered eyes, he spread his fingers over her hips and buttocks, relishing the shape of her. He showed her the movement, thrusting upward, bringing her down with care. He delayed her descent enough to let her slide a few inches down his length, and she let out a stuttering breath. Another boost of his hips, followed by a silky erotic plunge.

Kathleen began to move hesitantly, her face flooding with brilliant color. Following her instinct, she adjusted her position and moved on him with increasing confidence, finishing each drive with a forward sway that absorbed his upward thrusts.

God, he was being ridden, hard and well. She pleasured herself on him in an aggressive rhythm, faster and faster, striking a blaze of lust that made him sweat beneath his clothes and in his shoes. Perspiration trickled from his forehead. Closing his eyes, he tried to bring himself under control, but it was hellishly difficult at the pace she set. No, impossible.

"Slowly, sweetheart," he said hoarsely, reaching beneath her dress to take her hips between his palms. "I want you too much."

She resisted, driving him roughly, her body tightening.

The climax was rushing up to him. He could feel it intensifying no matter how he worked to stave it off. "Kathleen," he said through gritted teeth, "I can't . . . can't hold back . . ."

She was beyond hearing, working on him in repeated lunges. He felt her reach the peak, the supple quivers and throbs closing all around him. In an agony of self-discipline he held still, every muscle contracted and rock-hard. Forcing himself to wait, he let her take her pleasure, even though his heart threatened to explode from the effort. He managed to give her ten seconds . . . the most excruciating ten seconds of his life. That was all he could last before his release began. Grunting with effort, he tried to haul her off him.

What he hadn't bargained on, however, was the strength of her thighs, the muscles of an experienced horsewoman gripping him with a tenacity that even a thousand-pound Arabian couldn't have unseated. As he tried to buck her off, he felt her instinctively using the movements against him, her legs locking tighter with each backlash. She was too much for him. A scalding climax overcame him, pouring through him in a pleasure as absolute as death. He bucked a few more times while she rode him through it, her body wringing out every drop of sensation without mercy.

Devon groaned and collapsed back to the floor.

As the dizzying ecstasy faded, he was chilled by the realization that he had come inside her. He'd never done that with any woman before. In fact he'd always used rubber sheaths to make certain of it. But he'd arrogantly assumed that he would have no problem withdrawing from Kathleen—and the truth was, he'd wanted to be inside her with no barriers between them.

The price he might have to pay for that was unthinkable.

Kathleen lay over him, her slender body rising and falling on his wracking breaths.

"I'm so sorry," she gasped, sounding shocked. "I couldn't stop. I just . . . couldn't."

Devon was silent, trying to think through the panic.

"What should we do now?" she asked, her voice muffled.

Although he knew of ways to prevent pregnancy, the details and particulars of what to do *after* the sexual act were a woman's province.

"I've heard of using champagne," he managed to say. But he had only the vaguest idea about how a contraceptive douche was administered, and there was no way in hell that he would risk harming Kathleen by making a mistake.

"Drinking champagne will help?" she asked hopefully.

He smiled grimly above her head. "Not to drink, my innocent. But it doesn't matter—it would have to be done soon, and there isn't time."

Her weight on his ribs was making him ache. He eased her off his body and stood, restoring his clothes with vicious efficiency. Reaching down, he took her outstretched hand and helped her up.

As Kathleen stood and saw his expression, all the color leached from her face. "I'm sorry," she said once more, her voice unsteady. "Please believe that no matter what happens, I won't hold you responsible."

His fear transformed instantly into anger, the words setting off his temper like a keg of gunpowder. "Do you think that makes a damned bit of difference?" he asked savagely. "I'm already responsible for a thousand things I never asked for."

She replied with as much dignity as a woman could while trying to pull her undergarments back into place. "I don't want to be included on that list."

"For once, it doesn't matter what you want. If there is a baby, neither of us can will it out of existence. And it's half mine." He couldn't keep his appalled gaze from sliding low on her body, as if his seed were already taking root inside her. She took a step backward, the small movement infuriating him.

"When will your monthly flow begin?" he asked, struggling to moderate his tone.

"Two, perhaps three weeks. I'll send a telegram to you in London when it happens."

"If it happens," he said bitterly. "And you won't need to send a bloody telegram—you're still coming with me. Don't bother asking why—I'm weary of having to explain every decision I make to every person on this godforsaken estate."

He left her before he could say anything else, striding away as if the devil were at his heels.

# Chapter 28

THE RAILWAY JOURNEY TO London was accomplished in a miraculous two hours, at least four times faster than it would have been had they gone by coach. That turned out to be fortunate, as it soon became apparent that the Ravenel family did not travel well.

Pandora and Cassandra were both overcome with excitement, never having set foot on a train before. They chattered and exclaimed, darting across the station platform like feeding pigeons, begging West to purchase railway editions of popular novels—only a shilling apiece—and sandwiches packaged in cunning little paper boxes, and handkerchiefs printed with pastoral scenes. Loaded with souvenirs, they boarded the family's first-class railway carriage and insisted on trying every seat before choosing the ones they preferred.

Helen had insisted on bringing one of her potted orchids, its long, fragile stem having been stabilized with a stick and a bit of ribbon. The orchid was a rare and sensitive species of Blue Vanda. Despite its dislike of being moved, she believed it would be better off in London with her. She carried the orchid in her lap the entire way, her absorbed gaze focused on the passing landscape.

Soon after the train had left the station, Cassandra made herself queasy by trying to read one of the railway novels. She closed the book and settled in her seat with her eyes closed, moaning occasionally as the train swayed. Pandora, by contrast, couldn't stay seated for more than a few minutes at a time, jumping up to test the feeling of standing in a moving locomotive, and attempting to view the scenery from different windows. But the worst traveler by far was Clara, the lady's maid, whose fear of the train's speed proved resistant to all attempts at soothing. Every small jolt or lurch of the carriage drew a fearful cry from her until Devon had given her a small glass of brandy to settle her nerves.

"I told you we should have put her in the second-class carriage with Sutton," he said to Kathleen.

In the week since the episode in the morning room, they had both taken care to avoid each other as much as possible. When they were together, as now, they retreated into mutual and scrupulous politeness.

"I thought she would feel safer with us," Kathleen replied. Glancing over her shoulder, she saw that Clara was sleeping with her head tilted back and her mouth half open. "She seems to be faring better after a nip of brandy."

"Nip?" He gave her a dark glance. "She's had at least a half pint by now. Pandora's been dosing her with it for the past half hour."

"What? Why didn't you say anything?"

"Because it kept her quiet."

Kathleen jumped up and hurried to retrieve the decanter from Pandora. "Darling, what are you doing with this?"

The girl stared at her owlishly. "I've been helping Clara."

"That was very kind, but she's had enough. Don't give her any more."

"I don't know why it's made her so sleepy. I've had

almost as much medicine as she's had, and I'm not a bit tired."

"You drank some of the brandy?" West had asked from the other side of the railway carriage, his brows lifting.

Pandora stood and made her way to the opposite window to view a Celtic hill fort and a meadow with grazing cattle. "Yes, when we were crossing the bridge over the water, I felt a bit nervous. But then I dosed myself, and it was quite relaxing."

"Indeed," West said, glancing at the half-empty bottle in Kathleen's hand before returning his gaze to Pandora. "Come sit with me, darling. You'll be as stewed as Clara by the time we reach London."

"Don't be silly." Dropping into the empty seat next to him, Pandora argued and giggled profusely, until she dropped her head to his shoulder and began to snore.

Finally they arrived at one of the two train sheds at Waterloo Station, crowded with thousands of passengers searching for their correct departure platforms. Standing, Devon stretched his shoulders and said, "The driver and carriage are waiting outside the train shed. I'll have a porter assist Clara. Everyone else, stay together. Cassandra, don't even think about dashing off to look at trinkets or books. Helen, hold fast to your orchid in case you're jostled while we move through the crowd. As for Pandora . . ."

"I have her," West assured him, pulling the wilting girl to her feet. "Wake up, child. It's time to leave."

"My legs are on the wrong feet," Pandora mumbled, her face buried against his chest.

"Reach around my neck."

She squinted up at him. "Why?"

West regarded her with amused exasperation. "So I can carry you off the train."

"I *like* trains." Pandora hiccupped as he lifted her against his chest. "Oh, being carried is ever so much nicer than walking. I feel so flopsawopsy-doodly . . ."

Somehow the group made it through the train shed without mishap. Devon directed the porters and footmen to load their luggage onto a road wagon that would follow the carriage. Sutton reluctantly took charge of Clara, who was inclined to collapse and slump like a sack of beans as she sat next to him on a wagon bench.

The family settled into the carriage, while West elected to sit up top with the driver. As the vehicle left the station and proceeded toward Waterloo Bridge, a mist of rain accompanied the slow descent of pumice-colored fog.

"Will Cousin West be uncomfortable, riding out in the weather?" Cassandra asked in concern.

Devon shook his head. "West is invigorated by the city. He'll want to have a good look at everything."

Pandora stirred and sat up to take in the scenery. "I thought all the streets would be paved with stone."

"Only a few," Devon said. "Most have been paved with wood block, which provides a better foothold for horses."

"How tall the buildings are," Helen remarked, curving her arm protectively around the orchid pot. "Some of them must be seven stories, at least."

The twins pressed their noses to the windows, their eager faces on open display.

"Girls, your veils—" Kathleen began.

"Let them look," Devon interrupted quietly. "It's their first glimpse of the city."

She relented, settling back in her seat.

London was a city of wonders, alive with thousands of odors and sights. The air was thick with the barking of dogs, the clip-clopping of iron-shod horses and the bleating of sheep, the grinding of carriage wheels, the worrying of fiddles and the whines of street organs, fragments of song from street sellers and balladeers, and thousands of voices that argued, bargained, laughed, and called out to each other.

Vehicles and horses moved through the streets in a vigorous flow. Walkways swarmed with pedestrians who trod across the pale straw that had been scattered along paths and storefronts to absorb the damp. There were vendors, men of business, vagabonds, aristocrats, women in all manner of dress, chimney sweeps with their tattered brooms, shoe blacks carrying folding benches, and match girls balancing bundles of boxes on their heads.

"I can't decide how the air smells," Cassandra remarked, as a bewilderment of scents slipped through a gap in the slide window beneath the driver's box. There was smoke, soot, horses, manure, wet brick, salted brown fish, red butcher-shop meat, bakery bread, hot sausage pasties, oily plugs of tobacco, human sweat, the sweetness of wax and tallow and flowers, and the metallic tang of steam machinery. "What would you call it, Pandora?"

"Odorwhelming," Pandora said.

Cassandra shook her head with a rueful grin and curled an arm around her twin's shoulders.

Although smoke haze had grayed the street and buildings, an abundance of color enlivened the scene. Street sellers pushed barrows filled with flowers, fruit and vegetables past shops with painted hanging signs and picturesque window displays. Small jewellike gardens and lime walks had been set among stone houses with columns and iron balustrades.

The carriage turned onto Regent Street, where fashionably dressed men and women promenaded along rows of shops and clubs fronted with majestic terraced façades.

Devon reached up to slide the ceiling window open, and called up to the driver, "Go by way of Burlington Gardens and Cork Street."

"Yes, milord."

Lowering back to the seat, Devon said, "We're taking a slight detour. I thought you all might like to pass by Winterborne's."

Pandora and Cassandra squealed.

As they turned onto Cork, the heavy congestion of vehicles obliged the carriage to move at a snail's pace, past an unbroken row of marble-faced edifices that extended along the entire block. A central stained-glass rotunda added another fifteen feet in height.

The street-level façades were fronted with the largest plate-glass windows Kathleen had ever seen, with people crowding to view the exotic displays within. Columned arcades and arched windows adorned the upper floors, while a row of glass-paned square cupolas topped a triple-stacked parapet on the roof. For such a massive structure, it had a pleasingly light and airy feel.

"Where is Mr Winterborne's store?" Kathleen asked.

Devon blinked as if the question had surprised him. "This is all Winterborne's. It appears to be several buildings, but it's only one."

She stared through the window in amazement. The structure took up the entire street. It was too large to fit within any of her previous understandings of "store" . . . It was a kingdom in itself.

"I want to visit it," Cassandra said emphatically.

"Not without me," Pandora exclaimed.

Devon said nothing, his gaze resting on Helen as if he were trying to divine her thoughts.

Eventually they reached the end of Cork Street and

maneuvered to South Audley Street. They approached a large and handsomely appointed house, surrounded by an imposing iron fence and stone gate. It bore such a resemblance to the Jacobean design of Eversby Priory that Kathleen knew it belonged to the Ravenels.

The carriage stopped, and the twins nearly leaped from the carriage before a footman could assist them.

"You never visited here?" Devon asked Kathleen as they proceeded inside.

She shook her head. "I saw the exterior once. It wasn't proper to call on an unmarried gentleman at his residence. Theo and I had planned to stay here after summer's end."

Coordinated mayhem filled the entrance hall as servants retrieved luggage from the road wagon and escorted family members to their rooms. Kathleen liked the comforting ambiance of the house, with its solid, traditional furnishings and floors of inlaid oak and cherry, and walls filled with Old Masters paintings. The second floor contained bedrooms, a small drawing room, and an anteroom. Later she would venture up to the third floor, which Devon had told her consisted entirely of an opulent ballroom that extended the full depth of the mansion, with French doors opening to an outside balcony.

For now, however, she wanted to go to her room and freshen up after the journey.

As Devon accompanied her to the second floor, Kathleen became aware of strange ethereal music floating through the air. The delicate notes didn't come from a piano. "What is that sound?" she asked.

Devon shook his head, looking perplexed.

They entered the drawing room, where Helen, Cassandra and Pandora had gathered around a small rectangular table. The twins' faces glowed with excitement, while Helen's was blank.

"Kathleen," Pandora exclaimed, "it's the most beautiful, clever thing you've ever seen!"

She saw a music box that was at least three feet long and a foot tall. The shining rosewood box, decorated with gold and lacquer inlay, rested upon its own matching table.

"Let's try another," Cassandra urged, opening a drawer in the front of the table.

Helen reached into the box to withdraw a brass cylinder, its surface bristling with hundreds of tiny pins. Several more cylinders lay in a gleaming row in the drawer.

"You see?" Pandora said to Kathleen excitedly. "Each cylinder plays a different piece of music. You can choose what you want to hear."

Kathleen shook her head, marveling silently.

Helen placed a new cylinder in the box and flipped a brass lever. The brisk, jaunty melody of the William Tell Overture poured out, making the twins laugh.

"Swiss-made," Devon remarked, staring at a plaque on the interior of the lid. "The cylinders are all opera overtures. *Il Bacio, Zampa* . . ."

"But where did it come from?" Kathleen asked.

"It seems to have been delivered today," Helen said, her voice oddly subdued. "For me. From . . . Mr. Winterborne."

Silence descended on the group.

Picking up a folded note, Helen gave it to Devon. Although her face was composed, bewilderment shone in her eyes. "He—" she began uncomfortably, "That is, Mr. Winterborne—seems to think—"

Devon met her gaze directly. "I've given him leave to court you," he said bluntly. "Only if you desire it. If you do not—"

"*What?*" Kathleen burst out, fury pumping through

her. Why hadn't Devon mentioned anything about it to her? He must have known that she would object.

As a matter of fact, she objected with every bone in her body. Winterborne wasn't right for Helen in any regard. *Anyone* could see that. Marrying him would require her to fit into a life that was completely foreign to her.

The William Tell Overture floated around the room with ghastly cheerfulness.

"Absolutely not," Kathleen snapped at Devon. "Tell him you've changed your mind."

"It's up to Helen to decide what she wants," he said calmly. "Not you." With that obdurate set of his jaw, he looked exactly like the arrogant ass he had been the first time they'd met.

"What has Winterborne promised you?" she demanded. "What does the estate stand to gain if he marries Helen?"

His eyes were hard. "We'll discuss it in private. There's a study on the main floor."

As Helen moved to join them, Kathleen stopped her with a gentle touch on her arm. "Darling," she said urgently, "please let me speak to Lord Trenear first. There are private things I must ask him. You and I will talk afterward. *Please.*"

Helen contemplated her without blinking, her singular eyes pale and light-tricked. When she spoke, her voice was temperate and level. "Before anything is discussed, I want to make something clear. I trust and love you as my own sister, dearest Kathleen, and I know you feel the same about me. But I believe I view my own situation more pragmatically than you do." Her gaze lifted to Devon's face as she continued. "If Mr. Winterborne does intend to offer for me . . . it's not something I could dismiss lightly."

Not trusting herself to reply, Kathleen swallowed back her outrage. She considered attempting a smile, but her face was too stiff. She settled for patting Helen's arm.

Turning on her heel, she left the drawing room, while Devon followed.

*Chapter 29*

IT WAS WEST'S MISFORTUNE to have gone to the study at the same time that Kathleen and Devon went there to do battle.

"What's happening?" West asked, glancing from one set face to the other.

"Helen and Winterborne," Devon said succinctly.

Glancing at Kathleen's accusing face, West winced and tugged at his necktie. "There's no need for me to take part in the discussion, is there?"

"Did you know about the courtship?" Kathleen demanded.

"Might have," he muttered.

"Then yes, you will stay and explain why you didn't talk him out of this appalling idea."

West looked indignant. "When have I ever been able to talk either of you out of anything?"

Kathleen turned to glare at Devon. "If you truly intend to do this to Helen, then you're as cold-hearted as I first thought you were."

"Do what? Help to secure a match that will give her wealth, status in society, and a family of her own?"

"Status in *his* society, not ours. You know quite well that the peerage will say she's lowered herself."

"Most of the people who will say that are the same ones who would refuse to touch her with a barge pole if she decided to take part in the season." Devon went to the fireplace and braced his hands on the marble mantel. Firelight played over his face and dark hair. "I'm aware that this isn't an ideal match for Helen. But Winterborne isn't as objectionable as you've made him out to be. Helen may even come to love him in time."

"Given enough time," she said scornfully, "Helen could convince herself to love a plague-infested rat or a toothless leper. That doesn't mean she should marry him."

"I'm positive that Helen would never marry a rat," West said.

Devon picked up a fire iron and poked at the blaze on the grate, stirring up a storm of dancing sparks. "Until now, Helen never had a chance of making any kind of match." He sent Kathleen a hard glance over his shoulder. "What you seem unwilling to accept is that no gentleman of stature is going to choose a future of poverty with a girl he loves over wealth with a girl he merely tolerates."

"There might be a few." At his derisive glance, she said defensively, "There might be *one*. Why can't we allow Helen a chance to find him?"

West broke in. "That would mean giving up any possibility of marrying Winterborne. And then if Helen doesn't succeed in bringing someone up to scratch during the season, she'll have nothing."

"In that case, she can live with me," Kathleen said. "I'll find a cottage in the country, where she and I will live off the income from my jointure."

Turning from the fireplace, Devon gave her a narrow-eyed glance. "How do I fit into your future plans?"

A hostile silence followed.

"I really don't think I should be here," West said to the ceiling.

"You're able to take care of yourself," Kathleen told Devon. "Helen can't. She'll have no protection against Winterborne, if he should mistreat her."

"Of course she will. West and I will always protect her."

"You should be protecting her now."

West stood and strode to the door. "Is *this* what it's like to have a family?" he asked irritably. "Endless arguing, and talking about feelings from dawn to dusk? When the devil can I do as I please and not have to account to a half-dozen people for it?"

"When you live alone on an island with a single palm tree and a coconut," Kathleen snapped. "And even then, I'm sure you would find the coconut far too demanding."

West regarded them both sourly. "I've had enough of this. If you'll excuse me, I'm going to find a tavern where I can pay an underdressed woman to sit in my lap and look very pleased with me while I drink heavily."

As he left, he closed the study door with unnecessary force.

Folding her arms across her chest, Kathleen glowered at Devon. "Helen will never admit what she wants. She's spent her entire life trying not to be a bother to anyone. She'd marry the devil himself if she thought it would help the family—and she's well aware that Eversby Priory would stand to benefit."

"She's not a child. She's a woman of one-and-twenty. Perhaps you didn't notice just now that she behaved with far more composure than you or I." On a callous note, he added gently, "And although it might surprise you, a lifetime of living under your thumb may not appeal to her."

Kathleen stared at him, her mouth opening and closing as she tried to find words. When she was finally able to speak, her voice was thick with loathing.

"I can't believe I ever let you touch me."

Unable to bear being in the same room with him for another minute, she fled the study and rushed upstairs.

FOR MORE THAN an hour afterward, Kathleen and Helen talked intently in the small anteroom adjacent to the drawing room. To Kathleen's dismay, Helen seemed not only willing to be courted by Rhys Winterborne, but she was actually resolved to it.

"He doesn't want you for the right reasons," Kathleen said in concern. "He wants a wife who will advance his ambitions. And no doubt he thinks of you as an aristocratic broodmare."

Helen smiled slightly. "Isn't that also how men of our class judge the value of a potential wife?"

An impatient sigh burst from her lips. "Helen, you must admit that you and he are worlds apart!"

"Yes, he and I are quite different," Helen admitted. "That's why I intend to proceed with caution. But I have reasons of my own for agreeing to the courtship. And while I don't wish to explain all of them . . . I will tell you that I felt a moment of connection with him when he stayed at Eversby Priory."

"While you were nursing him through the fever? Because if so, that was pity, not connection."

"No, it happened after that." She continued before Kathleen could offer more objections. "I know very little about him. But I would like to learn more." Taking Kathleen's hands, she pressed them firmly. "Please, for the time being, don't object to the courtship. For my sake."

Kathleen nodded reluctantly. "Very well."

"And about Lord Trenear," Helen dared to say, "you mustn't blame him for trying to—"

"Helen," she interrupted quietly, "forgive me, but I can indeed blame him—for reasons you know nothing about."

THE NEXT MORNING, Devon escorted the Ravenels to the British Museum. Kathleen would have preferred West to accompany them, but he was staying at his private terrace apartment, which he had maintained even after moving to Eversby Priory.

Still outraged by Devon's deception, and his hurtful remarks of the previous night, Kathleen avoided speaking to him any more than strictly necessary. This morning they both wielded polite words and razor-thin smiles like weapons.

Faced with the museum's enormous quantity of art exhibitions, the Ravenel sisters elected to visit the Egyptian gallery first. Clutching pamphlets and guidebooks, they spent most of the morning examining every object in the exhibit . . . statues, sarcophagi, obelisks, tablets, embalmed animals, ornaments, weapons, tools, and jewelry. They lingered for a long time at the Rosetta stone, marveling at the hieroglyphs incised on its polished front surface.

While Devon browsed over a nearby exhibit of weaponry, Helen wandered to Kathleen, who was looking at a glass case of ancient coins. "There are so many galleries in this museum," she remarked, "that we could visit every day for a month, and still not see everything."

"Certainly not at this rate," Kathleen said, watching as Pandora and Cassandra opened their sketch tablets and began to copy some of the hieroglyphs.

Following her gaze, Helen said, "They're enjoying this immensely. So am I. It seems we've all been starved for more culture and stimulation than Eversby can offer."

"London has an abundance of both," Kathleen said. Trying to sound light, she added, "I suppose Mr. Winterborne has that on his side: You would never be bored."

"No, indeed." Helen paused before asking cautiously,

"Regarding Mr. Winterborne, may we invite him to dinner? I would like to thank him in person for the music box."

Kathleen frowned. "Yes. Lord Trenear will invite him if you wish. However . . . you are aware of how inappropriate that music box is. It was a lovely and generous gift, but we should give it back."

"I can't," Helen whispered with a frown. "It would hurt his feelings."

"It would hurt your reputation."

"No one has to know, do they? Couldn't we consider it as a gift for the family?"

Before she replied, Kathleen thought of all the rules she had broken and the sins she had committed, some small, some far more egregious than accepting an inappropriate gift. Her mouth curved in wry resignation. "Why not?" she said, and took Helen's arm. "Come help me stop Pandora—she's trying to open a mummy case."

To HELEN'S MINGLED consternation and excitement, Winterborne accepted an invitation to dinner the very next evening. She wanted very much to see him, almost as much as she dreaded it.

Winterborne arrived punctually and was shown to the main floor drawing room, where the Ravenels had gathered. His powerful form was dressed with elegant simplicity in a black coat, gray trousers, and a gray waistcoat. Although his broken leg was still healing, the cast had been removed and he walked with the use of a wooden cane. One could have easily singled him out in a crowd, not only from his distinctive height and size, but also from his raven hair and swarthy complexion. The coloring, thought to be the result of Spanish Basque influence in Wales, was not considered aristocratic . . . but Helen thought it very handsome and striking.

His gaze came to Helen, dark heat framed with black lashes, and she felt a nervous flutter. Maintaining her composure, she gave him a neutral smile, wishing she had the confidence to say something charming or flirtatious. To her chagrin, Pandora and Cassandra—two years younger than she—were both far more comfortable with Winterborne. They amused him with nonsense such as asking whether there was a sword concealed in his cane (regrettably, no) and describing the mummified dogs in the Egyptian gallery.

As the company went in to dinner, a moment of perplexity ensued when it was discovered that the twins had written the name cards in hieroglyphics.

"We thought everyone might want to guess which one was theirs," Pandora informed them.

"Thankfully, I'm at the head of the table," Devon said.

"This is mine," Winterborne said, gesturing to one name card, "and I believe Lady Helen is seated next to me."

"How did you know?" Cassandra asked. "Are you familiar with hieroglyphics, Mr. Winterborne?"

He smiled. "I counted the letters." Picking up the name card, he regarded it closely. "It's cleverly drawn, especially the little bird."

"Can you tell what kind of bird it is?" Pandora asked hopefully.

"Penguin?" he guessed.

Cassandra told her sister triumphantly, "I *told* you it looked like a penguin."

"It's a quail," Pandora said to Winterborne, heaving a sigh. "My penmanship is no better in ancient Egyptian than it is in English."

After everyone was seated and the footmen had begun serving, Helen turned to Winterborne, determined to overcome her shyness. "I see your cast has been removed, Mr. Winterborne. I trust you're mending well?"

He gave her a guarded nod. "Quite well, thank you."

She repeatedly smoothed the napkin on her lap. "I can hardly find words to thank you for the music box. It's the most beautiful gift I've ever received."

"I hoped it would please you."

"It does." As Helen looked into his eyes, it occurred to her that someday this man might have the right to kiss her . . . hold her in intimacy . . . They would do whatever mysterious things occurred between a husband and wife. A terrible blush began, the pervasive, self-renewing color that only he seemed to inspire. Desperate to halt its progress, she lowered her gaze to his shirt collar, and then a bit lower, tracking the perfect straight line of a hand-stitched seam.

"I see Mr. Quincy's influence," she found herself saying.

"The shirt?" Winterborne asked. "Aye, the contents of every wardrobe, drawer, and trunk have been under siege since Quincy arrived. He informs me that a separate room is needed for the sole purpose of maintaining the clothing."

"How is Mr. Quincy? Has he acclimated to London yet?"

"It took only a day." Winterborne proceeded to describe the valet's enjoyment of his new life, and how he had already become more familiar with the department store than employees who had worked there for a few years. The valet had made many new friends, with the exception of Winterborne's private secretary, with whom he bickered constantly. Winterborne suspected, however, that the two secretly enjoyed the exchanges.

Helen listened attentively, relieved to be spared the necessity of talking. She thought of bringing up the subject of books, or music, but she feared that might lead to conflicting opinions. She would have liked to ask about his past, but perhaps that was a sensitive area, in light of his Welsh heritage. No, it was safer to remain quiet. When her restrained comments could no longer sustain a conversation, Winterborne was drawn into a discussion with West.

Fearing that he thought her dull, Helen fretted silently and picked at her food.

Eventually Winterborne turned back to her as the plates were being removed. "Will you play the piano after dinner?" he asked.

"I would, but I'm afraid we haven't one."

"No piano anywhere in the house?" There was a calculating flicker in his dark eyes.

"Please don't buy one for me," Helen said hastily.

That produced a sudden grin, a flash of white against cinnamon skin, so appealing that it sent a shot of warmth down to her tummy. "There are at least a dozen pianos at my store," he said. "Some of them have never been played. I could have one sent here tomorrow."

Her eyes widened at the thought of so many pianos in one place. "You've already been far too generous," she told him. "The greatest kindness you could bestow is the gift of your company."

His gaze locked with hers. "Does that mean you've agreed to let me court you?" he asked softly. At her timid nod, he leaned a few degrees closer, barely an inch, but it made her feel overwhelmed by him. "Then you'll have more of my company," he murmured. "What other gifts would you like?"

Blushing, she replied, "Mr. Winterborne, there is no need—"

"I'm still considering the piano."

"Flowers," she said quickly. "A tin of sweets, or a paper fan. *Small* gestures."

His lips curved. "Unfortunately I'm known for making large gestures."

At the conclusion of dinner, the gentlemen remained at the table and the ladies withdrew for tea.

"You were so dreadfully quiet at dinner, Helen," Pandora exclaimed as soon as they had entered the drawing room.

"Pandora," Kathleen reproved softly.

Cassandra came to her twin's defense. "But it's true. Helen was as talkative as a fern."

"I wasn't certain what to say to him," Helen admitted. "I didn't want to make a mistake."

"You did very well," Kathleen said. "Conversing with strangers isn't easy."

"It is if you don't care what you say," Pandora advised.

"Or what their opinion of you might be," Cassandra added.

Kathleen sent Helen a private glance of comical despair. "They'll never be ready for the season," she whispered, and Helen bit back a grin.

At the end of the evening, when Winterborne was donning his hat and gloves in the entrance hall, Helen impulsively picked up her potted orchid from a table in the drawing room, and brought it to him.

"Mr. Winterborne," she said earnestly, "I would like very much for you to have this."

He gave her a questioning glance as she pushed the pot into his hands.

"It's a Blue Vanda orchid," she explained.

"What should I do with it?"

"You might wish to keep it in a place where you can see it often. Remember that it doesn't like to be cold and wet, or hot and dry. Whenever it's moved to a new environment, the Vanda usually becomes distressed, so don't be alarmed if a flower shrivels and drops off. Generally it's best not to set it where there may be a draft, or too much sun. Or too much shadow. And never place it next to a bowl of fruit." She gave him an encouraging glance. "Later, I'll give you a special tonic to mist over it."

As Winterborne stared at the exotic flower in his hands with perplexed reluctance, Helen began to regret her spontaneous action. He didn't seem to want the gift, but she couldn't very well ask to have it back.

"You needn't take it if you don't want it," she said. "I would understand—"

"I want it." Winterborne looked into her eyes and smiled slightly. "Thank you."

Helen nodded and watched forlornly as he departed with the orchid caught firmly in his grasp.

"You gave him the Blue Vanda," Pandora said in wonder, coming to stand beside her.

"Yes."

Cassandra came to her other side. "The most diabolically temperamental orchid of your entire collection."

Helen sighed. "Yes."

"He'll kill it within a week," Kathleen said flatly. "Any of us would."

"Yes."

"Then why did you give it to him?"

Helen frowned and gestured with her palms up. "I wanted him to have something special."

"He has thousands of special things from all over the world," Pandora pointed out.

"Something special from me," Helen clarified gently, and no one asked her about it after that.

*Chapter 30*

"I'VE WAITED A FORTNIGHT to see this," Pandora said in excitement.

Cassandra practically vibrated in the carriage seat beside her. "I've waited my *entire life*."

As he had promised, Winterborne had arranged for Kathleen and the Ravenel sisters to visit the department store after hours, and allow them to shop for as long as they liked. He had told the saleswomen to leave out their counter displays of items that young women might fancy, such as gloves, hats and pins, and all manner of adornments. The Ravenels would be free to visit any of the eighty-five departments in the store, including the book department, the perfume hall, and the food hall.

"If only Cousin West were with us," Pandora said wistfully.

West had returned to Eversby Priory after having spent less than a week in London. He had admitted to Kathleen that there was no more novelty left for him in any corner of London. "In the past," he'd told her, "I did everything worth doing multiple times. Now I can't stop thinking about all that needs to be done at the estate. It's the only place where I can actually be of use to someone."

There had been no concealing his eagerness to head back to Hampshire.

"I miss him too," Cassandra said.

"Oh, I don't miss him," Pandora told her impishly, "I was just thinking that we could buy more things if he were here to help carry the packages."

"We'll set aside the items you choose," Devon said, "and have them sent to Ravenel House tomorrow."

"I want you both to remember," Kathleen told the twins, "the pleasure of shopping lasts only until it's time to settle the bill."

"But we won't have to do that," Pandora pointed out. "All the bills go to Lord Trenear."

Devon grinned. "I'll remind you of this conversation when there's no money left to buy food."

"Just think, Helen," Cassandra said brightly, "if you marry Mr. Winterborne, you'll have the same name as a department store!"

Kathleen knew that the thought held no appeal for Helen, who didn't desire attention or notoriety in any form. "He hasn't proposed to Helen yet," she said evenly.

"He will," Pandora said confidently. "He's come to dinner at least three times, and accompanied us to a concert, and let us all sit in his private box. Obviously the courtship is going very well." Pausing, she added with a touch of sheepishness, "For the rest of the family, at least."

"He likes Helen," Cassandra remarked. "I can tell by the way he looks at her. Like a fox ogling a chicken."

"Cassandra," Kathleen warned. She glanced at Helen, who was staring down at her gloves.

It was difficult to tell whether the courtship was going well or not. Helen was sphinxlike on the subject of Winterborne, revealing nothing about what they had discussed, or how she felt. So far Kathleen had seen nothing in their interactions to indicate that they actually might like each other.

Kathleen had avoided discussing the subject with

Devon, knowing it would lead to another pointless argument. In fact, she hadn't discussed much of anything with him during the past two weeks. After the family's morning excursions, Devon usually left to meet with lawyers, accountants, or railway executives, or to attend the House of Lords, which was back in session. He returned late most nights, weary and disinclined to talk after having been sociable all day.

Only to herself could she admit how much she missed their intimacy. She longed for their companionable, amusing conversations, and the easy charm and comfort he had given her. Now he could barely bring himself to meet her gaze. She felt their separateness almost as a physical numbness. It seemed they would never find enjoyment in each other's company again. Perhaps that was for the best, she thought bleakly. After his coolness to her regarding her possible pregnancy—her monthly courses still hadn't started—and the way he had deceived her into coming to London merely as a pretext to push Helen together with Winterborne, Kathleen would never trust him again. He was a manipulator and a scoundrel.

The carriage arrived at the mews behind Winterborne's, where one of the back entrances would allow them to enter the store discreetly. After the footman opened the door and set a movable step on the pavement, Devon helped the young women from the carriage. Kathleen was the last to emerge, taking Devon's gloved hand as she stepped down, releasing it as soon as possible. Laborers passed through the nearby delivery yard, carrying crates and boxes to the loading dock.

"This way," Devon said to Kathleen, leading the way toward an arched entrance. The others followed at their heels.

A blue-uniformed doorman opened a large bronze

door and tipped his hat. "Welcome to Winterborne's, my lord. At your service, ladies." As they passed through the doorway, he handed them each a little booklet in turn. The ivory and blue covers had been stamped with gilt letters that read, "Winterborne's," and below that, "Index of Departments."

"Mr. Winterborne is waiting at the central rotunda," the doorman said.

It was a mark of the twins' awe and excitement that they were completely silent.

Winterborne's was a pleasure palace, an Aladdin's cave designed to dazzle its customers. The interior was lavishly appointed with carved oak paneling, molded plaster ceilings, and wood flooring with intricate insets of mosaic tiles. Instead of the small, enclosed rooms of traditional shops, the interior of Winterborne's was open and airy, with wide archways that allowed customers to move easily from one department to the next. Glittering chandeliers shed light on intriguing objects that had been heaped inside polished glass cases, with even more treasures artfully arranged on countertops.

In one day of shopping at Winterborne's, one could buy an entire household's worth of goods, including crystal and china, cooking utensils, hardware, heavy furniture, upholstery fabric, clocks, vases, musical instruments, framed artwork, a saddle for the horse, and a wooden ice refrigerator and all the food to store inside it.

They approached the central rotunda, six stories high, with each floor framed by gilded scrollwork balconies. It was surmounted by an enormous stained-glass dome with scrolls, rosettes, and other flourishes. Winterborne, who was standing beside a plate-glass counter and looking down at its contents, glanced up at their approach.

"Welcome," he said, a smile in his eyes. "Is this what

you had expected?" The question was addressed to the group, but his gaze had gone to Helen.

The twins erupted with happy exclamations and praise, while Helen shook her head and smiled. "It's even more grand than I had imagined," she told him.

"Let me take you on a tour." Winterborne slid a questioning glance to the rest of the group. "Would any of you like to accompany us? Or perhaps you'd like to start shopping?" He gestured to a stack of rattan baskets near the counter.

The twins looked at each other, and decisively said, "Shopping."

Winterborne grinned. "The confectionery and books are in that direction. Drugs and perfumery over there. Back there you'll find hats, scarves, ribbons, and lace." Before he had even finished the sentence, the twins had each grabbed a basket and dashed away.

"Girls . . ." Kathleen began, disconcerted by their wildness, but they were already out of earshot. She looked at Winterborne ruefully. "For your own safety, try to stay out of their path or you'll be trampled."

"You should have seen how the ladies behaved during my first bi-annual sale discounts," Winterborne told her. "Violence. Screaming. I'd rather go through the train accident again."

Kathleen couldn't help smiling.

Winterborne escorted Helen away from the rotunda. "Would you like to see the pianos?" she heard him ask.

Her timid reply was muffled as they retreated from sight.

Devon came to stand beside Kathleen.

After a long, uncomfortable moment, she asked, "When you look at them, do you ever see two people who feel even the slightest infatuation for each other? There's no natural ease between them, no sharing of mutual enthusiasms. They talk as if they were strangers on an omnibus."

"I see two people who haven't yet lowered their guards with each other," came his matter-of-fact reply.

Pushing back from the counter, Kathleen wandered to an elegant display of stationery supplies in another area of the rotunda. A lacquered tray of scent bottles occupied the countertop. According to a small framed placard, the scent was intended specifically for ladies who wished to mist their correspondence with fragrance that was guaranteed not to stain paper or cause ink to run.

Wordlessly Devon came to stand behind her, his hands coming to rest on the counter, on either side of her. Kathleen inhaled sharply. Caged by his hard, warm body, she couldn't move as she felt his mouth touch the back of her neck. She closed her eyes, her senses mesmerized by the vital masculine strength of him. The heat of his breath stirred a stray wisp of hair that lay on her nape, the feeling so exquisite that she trembled.

"Turn around," he whispered.

Kathleen shook her head mutely, her blood racing.

"I miss you." One of his hands lifted, his fingertips caressing her nape with erotic sensitivity. "I want to come to your bed tonight. Even if it's just to hold you."

"I'm sure you'll have no problem finding a woman who's eager to share her bed with you," she said tartly.

He pressed close enough to nudge the side of her face with his, the friction of his shaved chin brushing her like a cat's tongue. "I only want you."

She stiffened against the pleasure of feeling him all around her. "You shouldn't say that until we discover whether or not I'm with child. Although neither answer would ever make things right between us."

A gentle kiss nuzzled into the skin beneath her jaw.

"I'm sorry," he said huskily. "I shouldn't have reacted that way. I wish I could take back every word. It wasn't your fault; you have little experience in the act of love. I know better than anyone how damnably difficult it is to pull back at the precise moment that you want to be as close to someone as possible."

Stunned by his apology, Kathleen continued to stand facing away from him. She hated the vulnerability that had invaded her, the rush of loneliness and desire that made her want to turn in his arms and start weeping.

Before she could come up with a coherent reply, she heard the twins' vociferous chatter, and the clinking and rustling of a great number of objects being carried at once. Devon moved away from her.

"We need more baskets," Pandora said triumphantly, entering the hall.

The twins, who were clearly having a splendid time, had adorned themselves outlandishly. Cassandra was dressed in a green opera cloak with a jeweled feather ornament affixed to her hair. Pandora had tucked a light blue lace parasol beneath one arm, and a pair of lawn tennis rackets beneath the other, and was wearing a flowery diadem headdress that had slipped partially over one eye.

"From the looks of it," Kathleen said, "you've done enough shopping already."

Cassandra looked concerned. "Oh, no, we still have at least eighty departments to visit."

Kathleen couldn't help glancing at Devon, who was trying, without success, to stifle a grin. It was the first time she had seen him truly smile in days.

Enthusiastically the girls lugged the baskets to her and began to set objects on the counter in an unwieldy pile ... perfumed soaps, powders, pomades, stockings, books, new corset laces and racks of hairpins, artificial flowers, tins of biscuits, licorice pastilles and barley sweets, a metal mesh tea infuser, hosiery tucked in little netted bags, a set of drawing pencils, and a tiny glass bottle filled with bright red liquid.

"What is this?" Kathleen asked, picking up the bottle and viewing it suspiciously.

"It's a beautifier," Pandora said.

"Bloom of Rose," Cassandra chimed in.

Kathleen gasped as she realized what it was. "It's *rouge*." She had never even held a container of rouge before. Setting it on the counter, she said firmly, "No."

"But Kathleen—"

"No to rouge," she said, "now and for all time."

"We need to enhance our complexions," Pandora protested.

"It won't do any harm," Cassandra chimed in. "The bottle says that Bloom of Rose is 'delicate and inoffensive' . . . It's written right there, you see?"

"The comments you would receive if you wore rouge in public would assuredly *not* be delicate or inoffensive. People would assume you were a fallen woman. Or worse, an actress."

Pandora turned to Devon. "Lord Trenear, what do you think?"

"This is one of those times when it's best for a man to avoid thinking altogether," he said hastily.

"Bother," Cassandra said. Reaching for a white glass pot with a gilded top, she gave it to Kathleen. "We found this for you. It's lily pomatum, for your wrinkles."

"I don't have wrinkles," Kathleen said with dawning indignation.

"Not yet," Pandora allowed. "But someday you will."

Devon grinned as the twins snatched their empty baskets and scurried away to continue shopping.

"When my wrinkles appear," Kathleen said ruefully, "those two will have caused most of them."

"That day will be a long time coming." Looking down at her, Devon cupped her face with his hands. "But when it does, you'll be even more beautiful."

The skin beneath his gentle touch flamed with a blush more brilliant than potted rouge could have imparted. Desperately she tried to make herself pull away from him, but his touch had paralyzed her.

His finger slid around the back of her neck, holding her steady as his mouth sought hers. A shock of heat went through her, and she went weak, swaying as if the floor had tipped like the deck of a ship. His arm went around her, locking her against his body, and the feel of his effortless power devastated her. *I'm yours*, he'd once made her say in the carriage room as he had taunted her with sensual pleasure. It had been the truth. She would always be his, no matter where she went or what she did.

A soft moan of despair slipped from her throat, but his kiss absorbed every sound and breath. He feasted on her with controlled hunger, his head turning as he deepened the angle to fit their mouths together more closely. Touching her tongue with his, he enticed a response, his kiss tender and fiercely demanding. She was lost in a confusion of pleasure, her body flooded with ungoverned craving.

Without warning, Devon pulled back. She whimpered and reached for him blindly.

"Someone's coming," he said quietly.

Leaning against the counter for support, Kathleen fumbled to smooth her dress and tried to control her breathing.

Helen and Winterborne were returning to the rotunda. The corners of Helen's mouth were curved upward as if they had been tacked there with pins. But something about her posture reminded Kathleen of a lost toddler being led in search of its mother.

Kathleen's apprehensive gaze was drawn to the glitter on Helen's left hand. Her stomach dropped, all the sensuous warmth leaving her body as she realized what it was.

A ring.

After a mere two weeks of courtship, the bastard had proposed.

# Chapter 31

*Dear Kathleen,*

*I have just returned from the Lufton farm after inquiring about the welfare of their newest resident. Please convey to all concerned parties that Hamlet is thoroughly content with his pen, which, I might add, has been constructed to the highest porcine standards. He seems enthused about keeping company with his own harem of sows. I would venture to say that a pig of simple pleasures could ask for nothing more.*

*All other news from the estate pertains to drainage trenches and plumbing mishaps, none of it agreeable to relate.*

*I am anxious to know how you are taking the engagement between Helen and Winterborne. In the spirit of brotherly concern, I beg you to write soon, at least to tell me if murder is being planned.*

*Affectionately yours,*
*West*

Kathleen took up a pen to reply, reflecting that she missed West more than she would have guessed. How strange it was that the drunken young rake who had come to Eversby Priory all those months ago should have become such a steadying presence in her life.

Dear West,

Upon Mr. Winterborne's proposal to Helen last week, I will confess to initial thoughts of homicide. However, I realized that if I did away with Winterborne, I would also have to dispatch your brother, and that wouldn't do. One murder may be justifiable in these circumstances, but two would be self-indulgent.

Helen is quiet and withdrawn, which is not what one expects of a girl who has just become engaged. It is obvious that she loathes the engagement ring, but she refuses to ask Winterborne to change it. Yesterday Winterborne decided to undertake all the planning and expenses of the wedding, so she'll have no say in that either.

Winterborne dominates without even seeming to be aware of it. He's like a great tree that casts a shade in which smaller trees can't thrive.

Regardless, the wedding seems inevitable.

I'm resigned to the situation. At least, I'm trying to be.

Your brotherly concern is much appreciated, and returned with sisterly affection.

Ever yours,
Kathleen

DEVON RETURNED HOME late in the evening, filled with weary satisfaction.

The lease agreement with London Ironstone had been signed by both parties.

During the past week, Severin had turned the negotiations into a cat-and-mouse game. It had required inhuman discipline and a surplus of energy to contend with Severin's accelerations, delays, surprises, and amendments. At several points, the lawyers had fallen silent while the two of them feuded and sparred. Finally Devon had been able to force the concessions he'd wanted, just as he had found himself considering the prospect of leaping across the table and strangling his friend. The infuriating part had been knowing that Severin, unlike anyone else in the room, had been having a perfectly splendid time.

Severin loved excitement, conflict, anything to entertain his voracious brain. Although people were drawn to him and he was invited everywhere, it was difficult to tolerate his feverish energy for long. Spending time with him was like attending a fireworks display: enjoyable for a short time, but fatiguing if it lasted for too long.

After the butler took his coat, hat, and gloves, Devon headed to the study for a much-needed drink. As he passed the stairs, he could hear traces of laughter and conversation from the upstairs drawing room, while the music box played a glimmering cascade of notes.

The study was lit by a single table lamp and a fire on the hearth. Kathleen's small form was curled in the upholstered wing chair, her fingers forming slack loops around the stem of an empty wineglass. A pang of pleasure went through him as he saw that she wore the colorful shawl he'd given her. She stared pensively into the fire, flickers of light gilding the delicate line of her profile.

He'd had no time alone with her since Helen and Winterborne had become engaged. She had been quiet and disinclined to talk, obviously struggling with her unhappiness over the situation. Moreover, during the past week, the deal with London Ironstone had consumed Devon's attention. It was too important for the estate: He hadn't been able to risk failure. Now that the deal was signed, he intended to set his house in order.

As Devon entered the room, Kathleen looked up with a neutral expression.

"Hello. How did your meeting go?"

"The lease is signed," he said, going to pour a glass of wine for himself at the sideboard.

"Did he agree to your terms?"

"The most important ones."

"Congratulations," she said sincerely. "I had no doubt that you would prevail."

Devon smiled. "I had more than a few doubts. Severin is infinitely more experienced at business. However, I tried to compensate with pure stubbornness." Gesturing with the wine decanter, he gave her a questioning glance.

"Thank you, but I've had enough." She nodded toward the desk in the corner. "A telegram arrived for you just before dinner. It's on the silver tray."

He went to retrieve it, opening the gummed seal. Looking down at the message, he frowned curiously. "It's from West."

COME TO THE ESTATE WITHOUT DELAY

W.R.

"He wants me to go to Hampshire immediately," Devon said, puzzled. "He doesn't say why."

Kathleen glanced at him with instant worry. "I hope it's not bad news."

"It's no more than middling-bad, or he would have included an explanation. I'll have to take the first train in the morning."

Setting her empty glass aside, Kathleen stood and smoothed her skirts. She looked tired but lovely, a pucker of worry pinching the space between her brows. She spoke without looking at him. "My monthly courses started this morning. There is no baby. I knew you would wish to learn of it as soon as possible."

Devon contemplated her silently.

Strangely, the relief he would have expected to feel wasn't there. Only a sort of blank ambivalence. He should be falling to his knees in gratitude.

"Are you relieved?" he asked.

"Of course. I didn't want the baby any more than you did."

Something about her calm, reasonable tone rankled.

As Devon stepped toward her, every line of her body tensed in wordless rejection.

"Kathleen," he began, "I'm weary of this distance between us. Whatever is necessary—"

"Please. Not now. Not tonight."

The only thing that stopped him from reaching for her and kissing her senseless was the soft, raw note in her voice. He closed his eyes briefly, grappling for patience. When that failed, he lifted his wineglass and finished the drink in three measured gulps.

"When I return," he said, leveling a steady stare at her, "you and I are going to have a long talk. Alone."

Her lips tightened at his severe tone. "Am I to have a choice in the matter?"

"Yes. You'll have the choice of whether we go to bed before the talk, or after."

Letting out an indignant breath, she left the study, while he stood there gripping his empty glass, his gaze fixed on the vacant doorway.

# Chapter 32

THE INSTANT THAT DEVON stepped off the train at Alton Station, he was confronted by the sight of his brother in a dusty coat and mud-crusted breeches and boots. There was a wild look in West's eyes.

"West?" Devon asked in startled concern. "What the devil—"

"Did you sign the lease?" West interrupted, reaching out as if to seize his lapels, then appearing to think better of it. He was twitching with impatience, bouncing on his heels like a restless schoolboy. "The London Ironstone lease. *Did you sign it?*"

"Yesterday."

West let out a curse that attracted a slew of censorious gazes from the crowd on the platform. "What of the mineral rights?"

"The mineral rights on the land we're leasing to the railway?" Devon clarified.

"*Yes*, did you give them to Severin? *Any* of them?"

"I kept all of them."

West stared at him without blinking. "You're absolutely sure?"

"Of course I am. Severin badgered me about the mineral rights for three days. The longer we debated, the more exasperated I became, until I said I'd see him in hell before I let him have so much as a clod of manure from Eversby Priory. I walked out, but just as I reached the street, he shouted from the fifth-floor window that he gave in and I should come back."

West leaped forward as if he were about embrace him, then checked the movement. He shook Devon's hand violently and proceeded to thump his back with painful vigor. "By God, I love you, you pigheaded bastard!"

"What the devil is wrong with you?" Devon demanded.

"I'll show you. Let's go."

"I have to wait for Sutton. He's in one of the back carriages."

"We don't need Sutton."

"He can't walk to Eversby from Alton," Devon said, his annoyance fading into laughter. "Damn it, West, you're jumping about as if someone shoved a hornet's nest up your—"

"There he is," West exclaimed, gesturing to the valet, motioning for him to hurry.

At West's insistence, the carriage proceeded not to the manor, but to the eastern perimeter of Eversby Priory, accessible only by unpaved roads. Devon realized they were heading to the acreage he had just leased to Severin.

Eventually the vehicle stopped by a field bordered with a stream and a stand of beech. The rough fields and hillocks swarmed with activity; at least a dozen men were busy with surveying equipment, shovels, picks, barrows, and a steam-powered engine.

"What are they doing?" Devon asked, mystified. "Are those Severin's men? They can't be grading the land yet. The lease was signed only yesterday."

"No, I hired them." West pushed the carriage door open before the driver could reach it. He swung to the ground. "Come."

"My lord," Sutton protested as Devon made to follow. "You're not attired for such crude terrain. All that rock and clay . . . your shoes, your trousers . . ." He regarded the pristine hems of Devon's gray angora wool trousers with anguish.

"You can wait in the carriage," Devon told the valet.

"Yes, my lord."

A heavily misted breeze blew against Devon's face as he and West walked to a freshly dug trench marked with flags. The fragrance of earth, wet sedge, and peat wrapped around them, a fresh and familiar Hampshire smell.

As they passed a man with a barrow, he stopped and removed his hat, bowing his head respectfully. "Your lordship."

Devon responded with a brief smile and nod.

Reaching the edge of the trench, West bent to pick up a small rock and handed it to Devon.

The rock—more of a pebble—was unexpectedly heavy for its size. Devon used his thumb to scrape dirt from it, uncovering a ruddy surface banded with bright red. "Ore?" he guessed, examining the pebble closely.

"High-grade hematite ore." West's tone was filled with compressed excitement. "It makes the best steel. It commands the highest price on the market."

Devon glanced at him with sharpening interest. "Go on."

"While I was away in London," West continued, "it seems that Severin's surveyors did some test boring here. One of the tenants—Mr. Wooten—heard the machines and came to see what was afoot. The surveyors told him nothing, of course. But as soon as I learned of it, I hired a geologist and a mining surveyor to do our own testing. They've been here for three days with a rock-boring machine, pulling up sample after sample of that." He nodded to the hematite in Devon's hand.

Beginning to understand, Devon closed his fingers around the hard lump of ore. "How much of it is there?"

"They're still assessing. But they both agree that a massive bed of banded hematite lies close to the surface, just beneath a layer of clay and limestone. From what they've observed so far, it's eight feet thick in some places, twenty-two feet in others—and it extends for at least fifteen acres. All your land. The geologist says he's never seen a deposit like this south of Cumberland." His voice turned husky. "It's easily worth a half million pounds, Devon."

Devon had the sense of reeling backward, even though he was standing still. It was too much to take in. He gazed at the scene without really seeing it, his brain striving to comprehend what it meant.

The soul-crushing burden of debt that had weighed on him ever since he'd inherited the estate . . . gone. Everyone at Eversby Priory would be safe. Theo's sisters would have dowries large enough to attract any suitors they chose. There would be work for the men of Eversby, and new business for the village.

"Well?" West asked expectantly as Devon's silence stretched out.

"I can't trust that it's real," he managed to say, "until I know more."

"You can trust it. Believe me, a hundred thousand tons of stone is not going to vanish from beneath our feet."

A slow grin worked over Devon's face. "Now I understand why Severin tried so hard to obtain the mineral rights."

"Thank God you're so stubborn."

Devon laughed. "That's the first time you've ever said that to me."

"And the last," West assured him.

Turning a slow circle to view their surroundings, Devon sobered as he glanced at the woodlands to the south. "I can't let the estate's timber be razed for furnaces and forges."

"No, there's no need for us to mine or smelt. The hematite ore is so pure, we'll only need to quarry. As soon as it's taken from the ground, it can be transported."

Completing the circle, Devon caught sight of a man and a small boy walking around the rock-boring machine, viewing it with great interest.

"First an earldom," West was saying, "then the railway lease deal. Now this. I think you may be the luckiest sod in England."

Devon's attention held on the man and little boy. "Who is that?"

West followed his gaze. "Ah. That's Wooten. He's brought one of his sons to see the machine."

Wooten bent with his torso parallel to the ground, and the little boy climbed onto his back. Hooking his arms beneath his son's legs, the young farmer stood and carried him across the field. The boy clung to his father's shoulders, laughing.

Devon watched the pair as they retreated into the distance.

The sight of the child summoned an image to the forefront of his mind . . . Kathleen's blank face, limned in fire glow, as she'd told him there would be no baby.

All he had been aware of was a puzzling feeling of emptiness.

It was only now that Devon realized he had assumed she would be pregnant—which would have left him no choice to marry her. Having lived with that idea in the back of his mind for a fortnight, he had become accustomed to it.

No . . . that wasn't quite accurate.

Shaken, Devon brought himself to face the truth.

He'd *wanted* it.

He'd wanted the excuse to make Kathleen his in every way. He wanted his baby inside her. He wanted his ring on her finger, and every marital right that it conferred.

He wanted to share every day of the rest of his life with her.

"What are you worrying about?" he heard his brother ask.

Devon was slow to reply, trying to retrace the steps that had led him so far away from everything he'd always thought he was. "Before I inherited the title," he said dazedly, "I wouldn't have trusted either of us with a goldfish, much less a twenty-thousand-acre estate. I've always shunned any kind of responsibility because I knew I couldn't manage it. I'm a scapegrace and a hothead, like our father. When you told me that I had no idea how to run the estate and I was going to fail—"

"That was a load of bollocks," West said flatly.

Devon grinned briefly. "You made some valid points." Absently he began to roll the hematite between his palms. "But against all odds, it seems that you and I have managed to make enough of the right choices—"

"No," West interrupted. "I'll take no credit for this. You alone decided to take on the burden of the estate. You made the decisions that led to the lease deal and the discovery of the iron deposits. Has it occurred to you that if any of the previous earls had bothered to make the land improvements they should have, the hematite bed would have been discovered decades ago? You certainly would have found it when you ordered the drainage trenches dug for the tenant farms. You see, Eversby Priory is in good hands: *yours*. You've changed hundreds of lives for the better, including mine. Whatever the word is for a man who's done all that . . . it's not 'scapegrace.'" West paused. "My God, I can feel sincerity rising in my chest like a digestive disorder. I have to stop. Shall we go to the house for you to change into some field boots? Then we can return here, talk to the surveyors, and have a walk around."

Pondering the question, Devon dropped the pebble into his pocket, and met his brother's gaze squarely.

One thought was paramount: None of this mattered without Kathleen. He had to go to her at once, and somehow make her understand that during the past few months, he had changed without even being aware of it. He had become a man who could love her.

God, how madly he loved her.

But he had to find a way of convincing her, which would not be easy.

On the other hand . . . he wasn't a man to back down from a challenge.

Not any longer.

He glanced at his brother and spoke in a voice that wasn't quite steady. "I can't stay," he said. "I have to go back to London."

THE MORNING OF Devon's departure, Helen didn't come downstairs for breakfast, but sent word that she was suffering a migraine and would stay in bed. Unable to remember the last time that Helen had been ill, Kathleen was deeply concerned. After giving Helen a dose of Godfrey's Cordial to relieve the pain, she applied cool compresses to her forehead and made certain that the bedroom was kept dark and quiet.

At least once an hour, as Helen slept, Kathleen or one of the twins tiptoed to the doorway of her room to look in on her. She didn't awaken during any of the visits, only twitched like a sleeping cat and drifted through dreams that seemed far from pleasant.

"It's a good sign that she has no fever, isn't it?" Pandora asked in the afternoon.

"Yes," Kathleen replied firmly. "I expect that after the excitement of the past week, she needs rest."

"I don't think that's what it is," Cassandra said. She had perched on the settee with a brush and rack of hairpins and a fashion periodical in her lap, experimenting with Pandora's hair. They were attempting to copy one of the latest styles, an elaborate affair that consisted of locks of hair rolled and pinned into puffs atop the head, with a loose double chatelaine braid falling down the back. Unfortunately Pandora's chocolaty hair was so heavy and slippery that it refused to stay in its pins, the locks sliding free and collapsing the puffs.

"Be stern," Pandora encouraged. "Use more pomade. My hair will respond only to brute force."

"We should have bought more at Winterborne's," Cassandra said with a sigh. "We've already gone through half the—"

"Wait," Kathleen said, staring at Cassandra. "What did you just say? Not about the pomade, the thing you said about Helen."

The girl brushed out a lock of Pandora's hair as she answered. "I don't think she needs rest because of too much excitement. I think . . ." She paused. "Kathleen, is it tattling if I say something about someone else that's private and I know they wouldn't want it to be repeated?"

"Yes. Unless it's about Helen and you're telling it to me. Go on."

"Yesterday, when Mr. Winterborne came to visit, he and Helen were in the downstairs parlor with the door closed. I was going to fetch a book I'd left on the window ledge, but I heard their voices." Cassandra paused. "You were with the housekeeper, going over the inventory list, so I didn't think it was worth bothering you."

"Yes, yes . . . *and?*"

"From what little I could hear, they were quarreling about something. Perhaps I shouldn't call it quarreling, since Helen didn't raise her voice, but . . . she sounded distressed."

"They were probably discussing the wedding," Kathleen said, "since that was when Mr. Winterborne told her he wanted to plan it."

"No, I don't think that was why they were at odds. I wish I could have heard more."

"You should have used my drinking glass trick," Pandora said impatiently. "If I'd been there, I would be able to tell you every word that was said."

"I went upstairs," Cassandra continued, "and just as I reached the top, I saw Mr. Winterborne leave. Helen came upstairs a few minutes afterward, and her face was very red, as if she'd been crying."

"Did she say anything about what happened?" Kathleen asked.

Cassandra shook her head.

Pandora frowned, reaching up to her hair. Gingerly touching the pinned section Cassandra had been working on, she said, "These don't feel like puffs. They feel like giant caterpillars."

A swift smile was wrenched from Kathleen's lips as she regarded the pair. Heaven help her, she loved the two of them. Although she was not wise or old enough to be their mother, she was all they had in the way of maternal guidance.

"I'll look in on Helen," she said, standing. She reached

for Pandora's hair and separated one of the caterpillars into two puffs, using a pin from Cassandra to anchor it.

"What are you going to say if she tells you that she had a row with Winterborne?" Cassandra asked.

"I'll tell her to have more of them," Kathleen said. "One can't allow a man to have his way all the time." She paused reflectively. "Once Lord Berwick told me that when a horse pulls at the reins, one should never pull back. Instead, loosen them. But never more than an inch."

As KATHLEEN LET herself into Helen's room, she heard the muffled sounds of weeping. "Dear, what is it?" she asked, moving swiftly to the bedside. "Are you in pain? What can I do?"

Helen shook her head and blotted her eyes with the sleeve of her nightgown.

Kathleen went to pour a glass of water from the jug on the nightstand and brought it to her. She propped a pillow beneath Helen's head, gave her a dry handkerchief, and straightened the covers. "Is the migraine still bad?"

"Dreadful," Helen whispered. "Even my skin hurts."

Pulling a chair to the bedside, Kathleen sat and regarded her with aching concern. "What brought this on?" she dared to ask. "Did something happen during Mr. Winterborne's visit? Something besides discussing the wedding?"

Helen responded with a minuscule nod, her jaw trembling.

Kathleen's thoughts whirled as she wondered how to help Helen, who seemed on the verge of falling apart. She hadn't seen her this undone since Theo's death.

"I wish you would tell me," she said. "My imagination is running amok. What did Winterborne do to make you so unhappy?"

"I can't say," Helen whispered.

Kathleen tried to keep her voice calm. "Did he force himself on you?"

A long silence followed. "I don't know," Helen said in a sodden voice. "He wanted . . . I don't know what he wanted. I've never—" She stopped and blew her nose into the handkerchief.

"Did he hurt you?" Kathleen forced herself to ask.

"No. But he kept kissing me and wouldn't stop, and . . . I didn't like it. It wasn't at all what I thought kissing would be. And he put his hand . . . somewhere he shouldn't. When I pushed him away, he looked angry and said something sharp that sounded like . . . I thought I was too good for him. He said other things as well, but there was too much Welsh mixed in. I didn't know what to do. I started to cry, and he left without another word." She gave a few hiccupping sobs. "I don't understand what I did wrong."

"You did nothing wrong."

"But I did, I *must* have." Helen lifted her thin fingers to her temples, pressing lightly over the cloth that covered them.

*Winterborne, you hum-handed sod*, Kathleen thought furiously. *Is it really so difficult for you to be gentle with a shy young woman, the first time you kiss her?* "Obviously he has no idea how to behave with an innocent girl," she said quietly.

"Please don't tell anyone. I would die. *Please* promise."

"I promise."

"I must make Mr. Winterborne understand that I didn't mean to make him angry—"

"Of course you didn't. He should know that." Kathleen hesitated. "Before you proceed with the wedding plans, perhaps we should take some time to reconsider the engagement."

"I don't know." Helen winced and gasped. "My head is

throbbing. Right now I feel as if I never want to see him again. Please, would you give me some more Godfrey's Cordial?"

"Yes, but first you must eat something. Cook is making broth and blancmange. It will be ready soon. Shall I leave the room? I think my talking has made your migraine worse."

"No, I want company."

"I'll stay, then. Rest your poor head."

Helen obeyed, subsiding. In a moment, there was a quiet sniffle. "I'm so disappointed," she whispered. "About kissing."

"Darling, no," Kathleen said, her heart breaking a little. "You haven't really been kissed. It's different with the right man."

"I don't see how it could be. I thought . . . I thought it would be like listening to beautiful music, or . . . or watching the sunrise on a clear morning. And instead . . ."

"Yes?"

Helen hesitated, and made a revolted little sound. "He wanted me to part my lips. *During.*"

"Oh."

"Is it because he's Welsh?"

A mixture of sympathy and amusement swept through Kathleen. She replied in a matter-of-fact tone. "I don't believe that manner of kissing is limited to the Welsh, dear. Perhaps the idea isn't appealing at first. But if you try it a time or two, you might find it pleasant."

"How could I? How could anyone?"

"There are many kinds of kisses," Kathleen said. "Had Mr. Winterborne introduced you to it gradually, you may have been more disposed to like it."

"I don't think I like kisses at all."

Kathleen dampened a fresh white cloth, folded it, and laid it across Helen's forehead. "You will. With the right man, kissing is wonderful. Like falling into a long, sweet dream. You'll see."

"I don't think so," Helen whispered, her fingers plucking at the counterpane and twitching with agitation.

Staying by the bedside, Kathleen watched as Helen relaxed and drowsed.

She knew that the cause of Helen's problems would have to be addressed before her condition would truly improve. Having suffered from nervous distress in the weeks after Theo's death, Kathleen could recognize the signs in someone else. It made her heart ache to see Helen's cheerful nature crumbling beneath the weight of anxiety.

If it went on for too long, Kathleen was afraid that Helen might descend into a deep melancholy.

She had to do something. Driven by intense worry, she left Helen's bedside and went to ring for Clara.

As soon as the maid reached her room, Kathleen told her briskly, "I need a pair of walking boots, a veil, and my hooded cloak. I must go on an errand, and I need you to accompany me."

Clara looked disconcerted. "I can run the errand, milady, if you tell me what you need."

"Thank you, but I'm the only one who can do it."

"Shall I tell the butler to have the coach readied?"

Kathleen shook her head. "It would be much easier and simpler to walk. It's a short distance, less than a half mile. We'll be on our way back before they've even finished harnessing the team."

"A half mile?" Clara, who wasn't fond of walking, looked aghast. "Through London at night?"

"It's still light outside. We'll be walking through gardens and along a promenade. Now hurry." *Before I lose my nerve*, she thought.

The errand would have to be carried out before anyone had time to object or delay them. With luck, they would return home before dinner.

Once she was warmly dressed and ready to leave, Kathleen went to the upstairs parlor where Cassandra was reading and Pandora was cutting pictures out of periodicals and gluing them into a scrapbook.

"Where are you going?" Cassandra asked in surprise.

"Out for an errand. Clara and I will return soon."

"Yes, but—"

"In the meantime," Kathleen said, "I would appreciate it if one of you would make certain that Helen's dinner tray is brought up to her. Sit with her and see that she eats something. But don't ask questions. It's better to stay quiet unless she wants you to talk."

"But what about you?" Pandora asked, frowning. "What is this errand, and when will you come back?"

"It's nothing for you to worry about."

"Whenever someone says that," Pandora said, "it always means the opposite. Along with 'It's only a scratch' or 'Worse things happen at sea.'"

"Or," Clara added glumly, 'I'm only going out for a pint.'"

AFTER A BRISK WALK, during which Kathleen and Clara merged with the mainstream of pedestrian traffic and were carried along in its momentum, they soon arrived at Cork Street.

"Winterborne's!" Clara exclaimed, her face brightening. "I didn't know it was a *shopping* errand, milady."

"Unfortunately it's not." Kathleen walked to the end of the serried façades, stopping at a grand house that somehow managed to blend tastefully with the department store. "Clara, will you go to the door and say that Lady Trenear wishes to see Mr. Wintcrborne?"

The girl obeyed reluctantly, taking no pleasure in performing a task that was usually handled by a footman.

As Kathleen waited on the lowest step, Clara twisted the mechanical doorbell and rapped the ornate bronze knocker until the door opened. An unsmiling butler glanced at the pair of visitors, exchanged a few words with Clara, and closed the door again.

Turning toward Kathleen, Clara said with a long-suffering expression, "He's going to see if Mr. Winterborne is at home."

Kathleen nodded and folded her arms at her chest, shivering as a chilling breeze whipped the folds of her cloak. Ignoring the curious glances of a few passersby, she waited with determined patience.

A short, broadly built man with white hair walked past the steps, pausing to glance at the maid. He stared at her with undue attention.

"Clara?" he asked in bemusement.

Her eyes widened with relief and gladness. "Mr. Quincy!"

The valet turned to Kathleen, recognizing her even with the veil shrouding her face. "Lady Trenear," he said reverently. "How does it happen that you are standing out here?"

"It's good to see you, Quincy," Kathleen said, smiling. "I've come to speak to Mr. Winterborne about a private matter. The butler said he would see if he was at home."

"If Mr. Winterborne is not at home, he is most definitely at the store. I will locate him for you." Clicking his tongue, Quincy escorted her up the stairs, with Clara following. "Keeping Lady Trenear waiting outside on the street," he muttered in disbelief. "I'll give that butler an earful he won't soon forget."

After opening the door with a key that hung on a gold fob, the valet showed them inside. The house was smart and modern, smelling of new paint and plaster, and wood finished with walnut oil.

Solicitously Quincy led Kathleen to an airy, high-ceilinged reading room and invited her to wait there while he took Clara to the servants' hall. "Shall I have someone bring tea for you," he asked, "while I go in search of Mr. Winterborne?"

She pulled back her veil, glad to remove the black haze from her vision. "That's very kind, but there's no need."

Quincy hesitated, clearly longing to know the reason for her unorthodox visit. He settled for asking, "Everyone at Ravenel House is in good health, I hope?"

"Yes, they're all well. Lady Helen is afflicted by a migraine, but I'm sure she'll recover soon."

He nodded, his snowy brows knitting together over his spectacles. "I'll find Mr. Winterborne," he said distractedly, and left with Clara in tow.

As she waited, Kathleen wandered around the reading room. More smells of newness, coupled with a slight staleness in the air. The house felt unfinished. Unoccupied. A paltry number of paintings and knickknacks seemed to have been scattered there as afterthoughts. The furniture looked as though it had never been used. Most of the reading room shelves were empty save for a handful of eclectic titles that Kathleen would have been willing to bet had been pulled carelessly from bookstore shelves and deposited there for display.

Judging by the reading room alone, Kathleen knew that it was not a house that Helen could be happy in, or a man she could ever be happy with.

A quarter hour passed while she considered what to say to Winterborne. Unfortunately there was no diplomatic way to tell a man that, among other things, he had made his fiancée ill.

Winterborne entered the room, his larger-than-life presence seeming to take up every surplus inch of space. "Lady Trenear. What an unexpected pleasure." He executed a shallow bow, his expression conveying that her visit was providing anything but pleasure to him.

She knew she had put them both in a difficult position. It was wildly unorthodox for her to call on an unmarried man with no one else present, and she was sorry for it. However, she'd had no choice.

"Please forgive me for inconveniencing you, Mr. Winterborne. I don't intend to stay long."

"Does anyone know you're here?" he asked curtly.

"No."

"Speak your piece, then, and make it fast."

"Very well. I—"

"But if it has anything to do with Lady Helen," he interrupted, "then leave now. She can come to me herself if there's something that needs to be discussed."

"I'm afraid Helen can't go anywhere at the moment. She's been in bed all day, ill with a nervous condition."

His eyes changed, some unfathomable emotion spangling the dark depths. "A nervous condition," he repeated, his voice iced with scorn. "That seems a common complaint among aristocratic ladies. Someday I'd like to know what makes you all so nervous."

Kathleen would have expected a show of sympathy or a few words of concern for the woman he was betrothed to. "I'm afraid you are the cause of Helen's distress," she said bluntly. "Your visit yesterday put her in a state."

Winterborne was silent, his eyes black and piercing.

"She told me only a little about what happened," Kathleen continued. "But it's clear that there is much you don't understand about Helen. My late husband's parents kept all three of their daughters very secluded. More than was good for them. As a result, all three are quite young for their age. Helen is one-and-twenty, but she hasn't had the same experiences, or seasoning, as other girls her age. She knows nothing of the world outside Eversby Priory. Everything is new to her. *Everything.* The only men she has ever associated with have been a handful of close relations, the servants, and the occasional visitor to the estate. Most of what she knows about men has been from books and fairy tales."

"No one can be that sheltered," Winterborne said flatly.

"Not in your world. But at an estate like Eversby Priory, it's entirely possible." Kathleen paused. "In my opinion, it's too soon for Helen to marry anyone, but when she does . . . she will need a husband with a placid temperament. One who will allow her to develop at her own pace."

"And you assume I wouldn't," he said rather than asked.

"I think you will command and govern a wife just as you do everything else. I don't believe you would ever harm her physically, but you'll whittle her to fit your life, and make her exceedingly unhappy. This environment—London, the crowds, the department store—is so ill suited to her nature that she would wither like a transplanted orchid. I'm afraid I can't support the idea of marriage for you and Helen." Pausing, she took a long breath before saying, "I believe it's in her best interest for the engagement to be broken."

A heavy silence descended.

"Is that what she wants?"

"She said earlier today that she has no wish to see you again."

Throughout Kathleen's speech, Winterborne had looked away as if he were only half listening. At that last remark, however, she found herself the target of a blade-like gaze.

Perhaps, she thought uneasily, it would be best to leave soon.

Winterborne approached her as she stood by the bookshelves. "Tell her she's free, then," he sneered. He leaned his cane against a shelf and set a broad hand on a section of fluted casing. "If a few kisses are enough to make her bedridden, I doubt she'd live through her first night as my wife."

Kathleen returned his gaze without flinching, knowing that he was trying to unnerve her. "I'll see that the ring is returned to you as soon as possible."

"She can keep it as compensation for wasted time."

Her nerves crawled as he set his free hand on the other side of the bookcase, trapping her without touching her. His shoulders blocked the rest of the room from her view.

Winterborne's insolent gaze raked over her. "Perhaps I'll take you instead," he astonished her by saying. "You're a blue blood. One supposes you're a lady. And for all your lack of size, you appear far more durable than Lady Helen."

She stared at him coldly. "There's nothing to be gained by mocking me."

"You don't believe I'm serious?"

"I don't give a monkey's toss whether you're serious or not," she shot back. "I have no interest in anything you could offer."

Winterborne grinned, his amusement seeming genuine but not the least bit friendly.

As Kathleen began to sidle away, he moved to block her with swift efficiency.

She froze, fear beginning to hum through her.

"Never assume you know what someone's going to offer. You should at least hear mine before you turn it down." Winterborne leaned down until his face was close to hers. That small movement conveyed at least a half-dozen distinct threats, any one of which would have been enough to cow her.

"It includes marriage," he said, "which is more than you'll ever have from Trenear." Contempt gleamed in his eyes as he saw her surprise. "No, he didn't tell me that you and he were carrying on. But it was obvious in Hampshire. He'll tire of you soon, if he hasn't already. Trenear wants novelty, he does. But what I want is to go places where I'm not welcome—and for that, I'll need to marry a highborn lady. It doesn't matter to me that you're not a virgin."

"How fortunate," Kathleen couldn't resist saying acidly, "since virgins don't appear to be your forte." As soon as the comment left her lips, she regretted it.

That unsettling cold grin again. "Aye, a virgin sacrifice Lady Helen was, for the sake of Eversby Priory and the rest of the Ravenels." Brazenly he used his forefinger to trace the seam at the shoulder of her dress. "Wouldn't you do the same for them? For her?"

She didn't flinch at his touch, although her flesh prickled. "I don't need to. Lord Trenear will take care of them."

"Who will take care of Trenear? He'll have to scheme and labor a lifetime to keep his estate from falling to ruins. But with the smallest fraction of my fortune"—he snapped his fingers in front of her face—"all his debt will vanish. The house will be restored, and the land will be made fat and green. A happy ending for everyone."

"Except for the woman who marries you," Kathleen said disdainfully.

Winterborne's smile was edged with a sneer. "There are women who like it the way I give it. In the past I've even pleased a fine lady or two, who were tired of lily-white gentlemen with soft hands." He stepped forward, crowding her against the bookshelves. Suggestiveness colored his low tone. "I could be your bit o' rough."

Kathleen didn't know what he intended, or how far he might go in the effort to intimidate her.

She would never find out. Before she could reply, a murderous voice came from the threshold.

"Back away, or I'll rip every limb from your body."

# Chapter 33

WINTERBORNE TOOK HIS HANDS from the bookshelf casings and mockingly kept them in the air as if he were being held at gunpoint. With a gasp of relief, Kathleen skirted around him and hurried toward Devon. But she stopped in her tracks when she saw his face.

From the looks of it, Devon's grip on sanity was not at all certain. His eyes gleamed with violence, and the muscles of his jaw were twitching. The infamous Ravenel temper had begun to burn every civilized layer into bright-edged ash, like the pages of a book cast into a fire.

"My lord," Kathleen began breathlessly, "I thought you'd gone to Hampshire."

"I did." His wrathful gaze flickered to her. "I just returned to Ravenel House. The twins said they thought you might be here."

"I found it necessary to talk to Mr. Winterborne about Helen—"

"You should have left it to me," Devon said through gritted teeth. "The mere fact of being alone with Winterborne could create a scandal that would haunt you for the rest of your life."

"That doesn't matter."

His face darkened. "From the first moment I met you, you've tortured me and everyone else within reach about the importance of propriety. And now *it doesn't matter*?"

He gave her an ominous glance before turning to Winterborne. "You should have turned her away at the door, you conniving bastard. The only reason I haven't throttled you both is that I can't decide which one of you to start with."

"Start with me," Winterborne invited gently.

The air was charged with masculine hostility.

"Later," Devon said with barely restrained rage. "For now, I'm taking her home. But the next time I see you, I'll put you in a fucking *box*." Turning his attention to Kathleen, he pointed to the doorway.

She didn't like being commanded as if she were a disobedient poodle. When he was in this state, however, she decided it was better not to provoke him. Reluctantly she started forward.

"Wait," Winterborne said gruffly. He went to a table near a window and seized something. She hadn't noticed it before; it was the potted orchid that Helen had given him. "Take this bloody thing," he said, shoving the pot at Kathleen. "By God, I'll be glad to be rid of it."

AFTER DEVON AND Kathleen had departed, Rhys stood at the window to view the scene outside. A streetlamp shed a weak lemon glow over a line of cab horses, illuminating the puffs of steam from their nostrils. Groups of pedestrians hurried across the wood pavement toward the department store display windows.

He was aware of Quincy's sturdy footsteps approaching.

After a moment, the valet asked reproachfully, "Was it necessary to frighten Lady Trenear?"

Rhys turned his head to give him a slitted glance. It was the first time Quincy had dared to speak to him so impudently. In the past, Rhys had fired more valuable men for far lesser remarks.

Instead, he folded his arms and returned his attention

to the street, loathing the world and everyone in it. "Aye," he said with soft malice. "It made me feel better."

ALTHOUGH DEVON DIDN'T say a word during the short ride back to Ravenel House, the force of his anger seemed to occupy every square inch of the carriage's interior. Clara huddled in the corner as if she were trying to make herself invisible.

Vacillating between guilt and defiance, Kathleen reflected that Devon was behaving as if he had rights over her, which he did not. He was carrying on as if she'd done something to injure him personally, which she had not. The situation was *his* fault—he was the one who had encouraged Winterborne to court Helen, and he had manipulated Helen into the engagement.

She was vastly relieved when they arrived and she was able to escape the confines of the carriage.

Immediately upon entering Ravenel House, she discovered that a sepulchral silence had settled in her absence. Later, she would learn from the twins that Devon became so overwrought when he'd discovered her missing, everyone in the household had prudently disappeared from view.

Setting the orchid pot on a table, Kathleen waited as Clara took her outer garments and gloves. "Please take the orchid upstairs to the parlor," she murmured to the maid, "and then come to my room afterward."

"You won't need her tonight," Devon said brusquely. He gave the girl a dismissive nod.

Before Kathleen had fully absorbed the words, twitches of indignation chased across her shoulders and the back of her neck. "I beg your pardon?"

Devon waited until Clara had begun up the stairs, and then said, "Go wait for me in my room. I'll join you after I've had a drink."

Kathleen's eyes widened. "Have you gone mad?" she asked faintly.

Did he actually believe he could order her to wait in his room as if she were a strumpet being paid to service him? She would retreat to her own bedchamber and lock the door. This was a respectable household. Even Devon wouldn't dare make a scene when his actions would be witnessed by servants, and Helen and the twins, and—

"No lock would keep me out," he said, reading her thoughts with stunning accuracy. "But try it if you like."

The way he said it, with a sort of casual politeness, sent burning color to her cheeks.

"I want to see how Helen is," she said.

"The twins are taking care of her."

She tried another tack. "I haven't had dinner."

"Neither have I." He pointed meaningfully to the stairs.

Kathleen would have loved to decimate him with some scathing remark, but her mind had gone blank. She turned stiffly and ascended the stairs without looking back.

She could feel him watching her.

Her mind revolved in frantic dithering. Perhaps after a drink, Devon would become calmer and return to his old self.

Or perhaps he would have more than one . . . several . . . and come to her just as Theo once had, drunk and determined to take what he wanted.

Reluctantly she went to Devon's bedroom, rationalizing that it would be easier than trying to evade him and play out some farcical scenario. After trudging over the threshold, she closed the door, while her skin blazed and her insides turned cold.

The room was large and grand, the floor covered with thick soft carpeting. The hulking ancestral bed was even larger than the one at Eversby Priory, with a headboard that went up to the ceiling, and disproportionately huge columns adorned with imbricate carvings and strapwork. A richly embroidered counterpane of stylized forest scenes covered the endless plateau of mattress. It was a bed intended for the procreation of generations of Ravenels.

She went to stand near the hearth, where a fire had been lit, and flexed her cold fingers in the radiant heat.

In a few minutes, the door opened, and Devon entered the room.

Kathleen's heart began to beat so heavily that she could feel her rib cage vibrate from the blows.

If the drink had calmed Devon down, there was no obvious sign of it. His color had heightened to a shade of rosewood. He was moving too deliberately, as if to relax would unleash a storm of violence contained beneath the surface.

Kathleen was driven to break the silence first. "What happened in Hampshire—"

"We'll discuss that later." Devon removed his coat and tossed it to the corner with a carelessness that would have made his valet weep. "First we're going to talk about what impulse of madness caused you to put yourself at risk the way you did tonight."

"I wasn't at risk. Winterborne wouldn't have harmed me. He's your friend."

"Are you that naïve?" His expression was positively feral as he stripped off his waistcoat. The garment was hurled aside with such force that she could hear buttons crack as they hit the wall. "You went uninvited to a man's house and talked alone with him. You know that most men would interpret that as an invitation to do whatever they wanted with you. Holy hell, you didn't even dare to visit Theo in that manner when he was your fiancé!"

"I did it for Helen."

"You should have come to me first."

"I didn't think you'd listen, or agree with what I had to say."

"I'll always listen. I won't always agree." Devon yanked at the knot of his necktie and ripped the detachable collar from his shirt. "Understand this, Kathleen: You are *never* to put yourself in that position again. Seeing Winterborne leaning over you . . . My God, the bastard didn't know how close I was to killing him."

"Stop doing this," she cried fiercely. "You'll drive me mad. You want to behave as if I belong to you, but I don't, and I never will. Your worst nightmare is becoming a husband and father, and so you seem determined to form some kind of lesser attachment that I do not want. Even if I were pregnant and you felt duty-bound to propose, I would still refuse you, because I know it would make you as unhappy as it would make me."

Devon's intensity didn't lessen, but it changed from anger into something else. He held her with a gaze of hot blue infinity.

"What if I said I loved you?" he asked softly.

The question drove a spike of pain through her chest. "Don't." Her eyes smarted with tears. "You're not the kind of man who could ever say that and mean it."

"It's not who I was." His voice was steady. "But it's who I am now. You've shown me."

For at least a half minute, the only sound was the crackling, shivering fire on the hearth.

She didn't understand what he truly thought or felt. But she would be a fool to believe him.

"Devon," she eventually said, "when it comes to love . . . neither you nor I can trust your promises."

She couldn't see through the glittering film of misery,

but she was aware of him moving, bending to pick up the coat he had tossed aside, rummaging for something.

He came to her, catching her arm lightly in his hand, drawing her to the bed. The mattress was so high that he had to fit his hands around her waist and hoist her upward to sit on it. He set something on her lap.

"What is this?" She looked down at a small wooden box.

His expression was unfathomable. "A gift for you."

Her sharp tongue got the better of her. "A parting gift?"

Devon scowled. "Open it."

Obeying, she lifted the lid. The box was lined with red velvet. Pulling aside a protective layer of cloth, she uncovered a tiny gold pocket watch on a long chain, the casing delicately engraved with flowers and leaves. A glass window on the hinged front cover revealed a white enamel dial and black hour and minute markers.

"It belonged to my mother," she heard Devon say. "It's the only possession of hers that I have. She never carried it." Irony edged his voice. "Time was never important to her."

Kathleen glanced at him in despair. She parted her lips to speak, but his fingertips came to her mouth with gentle pressure.

"Time is what I'm giving you," he said, staring down at her. His hand curved beneath her chin, compelling her to look at him. "There's only one way for me to prove that I will love you and be faithful to you for the rest of my life. And that's by loving you and being faithful to you for the rest of my life. Even if you don't want me. Even if you choose not to be with me. I'm giving you all the time I have left. I vow to you that from this moment on, I will never touch another woman, or give my heart to anyone but you. If I have to wait sixty years, not a minute will have been wasted—because I'll have spent all of them loving you."

Kathleen regarded him with wonder, a perilous warmth rising until it pushed fresh tears from her eyes.

Cradling her face in both hands, Devon bent to kiss her in a brush of soft fire. "That being said," he whispered, "I hope you'll consider marrying me sooner rather than later." Another kiss, slow and devastating. "Because I long for you, Kathleen, my dearest love. I want to sleep with you every night, and wake with you every morning." His mouth caressed her with deepening pressure until her arms curled around his neck. "And I want children with you. Soon."

The truth was there, in his voice, his eyes, on his lips. She could taste it.

She realized in wonder that somehow, in the past months, his heart had indeed changed. He was becoming the man fate had intended for him to be . . . his true self . . . a man who could make commitments and meet his responsibilities, and most of all, love without holding anything back.

Sixty years? A man like that shouldn't have to wait even sixty seconds.

Fumbling a little with the watch chain, she lifted it and slipped it over her head. The glimmering gold timepiece settled over her heart. She looked up at him with swimming eyes. "I love you, Devon. Yes, I'll marry you, *yes*—"

He hauled her against him and kissed her without reserve. And he continued to kiss her hungrily as he undressed her, his mouth tender and hot as he ravished every exposed inch of skin. He removed everything but the little gold watch, which Kathleen insisted on keeping.

"Devon," she said breathlessly, when they were both naked and he had lowered beside her, "I . . . I should confess to a small prevarication." She wanted complete honesty between them. No secrets, nothing held back.

"Yes?" he asked with his lips against her throat, one of his thighs pressing between hers.

"Until recently, I hadn't really checked my calendar to make certain I was—" She broke off as he used the edge of his teeth to delicately score her throat. "—counting days properly. And I had already resolved to take full responsibility for . . ." His tongue was playing in the hollow at the base of her neck. ". . . what happened that morning. After breakfast. You remember."

"I remember," he said, kissing his way down to her breasts.

Kathleen grasped his head in her hands, urging him to look at her and pay attention. "Devon. What I'm trying to say is that I may have misled you last night . . ." She swallowed hard and forced herself to finish. ". . . when I said that my monthly courses had started."

He went very still. His face was wiped clean of all expression as he stared down at her. "They haven't?"

She shook her head, her anxious gaze searching his. "In fact, I'm quite late."

One of his hands came to her face, a tremor running through his long fingers. "You might be pregnant?" he asked huskily.

"I'm almost certain of it."

Devon stared down at her dazedly, a flush covering his face. "My sweet, beautiful love, my angel—" He began to look over her intently, pressing kisses along her body, caressing her stomach. "My God. This settles it: I am the luckiest sod in England." He laughed quietly, his hands wandering over her with reverent gentleness. "I have some good news to share as well, but it pales in comparison to yours."

"What news?" she asked, her fingers lacing through his hair.

He was about to explain when a new thought seemed to occur to him. His smile faded, his expression turning perplexed. Adjusting his position so that he could look directly into her eyes, he said, "Your condition would have become obvious before long. What were you going to do? When were you going to tell me?"

She glanced up at him sheepishly. "I had considered the possibility of . . . going somewhere . . . before you found out."

"Going somewhere?" He looked thunderstruck. "*Leaving* me?"

"I hadn't made a decision—" she began apologetically.

A low growl interrupted her, leaving no doubt as to what he thought of that idea. He leaned over her, radiating ferocious heat. "I would have found you. You'll never be safe from me."

"I don't want to be—" she began, and would have said more, but he had taken her mouth with a deep, aggressive kiss.

Grasping her wrists, Devon pinned them over her head to stretch her out beneath him. After anchoring with his weight, he entered her in a single thrust. As he slid deeper, again and again, she struggled to breathe around the jumbled pleasure-sounds in her throat, moans and half-formed words. Spreading herself wider, she tried to take as much of him as possible.

He was claiming her, pumping slowly, pausing almost imperceptibly before each thrust to allow her to brace against him. His fingers laced with hers, his mouth voracious, lavishing her with kisses. The pleasure advanced in rolling waves, causing her to writhe until her body was out of rhythm with his.

He reached down to her hips and pinned them firmly to the bed so that no movement was possible. She whimpered, receiving each thrust without being able to return it, while her inner flesh worked on him convulsively as if to compensate for her outward stillness.

His breath caught as he felt her reach the summit, shudders of physical joy making her press up against him so desperately that her slim hips almost lifted his weight. Groaning, he pushed deep and held, the heat of him flooding her, while she clung to him with every part of herself, pulling in every hard pulse of his release.

A long time later, as they lay entwined and talked drowsily, Devon murmured, "Will you tell Helen tomorrow that she no longer has to marry Winterborne?"

"Yes, if you like."

"Good. There's a limit to how much discussion of betrothals a man can endure in one day." Picking up the gold watch, still on its chain around Kathleen's neck, he traced its smooth casing over her chest in an idle path.

She pushed out her lower lip. "You still have to propose to me."

He couldn't resist bending to take her lip between his and tugging lightly. "I already did."

"I meant properly, with a ring."

The watch ascended the rise of her breast, the skin-warmed gold sliding over the tightening peak. "It seems I'll be off to the jeweler's tomorrow." Devon grinned as he saw the flicker of anticipation in her eyes. "That pleases you, does it?"

She nodded, sliding her arms around his neck. "I love your presents," she confessed. "No one's ever given me such beautiful things."

"Little love," he murmured, his lips grazing hers. "I'll shower you with treasure." Letting the watch rest between her breasts, he lifted his hand to caress her cheek. A wry note entered his voice. "I suppose you'll want a full-fledged proposal on bended knee?"

She nodded, the corners of her mouth deepening. "Because I do so love to hear you say please."

Amusement glinted in his eyes. "Then I suppose we're a well-matched pair." Covering her body with his, he settled against her intimately before whispering, "Because I do so love to hear you say yes."

# Epilogue

*SAFE AGAIN*, HELEN THOUGHT, wandering aimlessly through the upstairs rooms at Ravenel House. After the conversation she'd had that morning with Kathleen, she knew that she should be relieved that she was no longer betrothed to Rhys Winterborne. Instead, she felt stunned and disoriented.

It didn't seem to have occurred to either Kathleen or Devon that the decision about her relationship with Rhys Winterborne should have been hers to make. She understood that they had done it out of love and concern. But still . . .

It made Helen feel every bit as smothered as her fiancé had.

"When I said that I felt like never seeing Mr. Winterborne again," she had said to Kathleen unhappily, "that was how I felt at the moment. My head was splitting, and I was very distressed. But I didn't mean that I never *ever* wanted to see him again."

Kathleen had been in such glowing good spirits that she hadn't seemed to appreciate the distinction. "Well, it's done, and everything is back to the way it should be. You can take off that hateful ring, and we'll have it sent back immediately."

Helen hadn't removed the ring yet, however. She glanced down at her left hand, watching the massive rose-cut diamond catch the light from the parlor windows. She truly hated the large, vulgar thing. It was top-heavy and it constantly slid from side to side, making simple tasks difficult. One might as well tie a doorknob to one's finger.

*Oh, for a piano*, she thought, longing to pound on the keys and make noise. Beethoven, or Vivaldi.

Her betrothal was over, with no one having asked what she wanted.

Not even Winterborne.

Everything would go back to the way it was. Now there would be nothing to intimidate or challenge her. No dark-eyed suitor who wanted things she didn't know how to give. But she didn't feel the relief she was supposed to feel. The tight, trapped feeling in her chest was worse than ever.

The more she thought about the last time she'd seen Winterborne . . . his impatience, the demanding kisses, his bitter words . . . the more she thought that they should have talked about what had happened.

She would have at least liked to try.

But it had probably all worked out for the best. She and Winterborne hadn't been able to find their footing together. He unnerved her, and she was certain that she bored him, and she didn't see how she could have ever found a place for herself in his world.

It was only . . . she had liked the sound of his voice, and the way he had looked at her. And that sense he'd given her of being on the brink of discovering something new and frightening and wonderful and dangerous . . . she would miss that. She worried that his pride had been hurt. It was possible that he might feel lost and alone, just as she did.

As she fretted and paced around the room, Helen's gaze happened to stray across an object on the table near the parlor window. Her eyes widened as she realized it was the potted Blue Vanda she had given him. The orchid he hadn't wanted but had taken anyway. He had sent it back.

Helen hurried to the orchid, wondering what condition it was in.

Weak sunlight slanted across the table, flecked with glimmering, floating dust motes, some of them swirling around the light blue petals. Confusion spread through her as she saw the inflorescence of glowing blooms. The broad ovoid leaves were clean and glossy, and the roots anchored among the crushed clay pottery shards had been carefully trimmed and kept damp.

The Blue Vanda hadn't sickened in Winterborne's care . . . it had thrived.

Helen leaned over the orchid, touching the beautiful arc of its stem with a single fingertip. Shaking her head in wonder, she felt a tickle at the edge of her chin, and didn't realize it was a tear until she saw it drop onto one of the Vanda's leaves.

"Oh, Mr. Winterborne," she whispered, and reached up to wipe at her wet cheeks. "Rhys. There's been a mistake."

Do you love historical fiction?

Want the chance to hear news about your favourite authors (and the chance to win free books)?

Mary Balogh
Charlotte Betts
Jessica Blair
Frances Brody
Gaelen Foley
Elizabeth Hoyt
Eloisa James
Lisa Kleypas
Stephanie Laurens
Claire Lorrimer
Sarah MacLean
Amanda Quick
Julia Quinn

**Then visit the Piatkus website and blog**
www.piatkus.co.uk | www.piatkusbooks.net

**And follow us on Facebook and Twitter**
www.facebook.com/piatkusfiction | www.twitter.com/piatkusbooks

piatkus